THE PIE & MASH DETECTIVE AGENCY

J. D. BRINKWORTH

THE PIE & MASH DETECTIVE AGENCY

CENTURY

CENTURY

UK | USA | Canada | Ireland | Australia
India | New Zealand | South Africa

Century is part of the Penguin Random House group of companies whose addresses can be found at global.penguinrandomhouse.com

Penguin Random House UK,
One Embassy Gardens, 8 Viaduct Gardens, London SW11 7BW

penguin.co.uk

First published 2026
001

Copyright © Jo Dinkin and Catherine Brinkworth, 2026

The moral right of the authors has been asserted

Lyrics on pp. 109–110 from 'Blue (Da Ba Dee)' by Eiffel 65,
written by Jeffrey Jey, Maurizio Lobina and Massimo Gabutti
Lyrics on p. 149 from 'Barbie Girl' by Aqua, written by Søren Rasted,
Claus Norreen, René Dif and Lene Nystrøm

Penguin Random House values and supports copyright.
Copyright fuels creativity, encourages diverse voices, promotes freedom of expression and supports a vibrant culture. Thank you for purchasing an authorised edition of this book and for respecting intellectual property laws by not reproducing, scanning or distributing any part of it by any means without permission. You are supporting authors and enabling Penguin Random House to continue to publish books for everyone. No part of this book may be used or reproduced in any manner for the purpose of training artificial intelligence technologies or systems. In accordance with Article 4(3) of the DSM Directive 2019/790, Penguin Random House expressly reserves this work from the text and data mining exception.

Set in 13.4/16pt Fournier MT Pro
Typeset by Falcon Oast Graphic Art Ltd

Printed and bound in Great Britain by Clays Ltd, Elcograf S.p.A.

The authorised representative in the EEA is Penguin Random House Ireland, Morrison Chambers, 32 Nassau Street, Dublin D02 YH68

A CIP catalogue record for this book is available from the British Library

ISBN: 978–1–529–95044–1

Penguin Random House is committed to a sustainable future for our business, our readers and our planet. This book is made from Forest Stewardship Council® certified paper.

To: Simon Mash

Subject: Car Rental Ref #285101

Dear Mr S. Mash,

We regret to inform you that the condition of the vehicle you returned on 20 April was found to be unacceptable and in violation of our rental agreement. Our inspection revealed severe damage, including:

- bullet holes in the car's exterior
- smashed rear window
- wear on the tyre treads (suggesting the driver had been doing 'doughnuts')

Also, while not technically damage, someone has drawn the outline of a 'male organ' into the dust on the bonnet.

Significant costs have been incurred to get this vehicle back in service. We urge you to contact us immediately to resolve this matter amicably, and avoid legal action.

Sincerely,

Derek Pargeter

SwiftCar Customer Relations

PART ONE

I

Monday 8 April – Present Day

Dev Hooper came home from work to find his front door hanging open.

The hallway lights were on, and Nellie's handbag was missing from its usual spot on the banister.

'Nellie? Nellie!'

She wasn't in the kitchen, making one of her herby veggie stews. She wasn't on the sofa reading, or in the bathroom peeing, or hauling laundry from the dryer in the basement.

Dev strode upstairs in his outdoor shoes, shouting: 'Nellie? Are you here?'

Don't be silly, he thought. Yes, it was unlike Nellie to leave the front door open, but everyone made mistakes. She must have gone out. Dev established that they hadn't been burgled, as he'd first suspected. The TV was in its right place, and the thick cookbook on the shelf above still had his stash of cash tucked safely inside. Nellie must have taken her handbag and gone out somewhere. No need to panic. He always panicked over nothing.

In the kitchen, he poured a drink over ice, and his hand began to jitter, spilling gin on the counter. He cursed and moved things out of the way, unopened post, some papers, Nellie's handbag . . . Nellie's handbag?

*

'I will of course make a report, Mr Hooper, but please try not to worry. Many people who go missing turn up within twenty-four hours, with a reasonable explanation. Have you tried her phone?'

'As I said, her phone's here. In the handbag.'

'Oh, right. So this isn't like her, then? To go out without her things?'

'No.' In fact, Dev considered how it wasn't really like his girlfriend to go out at all.

He'd expected flashing sirens on his driveway to throw red and blue light through the hallway, for police radios to buzz and crackle, for the footsteps of the search and rescue team to pound through the house, sounding the hubbub of the investigation opening. Instead, two uniformed officers stood in the kitchen – PC Boughton, who'd cheerily introduced herself on the doorstep, and a large, silent colleague, who hadn't introduced himself and showed no desire to. He leaned on the countertop behind her, six foot four and silently solid, like a bouncer or a brick wall.

'I'll need to take some details,' PC Boughton said. Her police hat and strands of strawberry-blonde hair framed her freckled face. She pulled a tiny notebook from her vest pocket. 'Age?'

'Twenty-five.'

'Sex: female, and, uh – regular address is here?'

'Yes, 36 Shipwell Drive.'

'Are you worried about the missing person?'

'Yes, very!'

She wrote that down.

'Any particular reason to be worried? Has she gone missing before, or do you think she's likely to harm herself or another member of the public?'

'No! But, I mean, just because she wouldn't hurt anyone, I still think we should worry. This is very out of character.'

'Right . . . Oh, and what's her name, Mr Hooper?'

'Nellie Thorne.'

'Pardon?' PC Boughton didn't write this down.

'Nellie Thorne,' repeated Dev.

The silent partner bristled. Dev noticed how wide the man's shoulders were.

'And does *Nellie* have any friends we can talk to?' PC Boughton's voice had changed. It was snappy, impatient.

'Oh, well, I haven't really met her friends . . .'

'Have you checked any local favourite places?'

'Um, not yet . . .' Dev faltered. Did Nellie have favourite places?

'Is she likely to have travelled abroad? Any other countries she has links to?'

As the more talkative officer barrelled out questions, Dev felt dizzy. All he wanted was for them to get out their long poles and search every inch of town for Nellie.

'N-no, I don't think she has any links to other countries, no.'

'And I'm guessing she doesn't have a job?'

'Pardon?' Where had that come from? He hadn't said that, had he? 'Actually, Nellie *does* have a job,' said Dev. 'Well, she's self-employed. She has a little business where she buys clothes from the charity shop and then sells them on, erm, that app where you sell second-hand clothes? Depop? I think that's it.'

PC Boughton scribbled on her pad, mouthing along: 'No job.' She grabbed her radio.

'It's a Nellie Thorne.'

Dev felt the room spin.

'What's a Nellie Thorne? It's just her name. I know it's a bit old-fashioned—'

'Mr Hooper,' said the officer, putting the notebook back in

her pocket, 'you should be aware that wasting police time is an offence.'

'I'm not wasting your time, I'm reporting a missing person!' PC Boughton and her colleague exchanged a look. Dev's time was up. They turned to walk away, and Dev lurched after them. 'Where are you going?'

In the hallway, PC Boughton turned to him one last time.

'I'm sorry to inform you, Mr Hooper, that Nellie Thorne is not real. Maybe you knew someone using that name, maybe you didn't, but I need to escalate this internally before we take any further action. We'll be in touch about an interview at the station.'

'Are you even going to look for her?' wailed Dev, to no reply.

The words *not real* echoed around his head as the police car crunched off the gravel driveway.

Dev was white-hot and trembling. Part of him wanted to sit on the steps by the door, but his body wouldn't move. His neighbour Ian came outside holding a suspiciously half-empty bin bag, keen to see what the police had been called for.

'Everything all right, Dev?'

'Have you seen Nellie? She's missing. I can't— I don't know what to—'

'Nellie? That the girl you've been seeing?'

Dev nodded. His mouth was as dry as a tax return.

Ian shook his head. 'Sorry, mate. Wish I could help you. You've not brought her round to meet me yet. In fact, I don't think I've ever even seen her.'

2

Tuesday 2 April – Present Day

Jane Pye and Simon Mash, detectives in training, were in the middle of an important lecture.

'Next slide,' said their teacher to himself, clicking heavily on his mouse. He was a grizzled man in his forties who looked like he was in his sixties and occasionally vaped into his armpit between slides. 'Due diligence and background checks.'

Jane tapped brisk notes into her whirring laptop. Simon tried to play Toto's 'Africa' on the desk using pens.

On the outside of the door, a peeling sign read: PRIVATE INVESTIGATION LEVEL 1. In Jane's opinion, the classroom shouldn't have been signposted at all, and the first test should have been finding it.

During working hours, this room was used for what Simon called 'important things', like certifications in social care and food hygiene courses for managers of Wetherspoons. It had, in fact, been a bit of a struggle for Jane to get Simon to enrol in detecting with her.

'Ooh, look, Jane!' he'd said. 'You can get a qualification in running hairdressing exams for trainee hairdressers!'

But Jane had been sure: it had to be Private Investigation Level 1. That was her new hobby. So here they were, at the training centre in Croydon, in their brightly coloured raincoats, among a dozen ex-military men and bouncers who were squeezed into tiny school desks and plastic chairs. Even though the class had been running for a few weeks, the tougher students still occasionally turned and stared at Simon and Jane, sizing them up. She wished Simon hadn't worn his tie-dye bucket hat.

'. . . and I'll stress that again: while you can use this tool to find someone else's criminal record, there is nothing you can do to erase your own.'

A couple of the burly men groaned.

'Right,' continued the teacher. 'Coursework.'

Jane sat up straighter in her chair. The sleeves of her home-knitted jumper were already rolled up.

'As you'll know from reading the syllabus outline, this course finishes in three weeks, and to get your certificate, you'll need to submit coursework. A case of your very own.'

Jane grinned and turned to make eye contact with Simon, who was googling 'hot fashion looks for private detectives' on his phone.

'So, when we all meet back here next week, I'll be giving you real cases. It'll be up to you to solve them. But be warned . . . You might think you're tough. But not everyone passes Private Investigation Level 1. You'll soon find out why I assign coursework. It's where you'll find out if you can really handle the danger.'

Jane brought wine into the living room: small amounts in extremely large glasses, just like she'd seen on TV.

Their first-floor flat was in South London, close enough to Clapham Junction station that the trains sometimes rumbled the floor. Simon would boast that he lived next door to the busiest rail interchange in the world (a fact that wasn't true), and when the freight trains bulleted past they'd give a honk, which

Jane would mimic. Their living room was a bold terracotta red that the landlord still didn't know about. Their wide bookshelves were stacked high with books that had never been opened, and board games that had. Simon was lighting candles in the shape of women's bottoms.

'Ah, thank you, babe,' he said, taking his wine. He sank happily onto the velvet sofa and stretched his long legs out over the coffee table, showing off a pair of his signature patterned socks. Simon was a little over six feet tall, with a knack for making clothes look great. He liked using this skill to push fashion boundaries — especially in the office, where his collection of velour jumpers was causing a stir. He sighed, ready for a night of peace, and Jane sat beside him at the angle she always sat at when she had something bad to say. Feet flat on the floor, little body positioned at forty-five degrees to him so that eye contact was optional.

'Simon. I don't mean this to sound like an accusation or a criticism, but why are you always late?'

'Hmm?' Simon looked up from the inside of his wine glass. Jane pushed her glasses up her nose and tugged down the sleeves of her jumper.

'To detective class,' she said. 'I worry that you're not taking it seriously.'

'Oh, I'm not,' he said. 'I never take anything seriously. It's one of my top five Values to Live By.' He gestured to his homemade 'Values to Live By' wall chart. 'But it's a way for us to spend more time together, isn't it? A shared project?'

'Right. Yes. And that is lovely. It's just . . . I wonder if I'd enjoy the class more if I felt you were engaged?'

'Oh, OK. So you're getting the impression that I'm not "engaged"?' Simon swept his floppy brown hair out of his eyes. He couldn't believe he'd been rumbled.

'Well, you spent most of today's session reading an article about Cher's best Vegas stage looks, so no, I know you're not into it, or even learning anything at all, for that matter. I mean, just for example, which record would you check to see if someone's on the sex offenders register?'

He thought about it. 'You would ask at a nearby school.'

Jane sighed and pulled her legs onto the sofa, getting into a less combative, smaller and rounder position. 'It's just, I'm really enjoying the course, and I'm starting to wonder if it could be something I do for a job. Detecting, I mean.'

'Oh.' Simon leaned his head to one side like a Labrador.

'I know it sounds silly and like a pipe dream. But I'm not getting anywhere with applying for developer jobs either, so maybe having a nine-to-five is a pipe dream too – and in that case, I may as well do something I find interesting.'

'I didn't realise you hadn't been liking . . . umm . . . rear-end development.'

'Back-end development.'

'Yes, exactly.' Simon worked as a corporate collaboration consultant, which meant he was on hand to help teams in his company work together better. Or, at least, the teams that knew he existed. Judging by his very manageable inbox, most did not.

'I thought I liked being a developer, but now I haven't been doing it for a few months . . . well, it turns out I prefer not being a developer.' Jane put her wine glass on a geode coaster and lay back on the sofa, combing her scalp with her fingers. 'Or do I just like not working?'

'Not working is excellent,' mused Simon, who had plenty of experience in the field. 'But how are you doing for, you know, cashola?'

When Jane had been laid off, she'd seen it coming. First it had been 'The Nespresso pods are for clients only,' then the next thing she knew, she was handing back her MacBook and collecting one month's redundancy pay, which she'd been stretching out for three months with online survey work and one-pot tomato pastas.

'I don't think I have to worry about money just yet,' she said.

Simon looked down at Jane's big brown eyes and the spray of freckles across her nose; he found her beautiful in a nerdy way, and thought she could star in movies as a cheeky librarian or a clumsy archaeologist. Jane, on the other hand, saw herself as a 'little goblin', which Simon found too funny to correct.

'You don't have to worry about it at all. You know I don't mind lending you whatever you need.'

Jane sat up and tensely twirled a curl in her fingers. 'That's very nice of you.' But last week, she'd seen him stuffing their latest energy bill down his trousers as she walked into the room. She stared off into nowhere for a while. 'Anyway, there's an application I'm going to do tomorrow morning, and then maybe I'll watch another season of *Frasier*, and then, eventually, death . . .' Jane wished she had the coursework project now. Why make them wait another week?

'Jane. I hear you. You're enjoying the course, and that makes me feel happy for you. So I will bring some dedication to our coursework. It's just – and don't take this the wrong way – but I don't know if you really understand how serious crime is.'

'Huh?'

'As you know,' continued Simon, 'I'm a perfect example of how crime can ruin lives.'

'Oh yes, that.'

'And how some cases can just never be solved, no matter how much you want them to be. For example, when my mum was a victim of credit card fraud.'

Jane leaned forward and looked into his handsome, slightly beavery face. Were his eyes getting misty?

'Not only did they never find out who cloned her M&S card, but it was only a few short months after that that my dad moved to Marbella with his friend Francesca, and . . .' Simon's voice cracked. 'And I've always felt that the two things were linked.'

'Aw,' crooned Jane, as she always did when the subject of Simon's dad's friend Francesca came up. She leaned over to hug him and wiped a tear from his trendy stubble. 'There, there, love.'

'Thanks, Jane,' he said.

'Thank you. For agreeing to work hard with me on the coursework. And if we can't solve the case we're given, or if it gets to be a bit too much, then never mind.'

And with that, she kissed him on the head and went off to bed with the latest book she was reading on the Black Death, while Simon made his way to the kitchen to assemble a late-night charcuterie board for one.

3

Tuesday 9 April – Present Day

Dev had been sitting in Tonbridge Police Station for nearly an hour.

Making him wait was the freshest insult against him by the police, and he wouldn't let it stand. He'd stewed overnight on the way he'd been treated – how they'd suggested his girlfriend was imaginary. How they'd flipped from being helpful to getting irate and shutting him out.

He got up and paced the black parquet floor again, going through all the things he'd like to say, but knew it was best not to. Like: 'How do I find the right form to lodge the strongest possible complaint?' And: 'I don't know if you've heard of a little thing called the Police Ombudsman?' What was it called these days?

Ringing phones and chatter echoed off the clinical white walls, scuffed from years of scuffles. The waiting area was half full of hopeless victims on plastic chairs – an elderly couple clutching handbags and carrier bags, probably waiting to hear about a burglary that would never be solved, two teenage girls with bored expressions, a thirty-something man with his face in his hands – all waiting for what? For punishment? For justice? Either way, they'd be waiting forever.

Just as Dev was fantasising that his vitriol might be the final straw to topple the institution of British policing, a woman in beat uniform appeared in the corridor from the belly of the building, and she was walking— Yes, she was walking towards him! It was the officer from yesterday. When she reached Dev she stopped, and he noticed for the first time how short she was. What was the shortest you could be and still join the police? He remembered from yesterday that she was called PC Boughton.

'Mr Hooper? I've been instructed to apologise for implying that your girlfriend, Nellie Thorne, isn't real. As a victim of a potential crime, it's important you feel comfortable about the way we're conducting the search for Nellie. It's just, the name you gave me took me by surprise a little. If you'd like to follow me, I can explain the risk assessment, and we can agree on some actions?'

Was that an apology? Either way, Dev found himself struggling to respond and simply followed her into the machine of justice, and specifically, a small meeting room of justice off the next corridor.

'Name, we have down as Nellie Thorne.'

The meeting room wasn't one of those sterile blue interrogation rooms from crime dramas. In fact, it was quite a normal office: cramped, with yellow strip-lighting, box files on shelves, and a pair of polystyrene cups on the desk holding the drying dregs of instant coffee from the previous meeting. Dev bounced his brown brogues against the tired carpet. He was dressed in his usual work attire, a collared gingham shirt and chinos. He took shaky breaths, nostrils stinging with the cologne he'd oversprayed. PC Boughton's tiny, freckled fingers tapped away as she continued to answer her own questions.

'Age, you said twenty-five. And I've got here that nothing was missing from the house?'

Dev fidgeted. 'Ah. Well, her handbag with her phone and purse were still in the kitchen, but then after you'd gone, late last night, I noticed that a few of her clothes were gone, and my small suitcase. And I know what that looks like, but why would she take her clothes but leave her handbag? So I'm convinced that somebody took the clothes and the suitcase to make it look like she left.' He could tell he was losing her. 'She really wouldn't do this, and I just know something's wrong. I can feel it.'

PC Boughton stopped typing and gave him the kindest look she could manage. 'Let's stick with facts for now. You have the handbag: does it contain any forms of ID? Driving licence, passport? Anything like that would do.'

Dev frowned. 'I couldn't find any.' Yesterday evening, he had searched desperately for official proof of Nellie's existence. 'Maybe they were in her pocket when she was taken? But I've got the handbag here, so I'll look again. I mean, maybe there's another zip pocket I missed.'

He dived into his backpack to find the handbag, but the handbag was slightly too large and got stuck, and the silence lengthened as he tried to wrestle it out. Eventually, he left the bag wedged halfway out of his backpack like a calf struggling to be born.

'I'm sure there might be something in here, potentially . . .'

The rummaging was making him hot, and so far, the handbag still contained only half a packet of tissues with illustrated hedgehogs on them, a lip balm, and a lot of receipts.

'Actually, I don't think she drove, so there wouldn't be a driving licence, but . . .'

Did Nellie have a passport? He'd just assumed she'd have one, like anyone, but in their one year together they'd never been abroad. They'd had a trip to Broadstairs for their six-month anniversary, but hadn't progressed to the stage of their relationship where they'd go for a weekend in Brussels.

'Well, do you have her National Insurance number?' asked PC Boughton.

'I'm sure I could find it,' said Dev, unsure that he could find it, his hands still working the bag and sporadically pushing his round glasses back up his sweating nose.

'Right, so no workplace, colleagues or paperwork,' she said, nodding stiffly.

Dev looked up from the tangle of bags. He didn't need to be a detective to spot the same tone of voice she'd used yesterday, when she'd come to the house and told him Nellie wasn't real.

'Have any friends or family members come to mind that you might have forgotten about when we previously spoke?'

Dev paused for a second. Nellie had a brother called Jonah, she'd said. But they hadn't got around to meeting up with him yet. Any friends... did Nellie have any friends? He didn't remember her going out much. His default image of her was on the sofa, crocheting. Dev had unlocked her phone last night after guessing that, like everyone on planet earth, she'd set the code as her birthday. Thank god she had a birthday, at least. But the phone had been wiped somehow, reformatted, and everything was gone. Dev was starting to feel like he'd been reformatted.

'One of the problems we're having, Mr Hooper, is that we can't find Nellie.'

'Exactly! That *is* the problem!'

'No, what I mean is, we can't find any records of her. Anything official on file to prove she exists. Passport number, National Insurance number, employment records – anything.'

'But I can prove she exists!' Dev was struggling to restrain the volume of his voice. He pulled out his phone from his pocket and swiped through photos of himself and Nellie, selfies of them cuddling in the garden, on a windswept beach, silly faces pulled in their living room.

'I'm sorry, sir, and I believe you *think* you knew Nellie Thorne, but these photos can only prove that you knew a woman. We've run "Nellie" and every variation of "Nellie" we can think of – "Eleanor", "Ellen", "Helen", "Danielle" – but we might have missed one. Can you tell us what "Nellie" was short for?'

A silence as the world stopped. Dev realised he didn't know his girlfriend's full name.

'Dev,' PC Boughton said slowly, like a headmistress addressing a child, 'is there anything you want to tell us?'

She suspected him of something. He felt frozen, but found himself shaking his head.

'We also need to rule out the possibility that this might have been a romance scam.'

'A scam?'

'Did she take anything from you?'

Dev thought about the stash of cash in the cookbook. 'No.'

'Well, then.' She breathed out slowly. 'After leaving your house yesterday, we did enquire with neighbours on your street. Unfortunately, nobody had seen Nellie. We've also circulated the photo you provided around some local bars and cafes, and we have somebody looking through the CCTV at Tonbridge station to establish whether she got on a train.'

'Oh. Wow,' said Dev. That was quite a lot of work for one night.

'The thing is, Dev, this particular case comes with certain pressures. Since last night, it's been escalated quite high up the chain.'

'Why was it escalated?' His throat was dry.

'Because it has potential links to a series of historic cases dating back to the 1970s through the 1990s.'

'Not murders?'

'Murder was not a conclusion in the cases,' she reassured him. 'More like disappearances.'

Dev screwed up his face. 'Unsolved disappearances?'

'Yes. But if it helps – the fact Nellie packed clothes and took a suitcase reassures me. While we will of course investigate every avenue, in cases where belongings have been packed, there's a high likelihood she's left you.'

Dev was winded.

'I'm sorry, but I can't say too much more due to the sensitivity of the wider investigation. A supervising officer will need to speak to you soon, and maybe someone from the National Crime Agency. And on that note, please don't talk to any journalists who might come around. We'll handle the press side.' She wrote her email address on a Post-it and offered it across the desk. 'But I understand the need for you to be kept in the loop, so you can email me any time. Especially if you work out Nellie's full name.'

Dev took the Post-it, and PC Boughton stood up to make it clear that his audience was over.

'Oh,' she said, gesturing at Dev's bag, 'and I'll need to take the handbag.'

Dev tried once more to wrestle the handbag from his backpack, then handed over the whole thing.

The door shut behind him. What had he managed to accomplish? He'd found out that Nellie might have been a scammer, that this could have been a breakup, or that she was a part of something bigger. Something so horrific he wasn't allowed to hear about it.

The search would be getting underway without him. Dev had pictured himself helping – striding out in all-weather clothes to lead a team of volunteers with sticks, who would take turns patting him on the shoulder. As it was, he'd probably end up sitting in the house, drinking gin, and listening to Radio 4 to drown out his thoughts. Nellie was meant to be the one who was lost, and he was meant to be the one finding her.

As he leaned against a red brick wall outside, a woman in a smart suit and a lanyard left the station by the side door and squinted at him suspiciously, but Dev felt so deflated he didn't even care if he was loitering.

He found the phone number in his emails, and picked agitatedly at the police station's brickwork as it rang.

'You've reached Gavin Smith, private investigator. I'm out on an important mission, so please leave your message after the tone. Unless you hear a suspicious click, because historically, I've had some problems with the *News of the W—*' BEEEEP.

'Gavin, it's Dev Hooper. I emailed you yesterday about my girlfriend, Nellie Thorne? This is her second day missing, and, uh, I'd really like to hear from you. I am contacting other private investigators, too, so you know. Time is of the essence. I just . . .'

Hot tears stung his eyelids.

'I just really need somebody to give me some answers.'

4

Tuesday 9 April – Present Day

'Next slide. Unit Six, Part G: Service of Process. How to find a husband and serve him with the wife's divorce papers.'

A week on from his promise to be a dedicated detective, Simon had arrived for class on time. He and Jane sat at their usual desk at the back of the class (or, as Simon called it, the Naughty Seats). Simon's long legs stuck out from behind the desk. Jane's brown curls were tied up neatly in a pair of buns. On the table she had carefully laid out her laptop, notebook and a large Minnie Mouse pen with a fluffy head.

'I've figured out our detective agency name,' whispered Simon.

'Cool,' said Jane quietly, with a thin smile, not looking up from her notes.

'Well, you know how our names are Jane Pye and Simon Mash?'

'Maybe we should talk about this later.'

'We could be the Pie and Mash Detective Agency. Probably "pie" spelt like ham and mushroom, for googleability—'

'Is everything alright back there?' said the teacher sternly.

'Sorry, all good,' said Jane. 'Just very interesting, the difference between tracking down ex-wives and ex-husbands.'

'That's right. They're two very different beasts. And both as slippery as each other. Now, if you have any more questions on the legal ins and outs of service of process, you can download the worksheet on my website. But now for the important stuff. Coursework.'

Jane grinned.

The teacher hauled a battered backpack onto his desk and unzipped it up to the halfway point, where the zip always jammed on the bag's frayed fabric. He pulled out a dozen stapled sheaves of freshly printed paper.

'El Capitano.' He slapped the first pack down on the desk of an ex-army captain named Alex. 'You'll be having a go at a case I cracked back in 'ninety-eight. Started as a simple background check – wait until you find the herbal cigarette pyramid scheme at the centre.'

Alex picked up the papers and started reading. One by one, the rest of Simon and Jane's classmates received their cases: a woman cheating on her husband with her dental hygienist, a serial cat kidnapper, and even a potential murder that the coroner had ruled as an e-scooter accident.

Jane couldn't help but notice the detective teacher's hands were empty as he reached the desk next to theirs. He didn't stop at the Naughty Seats but strode back to the front of the classroom.

'Right, now you've all got your assignments—'

'Um, Gavin?' said Jane, a little too quietly.

'—in this game, it doesn't pay to keep a client waiting. Speed is part of your reputation. You'll present a case update next week, and the final deadline for submission is our bonus coursework presentation session on Friday of that same week. Less than two weeks away.'

'Gavin?'

Gavin heard Jane this time and rubbed his stubble as he noticed their empty, assignment-less hands.

'Oh. Right, yes, you two.'

He looked in his backpack.

'Yes, bigger class number than usual this term, but I've actually got something, uh, very special for you . . .' As he spoke, he unloaded several things from the tattered backpack: a vape charger, a glasses cleaning kit, a handful of GPS tags and a large ball of rubber bands.

Finally, he brought out a battered black tablet with a cracked screen. With a few dramatic swipes of his finger, he opened his emails.

'Right, yes, a very interesting one for . . . ?'

'Simon and Jane.'

'Yes. Simon and Jane, your case, if you choose to accept it, is the recurring disappearance of Nellie Thorne.'

'Oooh,' said Simon. 'Sounds Agatha Christie-y.'

Gavin approached their desk.

'The Nellie Thorne case is a bit of an urban legend in Kent. The story goes that every decade or so, a young woman named Nellie Thorne is reported missing somewhere in the county. And it's an odd name, isn't it? You don't meet many Nellies these days. But each time, the description of the woman is nearly identical. Same age, same look, same personality, decade after decade. Hasn't been one for donkey's years, but back in the day kids used to think she was a ghost and would wind each other up. They'd say that if you got too close to the edge of the playground, she'd snatch you up and make you disappear too.'

'Wow, the plot thickens,' said Simon, although Jane thought the plot sounded pretty thin.

'Anyway, the police have never solved it. There wasn't any quality evidence to go on, no bodies found or any of that business. The people who reported her missing were concerned neighbours, acquaintances and so on, nobody with useful info. The fuzz had to investigate, of course. There was a lot of pressure by the third one they looked into. But no missing persons case had ever thrown up so little evidence. It was notorious. Nowadays, most police suspect it was a hoax to waste their time, or some kind of scam.'

'Oh,' said Simon.

'Where you come in,' continued Gavin, 'is that yesterday, a bloke got in touch. Says his girlfriend is Nellie Thorne and that she's vanished. Now, you always get time-wasters in the game. Part of your job as detectives will be to screen them out. Maybe this . . .' He took his reading glasses from the chain around his neck and put them on to read the tablet screen. '. . . Dev – is part of a new generation of hoaxers. Or he could be running a scam himself, or covering up a real woman's disappearance, or anything like that. He could be a loony or an attention-seeker. I want you to find out what he's up to.'

He handed the tablet to Jane, who nudged her glasses up her nose and began speed-reading Dev's email.

'I'll forward that to you,' said Gavin. 'You don't mind sharing, do you? Sharing the one case, I mean.'

'Nope,' said Simon, 'it sounds like the perfect case for the Pie and Mash—'

'Can we have something else, please?' interrupted Jane.

'Hmm?' said Gavin.

'Well, this case is obviously a silly one. You've just told us he's probably a time-waster. But you gave Craniax a political assassination!' Jane pointed to the front row, where a leather-jacketed Hells Angel was scribbling a mind map in his Pukka Pad.

'Jane!' hissed Simon in the tone he used when she asked to try samples of wines at restaurants.

'I'm sorry, Gavin, and I don't mean any offence. I think the point I'm trying to make is that – well, you might get a certain impression of us from our age and from Simon's yellow raincoat, but we're not just silly millennials. We can handle a real case.'

'She's got plenty of time on her hands,' piped up a bouncer at the next table. 'Probably one of those stay-at-home types who watches true-crime documentaries all day.'

'Yeah,' said his desk neighbour. 'Go on, Gav – give her a proper horrible murder.'

'Excuse me!' said Jane. 'I'll have you know that I'm a back-end programmer in between positions!'

'She didn't mean that to come out sounding like an innuendo,' Simon added helpfully.

'Alright! No scuffles in class! I'll not have a repeat of Unit Three: De-escalation Exercises,' said Gavin, for the first time projecting genuine authority.

He turned to Jane, seeming a bit taller and maybe even wider, and spoke slowly. 'Janet, I understand that this case seems a bit more . . .'

'Diffuse?' offered Simon.

'. . . A bit more wackadoodle than the others. But when you've been a detective as long as me, you develop a radar for those cases that are ready to unravel like a jumper when you pull on the first loose thread. There's something here. And aren't you jumping at the chance to take the only case that's still open?'

Jane maintained a defiant look while she thought about it.

Gavin gestured around the class. 'The only case in the room that I haven't already solved?'

Jane sighed a very long sigh. 'Alright.'

'Good work, detectives,' said Gavin, returning to the desk at the front of the room and unplugging his laptop from the projector. 'Willingness, readiness, teamwork. All essential for the successful PI.'

The class packed away their things. The bouncer glared at Jane and Simon again, and Simon decided it wasn't the right time to get out the large vintage magnifying glass he'd bought on eBay. Maybe next week could be the soft brand launch of the Pie and Mash Detective Agency.

5

Wednesday 10 April – Present Day

The next morning, Jane called Dev. He answered after only half a ring, causing her to panic and hang up. But a quick half-hour later, having recovered and drafted a rough script, she tried again, and managed to arrange a meeting for that afternoon in Tonbridge.

When Jane arrived at 36 Shipwell Drive, she found Dev's living room neat and nicely decorated but impersonal. There was something about it that felt barely lived in, like a show home: scuffless pale grey walls and spotless patio doors showing off his peaceful patch of garden. Dev even made her a hot drink in a coffee machine so brand new that the latte left a plasticky taste in her mouth. The only homely touches were a vintage map of India on the wall and one framed photograph of a friendly-faced woman wearing a sari and a tall white man in a suit; presumably his parents. When Jane spotted it, she looked around for photos of Nellie, but found nothing. She couldn't read anything about this man from his possessions, except his neatness, and that he'd got his slender frame from his father and his smile from his mum.

Ten minutes into the interview, Jane had finished asking all the questions she'd prepared on the train. She paused to glance at the notes she'd taken, and doubted they'd hold up to a re-reading later:

Nellie Thorne
Headteacher, Depop
Suspicious leg bouncing
House boring, watercolour tulip prints
National Insurance number, hates police
Tell Simon we need pasta (wholegrain)

'So, Dev,' she began riffing. She flipped over a fresh page and said aloud, 'Oh, what's that?'

At some point, Simon had taken her notebook, randomly chosen a blank page, and drawn a Pie and Mash Detective Agency logo: a bloody knife sticking out of a pie, all being magnified by a magnifying glass. Still, knowing Simon's doodling habits, it could have been a lot worse.

'I mean – nothing! Sorry! So, you said you're a headteacher . . .'

'Head of Sixth Form.' Dev fiddled with his gold glasses. His usually smart hairstyle needed trimming, and he kept patting down the stubborn tufts on top. These were the types of tells Jane was looking out for – was he lying, or did he just not like his hair feeling tufty?

'Right . . . What was Nellie wearing when you last saw her?'

'Sorry, is there a connection between those things?'

'No.' Jane blinked.

'It's just, you said it as if there might be. Like I dressed her in clothes from the school's lost and found or something.'

'You dressed her?'

'No! What is this? Some kind of psy-ops thing to keep me confused so I'll say something incriminating?' He shifted on the edge of the sofa.

'Well, uh, even if it was, I wouldn't give that away, now, would I, Dev?'

This was going badly. Jane knew from Units 1 through 3 that while everyone was a suspect, when it came to clients, it was relationship, relationship, relationship. Unfortunately, Unit 7: How to Interview Persons of Interest – wasn't until next week. She took a deep breath.

'Dev, there's no easy way to say this, but are you sure she hasn't left you?'

'What? No! And you heavily implied that question earlier when you asked me twice – two separate times – whether the relationship was going OK.'

He definitely seemed grouchy now. Jane suddenly wondered why there weren't more boxes of tissues around for a man upset over the disappearance of his girlfriend.

'And before you ask, no, I didn't bloody kill her either, because if I'd done that, why would I report it to the police and then go to the trouble of hiring two private detective agencies to look into it?'

'Two? Who's the other one?'

'Well, Gavin, and you,' said Dev slowly, like she was stupid. 'Gavin said his caseload was full, and he had to pass me on to a reputable partner agency.'

'Oh! Yes, that. Yep. That's me. The reputable partner.' So Gavin had lied to Dev, and told him that Simon and Jane were proper detectives. Unbelievable! But also, score.

'And if I can just ask,' said Jane carefully, 'why do you want to work with a detective? I assume the police are already investigating?'

'Well, when they first turned up, they were dismissive, to say the least. I was worried they weren't taking it seriously. And then suddenly, it was all CCTV checks and top-secret intel. Now I'm being kept in the dark. I was hoping that a detective that I'd hired would be firmly on *my* side.'

Jane thought back to the unit on de-escalation, to any magic phrases she could say to defuse his annoyance. But it was too late; he'd begun to cry.

'She was the one. I know it sounds cheesy, but it just worked with us, and . . . she wanted kids. She didn't believe in the institution of marriage, and that was fine – well, a nightmare to explain to my parents, but not insurmountable. But I do like kids. What teacher doesn't?'

Plenty, thought Jane. This guy had an innocent streak. Jane wondered if he knew that nine times out of ten, it was the boyfriend who did it. Dev seemed nice, but those were tough odds to beat.

'We were . . . well, we were starting to try.'

After he said that, whatever dam was holding back full-on sobbing broke. Unsure of the etiquette here, Jane quickly wrote down 'baby' before moving onto Dev's sofa and giving him a hug.

'I'm sorry. This must be really hard for you.'

'I just keep having to go over and over it, and when I'm not talking to you or the useless police, my brain is stuck in interview-question-answering mode, so my whole inner monologue has become me explaining our relationship to a made-up outsider, and as I go over everything, I realise that I didn't really know anything about her. Was I that self-centred?'

Jane kept her arm around Dev as he pummelled his weeping eyes. 'You didn't know anything about her?'

He sat up a little but was still a slumped man.

'I mean, I knew she liked crafts, candles and depressing songs, and that she did cute stuff like make the oven mitt talk like a mouth.'

Jane nodded – those were the kinds of things that Dev would find impressive.

'But what did I actually know about her? Why did I just accept that she didn't have any friends? She was born in Kent too, but she just named a village that I didn't recognise, and now I've forgotten it.'

This made him cry more.

'How long were you two together for?'

'A year.'

'So, this all moved quite fast, then?'

'In some ways. She moved in a few months ago. Yes, you could say it was fast, but it felt right, and so time moved differently. You don't even think about time, you know? It was just easy.'

Jane thought about Simon and how he got very tetchy and perfectionistic while plating dinner and never asked if she wanted to use the shower first.

'And what about the other Nellie Thorne cases?' asked Jane.

'You hadn't heard about them before?'

'I bloody well know about them now. But "the mysterious re-disappearing woman" – whether it's a scam, or whatever it is, my Nellie has nothing to do with it.'

'Dev.' She looked him in the eyes. 'What do you really think has happened here?'

He looked stunned for a second, but when the answer came, it had a practised certainty.

'I think she's been abducted. Nellie would never go out and leave the door open. And if she'd decided to ditch me, why leave her phone and purse behind? She'd never leave me worrying like this, she was too nice. She would have sent a text, left a note, anything. And when it comes to "the mysterious re-disappearing woman", there's a highly simple, rational explanation.'

'There is?'

'Coincidence. Think about it. Many, many people have the

same name. Your name's Jane: there are loads of Janes out there. No offence. My girlfriend's called Nellie Thorne. She just happens to have the same name as a woman in a cold case.'

Jane spent a few minutes making Dev a cup of tea and checking that he had a friend to talk to later. All the while, she couldn't stop thinking how silly – or perhaps desperate – it was to think that a name like Nellie Thorne was common enough to be a coincidence.

Her watch buzzed. Five minutes until she really, really had to go. What had she forgotten?

'Dev, I'm sorry to ask, but could I look around upstairs? Just quickly.'

'Oh, sure. Why not? I hope it's tidy.' He tried to make a polite casual-joke-smile.

He carried his tea up the carpeted stairs with them. Camomile, with the bag left in. Jane always felt bag-ins were trustworthy. She noticed Dev's white ankle socks were starting to wear out at the heels. It felt odd to suspect him of murder.

'It never rains but it pours,' said Dev. 'On top of everything, the toilet's started flushing weirdly. The police were here for six hours turning the place over; I should've asked if they'd brought drain rods.'

Jane was holding her notebook, and she scanned her list of pre-prepared questions. She spotted a note she'd made of something Gavin had said in class: 'Could be a loony / attention-seeker.' Better not let Dev see that.

'I've just stopped using the upstairs one 'cos I can't face dealing with it—'

'There's no history of, say, histrionic personality disorder in your family, is there?' Jane cut in.

'Hmm?' Dev turned around.

'Or any, um, behavioural difficulties . . . ?'

'Well, my mum has her moments. That was a joke – sorry. I didn't mean it. No, no behavioural difficulties. Sorry. I'm tired.'

'Cool, cool. Just a standard detective question.'

In the bedroom, Dev showed Jane where the small suitcase had lived, in a built-in mirror-fronted wardrobe. Jane spotted a little dish of jewellery on a pine chest of drawers with a few tarnished necklace chains still in it. Next to it was a candle, half-melted and stuck directly on the wooden top of the dresser. Jane almost wrote down: 'N: didn't even put a coaster under her candles.'

In the wardrobe, Dev pointed to all the clothes left behind. Hanging up were hench puffer jackets, tie-dye dungarees, and T-shirts that were getting stretched out from being hung on hangers. There was an untidy storage box full of jumbled knickers and socks.

'The only thing is, Dev,' said Jane, 'I know all these clothes look like they've been left behind, but couldn't some of them have been for her to sell online? That was her business, wasn't it?'

'Oh,' said Dev. 'Well, yes, I guess some of them, but I'm sure I've seen her wear, uh . . .'

He thrust the hanging clothes back and forth, inspecting each garment for traces they might belong to Nellie.

'Did she have a favourite coat? Is it missing?' Jane continued. 'I mean, it's April: if she left on purpose she'd have packed a coat and jumpers.'

'I'm not sure.' Dev was getting flustered, and started throwing garments onto the carpet searching for knitwear.

'And had she been acting any different lately?'

Dev thought about it.

BRRING-BRRRRING.

'Argh! Sorry! Shit.' Jane scrambled for her phone and turned the alarm off. 'Shit. I have to go. Sorry.'

Jane strode left out of Dev's driveway. She had a purposeful, city-dweller walk. It looked silly on someone so short, and especially silly when she was wearing her novelty Cookie Monster backpack. Dev's street had houses along only one side. On the other was open nature, a thin forest, and a stream with fields visible beyond. There would be a place in there that Jane could take her urgent call. The one she'd been dreading. She felt her stomach tighten.

Her shoes slipped in the mud of the stream bank, but soon enough, she found a tree stump to sit down on. She looked at the time on her phone: 15:59. One minute to go. Down in the stream, a plastic bag had got trapped and looked tattered and translucent like a ghost. In the field beyond were two horses who had put the distance of the whole paddock between them. Maybe they weren't on speaking terms. Still 15:59. This minute was really stretching out.

6

'. . . Five different ways of thinking about a corporate problem. Each symbolised by a different hat. But I always like to say that the king of de Bono's five thinking hats is, in fact, the bit underneath the hat. You. The team who's wearing the hats. That's why, in fact, I like to think of a sixth hat, which is . . .'

Simon clicked onto a new slide: a drawing of a person wearing a hat, whose face was also a hat. It was reminiscent of Magritte's apple head paintings, or a terrible nightmare.

'You.'

'That's great, Simon,' said Simon's boss, Neil, on a video call. 'Except there are, technically speaking, six thinking hats to begin with.'

'Oh, yes, right, of course. Well, then, I guess you're the seventh hat.'

'Cracking,' said Neil. In the background of Neil's spacious countryside living room, several paddle boards were stacked up ready for an imminent non-work trip. 'Just change six to seven, or four to . . . whatever, and it's ready for the client.'

'Great!' said Simon, pleased with another day's toil.

Simon closed the presentation while still sharing his screen, and in its place popped up ten internet browser tabs: Nellie Thorne mystery; Kent's weirdest urban legends; Reddit r/kentmysteries; are male corsets bad for you; and several more. Neil squinted at the tabs as Simon rushed to end the screenshare.

'Anyway, Neil, on a completely different note, I know it's a bit last-minute, and I should go through the holiday request system, but I might need a few days off this week.'

'Have you had a bereavement?'

'Hmm?'

'I have to ask that for last-minute leave requests.'

'Oh, no.'

'Is it a "mental health" thing?'

'Well, I wouldn't quite put it like that . . .'

'Sorry, Simon. There's way too much on to think about time off right now. I really need you to stay laser-focused.'

Simon glanced at his empty inbox. He knew his calendar was bare, besides the blocks reminding him to eat lunch, and a virtual forum for the company's Women in Leadership network.

'Right, of course. No problem.'

'Now, if that's everything, I'll be off, as I need to attend to some urgent business.' Neil had already got up and started walking towards the paddle boards.

'Roger that. Better get back to the grindstone. Thanks, boss. Chat to you soon.'

With the *bloop* of the call disconnecting, Simon sat back in his chair. Out of the window, he stared at the stained brickwork of the houses on the next street. He admired his neighbour's palm tree, listened to a nearby dog barking, and noticed that the man in the bedroom opposite – who always exercised next to the window so that people could see him – was now achieving more pull-ups in a row than ever before. Simon considered what his job – corporate collaboration consultant – added to the world. Surely a lot? Who could argue with the mission statement 'Helping teams work together better'? Some people in the organisation had argued that the statement could be shorter or better written, sure; but fundamentally, who could argue that it wasn't a glorious goal?

Simon's phone buzzed and kept buzzing, and he felt the vibrations through the table, courtesy of caller ID Penny Mash. He rejected the call.

He sighed and got up, padding his fluffy-slippered feet towards the kettle to make a cup of tea. Later, he would have to call his mum back and help her deal with her latest drama. This one had been rumbling on for a while, and it involved a lot of tedious admin for Simon. He hoped he wouldn't be dragged in much deeper – wherever his mother went, chaos tended to follow.

There were other, more appealing things on his to-do list for now. Another Wikipedia hole waited for him, and soon he would be hearing from Jane about her chat with Dev in Tonbridge, and her job interview. He supposed that when the detective agency got into full swing, he could probably do it alongside his full-time job without anyone noticing. But the Women in Leadership network might have to make do without him.

In the woods, Jane was talking about how much she loved gambling.

'Fundamentally, I think that, for some people, I'm sure it's a . . . release, and people should have the right to a hobby that gives them a kick. If they can do that, uh, responsibly . . .'

She could see her bespectacled face taking up the phone's whole screen, her freckly nose magnified. As she rambled, she wore a big keen smile, the kind that would get painful if you maintained it at a networking event for several hours. She wished the interviewers would move on and ask about her fluency in NoSQL databases.

'Basically, while I'm not personally a gambler myself, I have felt excitement quite a lot of times . . .'

'And have you ever been to a major sports event, like the Epsom Derby or the World Cup?'

Jane furrowed her expression as if there was a possibility she really had been to either of those and just had to take a moment to recall it. She was cold, the tree stump she was sitting on had started to dig into her bottom, and she'd begun to wonder if she should be sitting here alone, in the woods, at the site of a potential recent abduction.

'I have been to some really excellent events that people have gambled on. For example, I went to the last Eurovision final.'

'In Tallinn?'

'At my friend's house in Bermondsey. But again, I think that sense of excitement, of all humankind participating in something and choosing to raise the stakes . . .'

The interviewers on the other end of the call nodded neutrally, giving little away.

'Oh, actually, for Eurovision, we did have a sweepstake! So, if it's not too late to change my earlier answer: yes, I have gambled.'

The interview concluded with a hollow 'We'll be in touch', which left Jane feeling deflated, but relieved. She phoned Simon, or, as he had saved himself in her phone: World's Sexiest Man.

'Hey, babe! How did the interview go?'

'So-so. I fumbled it a bit, but I still got a fair bit of information out of Dev, and basically, I kind of nailed it because I've got the answer. I think it's obvious Nellie just left him. A suitcase is gone. He says she left all her clothes, but he didn't know if the clothes she left behind were hers or just stock for her online shop. By the way, Dev asked if we'd help put up missing posters and search the area, and he looked sad, so I said we would. Are you free this weekend?'

'I meant the job interview?' said Simon.

'Oh. That was a big heap of balls.'

'Ah, I'm sorry. It's Mash's Law: never accept a job interview after two p.m. The interviewers' blood sugar levels are never up to it.'

'It's OK. I'm not sure working for a gambling app was my kind of thing anyway.'

'So, what did Dev tell you?'

'The police are pulling out all the stops because of the link to the cold cases. But they've turned up nothing, and they've also heavily implied to him that she's a scammer. He's convinced she wasn't, and that she wasn't using a fake identity, but also, he can't prove that Nellie exists. She was off-grid, in a way. No important documents or NI number that he can find.'

'Maybe she was from the travelling community?'

'Crap. I didn't think of that,' said Jane.

'Or maybe she was a ghooooost!' Simon oohed.

'I think the gambling odds on that one aren't great.'

'So if she left him, why didn't she send a breakup text? Did you look around to see if you could spot a note? Maybe he missed it. The old "note got lost under the doormat" situation.'

'I didn't look for one.'

'And did you get an alibi for him on the day she went missing?'

'Depends how you define an "alibi"—'

'Did you try good cop/bad cop?'

'Simon, I was only one cop.'

'You could have put on different hats to switch between the two. Metaphorically. You know how important it is to pull off a good power play.'

'I didn't need power plays! I just needed to have done next week's class on interrogations.'

'I wonder if they'll teach us how to swing a lightbulb into someone's face.'

'Oh god, Simon, I've really fucked this, haven't I?' said Jane, beginning to pace around the patch of woodland. She reached the fence that marked the edge of the horses' field and leaned against it with her full weight.

'Don't panic, Jane,' said Simon.

'You're right. It's not helpful for the case. I'm in nature, I'm going to try to relax.' She took a few breaths in, as deep as she possibly could.

'What's that sound? Is there a pig snorting?'

'Simon. It's me trying to be calm! I need an alibi for Dev which I can then check for reliability. I need to look around for a note. Although, if there was one, the police would have found it— Oh balls, I asked him if she was acting different lately, and he looked like he was going to say yes, but then my alarm went off and I had to leave to sell my soul to the devil!'

'Where are you, by the way?'

'I'm in some woodland near Dev's house, just across the street. After this, it sort of turns into fields and stuff.'

'Oh my god, Jane! You should get out of there!'

Jane looked around her, defensively pushing her back against the wire fence.

'What? Why?'

'Well, if Nellie was murdered, wouldn't this be the perfect place to hide her body? And thus, wouldn't Dev keep an eye on you to see if you went off looking for it?'

Jane exhaled. 'Simon, I really think she just left him.'

'I like that you've got a hunch, Jane. Good detectives are known for their hunches. But aren't they also meant to eliminate other possibilities before sticking with their hunch? "Hunch" is a weird word, isn't it? I've said it quite a lot now. Hunch. Hunch. A hunch over lunch.'

'You're right. We should be thorough. I'll have a scan around for clues. Just in case I can spot anything the police missed.' Even as she said it, she thought it sounded overconfident.

'Be careful. Is there anyone around?'

Jane looked up and saw that clouds were starting to gather, darkening the woods around her. 'I don't think so.'

She crouched and began looking at the soil, which looked very much like soil. She glanced up, taking in the large patch of woodland: it was about half the size of a football pitch and triangular in shape.

'It's a shame you refused to bring the magnifying glass. I did say you might need it,' said Simon.

'I don't think I've got long. It's getting all gloomy here and I think it's going to rain. Oh, I've got an idea!' Jane turned her iPhone torch on and began scanning it over the ground. 'I've put my torch on, so it'll catch anything shiny or different.'

'Jane, that's inspired!'

'I've got something!' She stooped to grub the dirt off her shiny clue. 'OK . . . It's an old bottle top.'

'Hmm,' Simon considered. 'I don't think that'll be Nellie's.'

Jane scanned the ground along the fence, then turned back and did another strip in a mowing-the-lawn pattern while Simon reeled off motivational quotes in an impressively serious voice.

'Come on, Jane. Nothing is impossible. The word itself says, "I am possible." Hold on, that's not right.'

'Wait a second!'

'Have you found something?'

'Just a condom.'

'Used?'

'Not sure. I'm trying not to look it in the eye.'

And so it continued until a growl of far-off thunder sounded, and Jane looked up to find she was in the woods in partial darkness.

'I think I might've done what I can for now, Si. But you were right. It's good to cover all bases.'

'That sounds about right, babe. Best get home now. And remember, fear kills more dreams than failure.'

'Thanks, Simon,' she said.

But she couldn't help herself scanning one more bit of ground. She stopped at the tree stump she'd sat on earlier and shone her torch around it. The ground was unbroken soil sprouting the odd weed, except for a patch that had been scrabbled at by an animal.

'Hmm,' she said. 'I'm just going to . . .' She dug into the scrabbled soil with her hand. A few centimetres down, she found something red. 'Argh!'

'"If you look after your staff, they'll look after your customers." Richard Branson. Sorry Jane, that's quite a business-specific one. Let me go back on my aunt's Facebook. Those were a bit more all-purpose.'

'Simon, I've found something!'

She poked at the shiny red something to find it was solid and cold.

'What is it?'

She excavated the evidence with her fingers. 'It's a red candle. Well, it's like the stump of a candle. It's been burned down. And it was buried.'

'That's odd.'

'Simon, I saw one like this in the house. A red candle like this, the same width and everything. It must be Nellie's. Or Dev's, I guess.'

'How did it get out there?'

'I don't know. Could she have had it in her pocket, and

then been kidnapped, and . . . and then it fell out, and an animal buried it?'

'I'm not sure, Jane. How often do you take your candles for a walk?'

Jane had been tracing her finger around the waxy molten rim of the candle stub, but she started to find it creepy and held it between two fingertips instead.

'So, is it . . . evidence in the case?' said Simon.

'I don't know. It must be. But it's weird,' said Jane. She found a packet of tissues in her bag, removed one, and carefully wrapped up the candle. 'We should buy some evidence bags on Amazon.'

'Yes! Great thinking. I'll order some,' said Simon. 'And are you going to come home now?'

'There's probably one more thing I should do. Seeing as I ballsed up the interview, and now I've just covered a clue in fingerprints, I should really go and talk to the neighbours.'

'Jane, go easy on yourself. Can't we do it tomorrow?'

'No, apparently people's memories fade quite quickly. That's why you do door-to-doors and get their statements as soon as possible. We learned that from Gavin in Unit One.'

'Ah, right. I guess my memory's faded quite quickly.'

Judging from the lack of lights at 36 Shipwell Drive, Dev wasn't home, but at number 35, a balding man in a shirt and cardigan opened the door. As soon as he'd established that Jane wasn't keen to clean his windows or clear his guttering, he was happy to help, providing plenty of information, some of which was useful, most of which was not. For example, that he thought Dev had left for school at the usual time on Monday morning, the day Nellie had disappeared, and that he, Ian, had worked as a marine engineer and could now only fall asleep to recordings of ships' engines, which had been hard for his ex-wife. He said Dev had come home at the normal time on the day of the disappearance, around 5.30 p.m. Of course, Ian pointed out, Nellie's disappearance could have happened before Dev had left for school, and no, he hadn't seen Nellie that day or ever. He hadn't so much as heard an argument through the wall.

By this stage, Jane had guessed that Ian was the type of person who'd listen for them. She wondered if, as a general project, she should make her own argument voice a notch quieter. She said goodbye and, after a quick story about straightening a bent rudder, Ian closed his door, but not before he had reassured her that he'd be there all night if she needed anything, and that she should pop back if she ever fancied a ride on a tugboat.

As Jane got back out onto the road, the first speckles of rain bothered her face, and she began thinking through her route back to the station. But before she set off, she glanced back at Dev's house, where there was now a light on downstairs in the living room. So he was home after all. She decided there was one more thing to do before she clocked off.

This final job fell under the 'sneaking around' section of the Detective's Weekly Task Planner, so she tried to make her footsteps as quiet as possible on the gravel of Dev's driveway. As a roly-poly, frizzy-haired child, Jane had dreamed of being an elegant Tolkienesque elf, and she had practised walking silently, because she'd read that elves could mute their footsteps. Jane had never had that kind of bodily control, not then nor now, and a rustle at Dev's drawn curtain spooked her. She ducked and ran straight for the doorway on all fours like a weird little animal.

Once there, she was hidden by a potted shrub from the sightline of the window. Breathing unfitly, she lifted up the doormat: no breakup note. Well, it had been a long shot. But there was a silver Yale key: almost certainly for the front door. Shit. *Would Gavin take the key?* Jane's cold fingers fumbled three attempts to pick up the flat key from the doorstep. She slipped it into her back pocket as silently as an elf.

'Jane?' said Dev, as he opened the front door.

'Dev!' She nudged the doormat into place just in time and shot up as quickly as her back would let her. 'Sorry, I dropped a headphone. I was just coming back to, um, to . . .'

'I saw you go to Ian's house. Did he have anything useful?'

'Oh, he wasn't much help! But I felt I should go over there. It's just standard detecting practice to go house to house, talk to everybody, get his alibi.' Her cheeks were singeing hot.

'Right.'

'. . . Which is actually the reason I'm here! I forgot to get yours. Just to eliminate you. God, the word "eliminate" seems a bit insensitive for murder investigations, don't you think? I can't believe no one's noticed that before. Not that Nellie's— Sorry, I mean, of course, we'll find her.'

The limits of Dev's patience had been reached. He looked at her suspiciously.

'Yes. I was at school. Anyway, I'll see you on Saturday if you still want to help with the posters? I've done a lot this week, but I want to put up a few hundred more.'

'Sure. I'll see you on Saturday.'

'Who is it?'

Both Dev and Jane froze, because it wasn't either of them who'd spoken. A woman, clear as a crystal lake, was talking from inside the house.

'Sorry,' said Dev. 'I'm watching *EastEnders*. I've got it turned up loud. See you soon,' and he shut the door before Jane could say anything. Of course, she crouched to listen at the living-room window, wishing she could see through the closed curtains, hearing nothing but the rain thumping the driveways and gardens. How much rain should a detective let trickle down the back of their neck before they give up? For Jane, it was just the one rivulet.

7

KENT NEWS ONLINE, 11 APRIL

WOMAN MISSING FROM TONBRIDGE

There are concerns over a woman who went missing in Tonbridge on Monday. Nellie Thorne was last seen at her home at 8.15 a.m., and went missing some time before 5.25 p.m. Police are appealing for help finding her. Ms Thorne, 25, is described as 5'8", white, with a slim build and long brown hair. Anyone with information on her whereabouts is urged to contact the police immediately.

Saturday 13 April – Present Day

It was Saturday, three days since Jane's trip to meet Dev, and now Simon Mash, weekend detective, was ready to join the case. He looked up from his phone.

'Well, Kent News Online is all over it,' he said. 'There's not much information in the article, but you never know. We might end up with the only viral case in class.'

Jane wasn't listening. She was absorbed in the 'Missing Persons' section of her *Little Book of Detecting* – the stocking-filler that had sparked her sleuthing obsession.

'The first few hours are crucial,' she said. 'Crap.'

The book was part of the detective's day bag she'd packed for their trip to Tonbridge, which also contained a blue light, wet wipes, gummy sweets and Simon's antique magnifying glass. They'd managed to get a table on the train, and Simon ran his fingers along the plastic edge. He was wearing his best driving gloves.

'Hmm. She disappeared on Monday, class was on Tuesday,' he said, counting on his fingers. 'Well, I'm sure the first six days are crucial, too.'

'I feel bad,' said Jane, who'd been spooked by the 'Outcomes' section of the chapter. 'Why haven't I been more worried about this woman? She could be dead! I mean, I've been worried. But it hasn't felt real. I've been convinced that she just left him.'

'Those are all possibilities,' said Simon. 'But remember, we're two young professionals doing a detecting class. We're not social services, or Batman. We're Robin at best. If we can help, then great, but don't beat yourself up about it.'

'I did hear that woman in his house. Maybe it was her? Or maybe it really was the telly, and Nellie's dead.'

Jane had opened the sweets without realising, and suddenly noticed she was chewing.

'Should we be eating sweets?' she said. 'Is it a bit disrespectful?'

'No, I think it's alright,' said Simon wisely. 'We'll need the energy. Imagine if Poirot hadn't had his breakfast of eggs and toast squares. He wouldn't have solved anything. Cutting the little squares helped him get into a methodical frame of mind for the day.'

Jane stuck four gummy cherries in her mouth at once. 'I think I'd better go back to Dev's house today and re-hide the key under his doormat,' she said. 'He might've already noticed it's missing, but he can't say anything if I put it back. That would be too awkward, right? "Did you steal my house key and borrow it for a few days?"'

'Absolutely,' said Simon, sweeping his floppy hair off his face with a leather-gloved hand. 'And if he brings it up, we go full Bill Clinton. Deny, deny, deny.'

'Cool.' Jane looked out of the window. She was hoping to enjoy the trees and house-backs whipping past, but they made her feel a bit dizzy. 'Why did I steal someone's house key?'

'I think it was good detective instinct,' said Simon. 'I mean, if we were movie detectives, we'd get in there and see if we can find Nellie. If you heard what you think you heard, she could be sitting around in there eating cereal. And if we find her, it's case closed. Coursework donezo.'

'Simon, there's no way I can get away with breaking and entering. I can't even lift a doormat without getting busted.'

'I reckon I could get away with it,' said Simon Mash, master criminal.

'Yes, you could get away with murder.'

Jane got her phone out and went back to the Nellie Thorne Wikipedia page. She re-read everything she'd found that morning: in 1971, the first Nellie had gone missing. Or, at least, the first one that anyone had recorded. There was a bullet-point list of all the years there'd been a Nellie-related investigation: 1971, 1976, 1987 and 1997.

'It's weird you hadn't heard of this one, Jane,' said Simon through a mouthful of colourful bears. 'Thought you loved crime.'

'I do,' she said. 'But most of the books and podcasts are about American crime. I guess there's not as much appetite for four disappearances in Kent. A humble Home Counties mystery,' said Jane.

'Hmm,' said Simon. 'Like the mystery of who stole my dad's tennis racquet at the David Lloyd gym.'

The Wikipedia page didn't offer much information on the women, beyond their towns of residence – all in Kent – and dates of disappearance. There were no updates about anyone being found.

'Jane!' Simon sat up straight, having discovered something massive.

'What is it?!'

'There's a pub in Tonbridge that Oliver Cromwell visited!' He kept scrolling. 'There are so many good pubs we could go to.'

'This isn't about going to the pub, Simon! We're on duty.'

'Jane! What would Inspector Morse do?'

'I'm not sure it's good that all our detective role models are fictional.'

'OK,' said Simon, 'then what would Gavin do?'

Jane thought about it. 'We don't know him that well, to be honest.' She looked back at her phone. 'It's one thing helping Dev put up posters to find his girlfriend. But what about the cold cases? How are we going to link our Nellie to them?'

'No point worrying about that while we have real leads to follow up with,' said Simon. 'Chuck it on the laterbase.'

It didn't sit well with Jane to kick problems down the line just because they weren't easy. She preferred to worry about everything, constantly, all at once. But she had to admit, tracking down a possibly kidnapped woman was enough to be getting on with.

'OK,' she agreed. 'Let's think of it this way: it's a mystery of two halves. Dev's missing girlfriend, and the Nellie Thorne legend stuff.'

'And right now,' said Simon seriously, leaning forward to cram a gummy ring onto his finger then nibble it off, 'we could be hot on the trail of a kidnapper.'

On Shipwell Drive they met another new recruit on the kidnapper's trail.

'Are you allowed to call a dog Hotdog?' said Jane. 'I can't tell if it's clever or stupid.'

'If in doubt,' said Simon, 'I tend to assume things are clever.'

'She belongs to one of the administrators at school,' said Dev, reaching down to pat the panting dog's flank, a gesture of goodwill before the search. 'Look, I don't know the science around how good chocolate Labradors' noses are, but they've got to be better than mine, haven't they, Hotdog?'

Hotdog huffed out a little sneeze.

'The police have searched this area, but they haven't been back in a few days,' continued Dev. 'I feel we should be searching for clues repeatedly, perhaps daily, just in case something was missed. So, we're going to search in the three directions a kidnapper could have taken Nellie. Left along the road, right along the road, or straight ahead into the wooded patch.'

'Good deducting,' said Simon, nodding.

Dev swung a backpack round onto his front and started rummaging. Hotdog cocked her nose up hopefully, smelling pork balls in the side pocket. Instead, out came a hairbrush disgustingly knotted with mousey-brown hair. Dev offered it to Hotdog to sniff.

'Interesting,' said Jane. 'Why a hairbrush?'

'Well,' said Dev, a little defensively, 'as I wasn't sure which of her clothes had been washed recently, or were even, you know, worn by her . . . I thought the hairbrush would be the most Nellie-smelling thing.'

All eyes were on Hotdog as she took a moment, considering the scent of the hairbrush. Then she began eating it. Not wanting to wrestle a dog, Dev reasoned with her.

'No, no, let's not eat that.' His teacher voice was useless here. 'No, please . . .'

With a bit of effort, Dev nudged the hairbrush out of her mouth.

'OK,' Dev told her. 'Um, go.'

Hotdog sat down and then lay down on the pavement.

'Right.'

'Yes, I've had that feeling,' said Jane.

Dev crouched down and began giving the dog a pep talk. 'Listen, Hottie—'

'Not sure you should call a dog that,' advised Simon.

'If you can get up and search the area, I'll give you a treat.'

Treat? said the dog's hopeful face.

'Try giving her a treat after smelling the hairbrush,' said Jane, despite her doubts about this languid pet becoming a ruthless police hound.

Whether the hairbrush-treat method worked remained unclear, but they did use it to lure Hotdog onto her feet and into the wooded patch, crossing the road carefully.

'I searched round here the other day,' said Jane, 'but it was a bit dark, so I probably didn't cover the area as thoroughly as I should have. Like, for example, I missed that far corner.'

'I think we want to be out here for at least an hour or two, seeing what Hotdog can sniff out in various directions. Then after that, I've got about five hundred missing posters we can put up around town.' Dev slapped the backpack. 'Used the last of Year Nine's printing paper, but this has got to be more important than *The Great Gatsby*.'

'Certainly,' said Jane, the evil light of an idea arriving in her eyes.

She hung back as Dev and Hotdog started sniffing around.

'Simon, I think we ought to do that thing we discussed.'

'Megabus mile high club?'

Dev was still in earshot. Simon, almost a foot taller than Jane, had to lean down to hear her.

'That . . . thing . . . we discussed on the train.'

Simon looked blank. Dev followed Hotdog down to the little stream.

'Should she be hungry for this?' he yelled from afar. 'Maybe I shouldn't have given her breakfast?'

'No, I think that's attack dogs,' Jane called back. Dev gave a thumbs-up.

'Get into the house, Simon,' she said, and slipped him the key from out of her back pocket.

'Really?! I was kind of bluffing on the train, you know,' he said.

'I know, but you still have a better chance than me. Anyway, it'll be quick: in, is Nellie chained to the radiator, out.'

'Oh no, oh no,' Dev called out. 'Yep, that's a hairball. I don't think we should have let her chew the brush earlier.'

'I'll cover for you,' said Jane.

Before Simon could make any excuses, she began making them for him.

'Dev,' Jane strode up to him, 'I'm so sorry about this, but Simon's feeling squeamish.' Dev looked up from prodding the forest floor with his shoe as she continued: 'He's worried that we'll find a—' *Don't say dismembered hand* . . . 'He's just squeamish when it comes to, you know, all the emotions around this. But I was wondering if he could get a head start on the missing posters instead, and we'll meet him in town?'

'Yeah, OK.'

'Great! Thanks,' said Jane. 'Can I get some posters?'

Once she had an inch-thick chunk of posters, she brought them back to Simon. 'You've got this.'

'Smash,' he said weakly. He'd been hoping to try out his new detective catchphrase under more empowered circumstances.

When Simon returned to the end of Dev's driveway, he found a cardiganed man in the front garden of the next house, pruning shrubs. Simon's confident stride often turned heads, and the neighbour eyed him as he approached.

'Howdy,' said Simon, raising a hand. 'Friend of Dev's. I'm just picking something up.'

The man nodded but didn't smile. Crap. What would James Bond do in this situation? Probably silence him with garrotte wire, but Simon would have to rely on the fact that neighbours didn't talk to each other in real life.

Simon could see the search party of three small figures, two human and one canine, far away in the copse. When he was sure they were looking at the ground, he slipped the key from his pocket and rattled it into the lock, hand shaking like a caffeine fiend.

Inside it was cool and luckily free from the beeps of a burglar alarm needing to be silenced. Simon scanned the hallway: very modern in design, a relatively new build. It would be a stylish space with the addition of some neon lettering or a brightly coloured statement ceiling. He opened a cupboard door to the right: just brooms. Why would someone own so many brooms?

'Hello?' he said. Was that a good idea? If Nellie was here, perhaps he shouldn't let her see him?

'Forget that,' he added out loud. 'There's no one here.'

He crept into the open-plan living room/kitchen area. The coffee table was strewn with a light mess of pens and papers, the detritus of homemade posters and note-taking. But no mystery woman. Not quite knowing why, Simon looked in the fridge and then in the biscuit tin. Did the front door have a video doorbell? He should have checked! Too late now. Perhaps he could destroy it? Was it worth getting some coffee on to brew so he could pour it over the doorbell on the way out? No, that didn't seem like the kind of thing Jane would rubber-stamp.

He moved out into the hallway for a quick scan of upstairs. A bit of woodland mud had rubbed off his shoe onto the cream hallway carpet.

Crunch, crunch, crunch, came the footsteps up the driveway. Oh no. Filled with total panic, Simon ran muddy-booted up the stairs and did the only thing he could think of. He locked himself in the bathroom.

Downstairs there was a metallic *ker-lunk* – the front door opening?

Simon wasn't prone to anxiety, but he found himself breathing heavily and thinking about how well he might do in prison. He'd always felt he would either thrive or crumble, but there'd be no in-between.

TACK-TACK-TACK.

Someone was banging the door knocker. Simon felt dizzy. At least it wasn't Dev at the door: he wouldn't knock his own knocker. But it could be the nosy neighbour, phone in hand and ready to call the police. It was time for Simon to get out. First, he had to get the mud off his shoes and the bathroom tiles. He wetted a wad of toilet roll in the sink and clumsily cleaned his soles, shedding soil and clumps of baby grass onto the floor.

'Bollocks,' he muttered, trying to wipe the vinyl floor tiles clean, but smearing the mud around instead. By the time he'd finished, he had two handfuls of wet, mushy, muddy paper. He tipped it into the toilet, wanting to flush all evidence of his presence, and pressed the button.

Instead of swirling and draining, the papery water rose up, about to spill over and flood: the wodge of muddy paper had blocked the toilet.

'Oh, Christ on a pedalo.'

The water stopped centimetres from the top of the bowl. Simon couldn't risk another flush – that would flood the floor. Deeply upset, he pushed up his sleeve and sunk his hand into the depths. Disintegrating toilet paper tickled him like seaweed. How much hand-washing would it take to feel clean after this? It was one for the philosophers. He searched deep into the toilet's exit hole for a blockage. But instead of connecting with a ball of loo roll, his fingers nudged a plastic stick. He pulled it from where it was wedged in the pipe, brought it to the surface, and saw something that no adult could fail to recognise.

He looked at the results box: did one line mean pregnant, or two lines? He had absolutely no idea.

8

'Well, I've got no idea either,' said Jane, steering Simon into Tonbridge's big Sainsbury's. In the woods, Jane had announced that she was going to help Simon stick up posters, and had left Dev chasing Hotdog, who'd been chasing squirrels. The supermarket was the meeting point because, after his mission impossible, Simon had insisted that he needed a bottle of chocolate milk.

'Why did you think I'd know what a pregnancy test result means?' said Jane. 'Because I'm a woman?'

They strode fast, swerving round families' capacious trolleys.

'Um, well, sort of. Sorry. I mean, have you ever done one?'

'Yes, of course, everyone has, but not for a few years and then a few years before that, so I can't remember what the lines mean. Actually, hold on.'

She rearranged the missing posters in her arms to get out her phone and start searching.

'Yeah, that's right! It's two for pregnant, which would make sense, because one of the lines is to ensure the test is working. Then if the second line goes, you're Preggers McGregors.'

Simon pulled the test from his pocket.

'Well, it's positive.'

He shivered, perhaps due to the chill of the fridge aisle, or perhaps because he was holding a stick someone had peed on. Jane had noticed straight away that he was in a weird mood, pale and full of energy, but not in a good or useful way.

'Christ,' she said. 'Well.'

Simon found his favourite brand of chocolate milk and grabbed two bottles.

'Oh, I'm fine, thanks,' said Jane.

'They're both for me, Jane. In fact . . .' He pulled a third bottle off the shelf. 'Maybe I want a Müller Corner too.'

'I think this is potentially much more serious now,' said Jane, picking up yoghurts. She stared at the labels, their happy cows and fresh tumbling fruit. 'If she was pregnant, we're talking about two missing people. It's less of an incentive to run away. Or is it more of an incentive? God, I don't know.'

'So you didn't find anything with Dev and Inspector Hound?'

'No, thank god. I mean, it wasn't likely we would after the previous police searches.'

'Did you tell him about the candle?'

'No,' said Jane. 'I had a feeling I should keep that one back.'

'Maybe we should do the same with the pregnancy test. Why would you flush it down the loo?'

'If you didn't want anyone to find it in the bin,' said Jane. 'And if you didn't understand the first thing about plumbing. But people flush all sorts.'

'I know,' said Simon glumly. 'My mum once flushed my goldfish.'

'That's terrible!' said Jane. 'I think you're meant to bury them these days.'

'Oh, it wasn't dead. She'd just decided it had "sided with Dad".'

They were just wandering around aisles now, looking at stacked juice cartons and racks of fresh milk, taking in the supermarket smell of plastic packaging and baked bread. Simon cracked a chocolate milk and magnanimously handed his third one to Jane. They sipped them quietly.

'So . . . ?' said Simon, breaking the silence in the cheese aisle. 'Aren't you going to congratulate me? I did a crime!'

'Come on, Simon, that can't have been your first crime. I'm not even convinced we're allowed to be drinking these before we've paid for them.'

'It's the first non-socially acceptable one I've ever done.' Simon was guilty of a drunken traffic cone theft or two, and he'd once accidentally shoplifted a book of fabric swatches from the home furnishings section of John Lewis at Bluewater. 'I remembered to leave the key under the mat on the way out. And I've learned how to use carpet cleaner.'

'Well done, Simon,' said Jane.

'There was a moment I thought I was rumbled. The only reason I found the pregnancy test was because I hid in the bathroom. I heard someone walking up the driveway, and then they banged on the door! But then there weren't any other sounds, and I waited for ages, until I was sure I couldn't hear anything.'

'Don't forget to breathe, Simon.'

'And when I finally came out of the bathroom, there was something on the doormat, and it turned out what I'd heard was someone dropping off a handwritten note!'

'What did it say?!'

'It said: "Hello, I'm cleaning gutters in your area. Please call me on this number if you need your gutters cleaned." I mean honestly – how needy is that, to bang on the door? "Knock-knock, please read my flyer."'

They mooched back through squash and sparkling water towards the tills.

'Right,' said Jane, trying to picture a detective's pinboard in her mind. 'First things first: good work, Simon, on the pregnancy test and the sneaking you did to get it. It's not often a man finds himself locked in a bathroom sweating over a pregnancy test, so it was probably a useful life experience. Second: I think we should keep our focus laser, er, focused on the actual missing Nellie and – as we now know – her baby.'

'Laser focus is always good,' said Simon, whacking out a brightly coloured debit card to pay for the treats.

'And I've been thinking about what you said. This does feel a bit above our pay grade. It's kind of irresponsible to keep it to ourselves if we think Nellie and the baby could be in danger.'

'Should we ping Gavin?' suggested Simon.

'No, I don't want to lose points for initiative,' said Jane. 'But I do think it's time to talk to the police.'

They paused by the noticeboards that lined the way out. Jane held pins in her mouth and stuck posters to the boards, each with a black-and-white photo of Nellie (Year Nine had been out of colour toner). Nellie's pretty heart-shaped face was covered in straight strands of blown-about hair on Broadstairs beach, Dev's shoulder cropped out beside her. Was it interesting, Jane wondered, that he hadn't been able to find a picture of her alone? Not just somebody's girlfriend, attached by the shoulder.

Simon cracked the lid off his second drink and read the other bulletins.

'Spa and wellness retreat, chakra-cleansing classes every Tuesday and Thursday.' He stabbed the chakra-cleansing poster with his finger. 'When all this is over, I think you owe me a week here.'

Jane and Simon didn't find the Tonbridge Police Station waiting area to be any more appealing than Dev had.

The entrance was small and clinically white, with red plastic chairs lined up along the right-hand side of the wall, and above them a pinboard of ageing flyers warning women not to wear jewellery (it attracted thieves) and missing pet posters (including a ferret called Bertie who'd been on the lam since 2014).

Simon had hoped to get to the reception desk before Jane. He wasn't a bragger, but knew he had the stronger ability to charm people into getting what he wanted. However, Jane's power-walk was too strong.

'Hello,' she said. 'We want to talk to somebody about a crime, please, and as soon as possible, because it's urgent.'

Simon took in everything he could about the receptionist: floral M&S top, mid-length dyed blonde hair, probably mid-fifties. Seemed like the type to have tea before bed, not wine. Almost certainly liked *Strictly*.

'Alright,' she said heavily, clicking her mouse with a pearlescent-pink-nailed finger. 'Do you have a crime number?'

Jane turned to Simon.

'I'll have to text Dev and get it.'

'Well, is it not your crime?' asked the receptionist.

'Our crime?' said Simon. 'Well, we didn't do it, if that's what you mean.'

'I hear that a lot. But I can't let you speak to someone if it's not your crime. There are confidentiality rules, so . . . I'm sorry.' She shrugged un-sorrily.

'No, no, it is our crime!' Simon stepped forward. The receptionist raised an eyebrow.

'Listen here, madam,' said Jane, pushing past Simon to poke the desk with her index finger. 'As, er, tax-paying members of the public, we'd like to talk to your . . . commanding officer!'

'Excuse me,' Simon cut in, 'could I just borrow my partner for a minute?'

He gestured for Jane to step aside with him.

'What? I was doing a power play.'

'A power play isn't just being rude, Jane! A power play is an elegant dance. It's the feathers of a weedy bird fluffing up to make it look bigger. It's pretending you haven't heard of the A-list celebrity your co-worker saw in Whole Foods. It's going to your boss's awards ceremony presentation, but not staying to congratulate her after. It's big, it's bold, it's outrageous. It's part of a long tradition of power pageantry.'

'It sounds like part of a long tradition of absolute bollo—'

Simon stepped back to the reception desk.

'I'm very sorry about that, Ms . . . ?'

'Becca.'

'Becca. Becca, I understand you're all very busy around here and I'm sure you understand too that we're in a difficult situation. Grief makes people act, well, you know.' He gestured towards Jane in a 'poor old thing' way. 'See, a relative of ours was reported missing on Monday, and all we really want is an update to see whether any new information has come in. Her name's Nellie Thorne.'

'Ah, yes,' said Becca. 'I've heard about that one.'

'Great! So perhaps you can tell us anything you've heard. We're desperate to find out what happened to Nellie.'

'So you're relatives of Miss Thorne?'

'We're her cousins,' said Simon. Jane winced; Nellie had no friends or family. It was one of the main problems with the investigation. But Becca might not know that. And how else could they worm their way in?

'Yes,' said Becca, looking at Simon and Jane, 'I can see the sibling resemblance between you two.'

Simon breezed onward with the steadiness of a talented

corporate professional or perhaps just a man who'd been mistaken for his girlfriend's brother before. 'Now, as you can imagine, we're gutted that our cousin has gone missing. And what I really want to ask you is: is there a vending machine nearby?'

'Oh. Um, yes, just round this corner here, to the left of the desk.'

Simon went to the machine. Jane heard his card beep, mechanisms whirring, and the thuds of three chocolate bars hitting the deck. When he returned to Becca, he laid a Twix, a Bounty and a Lion bar out in front of her in a fan shape.

'Here's the situation: if I can guess your favourite, you have to keep it. Grief gives me sugar cravings, and I'm at genuine risk of eating all three.'

'Oh,' said Becca, visibly trying to figure out the catch. Jane was certain he must have read this in some pick-up artist manual.

'Now, my guess is . . .' Simon folded his arms in a thinking pose and scratched his chin. This was just theatrics: he was the magician who already knew the ace of spades was up his sleeve. 'I think you're a Twix fan. There's more than meets the eye to you, Becca. There are layers, complex layers – some are crunchy, some are caramel, and you keep it all behind that chocolate-coated facade. But just when people think they have you figured out, they forget: there are two sides to you.'

Becca took the Twix and put it carefully by her keyboard, lining it up exactly parallel, holding back a chuckle. 'I suppose that would have been my first choice.'

'If there did happen to be anything you could do to help us get an update on our cousin's case, we'd be so, so grateful.'

She paused, taking in Simon's smiling, handsome face. He'd cracked her like an egg. The drawbridge was nudging down.

'Look,' said Becca, leaning forward, 'if you're not the person who registered the crime and received your letter with your active crime number, I can't tell you anything. I'm sorry.'

She watched their shoulders drop.

'But . . .' She looked around as if somebody might be bothering to eavesdrop. 'Well, there is one thing. There's a man who retired a few years ago who managed several similar cases. Bernard Parker. He was the Kent DCC for the last few years of his career. He won't be able to talk about this specific case, but he's a nice man, and he might be willing to give you a bit of reassurance about how these kinds of investigations are carried out. He drinks at the Miller's Arms most days from about five o'clock.'

'The Miller's Arms!' Simon gaped. 'Isn't that the pub Oliver Cromwell drank at?'

'It is!' Becca glowed. 'If you haven't been, you must. They do a great Sunday roast, with real crackling.'

'Thank you, Becca,' said Simon, with a big, warm smile. He pocketed the other two chocolate bars and pointed at Jane. 'This means a lot to me and my sister.'

'Wow,' said Jane as the building's automatic doors closed behind them. 'How did you know she wanted a Twix? Is that from the psychology module you did at university? Or did you just know that nobody likes Lions or Bounties?' Jane did, in fact, like Bounties. She felt it made her unique.

'Not quite,' said Mash the magician. 'I saw a Twix wrapper poking out of her lunchbox.'

9

It turned out being a detective did involve some working from the pub. The Miller's Arms was airy and wood-panelled, the type of pub that used to be ancient but had been expensively refurbished by the parent company. There was a solid wooden bar at its heart, and cosy corner tables dotted around the edges. It was designed to please everybody; from the men at one end of the bar watching football, to the people like Simon, who imagined it was the kind of place George Orwell might go for a stout.

'Being a detective is all about stakeholder management,' said Simon, taking a sip of his craft IPA, drinking in the pretty pub over the brim of the glass. 'It proves my point, really, that everything in life is stakeholder management at the end of the day. It's humbling. Awe-inspiring. I might present that at a steering committee next month.'

Jane was too frustrated to speak. Almost. 'I know what's going to happen now. You're going to spot Bernard Parker, you'll buy him a Jägerbomb, he'll tell you they've solved the case, next thing we know the Kent chief of police will have turned up for a round of shots, and by chucking-out time they'll have offered you a job.'

Jane had chosen Diet Coke because they were on duty, and only half a pint of it, because she wanted to be able to sleep tonight.

'Jane,' said Simon gravely. 'Be honest. Is there something wrong?'

'Well – I'm crap at this, aren't I? But you don't even care about it, and you're amazing! Today alone, you've broken into a house and as good as broken into the police records system, and now it's half past four in the afternoon and you're having a pint!'

Simon knew it was crucial to address these points in the correct order. But would he begin with (a) 'You're a good detective'; (b) 'I do care about this'; (c) 'When it comes to breaking into houses, I'm an up-and-comer at best'; or (d) phone a friend?

'Jane. Come on. You're a great detective!' He monitored her face. This seemed like a hopeful tack. 'You're the one with the logical mind who can keep all these bits of information up in the air and put them together! And I'm here for you, to put my hand in toilets and charm the Kent police version of my mum, but you know we wouldn't have achieved anything today without the combination of my practical magic and your brilliant brain. Smash!' He lifted his pint hopefully.

'I guess so. "Smash" because ... Simon Mash, right?' She ignored his beaming grin and got out the *Little Book of Detecting* from her bag, just to turn it around in her hands. 'I understand everything in here, easily, and I can remember it all. Until the time comes to put it into practice in the real world.' The real world. Jane's long-term nemesis. 'You know what, screw it, I'm having a pint. Do you want another one?'

At the bar, Jane was waiting for her drinks when a square-faced, thickset man with neat iron-grey hair asked if she would mind moving so he could reach his bar stool.

'Oh, sure,' she said. It was a prime location, near the end of the bar, with a view of the whole room and a wall behind for leaning. But while he settled on the stool and hung his coat on the under-bar hook, Jane didn't move a polite distance away, but studied his face instead. Earlier, she'd looked up DCC Bernard Parker online and had found a picture of him in the *Tonbridge Gazette*, from when he'd cut the ribbon at a new fudge stall in the shopping centre.

'Um, by the way . . .'

'Yes?' The man smiled, but only below the eyes, and he was already unfolding his newspaper.

'The thing is . . .'

The man took a thin glasses case from his overcoat pocket, removed the glasses, and put them on his nose with a wiggle.

'Yes, usual, please, Jay,' he said to the barman. 'Can I help you with something, Miss . . . ?'

'Jane, I'm Jane. It's just that, um, are you Bernard Parker?'

'That's me,' he said, taking off his glasses.

'I was wondering if I could ask you something?'

'Fire away.'

Jane wasn't sure what she should keep close to her chest and what she should reveal. This was going to require poise and confidence. But right now, she felt like a trainee doctor holding a lung. She waved to Simon at their corner table, who understood the severity of the wave and came to the bar, trailing their bags and coats with him.

'Hello there. Simon Mash,' said Simon, moving the coats and bags around to shake Bernard's hand.

'We're cousins of the missing woman, Nellie Thorne,' said Jane, 'and we heard from— We heard that you might know something about her case?'

'Cousins?' repeated Bernard, not buying it.

'Sorry. We're not her cousins. That's a cover story. We know Nellie doesn't have any family,' Jane blustered.

'I can see the resemblance between you two, though,' said Bernard.

Jane took a big breath, preparing to tell him the truth.

'We're podcasters!' Simon chipped in brightly. 'And we're working on an episode about the Nellie cases.'

Jane blinked hard, trying to absorb the cover story: they were now civilians pretending to be detectives pretending to be podcasters who, until a moment ago, had been pretending to be siblings.

'Well,' said Bernard, watching the barman put a large glass of red wine down in front of him. 'I'd love to talk about the case. Love to.'

'Oh, great,' said Jane.

'But I can't. Sorry.'

'Are you sure?' said Simon.

'Completely sure.'

'Not even if we bought you a big bag of fudge?' offered Jane.

'Not even then, and luckily for you, since I'm retired, that doesn't count as attempting to bribe a police officer.'

Jane's stomach went cold, but Bernard was smiling.

'Like I say, absolutely love to. Great case. A real challenging one. Some of the theories I've seen online . . .' He shook his head. 'But rules are rules. We keep information strictly within the force, and once we retire, we can never speak of it again. Unless you get asked back as a consultant, which sometimes happens, if a case is re-opened that you know a lot about.'

'Have they asked you back to help with this latest Nellie case?' said Simon.

Bernard tapped his nose. But the sad look in his eyes said *no*.

'That must be frustrating,' said Simon.

The detectives paused, both scheming something to say to keep him talking.

'Here's an interesting fact about the Official Secrets Act,' Bernard continued, not noticing the gap in conversation. 'Did you know there are very few convictions from it? Fewer than one per year.'

'Wow. Interesting,' said Simon convincingly.

'The current Act was drafted all the way back in 1911,' said Bernard, waving a finger in the air. 'And in my opinion, the outdated language leaves loopholes. Most of the time, it's more appropriate to charge someone with corruption instead.'

There was another pause. Bernard was talking, but was any of it useful?

'Did you say you were writers?' he continued.

'Podcasters,' said Jane, a slight shake in her voice.

'I'm a bit of a writer, you know. I've found it a real outlet for all the things I want to say.'

'Oh, really?' Jane wondered whether facts about the Official Secrets Act could prop up the plot of an average-length novel.

'Ooh, we'd love to hear about your work!' said Simon. 'Jane's day job is in the publishing industry.'

'It is?' she asked quietly.

'She's very important in publishing. The podcasting is more of a hobby for her,' said Simon. 'And also, I'm a top DJ.'

'Well, then!' Bernard smiled heartily. 'That's very interesting. You'd better pull up a couple of stools!'

'This one here is called *Year of the Lexus Thefts*. It's the story of eight cars being stolen from a town in Kent in the space of twelve months. Not all of them were Lexuses, of course – a luxury car thief will target a range of models – but my wife suggested cutting down to just one in the title, to make it snappier.'

'Sounds wonderful,' said Simon. Under these circumstances, even he was struggling to lie.

Bernard had got out his phone and was swiping through pictures of the covers of his books. They were moody and dramatic, but the pictures on them had been pasted together crudely, like a collage.

'I put them together in PowerPoint,' he said. 'I can't seem to get the watermark off that stock image of a car, but I think you can barely notice it. You'd think it would be challenging to come up with so many ideas, seeing as most of my on-the-ground work was done in Tonbridge, the third-safest medium-sized town in Kent. But I always manage to draw some inspiration. Loose inspiration, obviously.'

'So, hold on,' said Simon. 'You can't talk about real cases you worked on. But your novels are inspired by real cases?'

'Well,' said Bernard, getting a bit sheepish. 'Like I say, loosely. I'll always change sensitive information. Like if a victim of crime had dark hair, I'll say they had blonde hair. I'll never use real names or locations or dates. I'll describe a crime similar to what happened, but not the same. In *The Hooligan*, for example, the titular criminal likes to start fights at cricket games instead of football matches.'

'I see,' said Simon.

'I'd be surprised if you recognised any similarity to real cases, and I use a range of different pen names.'

He swiped onto the next book cover. Jane looked at it carefully, as the title was very long and cramped on the small image.

'*The Mystery of Missing Shirley Bourne (Who Went Missing Several Times)*,' Jane read aloud. She looked at Simon. His eyes lit up. Bernard went a little red.

'Well, I couldn't resist writing an homage to one of my most challenging cases,' he said. 'But like I say, it's loose, and I might take out a few sections before publication...'

'This one,' said Jane, pointing at the screen. 'I'd love to read this one.'

'Hmm, well, I suppose I can see why you'd pick that one, but you won't find anything useful for your podcast—'

'Forget about the podcast,' interrupted Simon. 'The title alone gives this publishing potential. Think how it would pop on an airport bookshelf, Jane!'

Jane nodded in agreement.

'Brilliant. Well, I'll send it over. Forgive any typos. I don't know if you find this, but once I've typed something out, I can't bring myself to look at it ever again.' Bernard drained his drink, swallowing the wine dregs, and stood up. 'Anyway. Got to be home for dinner. My first time trying to make beef rendang, so wish me luck. Or wish my missus luck.'

He shrugged on his jacket and overcoat. Simon and Jane stood up with him and clumsily gathered their things. Jane lined their empty glasses up on the bar, and they made their way out into the night. Bernard was taller than Simon and strong in proportion, towering over them as he held the door open. Out in the night air, Jane noticed she was woozy. Maybe she needed to get out more.

'Funny old case,' said Bernard, his eyes set on a target in the distance. 'There's a good Wikipedia page for it, I believe. You've read that, have you? You can find plenty of info on the net: the years each Nellie went missing, the towns she'd been living in beforehand. The rumour that the women were always pregnant when they disappeared.'

'They were pregnant?' said Jane.

'Oh.' Bernard straightened his coat. 'That's not on there, is it? Bugger.'

'I don't think it is, no,' said Simon, trying to keep his tone breezy.

'Well,' replied Bernard, 'you didn't hear it from me.'

And with that, the great detective-author gave his nose another tap and walked off into the night.

PART TWO

PART TWO

10

6 January 1997

In a packed South London pub, a fireplace rumbled and snapped, tables hummed with chit-chat, and a young man in a massive duffel coat sat at the bar feeling sorry for himself, wondering why there wasn't such a thing as hot beer for winter.

'Cheer up, mate,' said a punk in a rumpled band T-shirt pulling up at the bar. 'Might never happen.'

Gavin hated that phrase.

'I wouldn't be sat here with a face like arse if nothing had happened,' he said gruffly, and sipped his lager.

'Oh yeah?' The man swivelled his bar seat towards Gavin. 'So what's happened?'

Gavin looked up, revealing his plum-coloured black eye.

'Christ. Where'd you get that?'

'Workplace accident,' said Gavin.

'Where do you work? Millwall?' The man chuckled to himself. 'Foster's top,' he added to the woman behind the bar.

'Construction,' said Gavin. The truth was, he'd been trailing his very first cheating husband. He'd followed the guy to a New Year's Eve party at his mistress's flat, which had looked busy from the outside. Unfortunately, when Gavin had let himself in, he'd found four guests sitting on bean bags drinking wine. Awkward hadn't begun to describe it. Even worse, the philanderer had recognised Gavin as the bloke who'd been going through his bins. Gavin was sorry it had gone that way. So far, being a PI had been more humiliating and poorly paid than he'd hoped.

'I work down the dog track at Wimbledon,' said the man as his pint was plonked on the bar. He reached into his pocket and counted out change. 'We do a sweepstake on which of us is gonna get bit next.'

Gavin decided to give detecting a few more months.

'Anyway,' the man continued, 'least you're not being haunted.'

'Haunted?' Gavin snorted, and it made his eye hurt. The fire crackled. A bunch of old bald men in the corner laughed at what must have been the joke of the century.

'By my ex-girlfriend,' said the man. 'Turns out . . .' He spread his arms wide and wiggled his fingers like a spooky magician, 'she's a ghooost!' He chuckled at his own joke again. But now Gavin noticed something hollow about him.

'Go on,' said the detective, even though he believed that all those ghost and alien stories run by the tabloids were destroying his generation's critical thinking skills, and felt like writing a letter to the non-tabloid papers about it.

'Well,' said the man, 'it was last summer. I met this girl down at the stadium. She was hanging around as we were closing, and she was asking me what greyhound racing was. Who doesn't know what greyhound racing is?'

Gavin listened carefully. He found he was suddenly on duty — his ears tuning in hard to everything the man said. Detectives had to listen for information, clues, and for the things left in the gaps, the things your informants didn't want to give away. It was like being a head-shrinker. Which this guy might need, if he really thought he was being haunted by the ghost of his ex-girlfriend.

'I just thought she was being funny. Like she had a weird sense of humour. Or she was trying to flirt, get me talking. Anyway, it worked. I liked her. Nice hair, pretty face.'

He took a long drink. Gavin waited.

'Whatever. She's gone,' said the man. Gavin made a mental note: *Emotional pain, recent.*

'Was she allergic to greyhound hair?'

The man smiled at that, but it was a tight smile.

'So . . . she's a ghost?' Gavin prompted.

'Right!' said the man. 'So, get this. First things first. She's a bit pale. Like Casper. Also, when I say she's gone – I mean she disappeared. Bang. One day about a week before Christmas – just wasn't answering her door. Didn't leave a single thing at my place in five months. Didn't have a bleeding phone. Who doesn't have a phone? And then I thought about it. She didn't know about the dog-racing at the stadium. But she also hadn't heard of Blur.'

Gavin nodded. That did seem like a dumpable offence.

'Her clothes were weird and old. And she did all these cuckoo remedies, like your granny might. Like once, she had a cold, and she wouldn't take a paracetamol. Oh no. What did she do instead? Put half a chopped onion under the mattress.'

'At least with a cold you wouldn't be able to smell it,' offered Gavin.

'And . . .' The man looked around him, like she could be anywhere. 'I think she was making me ill.'

Paranoia, thought Gavin, noticing the bags under his eyes, the thin cheeks. The man ordered another beer. Gavin wondered if he was eating.

'Have you reported her missing?' asked Gavin.

'Missing? Nah, mate. At first I thought she'd just taken off. Like they all do in the end.'

Gavin left a pause.

'I've got this kidney problem,' continued the man.

You've got all kinds of problems, thought Gavin. But he kept quiet, compelled to hear where this was going. And avoid another black eye.

'I have meds, but Nellie was always on at me to stop taking them. Something about chemicals in the body.'

'So you stopped taking them?' That would explain why he looked so terrible.

'No, I've been taking them. But they've stopped working now. I feel dreadful.'

'Maybe she swapped them out for sugar pills,' said Gavin.

The man shook his head.

'She didn't do anything, mate, because she wasn't real! She never existed. I've seen her grave.' Gavin felt a chill. 'A bloke at the track drove me down to Kent to see it. Turns out she's an urban legend. She comes into your life for a few months and then disappears. He took me to this cemetery out in the middle of nowhere – Nellie Thorne, died 1926. And now I've just got this feeling . . . like she's cursed me. Like the clock's ticking.'

'Nellie Thorne? You mean like the woman who went missing ten years ago?'

'What?'

'It was all over the papers. Twenty-five-year-old nanny who went missing. They never found her. It was a weird one, 'cos two other women with the same name had gone missing in the seventies.'

The man shrugged. 'Never bothered with the papers much. Besides, couldn't be the same girl as my Nellie. She was only twenty. Unless . . .' The man's sunken eyes widened. 'It's the same ghost! Come back ten years later! That just proves it!'

'Well, do you want me to look into it for you? I'm actually a private investigator,' said Gavin, against his better judgement. 'She's got to be a real woman because there's no such thing as ghosts. So if it'll give you some closure, I can find her, prove that she's just a person. Get her to explain why the relationship wasn't working out. It might make you feel better.'

The man looked hopeful for the first time all night. So Gavin took a few details and promised to meet him back at the same pub in two weeks.

Those two weeks were hard. The man was right – there was nothing to go on. Gavin's first port of call was the phone book, where nobody named Nellie Thorne existed. He'd gone to her flat, where a young family, newly moved in, had never heard of the previous tenant. He'd stupidly failed to ask his client where the gravestone had been, so he couldn't go there and ask around. He'd managed to find a Kentish friend who'd heard the legend, but she didn't have any light to shed on it.

Gavin was tense, worrying about how the man might react when he turned up back at the pub empty-handed. He was ready with an apologetic speech about how some mysteries couldn't be solved, and how there'd be no fee since there'd been no result. But he needn't have worried about disappointing his client. When he returned to the pub on the night they were meant to meet, the man never showed up.

J. D. BRINKWORTH

THE MYSTERY OF MISSING SHIRLEY BOURNE
(WHO WENT MISSING SEVERAL TIMES)

BY P. BERNARDSON

It was a cold and atmospheric night on the fancy Kent lane. The alluring police constable, Mike, could smell criminal misconduct in the air. He tightened his coat around him and hummed Rick Astley's new hit, 'Never Gonna Give You Up', which was 1987's song of the summer, and was considered a genuinely good tune (its misappropriation by internet youths would come much later, along with the internet). Mike was pleased to be out of the patrol car, because he was too tall for it, and often hit his head on the roof when driving over speed bumps.

There were plenty of officers milling around the swanky mansion. PC Mike assessed the house. It was three storeys tall, with huge windows and ivy growing all over. Majestic. But he reckoned the heating bill made a thump when it came through the letterbox.

The also alluring PC Sidney shuffled over. 'The nanny's gone missing. It's all hands on deck,' she said, because even though the 1980s were regressive in lots of ways, there were a few policewomen.

Together they went to scour the garden for clues. The garden smelled of cut grass. The young PC wondered if the missing woman had been concreted under the family's brand-new pool. Here's an interesting fact: pools became very popular for wealthy people in the 1980s, with a 350 per cent rise in sales on the 1970s, probably because of Hollywood and that kind of thing.

'It's a waste of our time looking,' PC Sidney muttered. 'I've heard it's another Shirley Bourne.'

A shiver went down PC Mike's spine. If he'd known, he might have used a clever excuse to stay at home that night (for example, 'My wife's cut my hair today, and she's absolutely botched it.' [See Appendix B for further handy excuses you can use yourself]). Because in Kent back in the 1970s and '80s, Shirley Bourne may as well have been the bogeyman. Men weren't allowed to be scared of things at that point, but if they had been, they'd be scared of Shirley. It had started as two unsolved missing persons cases in the 1970s. Now, folks were afraid she was an evil ghost hiding under the bed or in the wardrobe, ready to kill them with her long magic fingernails and leave no evidence on the body, which would make the murder basically unsolvable. Not to mention the headache that would cause for the coroner. He wasn't sure how the ghost rumour had started, but he'd heard it in the pub once or twice. If it was true that this was a Shirley, then it would be the third time she'd gone missing in sixteen years. (For comparison most people, on average, don't go missing at all.)

'They're pretty sure it's a Shirley,' said PC Sidney, 'because she fits the description. Long blonde hair, no next of kin.'

PC Mike nodded. That sounded about right. Both the Shirleys from the previous decade had had long blonde hair. Despite what you might have read in the papers, the police had done their very best on those cases. But they'd never found any friends or family members to follow up with, and outside of the person who'd reported her missing, no loved ones had come forward to help. There was no paperwork, or record of her, and the excuses were always the same: 'Oh, she told me she was a home birth. Perhaps her parents forgot to register her.' 'She's afraid of flying, so she doesn't have a passport.' (These types of excuses are not included in Appendix B.)

'I don't believe she's a ghost,' said PC Mike to his colleague. He had a theory of his own, that he'd been working on for some time, although nobody in the force would take it seriously, no matter how many urgent letters he sent about it. 'I think this is all a hoax to waste our time.'

'Really?' said PC Sidney.

'Really,' Mike replied. He spoke in a quiet, mysterious voice, and PC Sidney had to lean in to hear him better. 'It's activists. Protesters. Think about it – the name can't be a coincidence. So it must be an alias. And if it's an alias, that means the disappearances are part of an organised plan. Come on – three linked disappearances, and barely a scrap of evidence? No last sightings, or diaries to check, or signs of a struggle at their houses – have you ever heard of a missing person case like it?'

PC Sidney had to admit she hadn't. Mike carried on explaining.

'One day, they'll come out and admit this was all a protest against the establishment. A piece of long-running theatre designed to show up the police in the eyes of the public. To make some twisted point – like we're incompetent and can't do our jobs.'

For the rest of Mike's career, the 'protest' theory would remain his top explanation for the mystery of the missing Shirley Bournes. He loved the idea that it was a kind of angry art, like graffiti, or Eminem.

(NOTE TO JENNIFER: Given nobody ever did come forward to claim responsibility, maybe I should rewrite to have Mike's theory be the bogeyman after all? I'm not sure what to think any more. Would the public have been better off calling Ghostbusters?)

11

Sunday 14 April – Present Day

As the day broke in Clapham Junction, Jane shifted in her bubble bath and noticed it was going cold. She wasn't sure she'd enjoyed the first three chapters of Bernard Parker's novel, but on the plus side, there were only four more chapters left in the whole tome.

'Simon?' she called out. But Simon didn't hear her. He was sitting at the kitchen counter on his laptop, once again googling himself.

'Oh!' he said indignantly, discovering that his LinkedIn profile didn't even reach the front page. 'Who's this?' Simon had an identity interloper. No, two! The first he already knew about: an American college football player called Simon Mash, who was about twice the size of his British counterpart. But now there was a second, a jazz musician named Simon Walker-Mash. He had a Wikipedia page, a fan website with a discography, and even a Facebook group. Simon considered whether he – himself, Simon single-barrelled Mash – might not be as much of a big deal as he'd thought.

He got up, turned on the kettle, slid some bread into the toaster – white for him, wholegrain for her – and got out a polka-dot tray from their kitchen cupboard. Jane had been down since she'd been fired, and had started doing weird things, like taking bubble baths first thing in the morning. He hoped that little touches like using the spotty tray would lift her mood.

While he waited for the toast and the kettle, he went back to his laptop. It lagged a little, as it hadn't been shut down properly for months, just closed and shoved into bags. A peeling sticker by the keyboard bore a barcode and read PROPERTY OF GL PROFESSIONAL SERVICES. Next to that Simon had stuck a sticker of a cute cappuccino smiling.

He began re-googling: Nellie Thorne. The usual results came up – the top half a dozen links were already purple, roads he'd been down before.

Simon was well versed in looking people up on the internet. In his single days, he'd liked to turn up to first dates with a few discussion topics in his pocket that were guaranteed to land well. He had looked up Nellie on every social media site he could think of, and had scribbled sites off his list as he'd failed to find her on Pinterest, Etsy or Spotify. She had never posted a video on YouTube, nor tweeted anything, not even an embarrassing seven-year-old complaint to a delivery service or an off-the-cuff restaurant review. But then, Jane had been this digitally elusive too.

They'd had their first date just over a year ago. Simon had arranged for them to meet at On Cue, an underground concept bar where sixteen vintage pool tables had been installed. Here, the after-work crowd could enjoy some laid-back, good old-fashioned pub pool, a carefree night of retro fun, which had to be booked in advance in eighty-minute slots. Since Simon couldn't impress Jane with targeted facts based on her internet presence, he'd instead played trick shots he'd learned on the table in his Uncle Nick's garage. Jane had been grudgingly impressed. Later, she'd said it felt like falling for a stage magician.

POP! The toaster propelled their toast into the world. As

Simon went to spread it with enough butter to cause health problems down the line, he noticed Jane's detective notebook on the counter. The one Simon had drawn a tiny phallus on the front of. He wondered yet again why she'd acted so annoyed at that when it was obvious that she loved his high jinks.

He put down the toast and picked up the notebook, leaving butter prints on the cover. This was it – Unit 2: Effective Search Terms!

Simon sat back at his laptop and tried a few search tools. "Simon Mash" in double quotation marks. Now it was just Simon and the American football player. Take that, jazz man.

Another look at the notebook and Simon tried using a hyphen to remove results: "Simon Mash -football"

Ha-ha! Now the results were him alone: king of the internet. There was his LinkedIn, Instagram, and – oh god, some think-pieces he'd written ten years before for the student paper about how the reggae genre was evolving. It turned out that an ex of his had successfully pitched an article to *Cosmo* called 'Why I'm Staying Single Forever'. It was a bit surprising she'd used his real name in it. How had his phone number and parents' address ended up on a directory site? Was that his teenage email address (x-gossipguy99-x@i-mail.com)?

'Morning. What are you up to?' Jane was in the doorway in her dressing gown, detangling her wet hair with an industrial-strength brush.

'Google search, Jane!'

'Simon, come on, we've talked about this. There feasibly wasn't a way you could have become an American football star—'

'No, look: using search modifiers we can find all kinds of other stuff. We might be able to find an old social media account of Nellie's or something.'

Jane came and sat at the counter on a high wooden chair, pulled Simon's laptop towards her, and started typing.

'This is great. I'm so annoyed I didn't think of this.' In Jane's world, this was a compliment.

'Thank you.'

'Look, you can filter by just stories that appeared in Kent papers!'

Jane had that rabbit-hole look in her eyes. Occasionally, Simon worried that she might one day become a conspiracy theorist, and that he would be forced to leave her after a string of embarrassing online posts and public debates with strangers.

'We should use this to go deeper into the historic cases,' she said. 'Maybe we can find out what the link is between them and our Nellie.'

'Sounds perfect,' said Simon. Since his laptop had been commandeered by his detecting partner, he was using his phone to search. 'Jane, I don't want you to freak out, but I think I've found a website where I can buy some of your passwords.'

Jane wasn't listening; she peered and scrolled.

'Kent News Online has coverage of this week's stuff, and then there's one article about the 1997 case, from . . . Oh, back then it was the *Tonbridge Gazette*. There's nothing else under the Nellie Thorne search tag. Apart from this man who'd lost his chameleon for the third time but found it a year later.'

'I can't believe that not one of your passwords is "IloveSimon". Oh god, Jane, I've found nudes!' Simon's face was very pale. 'They're not even my good nudes!'

'OK, it looks like the *Tonbridge Gazette* don't keep all their old articles online, but it says for older articles, you can search the archive kept in Tonbridge Library!'

She gave him a pat on the back before getting up.

'Where are you going?' Simon felt he was going to need some help today, as a lot of research lay ahead of him on the logistics of getting one of those EU injunctions that removed search results about you.

'I need to get dressed and so do you! We're going to Kent again – I want to see these archives.'

'Do we have time to eat our toast first?'

'This is perfect, because I need to go up to Dev's school and see if I can confirm his alibi. I mean, it's not really an alibi at all because, of course, she could have disappeared before school—'

'No point checking the school on a Sunday, it'll be a ghost town,' said Simon.

'It's a posh boarding school: there'll be staff there every day.'

Simon's phone rang. He looked at the screen, and his face darkened. He put a finger up to say sorry.

'Hi, Mum.' He rolled his eyes at Jane and moved off towards the bathroom to take the call. 'Yeah, yeah, I've got it, thanks. No, Mum, I've told you she doesn't have Instagram. And regardless, as I've told you plenty of times, even if Francesca did have Instagram, I wouldn't print her pictures out for you. No, Nick won't do it either. Well, for a start, he doesn't have a printer, Mum. Right. I don't think I can today . . .' Simon frowned and closed the bathroom door.

Jane reached for her toast, which was now cold, exactly how she liked it. Simon had been getting a lot of calls from his mum lately. Penny Mash, the woman, the legend; a Kentish village socialite who had once won a tea towel from Waitrose for buying the most bottles of own-brand gin of any shopper in the southeast. Jane got a text and saw it was from Simon.

> Sorry, babe. Probably can't come to Kent today. Lots of admin to do. Good luck!

And then a detective emoji. So Jane and the detective emoji were on their own. She used Simon's laptop to find a train to Tonbridge, which left in twenty minutes. Remembering what she so often forgot, she went to Simon's jacket, hanging by the door, to reach into his wallet for their Two Together Railcard. It had been Simon's idea of taking their relationship to the next level. If a ticket inspector asked where he was, she'd have to say the toilet. She rehearsed explaining Simon's terrible gastrointestinal problems: 'Best not get too close to me, I think it's catching, and I'm starting to feel a bit rumbly myself.' Would the machine even let her buy just one ticket? It was a hassle, but what price could you put on saving a third on rail fare?

She opened Simon's wallet, Italian leather and battered, a gift from Penny, and found the railcard, and a thin wodge of fifty-pound notes, which she counted out to be three thousand pounds. Now her stomach really did feel rumbly. She looked at the notes for a moment. It was more cash than she'd ever seen at once. She shoved it back into the wallet with shaking hands and went to get dressed.

12

Jane spent an hour at Dev's school but learned nothing. By an empty basketball court she'd caught the attention of a matey young teacher, Mr Sullivan (geography), sandy-haired and keen to please, who had invited her to the staff room for a chat about his good mate Dev Hooper. It had been exciting for Jane to be let into the school staff room, even though it was drab, and as she'd always imagined, it smelled like instant coffee.

Mr Sullivan ('but call me Paul') had smiled hopefully at Jane throughout their chat. His smile was like a lighthouse beacon scanning life's waves for someone nice to marry and complete his teacherly life. But settling down with a teacher in Tonbridge wasn't as cushy as you'd think, Jane knew, since there was a risk that you might randomly disappear. Still, a teacher in Tonbridge might not mysteriously hide thousands of pounds from you.

Mr Sullivan had seen Dev locking up his bike in the car park on the morning that Nellie had disappeared, and they'd walked into school together. On the staff-room pinboard, Jane had seen that Dev's timetable only had one free period on Mondays. Neither the single free period nor lunch or breaktime were long enough to bike the twenty minutes back to his house, do something heinous, clean up after it, and get back without the students noticing his absence. And school students were very hot on teacher absence.

Of course, since Nellie could theoretically have been murdered at any time before the start of the school day, this wasn't a meaningful alibi that could clear Dev, but at least his movements were accounted for. Jane had asked Paul whether he'd consider himself a good friend of Dev's. The answer was a beaming yes. She'd asked how his relationship with Nellie had seemed. The answer was that they didn't really talk about that kind of thing. Paul also didn't know whether Dev had grown up in Tonbridge, whether he had any family there, exactly how long he'd been teaching at the school, or whether he seemed, in general, happy.

Paul's smile had gradually faded. Hoping to get some leads to follow up with, Jane had ended by asking whether Dev had any other friends she could talk to. Paul had stared over her shoulder and replied, 'Do any of us have any real friends to talk to?' Jane had told him that was one for the philosophy teacher.

The route to her next stop took her back past the now-familiar Tonbridge station. A drizzle was beginning, and the wind whipped stinging cold raindrops into her face. She wanted to call someone, talk to someone about the three grand, but who? Her mum, maybe? That was a terrible idea. Her mum was very keen for things to work out with Simon, regardless of what Simon might be up to or might be like. She'd say, 'Well, why shouldn't Simon carry cash around in his wallet? He doesn't have to tell you everything, does he? Why are you always so suspicious of the poor man?' If Jane woke up to find Simon harvesting her organs, her mum would probably say, 'I don't think he'll get a very good price for *your* organs, love. You eat too much dairy.'

Anyway, there wasn't time to have problems, as central Tonbridge was small, and Jane had almost reached her destination. Perched on Tonbridge's artery, the high street, on the edge of a mini roundabout, was a large red-brick Victorian building. It was awkwardly grand for the street, towering between squat pubs and pizza places like a tall cousin in a wedding photo. Curly words had been carved into sandstone on the facade: PUBLIC LIBRARY.

Inside, the library was chilly and quiet, with white walls and a grey carpet. The entrance corridor, lined with pinboards, opened into a main space where small shelving units on wheels bore collections of children's books.

A sucker for books, Jane stopped at a trolley in the corridor, running a finger along the wrinkled spines of a row of paperbacks. She wondered if she could find the new history of American UFO sightings she'd been trying not to buy online. Unfortunately, this trolley was stacked with Tonbridge Library's main stock: romance novels in series that ran thirty books long. On the bottom of the trolley were some of the crime thriller big hitters of the last few years, with their authors' names in huge neon letters, all looking very well used. Jane crouched to pick one up, and it fell open to a page where a chunk of a Twister lolly, plus the stick, was wedged inside. She shuddered, shoved the book back on the shelf and wiped her hands on her jacket. As she sprung up cringing, she came eye to eye with the library's pinboard, and realised something was wrong.

The pinboard was bare. Looking left and right, she checked every board. There were a few business cards for gardeners and taxi drivers, and one tatty flyer for toddler drum lessons. But she knew that Dev had put up posters in the library. She got out her phone and checked the text he'd sent her on Saturday: Don't bother postering library, lampposts, Costa Coffee, I did those earlier in the week. Yet now, just days later, there were no traces of Nellie's photocopied face. What did it mean? Jane had no idea. She would have to ask a helpful librarian.

The librarian was a woman dressed all in black with heavy dark eye makeup. She was slightly older than Jane, and sat behind a large semicircular wood-veneered desk, covered in parapets of books like a fortress. She was reading and didn't look up as Jane got closer. Rain tip-tapped on the skylight above.

'Hello. Excuse me,' Jane whispered. 'Do you take posters down off the pinboards? Have you done that, say, in the last few days?'

The librarian looked up from her book, her face blank. 'I don't approve of baby yoga and community art, but I don't interfere with their posters. Live and let live.'

'Are you sure?' Jane tried again.

This time the librarian didn't answer but glared at Jane, who decided not to push it further. She didn't want to piss the woman off. After all, she'd need her help for the primary mission. Figuring out the meaning of the missing missing posters would have to go on what Simon called 'the laterbase'.

'I'm looking for the archives of the *Tonbridge Gazette*?' Jane channelled her inner Simon and attempted a charming smile.

'Why do you need them?' The librarian spoke at a volume that would have been normal in most places but was loud in a library. Jane instinctively looked around. Sure enough, a woman at the communal computers had started staring, her train of thought interrupted, and a man in moth-eaten clothing had woken up from a slumber on two pushed-together chairs by a THIS MONTH'S SPOTLIGHT display.

'Um, well, I'm looking for some very important information on . . .' Jane was whispering as urgently as it was possible to whisper. 'A friend needs to find some information about his girlfriend.' Jane was getting hot. What had Gavin said about concealing your back story?

'Setting you up with the archive is a lot of work,' bellowed the librarian, who was also chewing gum, 'so we usually ask that people prove they're using it to study for a university project or something.'

Jane looked around again – more library punters were getting irate.

'Look, uh . . .' Jane examined the woman's top for a name badge, but there was nothing. 'Sorry, what's your name?'

'LINDA.'

'Shh! Sorry, I mean, look, Linda . . .'

'Do you have an email showing you're enrolled on a course?'

'Does it matter? Isn't a citizen doing research entitled to as much public library access as someone who's paid for a course?' Jane was managing to shout quietly.

'I don't make the rules,' replied Linda. 'Well, I do, but that's why I don't want to break them.'

Jane took a breath and looked around for more clues. How would Simon schmooze his way into the archive?

'Oh, your book!' said Jane, this time a little louder than she meant to, pointing down at the thick paperback Linda was holding, thumb marking her place. 'I've read that one! *The Worst Great Hunger: The Untold Story of Chairman Mao's Famines*.'

Linda's expression changed. 'This one?'

'Yeah. I'm surprised, actually. I didn't think that would be the kind of book you had here.'

'It isn't,' said Linda. 'I have to bring good books from home.'

Jane could finally sympathise with her, if only slightly.

'Have you ever read *The Abominable Pestilence*?' said Jane. 'It's my absolute favourite book on the Black Death.'

Linda's eyes and mouth opened wide in synchronised shock. 'No way, *The Abominable Pestilence* doesn't even make my top *five*. It's lightweight. Alright for an overview, sure, but you have to go elsewhere for the detail. It shies away from describing the disintegration of the internal organs.'

'Well, what's the definitive plague book, then?' Jane was starting to forget about volume herself.

Linda ignored the question, rolled open a deep desk drawer, and pulled something from it. It was a book, but she concealed the cover with her hand.

'You'll never guess what this is. Go on, take a guess.'

'Umm . . . Martin Hansen's history of CIA torture?'

'*Pffft*. That's baby stuff for Hansen fans.' Her hand slid off the cover. 'This is an advance copy of *Two Hundred Murders, Two Men*.'

'There's no way you've got the new Hansen. It's not out for six weeks!' Jane had it on pre-order.

'Got it at his special talk—'

'You went to Coventry for his talk?!' Jane had been unable to make it to the launch of her hero's new book *Two Hundred Murders, Two Men: The New Identical Twin Theory Behind America's Most Gruesome Serial Killings*.

'—*signed* by Hansen.' Linda opened the cover to deliver the slam-dunk: the spiky Sharpie signature of a wizened American septuagenarian.

'No way!' whined Jane. 'I can't believe you got that!'

'Keep it down,' gruffed the homeless man trying to sleep on two chairs.

'Hold on,' whispered Linda, pointing at the drawer. 'I'm going to give you something. It's the only true crime I've got in stock.' She rummaged and pulled out a thin, cheaply bound paperback. 'The author stopped by and left us a lot of copies.' It only had about twenty pages, all of them extremely shiny. 'Well, it's a novel, technically, but it's based on a real case.' Linda offered it to Jane.

'Thank you.'

The cover read: *The Tonbridge Strangler: Local Legend, Local Man*, by Pernard Barker.

'Although isn't something this length technically a leaflet? I suppose it would have been considered a pamphlet back in the day?' Jane put the tiny tome in her bag. 'Er, but I really, really appreciate it, and now we know each other a bit, maybe I could just go and access the archives?'

Linda leaned back in her chair and examined her dark-painted nails.

'As I said, I can't let every member of the public down there. There'd be a stampede.'

Jane scanned her brain, looking for a way out of this impasse.

'Look, Linda,' she said, as coolly as possible, 'I shouldn't really be telling you this, Linda' – Simon said that when you wanted something, you should use the other person's name as much as possible – 'but I'm a private detective, Linda. With the Pie and Mash Detective Agency. And we're on a serious case. A woman is missing. In fact, she could be in danger right now.'

Linda's eyes lit up. She leaned forward with a big smile. 'Of course. I understand. You'd be surprised how many PIs we get in here.' She sounded excited. 'Looking at the archives. Not as many as we used to, of course, but still a good few. Once, we even had Perry and Llewelyn.'

'Oh, wow,' said Jane, pretending to know who they were. But Linda seemed to be on her side now. More than that, she was being a bit flirty.

'I'll set you up with the archives right now: if you're a PI, you'll already know how to operate microfilm, right?'

'Um, well, yes, but seeing as you're such an appreciator of crime, I suppose you could tag along, maybe offer an opinion on the case?'

'It only seems fair,' said Linda. 'After all, I'm the one who's fought tooth and nail to keep the microfilm here.'

Jane didn't like the thought of fighting Linda tooth and nail. Her nails were long, and pointy, and painted with black and silver spiderwebs, and her teeth were lined with sharp-looking braces. So instead, she followed her to a big cold concrete stairway and down into the library's basement.

13

'Most of what we have on microfilm are burial indexes, cemetery registers, death registers, that sort of thing,' said Linda, gesturing around the basement. 'I read them for fun.'

The basement's white walls were lined with grey filing cabinets. The atmosphere was gloomy and heavily silent. Linda led Jane to a thick wooden table at the far end of the room. On the table was the type of microfiche reader Jane recognised from TV and movies: a big, grey 1980s box of a machine. She thought of Simon's joke magnifying glass. Her detective-stereotype toolkit was coming together. Perhaps next she should get a fedora, or a Dr Watson.

'The only paper we have in full is the *Tonbridge Gazette*. Every issue since 1971, but I'm— we're working on collecting other local papers too. It's good to have the history. You can't trust the official system to keep hold of things. One spilt coffee could take the internet down. Look it up, sheeple.'

'Right,' said Jane, taking in the surroundings, looking for emergency exits, and trying to put her finger on the smell. It wasn't quite damp, antique bookshop or schoolboy – more like a fight between all three.

Linda reached over the table to turn the microfilm machine on at the plug, and it made a loud pop. The machine was attached to a modern screen, rotated to portrait mode, and Linda leaned over to switch that on too. As she leaned, Jane noticed she smelled of fresh laundry.

'My name's not Linda, you know,' said Linda.

'What?'

'I like to keep my real name low-profile. You're probably the same. I just picked it out from an old name badge I found in the desk drawer.'

'Oh, right. So what's your real name?'

'Nice try. But you get it now, right? I don't look like a Linda?'

'You don't. It adds to your mystery.'

Linda winked at her. Well, that was unmistakably a flirt. Jane's stomach clenched. It was either fear from the odd aura in the basement, or attraction. Jane always struggled to tell the difference.

'Right, what can I get you?' said Not Linda.

'Hmm? Oh, the *Tonbridge Gazette*, please,' said Jane.

'Which issue?' Linda went to the nearest grey filing cabinet, taller than she was, and started grabbing rolls of film from the drawers. 'These are the last three years, up until it rebranded in 2014, but we've got it all,' she said temptingly.

'A bit further back, please,' said Jane. 'How about 1987?'

'Nineteen eighty-seven?' Linda smiled as if she could see Jane's secrets. She moved to a different cabinet, around the corner. 'A private investigator, on a cold case. Super weird.'

Jane heard her roll open a large metal drawer.

'What date?' Linda called out.

Jane realised she'd have to go through every single article in all fifty-two weekly editions to find anything about the 1987 Nellie case.

'I'll start at the beginning,' she called back.

'Sounds like we're in for a long night.'

Jane had never read a local newspaper all the way through

before. Was Linda going to stay here watching? For a moment, Jane imagined life with Linda instead of Simon. If Simon turned out to be a money launderer, and she decided that was a deal breaker, she might find herself with Linda in Tonbridge. She could cook nice bean stir-fries and they could stay up all night talking about crime. Above Jane's head, a buzzing strip-light crackled and puttered out, leaving the room halfway darker than it was before.

"Eighty-seven! King's Cross fire and the Great Storm. Sevenoaks became Oneoak, but they still haven't updated the sign,' Linda re-emerged from the gloom with armfuls of circular tape reels and sat bouncily in a desk chair at the microfilm reader.

'Great year for disasters,' Jane replied weakly.

Linda began freeing a reel from its protective layer of paper. The tape looked like old camera film: dark, and burned with tiny images of newspaper pages.

'I see the lights are going out again,' said Linda grimly as she threaded tape through the machine. 'It's like we're cursed down here. Bulbs don't last six months. Let's hope they don't all go out at the same time. Come on, sit down.'

Linda smiled villainously and patted the chair next to her, a small wooden one that might have started its life underneath a Victorian schoolboy. Jane sat down carefully.

CLICKCLACKCLICKCLACK! Jane jumped. Linda was turning the direction knob on the front, causing the machine's reels to whir and clap loudly. On the screen, the front page was blown up to life-size brightness.

'Wow,' said Jane. 'It's quite magical, isn't it?' The headline read: CRAZY PAVING: WHEN WILL COUNCIL U-TURN ON BONKERS DROPPED KERB APPLICATION REFORMS?

'So, what's your case?' asked Linda. 'Council corruption?

The mystery of the declining acting quality in Tonbridge school nativities?'

'Oh, it's OK. If you just leave me here with the machine, I think I've got the hang of it now.' Jane wanted to be rid of Linda: she wanted to keep the mission close to her chest, avoid having an emotional affair, and get out of the creepy basement quickly. 'Maybe I could . . . ?' Jane gestured at Linda's desk chair.

'Oh, right, of course.' They swapped. Jane began carefully turning the wheel across a page, and then the next one, scanning headlines: LEAVE YOUR CHRISTMAS TREE OUT BY THURSDAY OR FACE FINES, SAYS COUNCIL; COUNCIL UNDER FIRE FOR DANGEROUS BOLLARDS; BAD KARMA? MAN LOSES CHAMELEON FOR SECOND TIME. There was a cold silence in the room.

'You want July. Second issue. Front page,' said Linda, her voice suddenly sinister.

Jane turned from the screen – Linda was watching her, totally unblinking, deep in a one-woman staring contest. She held up a reel and offered it, smiling as if something delicious was waiting there.

Jane was feeling very chilly now, but in much the same way as you'd hand over your phone to muggers, she sat back and let Linda replace the reel.

'Go on,' said Linda. Jane zoomed in a few nudges.

ANOTHER KENT WOMAN MISSING. NELLIE THORNE MYSTERY DEEPENS.

She turned to Linda.

'How did you know that's what I was here for?'

The backs of Jane's thighs were getting sweaty. She heard a click or a creak in the dark distance – somebody moving, or just the old building breathing?

'Because you're not the first person to come here looking for

Nellie,' said Linda. 'You're not even the first this week. I can tell you're one of us. The ones who can't let the case lie. Who know there's a deeper conspiracy.'

'Yeah. Perhaps. What is the conspiracy?'

'Well, look, if you're new to this, I should warn you.'

'Warn me what?' Jane shivered. That she was going to be murdered by Linda?

Linda sat back as dramatically as was possible in the Victorian schoolboy's chair. 'That Nellie's ghost appeared many, many more times than what's on the official records.'

Jane snorted. She couldn't help it. 'Sorry! Sorry. It's just, what do you mean "Nellie's ghost"? Not a literal ghost?'

'A sceptic.' Linda smiled. 'I love a challenge.' She rushed off to get something. 'If you'd just admitted you were here for Nellie in the first place I would've got out my folder!' She reappeared with a packed blue ring binder, which she put down on the table in front of Jane. She opened the cover and flicked through the plastic-bound pages. 'See, I've been printing out the articles. This one here's the piece you just saw on the microfilm: 1987. One of the canonical four.'

Linda flipped a few pages back. Jane started scanning the tiny text.

'Are these the articles from the 'seventy-one and 'seventy-six cases?' she said. 'They're short.'

'Yep,' said Linda. 'Nobody really cared back then. So here' – she pointed at the printout – 'in 1971, the boyfriend goes to her place, finds she's not there, and reports her missing. There isn't much of an investigation, because most of her things were gone, as if she'd taken them with her. And also because it was the seventies. In 1976, there's more of a fuss, because she's stolen some money from the farm she worked on. Just fifty quid or so. Have you ever seen this article from the *Mirror*? It's only a couple of inches long, but it's the first time she's ever mentioned in the national papers. You can't get this article online,' she added proudly.

Jane read the grainy headline: RUNAWAY SCAMMER DEFRAUDS FARMING FAMILY. SCAM LINKED TO HEARTBROKEN BOYFRIEND?

She paused for a moment, trying to keep hold of all the new information. 'Just now, did you say the "*canonical* four"?' she asked. 'So that's what, the official four? And the rest aren't on the Wikipedia page?'

'Duh,' said Linda. 'You're *really* new to this, aren't you?' She pulled the binder back and turned to the 1987 article. 'See here? There's a description of Nellie: "Ms Thorne is described as tall, white, slim build, with long, mid-brown hair. If anyone sees her, please contact Kent Police on blah-blah-blah."'

'OK,' said Jane. That matched the description of modern-day Nellie.

'Now what about this,' said Linda, flipping through pages. 'September fourth, 1974.'

Jane had memorised the disappearance years: 1974 wasn't one of them.

'"Still no news in the search for Lily Jones, whose partner, Alvin Myddle, was released without charge yesterday, after twelve hours of questioning." That was in Maidstone,' said Linda. '"Myddle is offering a five-hundred-pound reward for anyone who finds Lily safe and well. He has no photographs of her, but is asking people to look for a tall, pale woman with waist-length mid-brown hair."'

'So they looked similar. You're not saying that . . . ?'

'They're the same woman,' Linda said. 'Look at this.' She skipped a few pages forward. '*Margate Herald*, letters to the editor, July 1990, issue three.'

Linda pointed to the letter's tiny font with her long fingernail. Jane leaned closer and read it aloud.

'"Dear Sir – why do young people these days think it acceptable to abandon their posts? If we'd done that back in the war—"'

'You can skip that first bit,' advised Linda.

'"An example of this is a young employee at my fish-and-chip shop, a teenage, long-haired 'alternative' type called Lily Jones, who decided to tender her resignation last Friday by not turning up for her shift. I ask – what is wrong with this generation's moral fibre?"'

'See? Same name. Lily Jones. Sixteen years after she went missing from Alvin's life, but her boss describes her as a teenager. And there are more,' said Linda quickly. 'Here in 1979. A woman who *did* put in her resignation at work, and told everyone she was leaving, but when she took off, she still owed her housemates rent. So they went to the paper to try and find her. Identical description. Same as every other article in this folder. Name is Daisy Brown. That name crops up twice more. Like in 1992, when a woman called Daisy Brown places third in a beauty contest called Miss Whitstable.'

Jane looked at the ring binder, and its thick stack of articles.

'I see what you're saying, Linda, but you can't really think they're all the same woman?'

'It's the urban legend round here. My grandma told me about it when I was a kid. The recurring disappearing woman. The way my grandma told it, there were more than four. So I'm saying she's not always called Nellie Thorne. And if you look really carefully, you start seeing names recur. Like Lily Jones and Daisy Brown.'

'And the police didn't pick up on that during the Nellie investigations? Other missing women with recurring names?' said Jane.

'Well, when Daisy left her housemates in 'seventy-nine, she wasn't missing. She'd told everyone she was moving away from the area. Not suspicious. Loads of them are like that – only suspicious if you know what you're looking for.'

'If you're right,' said Jane, rubbing her temples to stretch her brain, 'and there is a link between the Nellies and the other women in this folder, how many women are we talking about?'

'One. She's a ghost.'

'How many *disappearances*?'

'Oh. Twenty upwards? Not so many since the 2000s. And imagine how many didn't make the papers!'

Jane's brain buzzed. Ghost theories aside, the number of missing women had just more than quadrupled.

'You can see why the police wouldn't have put it together,' said Linda. 'Tall, long brown hair. It's quite a common description unless your senses are really honed to the energy of the case.'

The word 'energy' dampened Jane's excitement. 'Well, maybe they were right,' she said, getting back into a logical frame of mind. 'How would you describe my hair colour?'

'Brown?'

'Exactly. It's a very common hair colour, and "long" is just the default hairstyle for women. It's to hold us back, so that we have to spend all our time detangling it and unblocking our shower drains.'

'Think about it. It's not just the hair. It's the disappearing act. The height. The lack of any family members chiming in. The fact that none of them ever, ever turn up.'

Jane sighed. 'It's just a bit much to take in. I'm sorry. I see what you're saying, but I'm not totally convinced.'

Jane flipped through the binder. Alvin Myddle had drawn a sketch of his missing girlfriend, which would have been helpful if he'd been a more gifted artist. He'd made her look a bit like an alien, or a triangle. Jane reached out to touch the picture in the binder, and the second her fingertips hit plastic, *PHUT* – the lights went out.

'Oh no.' Linda giggled before whispering in Jane's ear: 'Nellie doesn't like it when you question her existence.'

14

TONBRIDGE GAZETTE, 10 JULY 1987

CAN POLICE FIND MISSING GIRL? NOT ON YOUR NELLIE
'BLUE CAR' ONLY CLUE IN STRANGE SEARCH FOR MISSING NANNY

Police in the search for Sevenoaks nanny Nellie Thorne, who vanished three weeks ago from the family home where she worked, have now revealed she was last seen by a neighbour in a small blue car on her posh Kent lane. The short-sighted neighbour failed to catch the number plate or make of the car, just as police have failed to catch Nellie's abductor. The vehicular sighting is the only clue so far in a mystery that has baffled investigators. No friends or relatives of Nellie have come forward to help with the search. There are no known photographs of Nellie, but the family she worked for described her as a 'lovely girl, tall, with long brown hair'. If you think you have seen Nellie or the blue car, please contact the police at the number below.

Simon's search-term skills were reaching creepy levels. He'd struck cloth gold: Nellie Thorne's Depop page. The handle was @nelliesvintage, and there were hundreds of items of vintage clothing listed with prices. About a third of them were marked as sold.

'Come to Papa,' he muttered.

'The next station is Hartwell,' said the train, which was taking

Simon to another part of Kent. Not in the direction of Jane, but towards a secret meeting. 'Due to a short platform at Hartwell, please use the front four carriages only.'

Simon wasn't listening. 'Bingo.' He'd scrolled upon the mother lode.

Pictures of Nellie modelling the clothes. Her skin was so pale, her limbs long, the clothes baggy like a disguise – Simon wouldn't recognise that body if it sat next to him at the bus stop. The only noticeable feature was her long hair, which fell nearly down to her elbows and possibly had never been cut. This would have made her the princess of primary school, but hinted at a strange adult. Every picture was missing her head, which had been cropped out.

It was comforting to find something new that backed up Dev's story, because surely he wouldn't have gone so far as to set up the page, hire a Nellie model, and post off all the clothing just to keep up a deceit? Simon wondered for a while what else he could do with the information on the page. Inspired, he opened a direct message with her.

'Hi Nellie,' he typed and read aloud. 'Would you sell the whiskey-scented men's bubble bath set for six pounds?' There. If she responded, he'd found both Nellie and a bargain.

Yet he couldn't stop scrolling. This was the closest he'd felt to her, the first time she didn't seem like an abstract concept— Ooh, vintage coats and hats! Simon clicked onto another profile: Vintage Coats and Hats, Margate, UK.

Simon had been extremely keen to buy himself and Jane matching trench coats. She'd said that would make them look less CIA, more M&S – but these vintage coats were just sublime. There was a navy one that would be perfect for Jane and a subtle yet stylish orange tartan one for himself. And they were both available for next-day delivery! The orange tartan was listed as in 'bad' condition, but Simon decided this would only make him look more like a field veteran. He couldn't wait to show it to Gavin.

Simon finally sat up straight and looked out of the window. He half-heartedly did one of the stretches his physio had printed out for him, and nearly hit a passing teenager in the face.

He turned back to his phone and opened a new tab without realising he was doing it.

"Nellie Thorne" + "hoax"

Top result: The truth about immortal succubus Nellie Thorne. It was a comment posted on a message board dedicated to Kentish paranormal mysteries. Simon read on.

msweeney89

What some call a hoax and others an urban legend is, in fact, the ultimate paranormal case. Run from any woman with this name because she is not a human being but a powerful force roaming the countryside seeking the life energy of men on which to feast. Proof? I have it, but I can't post it here for now.

The train ended its long deceleration into Hartwell station, and the doors beeped green but didn't open. As Simon joined the straggling herd of punters jogging to the front half of the train, he wondered if he was now on the trail of a ghost. If that was the case, he and Jane could be getting into something dangerous, something they weren't prepared for. Perhaps, instead of matching trench coats, he should have bought some exorcist robes. Or he could always repurpose the vicar's outfit from his fancy-dress box.

15

TONBRIDGE GAZETTE, 24 APRIL 1997

CONCERNED NEIGHBOUR ISSUES PLEA FOR
HELP IN SEARCH FOR MISSING GIRL

Days after police issued an appeal for information, the neighbour of missing Kent woman Nellie Thorne has pleaded for help finding her. A visibly emotional Terence Hancock, 82, said: 'Yes, if anyone has seen her, that would be good.' Amid allegations of bungling, Kent Police say the search for Miss Thorne is ongoing. But so far, no clues have been revealed to the public, not even a photograph of Miss Thorne. 'I've a good mind to solve it myself,' added Hancock, of Elm Crescent, Hildenborough. 'If anyone has any information at all, or happens to be a detective, please contact me on the number listed at the bottom of the article.' Officers have stressed that any clues should be reported to Kent Police.

29 April 1997

Gavin swung his arms to the beat. He brought his flat palms up to his face for a vogue. He tipped his head from side to side. His tape player vibrated with bass.

'*I'm blue, da ba dee da ba di!*' he sang along.

The kettle rumbled. Three teaspoons of Maxwell House granules waited in the mug. This was his morning routine for energy.

The post clattered its way through the letterbox and onto the mat. The noise tripped dread in Gavin's stomach, as the wedge of envelopes were rarely work enquiries, and almost always bills.

He tried to ignore it. He wiggled his hips. He needed to stay focused, poised, dangerous. *'Blue are the feelings that live inside me!'*

This wasn't his kitchen, strewn with his important papers and cigarette ends. It was his friend's, a prime South London one-bed, which Gavin was looking after (and paying the bills for) while the friend was in Morocco. It needed a bit of decorating and something done about the damp problem. Plus, there was a pane missing in the bedroom window, which he'd had to stuff with a Depeche Mode T-shirt to stop pigeons getting in. But he hadn't yet got around to finding a new squat to mooch into. He'd been completely consumed with his case.

Although calling it a case might have been a tad generous. The sickly punk in the pub – whose ghostly girlfriend had disappeared – had never shown up for his appointment with Gavin. But Gavin didn't believe in 'unsolvable', especially on cases where he was involved, and four months later, he was still working on it pro bono. The puzzle had got stuck in his brain like chewing gum in hair; plus, he didn't have much anti-bono work on anyway. His notebook sat open on the kitchen counter on a page headed WHERE/WHAT IS SHE?

Punk worked Wimbledon dog track. Can't find him there. Dead?

'Nellie Thorne' – Nanny vanished 1987 (Sevenoaks). Couple of others in seventies.

New disappearance! No photos, suspects, leads. Keep checking local papers (see cutting glued on previous page – CALL Terence Hancock – phone number at bottom of article!)

Recon trip to Kent (Hildenborough) – kids in a playground were yelling, 'Watch out for the witch, Nellie Thorne is coming to get you!'

Whole thing = bizarre

Today, Gavin was meeting Terence Hancock, possibly the last person who'd seen this mysterious woman. Terence had rambled quite a lot on the phone, but one of Gavin's rules of detecting was to separate the kook from their information – just because someone was absolutely batshit didn't mean they had bad intel. Gavin would be scooping that intelligence out of Terence's head at ten-thirty, as long as he could re-spray his armpits with deodorant, drink a scalding coffee in the next five minutes, skip over the red-stamped bill letters on the doormat, and dodge the ticket inspectors all the way down to Kent.

Gavin felt this must be his lucky day, as he'd found a pair of sunglasses on the train. Not only had he avoided £3.50 in fares, but he was also quids-in sartorially. This seemed especially lucky as the sun outside Terence's terraced house was disgustingly bright. He made his way up the concrete steps to the front door, where he found two doorbells for two flats. Unable to remember which one was his client's, he buzzed both.

TSRRRSK. 'What is it?' said a voice grumpily.

'Mr Hancock?' Gavin's third rule of detecting: Always confirm the other party's identity before giving away your own. But there was no answer. 'We have a meeting at ten-thirty?'

CLICK. The intercom disconnected. Silence. A drop of sweat formed on Gavin's forehead. Another one ran down his back.

After a while, there was a creak from inside the house, a few footsteps, and the door was opened. Terence stood at a proud stoop of five foot three and wore a knitted waistcoat over a yellowing striped shirt, held around his thin bicep with a stainless-steel sleeve garter. His eyebrows were thick and thriving, boasting more hair than his greying combover.

'In you come.'

Gavin followed this instruction.

Instead of leading him up the stairs to the top-floor flat, Terence paused at the downstairs flat's front door, where the silver letter A had come un-nailed and now hung upside down. Terence tapped on the door, not to get his neighbour's attention but more to indicate that the door was there.

'This is her flat,' he said, his serious face craned upwards towards Gavin, 'and it's been sitting empty for nearly two weeks, Detective.'

Gavin loved being called 'Detective'. He tried to look very sombre.

'She was a nice girl. Sometimes brought me a bit of spag bol. Now she's gone, and the police won't tell me anything. It's a criminal conspiracy.'

'I see, Mr Hancock.' Terms like 'criminal conspiracy' tended to shift the nutjob needle in Gavin's mind, but if flat A was really lying empty . . .

Terence Hancock led Gavin upstairs to his flat, which was kitsch rococo in the extreme. Mr Hancock had an enthusiasm for Toby Jugs. Leering eighteenth-century faces with handles watched Gavin from all corners of the small apartment.

'Sit down,' gruffed Terence, indicating a buckled sofa covered by a beaded doily.

'Thank you,' said Gavin. He sat down carefully, his buttocks inches from the ground.

'If you see a moth,' said Terence warningly, 'you must squash it immediately. I've an infestation.'

The flat was cool, a grubby net curtain filtering out the sun. Without asking Gavin if he wanted a cup of tea, to which the answer would have been no, Terence filled a steel whistling kettle from the kitchenette sink.

'Now, let me tell you everything I know, Detective, and then you can go off and catch whoever took Nellie,' said Terence. He sat down in a rocking recliner opposite the sofa. 'I last spoke to her two weeks ago exactly. A Tuesday. I was on my way down to the registry office. As you will know' – Terence poked his wrinkly cocktail-sausage finger at Gavin – 'all couples intending to marry must file that intention in writing, which is then displayed by the registrar, and I like to go down there from time to time to keep an eye on who's getting married and whatnot. Now, on my way out, I saw Nellie. I said, "Good morning, Nellie," and she said, "Good morning, Mr Hancock," because she has good manners.

'I remember it was the Tuesday, because that was her shopping day, and she said, "Mr Hancock, will you be wanting anything from the shops today?" I said, "No thank you," and would you believe it, when I got back from the registry office, I found a shepherd's pie on my doorstep. It was cool, mind, so she hadn't just left it. Anyway, a couple of days later, when I went down to give her back the – the, um . . .'

'The dish?'

'The whatnot, she wasn't in. *Not too odd*, I thought. But then later, I happened to be looking out the window, and I saw her get in a car. I watched out for that car to come back, so I could give her the dish. But it didn't. By the Friday, I stood on the street all night watching to see if she had put her front room light on. But she didn't. And then I did the same all Sat'day. Stood out there on the street, and her lights didn't go on all night either. Monday, I went down to the station to report the crime.'

Gavin wasn't convinced a crime had taken place.

'Just to get this straight, Nellie was the type to cook for her neighbours, get things from the shops. She wasn't . . . how can I say this? . . . kooky?'

Terence's wrinkled eyes opened wide enough for Gavin to finally see them.

'I should say not! I know she's been kidnapped, Detective. She wouldn't have just gone like that.'

'Did it seem like she was putting up a struggle getting into the car?'

Terence shifted. 'Well, not as such, but she wasn't the type to make a fuss.'

'I don't mean this question to sound accusatory towards her, Mr Hancock, but I have to ask. Did she ever ask you for money? Or do anything that made you nervous?'

'No, no. Nothing. She would even go down and get my pension for me if my back was playing up. Detective, she was a nice girl. Why would she give me the shepherd's pie if she was leaving? Wouldn't she wait a few days to get her bowl back?'

Gavin sighed. 'Mr Hancock,' he said gently, 'do you have any evidence that Miss Thorne isn't just on holiday?'

He pictured the legendary Thorne on the beach at the Costa del Sol. She could be in a taxi back from the airport at this very moment. Knowing Gavin's luck, she wasn't even named Nellie Thorne. Terence had probably misheard her name, and she wasn't an infamous unsolvable mystery, just a local woman with a disregard for the location of her pie dishes.

'When she got in the car, she didn't have a suitcase or even a jacket. Why would she leave for two weeks without any of her things?'

'Mr Hancock, can you describe the car for me?'

'I can do one better than that, Detective.' With a lot of effort, Mr Hancock got up and gradually retrieved a notebook from a drawer in the sideboard. 'I can give you my log of all the number plates that park on the street.'

On the sideboard, Gavin noticed a framed black-and-white photograph: a short, serious, bushy-eyebrowed young man in military uniform, sitting on a motorbike under the blazing sun... in Algeria? Maybe Tunisia?

'And my working theory,' said Terence as he doddered back to his seat, 'is that the car belongs to that no-goodski she was seeing.'

'Which no-goodski?'

'Her boyfriend.'

Gavin wondered if there was a logbook for male visitors, too.

'He didn't look a good sort. Greasy hair. Leather jacket. I heard them fighting a lot. Nearly went down there myself more than once.'

It occurred to Gavin that there might be a service revolver somewhere in this flat.

'And on top of that, every time I saw them together, he never smiled at her. I didn't like him at all. And I always have a very strong and accurate feel for people.' With that, he gave Gavin a small glare, as if to hint that the jury was still out on his personality.

'Could you hear what they were fighting about?' Gavin asked.

'No. Not even with my ear to the floor. But it wasn't too long after a big argument that I saw her get in the car and leave.'

'The boyfriend's car?' asked Gavin.

'Well, no, she left in a car I hadn't seen before. Maybe he had two cars. I only just managed to get the number plate.' Terence was looking off into a far corner of the room now. 'Anyway, like I say, the police won't tell me if they've got close to finding her. Just because I ring up regularly with a number of concerns, they think I'm a nuisance. They've threatened to put a blocker on my telephone number for years.'

'Did you show them the list of number plates?'

'Well . . .' Now the old man was coy. 'I felt I'd best save them for someone who could prove themselves more useful.'

This was the first time in Gavin's career that he had more evidence in a possible criminal investigation than his colleagues in blue. Without thinking, he made his voice more plummy.

'If it helps, Mr Hancock, I don't think they're allowed to block your phone number. If they're withholding details about the case, I'm sure it's all in Ms Thorne's best interests.'

'Well, that's it, Detective. You've got the number plate. The one she left in is circled. The boyfriend's has a star next to it. I still don't know what to do with her dish.'

Terence looked sadly towards the kitchen countertop, where Gavin now noticed the shepherd's pie dish crusted with bits of old mince and potato. He had separated the kook from his information. He shook Terence's hand and let him get on with whatever snooping he had planned for the rest of the day.

There was plenty of new information to pore over. While Gavin hadn't bought into the idea of Nellie as a paranormal being, he'd become convinced that he was dealing with one woman moving from place to place on some kind of nefarious business. Why had she turned up here acting like a saint? Who had picked her up in the car? Could Gavin finally find a good contact at the

DVLA, or was he going to spend the next four days sneaking around Kent streets with a pencil and pad, and schmoozing owners of the local dealerships? If he kept writing down number plates in a notebook, would he eventually turn into Terence Hancock?

'Oh, there's just one more thing, Mr Hancock, and I appreciate that it's a little awkward, but it's the matter of my fee.'

Gavin's sixth rule of detecting was: Half now, half on completion of the task – because it reassured clients that you were a proper professional. Also, he'd be able to get a new loaf of bread on the way home.

'Oh yes, there was a small problem with that – you see, my back. And the pension, and since Nellie's left, because she used to get it for me, you see . . .'

And so Gavin's next destination became the post office. On his way out he spotted a silvery sliver: a clothes moth on the doorframe. He smacked the wood, but his hand came up clean – it had given him the slip.

16

Monday 15 April – Present Day

Although he used to hate it, Dev no longer minded being out after dark. Anything to avoid another restless night, tumbling from one nightmare to the next. Even worse, tonight was Monday, the grim marker of a full week since Nellie's disappearance. So, seeing as this was a chance to distract himself, as well as a chance to help her, he'd come to Wylebrook Woods, a few miles outside Tonbridge, at ten o'clock at night. He was waiting in the place he'd been told to wait, in a clump of trees on the edge of a sheep field. With two idiots in matching trench coats.

'We can't get murdered, Jane, because I've shared my live location with Sami from work.'

'Simon, we can too get murdered. What's Sami going to do with our location? All he could do is get the killer caught marginally quicker. Sorry, Dev, this is all very insensitive.'

'Jane! Don't say it's insensitive – that implies that Nellie's been murdered, and we don't know that yet. We just suspect it.'

'Thanks, Simon,' said Dev.

'Dev,' said Jane, searching for something nice to say, 'I'm not sure we really explained who we're meeting here tonight. Simon found him on a niche message board. His name's Mark Sweeney and he's an online sleuth.'

'Of the paranormal,' added Simon.

'Right,' said Dev. 'The careers advisor never mentioned that one to me.'

Dev and Jane had the group's torches. They'd used them to have a good look around the area's twigs and shrubs before deciding to turn them off to save the batteries. Now they stood in the dark listening to their surroundings.

'We don't know what he looks like, despite quite a lot of googling around, so he's either got a very locked-down online profile, or "Mark Sweeney" is a fake name,' said Jane.

'Although there is a Mark Sweeney who lit a fertiliser silo on fire in Canada a few years ago.'

'Thank you, Simon.' Jane pulled her trench coat tighter around herself. Only now, in the woods, was she realising that trench coats weren't famed for warmth.

In the darkness woodland rodents scuffled and distant birds hooted. Jane felt a tingle on the back of her neck. If she'd been in touch with her intuition, she might have sensed that they weren't the only three people there.

'Can you get cold sores on the back of your neck?' she asked.

This question hung in the air, getting the response it deserved. A bird cawed and made Simon jump. It was hard to tell if they'd been waiting for two minutes or twenty.

'Oh!' said Jane. 'Dev, I have a bit of bad news, potentially.'

'Fantastic.' Dev crossed his arms tightly across his front.

'Did you put your missing posters up in Tonbridge Library?'

He looked startled. 'Oh, uh, yes. Well, I put them everywhere, all around town.'

'I'm so sorry, Dev, but I think some of the posters have been taken down. When I was at the library yesterday, I had a look at the boards, and I noticed there weren't any up. It made me realise I hadn't seen any of them on lampposts that day either. So I went to the supermarket to check if the ones Simon and I did were still up.'

Simon waited hopefully, but Dev looked resigned.

'Well, they were gone too,' said Jane.

'Shit,' said Dev, rubbing his face.

'Wow. Who do you think did it?' Simon asked.

Jane shrugged. 'Whoever it was, they don't want us to find Nellie.'

'Well, that's a huge tick for the abduction theory,' said Simon. 'Unless Nellie took them down herself. She might have done that. But it's a bit extreme for a breakup.'

'Exactly,' said Jane. 'Somebody's hiding something. But the question is, who?'

CRACK! A stick broke.

'There's someone else here,' said Simon.

Dev spun round, but all he could see were the dark woods on one side and the moon glimmering off the stubbly field on the other. Behind him, there was an unmistakable swoosh of fabric.

'Mark?' said Simon. Dev's breathing shallowed. Jane clicked on her torch and shone it in random directions, lighting up the spindling trunks of trees.

'It's too early to be Mark. Don't get spooked. It was probably just a badger,' said Jane.

'Don't badgers eat people if they get the chance?' said Dev, panicking. 'Or is that pigs? I can't think straight.'

'It's quite the power play,' said Simon. 'Leading us into the woods, where city dwellers are vulnerable and helpless.'

'This is a terrible idea,' said Dev. 'Why did I go along with this?'

'Mark!' yelled Jane. No reply. But there was a crunch and a shuffle nearby: someone of human weight moving around on the forest floor.

'If that was Mark, he'd be replying. That's not Mark,' said Dev, who was moving around in a defensive spin.

'Who else would be out here?' said Jane.

'Guys,' said Simon, 'lots of people enjoy a nighttime visit to the woods, and I want to say, there's no reason to knock dogging just because we haven't tried it.'

Jane threw her arms in the air and made a big starfish shape. Feeling she wasn't big enough yet, she began doing star jumps.

'What are you doing, Jane?' said Dev.

'A power play! If Mark's a murderer – well, we may as well try and do something! Scare him off with our own manoeuvres!'

'Aren't you thinking of power poses?' said Dev, who'd done an assembly on the topic. It had played well, but to much more laughter than he'd have liked.

Jane kept jumping, which took some effort, since she didn't have the stature of a natural athlete. 'Don't even think about it!' she yelled into the distance. 'I've got a heavy torch!'

'I'll tell you what, Dev,' said Simon, 'this would be a terrible time to find out you really are a murderer.'

'Oh, for Christ's sake!' came a gruff Liverpudlian voice from nearby.

'Arghh!' said the detectives, spinning in the direction of the voice.

From the undergrowth emerged a large dark shape, a tall and proportionally well-built man in a cape, which he swished dramatically.

'No, I'm sorry, but you've absolutely ruined my entrance,' he said. 'Yammering on and on and on. I was waiting for a break in the conversation, but with you lot that was never going to happen. You know, when I do this bit for tourists, it's considered the highlight.'

'Oh my god,' said Jane.

'Nope, no, no, thank you,' muttered Dev, who had optimistically opened a taxi booking app and was searching for a way out.

The man mountain offered each of them his big, cold hand to shake. 'Mark Sweeney, Fortean researcher, expert in Tonbridge's history and mythos, PhD candidate (fully remote).'

'Licence to kill?' said Dev quietly.

Jane shone her torch towards Mark's face. He had chestnut-brown hair cut in a short, slightly monk-like style, large clean-shaven cheeks, a small button nose, and bright blue eyes that were scrunched up in a pained expression.

'Oh, bloody hell!'

Jane lowered the torch. 'Sorry, Mark. Just wanted to verify your identity.'

'Well, maybe next time you could do it without breaking the Geneva Convention?'

'Right, Mark,' said Simon in the voice he used for Zoom meetings. 'Perhaps we can kick off the session with some introductions, then move it to the pub for an informal roundtable on what you know about Nellie Thorne?'

Mark squared up to him. 'I was thinking we could commence the tour right here, at the gateway to a powerful ancient energy of which you lot know nothing.' Mark began striding around them in full tour-guide mode, swishing his cape. 'For this land holds the key to the mystery you have come to me enquiring about. I will be the one to walk you through it, and by the end of the night, you might have seen the spectre of Miss Nellie herself.'

'Now that,' Dev whispered to Jane, 'is a power play.'

'I am sorry you've been through that, mate,' said Mark, who had begun to soften now he was in charge of proceedings. The four of them trudged through wet mud, weaving between trees and roots, on a barely-there track that was winding them through the woods uphill.

'Thanks,' said Dev. 'In a way, it's nice to get some space to talk about it. Out here, away from everything. I can sort of look at myself like a third party. They've set me up with the school counsellor, but she's way out of her depth. Her bread and butter is a posh kid's pony dying.'

'*Tch*. Well, I totally hear you, mate,' said Mark, who had picked up a gnarly five-foot-long stick and was using it as a sort of wizard's walking staff. 'Not many people understand what we've been through.'

'Oh – Mark, I'm so sorry. Have you . . . lost a partner?'

'I was in a relationship with a succubus.' He put the hand that wasn't holding his staff to his forehead to rub at the pain.

'Jane?' whispered Simon.

'Yes?' Jane whispered back.

'Let's keep an open mind, OK?'

'Met her about five years back,' said Mark. 'She was working in the Starbucks drive-through on the M6. Corley services. Hiding in plain sight. She kept me on the hook for eight months. But don't worry, mate. Your essential lifeforce will come back to you. You've just got to give it a bit of time.'

'Right. Thanks, Mark,' said Dev, feeling a little better, but not for the right reasons.

'Mark has spent many years finding victims of succubi and incubi,' Simon whispered to Jane. 'He thinks Nellie Thorne is one of the most famous examples.'

'Very haunted, these woods,' said Mark to everyone. 'I'm taking you to see the most active paranormal site in Tonbridge, so it's highly likely we'll see ghosts on this stakeout.'

'Sorry, stakeout?' said Jane. Gavin had covered stakeouts in week four of the course, but there had been no mention of hiking in the woods with a caped pseudo-wizard.

'Ghost stakeout. You wanted to know about Nellie. I thought I'd go one better and show her to you. But please, save your questions 'til the end because this story needs to be told in the right order.'

As the group trudged on, Mark used his hands and staff to add drama to his tale.

'Once upon a time, ancient peoples walked this part of what we call Kent. People who worshipped their gods at large stones we call megaliths. *Lith* meaning "stone", *mega* meaning "massive". A bit like the stones that make up Stonehenge. And there is one here in these woods.'

'That's fascinating,' said Dev. 'I teach history. So is the stone an example of the area's Early Neolithic long barrows?'

Mark hesitated. 'It's very ancient,' he said confidently. 'Nobody knows how the stones in this area appeared. Some say they were placed by aliens.'

'Actually, don't archaeologists think they were rolled on logs?'

'No,' Mark said flatly. 'Anyway, throughout the centuries, people have felt connected to stones like the one we're going to see tonight. This is because they were placed along ley lines. Some ley lines are sources of great positive energy.'

'Ooh, I love positive energy,' said Simon.

'But other ley lines are wells of pure evil,' said Mark.

Simon gasped.

They arrived at a clearing in the woods, an open expanse of grass as large as a football field, with Mark's circular megalith standing at its heart. The silvery stone was bigger than a car, with smooth edges and a flat top, and gleamed like an ancient CD-ROM under the moonlight. Mark halted the group to admire it from afar, lifting his arms as if to savour the moment.

'Here is the intersection of ancient energies where the prehistoric peoples of Tonbridge chose to lay their stones.'

Simon snorted. 'Lay their stones.'

'I usually say, "I'm dropping the kids off at the pool,"' said Jane, and laughed at her own joke. Simon low-fived her.

'Unbelievable,' said Mark. 'Can I finish?'

'Sorry,' said the two detectives in unison.

'As I've mentioned,' Mark continued, 'over the centuries, this site has served many a mystical purpose. The most famous one we know of is the terrifying ritual of the Wylebrook Witches.'

Jane nodded. More terrifying women.

'The first known sighting was by a group of teenage boys who came out here during the sixties looking for birds' eggs. What they reported was an ensemble of witches in white robes casting incantations. But as the witches reached the climax of their spell, they disappeared!'

Jane had stopped listening. She thought she'd seen something poke its head out from behind a tree on the opposite side of the clearing. She wanted to tug Simon's sleeve, but she was frozen with fear. Mark continued his tale.

'Since that night, many others have been fortunate enough to witness the same apparitions: women in white chanting around the stone.'

'Wow,' said Simon.

'However, I believe these women are in fact the spiritual materialisations of Kent's most notorious spectres: the infamous Nellie Thorne and her phantom sisters!'

Jane, still speechless, watched as a figure in white emerged from the opposite side of the clearing. It walked a few slow steps towards the megalith. Her throat felt sewn up.

'Mark,' she croaked. Simon and Dev followed her eyeline about a hundred metres; the figure was small and slow, and looked almost translucent. Simon grabbed Jane's arm. A breeze blew into the clearing from all directions, lifting leaves from the forest floor.

'What?' said Mark. He turned to look around. 'What are you lot staring at?'

'It's . . .' Again, this was the best Jane could manage.

The figure seemed oblivious to their presence. It started pacing a circle around the stone.

'Recent sightings have been reported by a chef from the local gastropub scavenging for mushrooms, and a few fly tippers,' Mark continued, 'but they're getting less common these days. Sometimes I wonder if ghosts are dying out, as it were. But I still bring people out here at night hoping for a spiritual sighting.'

The ghostly figure finished its lap of the megalith, and jolted into a run directly towards the group, arms reaching out towards them. The stakeout party screamed with terror.

17

'Incredible,' said Simon, clapping. 'That is incredible. This man's dedication to creating thrilling experiences for his stakeholders. It's just . . . Wow. Mark, have you ever done any in-house corporate work? Because my department will be hiring a few newbies soon.'

Mark shook his head. 'No, no, the corporate world isn't really my . . . well, maybe you could send me a link.'

'I was completely convinced,' said Simon, shaking the ghost's hand.

'Oh, thank you, I do quite a bit of local theatre actually,' said the ghost. 'It's rewarding to create a reaction in someone like that.'

The apparition's name was Clive, and he had turned out to be a 66-year-old grey-haired allotment fan with a kindly energy, who had sold his IT company in the 2000s and had enjoyed retirement since then.

'Hope I didn't scare you too much!'

'It's fine, Clive, don't worry about it,' said Jane. 'We're all just a little bit on edge because we're investigating a disappearance.'

'Potentially a murder!' added Simon.

'Oh my goodness, that's awful,' said Clive, wringing his hands in his thermal black Gore-Tex gloves. He began packing his ghost costume – a white dressing gown – into his backpack. Clive's eagerness, dainty stature and grey-white frizzy hair, plus the rust-red fleece under his black coat, gave him the air of a people-pleasing robin. 'Have you got any leads?'

'Um . . .' Jane searched her brain for their list of leads. 'Yes, a few. Anyway, we'd best get home. We're going to walk Dev back to his house and then on to the station for the last train,' she said.

'You ought to ask Clive about his ghost story,' said Mark. 'I get him out here for these because he's one of the few people still in the area who's seen the ghosts.'

'That's right.' Clive nodded. 'But who's Dev?'

Everyone looked around.

'Oh dear,' said Clive, realising he might have caused a second disappearance.

'He's legged it,' said Mark. He puffed his chest out. 'Wouldn't be the first time this has happened on one of my ghost walks. You often get a runner. They can't hack it, is what it is.'

Jane panicked. She jogged back into the woods. 'Dev?' she called out, causing birds to shuffle into flight overhead. Simon's footsteps joined behind her. Jane pulled out her phone. 'Simon, do you have signal? We need to try ringing him.'

She paced back into the clearing to the megalith, crouched and looked around the bottom of the stone, as if Dev could have somehow got lost underneath it like a bra under the bed.

'Jane,' said Simon, in a feeble voice that Jane had never heard before. She slowly stood up and looked where Simon was looking.

Across the clearing was another shadowy figure, standing a few metres back into the woods. They both turned around to confirm that Clive and Mark were still where they'd left them. Maybe this was a woman; the figure was certainly too short to be Dev. They couldn't work out any features, like a silhouette, because it was lit up from behind with a halo of white-gold light.

Jane tried to say something like, *It's a trick of the moon*. But she was stuck with fear.

The figure lifted a small hand and waved at them slowly. The light behind it went out, then flashed once more, leaving a harrowing imprint of its shape in their eyeballs.

'Have you found Dev?' Mark's voice interrupted the suspense.

'Mark, look,' Simon managed to say, and pointed in the direction of the mystery guest.

'At what?'

The figure and its mysterious glow had gone. Jane's fear turned alchemically to anger.

'Mark, once is enough! How could you? Scaring us twice in one night. How many more people do you have waiting to jump out? It's like a fairground ghost train!'

'Jane, what are you on about? There isn't anyone else.'

18

When they got to the pub and re-established wi-fi connection, Jane received a text from Dev that said simply: Sorry. Had to get out. Walked home.

'Well, that was a waste of our time and energy,' said Jane, putting her elbows firmly on the bar.

Simon thought she looked more stressed than usual, and noticed she'd uncharacteristically ordered a pint of stout. 'Are you sure you want to drink that?' he asked gently.

'Yes, definitely. It's warming.' She brushed at a wet beer stain on her elbow.

'Here you go,' said the bartender. 'One Guinness Extra Cold. And for you, sir?'

Behind them, Mark was giving Clive notes on his performance.

'I think you could enter the clearing more slowly next time, and maybe limp a little?'

'Right, right, yes.'

'I've got the Greater Manchester Fortean Society coming in two weeks, so it'll need to be a belter.'

There was a round table free in the corner. Jane and Simon slipped into the bench seats, and Mark and Clive took the outer two. Next to them, the bartender came over and used a wrought-iron set of tongs to put two fresh logs on the glowing, dying fire. Jane watched as the logs slipped, settled, and began being licked by flames.

'Look, gents,' said Simon. 'I'd love to get your take on what you think Jane and I saw out there. It was quite small. Maybe a goblin? I know you didn't get a look at it yourselves, but maybe you've got some experience of woodland goblins in the area?'

'Hmm,' said Clive, considering it. 'I've not heard much about goblins in this area, but nothing's impossible, I suppose . . .'

'It definitely wasn't a long-haired woman wearing white?' Mark asked again.

'Hmm. No, sorry,' said Simon. 'It was small, and if it was wearing something, it was figure-hugging, and black. Like a cat burglar. Could it have been a cat burglar?'

'In the woods?' said Clive, rubbing his chin. 'I've mostly only heard about them in detective fiction, but you never know . . .'

'I suppose ghosts don't necessarily have to wear white,' pondered Mark. 'Maybe ghosts can change their clothing.'

'It didn't feel totally human,' said Jane, tracing her fingers around the condensation on her pint glass. 'Though, of course, it had to be. Do people go camping in those woods?'

'No!' said Mark. 'Because they're bloody haunted.'

'Well, of course, that's your line of work, to tell people they are,' said Jane.

'They are, I'm afraid,' said Clive. 'I didn't get to tell my bit of the story up there. Usually, at the end of Mark's walks, I tell people what I saw back in 1982.'

'What did you see?' Simon leaned forward, rapt. Jane wondered if he was about to make Clive a job offer. Could he make Jane a job offer too? No, that would be inappropriate.

'Go on, Clive: tell your story,' said Mark.

'Well,' Clive cleared his throat gently and nudged his pint around on the beermat. 'I was born in Guyana, a few more years ago than I'd care to mention—'

'The ghost bit, Clive.'

'Right, sorry, Mark. I was quite a young bloke in the early eighties; I'd just finished college and I was working in computers for the insurance company with the big offices on Wellesley Street when I met this bloke, Eddie. Bit of a weird one – always wore a donkey jacket, which was quite smelly, and he liked starting fires. Anyway, he was a big birder.'

Simon shook his head. 'Those days were so unenlightened.'

'Simon, I think he means "birding", as in "birdwatching",' said Jane.

'That's right, Jane,' said Clive, smiling. 'But Eddie did also happen to love pulling birds. Now, one night, we're having a pint here, and he convinces me that we ought to go up to Wylebrook Woods to see the famous European nightjar, or common goatsucker.'

'I used to play drums for them,' said Jane.

'The catch is, they're nocturnal. So you've got to go to the woods at night.'

Clive was using his finger to point, conducting the story. Behind him, the fire crackled as a log caved in.

'Now, I wasn't sure the European nightjar existed. But Eddie reckoned he'd read about them in a birding book, and back then, you just had to take it at face value. There also wasn't too much to do, so after a few pints, it seemed like a good idea. But when we got up to the woods, we could hear singing. So we followed it. We hid near the clearing, and crept towards the stone. Standing all around the clearing were a load of women.'

He emphasised 'women' as one might say, 'a load of ghouls'.

'About a dozen, all dressed in white robes. Doing a sort of dance. It looked a bit like t'ai chi. That was trendy at the time. We were terrified, and started to run, but then Eddie said he'd dropped his birding book. After a bit of an argument, we went back up there. And what did we see?'

The group put on expectant expressions.

'Nothing. The women were gone. There was just one thing. Blood on the stone. Big thick drops of red blood, except it wasn't like ordinary blood. It was sort of solid. I told Eddie not to touch it, but . . .' He shrugged. 'After we found that, I wanted to get out of there sharpish.'

'So, what you saw was . . . ?' prompted Mark.

'Ghosts.' Clive nodded.

'Wow,' said Simon, sitting back. 'Where's Eddie these days?'

'Oh,' said Clive. 'He accidentally drove his Harley Davidson off a cliff at a bike rally around the turn of the millennium. It was very sad.'

CLANG – the bell rang for last orders. Jane jumped. 'The time!' she said. 'Simon, what time is it?'

Simon looked at his bright blue calculator wristwatch.

'Not sure. I've got it stuck on long division.' He looked at her. 'But don't worry, babe. We won't miss our train. I'll sort everything out.' He got up and went over to the bar with his wallet in his hand.

Jane tapped her fingers against her glass. 'Clive, are you sure there wasn't just a group of women in the woods, and they ran away when they heard you?'

'No, no, there wouldn't have been time,' said Clive.

'There wouldn't have been time,' echoed Mark.

'And besides,' said Clive, 'over the years, lots of people have seen the ghost women. They always look exactly like the Nellies.'

'Let me guess: tall, thin, long light brown hair?' said Jane.

'Exactly!' said Clive. 'That is the exact description.'

'In fact, I got a bit of a shock when I eventually met a Nellie,' said Mark. 'Because of the resemblance to the ghosts.'

'What?' said Jane. 'You met a Nellie?'

Simon strode back to the table. 'The day is saved!'

'We haven't missed the train?'

'We have missed the train. But we're going to stay here for the night!'

'We're what?!' Jane forgot about Clive and Mark for a moment.

'They've got rooms! And there was one free, so I booked it.'

'Simon, with what money?'

Clive and Mark looked into their pints. Jane stood up and led Simon to the bar by the elbow. 'Simon, we can't afford a spontaneous holiday to Kent. I'm unemployed, remember?'

'Credit card! We get the airline points too, so in a way, it's even cheaper.'

'Simon, we have no use for airline points. I've just told you we can't afford a holiday to Kent.'

'But what else are we meant to do? Ask to sleep on Clive's sofa?'

Jane rubbed her eyes, which were feeling quite foggy now. The only thing she wanted to do was say goodbye to the amateur-dramatic cast of Kent's *Most Haunted*. 'That would've been the cheaper option. But fine, you've booked it, so I guess we'll have to figure it out when the bill comes in.'

'Jane,' said Simon encouragingly, stroking her arm, 'you're having a crisis of confidence in our ability to sort everything out. But I really believe in us. Together, we can do anything. We're going to be fine.'

Jane looked sideways, spotting a stairway marked ROOMS THIS WAY in the corner.

'And you know what they say,' continued Simon. 'You've got to spend money to make money.'

'Funny,' said Jane. 'I always thought you had to make money

to spend money.' She was suddenly reminded of Simon's secret wad of cash. She looked at the barman, who was on his phone, probably booking a holiday with the mystery Mash millions.

After some soul-searching and reading relationship advice online, she'd accepted that the only person she should be asking about Simon's secret cash was Simon. There were a few too many mysteries going on at the moment, and if it took a painful conversation to solve one of them, it might be worth it.

'We'll be off then, lads,' said Mark, as he and Clive put on their woollen hats and headed to the door.

'Hold on!' said Jane. 'I still have things I want to ask you.'

'Well, you can drop me a line on the message board,' said Mark. He and Clive were already halfway out into the night. 'Ta-ta!'

19

The room's wooden door had a wrought-iron hoop for a handle that Simon had to rattle to get open, and the ancient beam that topped the doorframe was crooked and sloping so that he had to duck not to hit his head on it, but still hit his head on it anyway.

'Ow!'

He flopped onto the bed and started doing snow angels.

'This duvet's a great tog,' he said happily.

Jane came to perch on the side of the bed and ran her hands over the stiff cotton that still smelled of laundry.

'Mark and Clive's theory is the same one I found at the library. All the Nellies look the same. Therefore, they must all be the same. Therefore, they must be a ghost. A ghost that hangs out in a bit of local woodland and casts spells.' She sighed.

'I quite like the ghost theory – I bet it would knock Gavin's socks off,' said Simon, plumping pillows to lie back on. They were feathery and about twice the size and softness of their pillows at home.

There was a rare moment of silence between them. And yet, so much to say. Normally, Jane would've told Simon about the flirt with Linda. But since he was keeping a secret, it had felt harder to say.

She took a slow breath in, hoping that air would come back out as words along the lines of: *Simon, why are you carrying around thousands of pounds in cash? It feels a bit like lying given that I'm under the impression we have no money.* But before those words came out, she saw his eyes were teary.

'Simon, what is it?'

He sat up, and she cuddled him into her shoulder. 'I was just thinking about how one day you're going to die.'

'Oh dear,' she said, patting his back.

'It makes me wish I believed in an afterlife because . . . well, how long have we been together? A year and a bit? And it's gone so fast, and we'll only get about sixty of them if we're lucky. And sixty of anything is nothing. What if someone told you that you could only see sixty more movies in your life? Or eat sixty more chips?'

'Aw, Simon, try not to worry. I'm not going to die any time soon. I mean, I don't know the normal life expectancy for a PI. Obviously, it's not going to be as good as the average, but probably better than a North Sea fisherman or a dog astronaut.'

He nodded, remembering those great hounds.

'By the way, Simon, why are you carrying around several thousand pounds in your wallet?'

'What?' He let go of the hug.

'If we have that kind of cash floating around, I would've liked to know about it,' said Jane, who was now looking not at Simon but out into the distance through the leaded window.

'Have you been detective-ing around in my wallet?'

'I'm sorry, but I had to go in there to get our railcard.'

'Well . . .' He looked deflated, having been faced with the thought of his girlfriend's untimely death and now with being in trouble. 'It's just a favour I'm doing for my mum. It's not our money – yours and mine, I mean. But she's asked me not to tell anyone about it, so I can probably explain at some point, but . . .'

Jane looked at him, his red eyes sad and saggy. She knew that when Simon had been little he'd once played hide-and-seek in Waitrose, and Penny, with her perennial Sauvignon-region hangover, had driven home without him as a punishment.

'I'm sorry. I should've just asked you about it straight away. It's just a bit discombobulating finding the most cash you've ever seen in your boyfriend's wallet.' She hugged him again. After all that, Jane felt disappointed it wasn't a secret windfall. She breathed in his nice smell through the shoulder of his shirt. You couldn't put a price on getting along. Well, maybe you could. Three thousand pounds, for example.

'Hey, I've had an incredible thought,' said Simon excitedly.

'Oh yeah?' Jane beamed. Incredible Thoughts was one of their favourite games.

'I've just realised that if the millennium was now, we'd do nothing to mark it. You know, as a nation.'

'God, you're right. You can barely get an ambulance to come to an emergency these days. Imagine building a dome! Not to mention a giant Ferris wheel.'

'Exactly!'

'I think, at best, we'd get a crap firework display and Take That playing on the roof of Buckingham Palace.'

'And by the way, that's not the most cash you've ever seen. Don't you remember the room in the Millennium Dome that had a million pounds, just so people could see what a million pounds looked like?'

And so it went on in the candlelight for a while, the two of them lying on the fresh bed with their shoes kicked off, talking nonsense. Even the room they were staying in was supposedly haunted, according to a laminated factsheet on one of the bedside tables, by the ghost of a monk called Sad Harry, and every now and then there was a creak on the ceiling, as if from footsteps on the floor above. Except there was no floor above, just the roof.

'Wow, spooky. Haunted is the theme of the day,' said Simon, who loved being away from home overnight. The weirder the location the better.

'Must be pigeons,' said Jane.

'We did see something out there in the woods, didn't we?'

'We did.' Jane sighed. 'But . . . my instincts are all off-whack at the moment. For a second there, I really thought Dev had vanished. It's so silly. Of course he'd just had enough. Hadn't you?'

'I thought the whole thing was sort of brilliant. I'm still a bit cold, though.' Simon sat up and scanned the room. 'Do you think we have a bath in here?'

'Hold on,' said Jane, tensing up.

'Have you had an incredible thought?'

'Mark said he met a Nellie!'

'Did he?' said Simon, screwing up his face to access his memory.

'Yes, right before you got back to the table, after last orders! He said, "When I met a Nellie." God, do you think we can talk to him again? Maybe we should drop him a message now,' she said, meaning: *Simon, you should drop him a message now.*

'Gosh, we're always on duty.' Simon picked up his phone, but he wasn't typing. In fact, he'd frozen with his mouth open, like a fishmonger's haddock on ice.

'Jane, she's alive!' Simon showed her the screen. It was the page for Nellie's Vintage: Last seen online less than a minute ago.

'The person using her account is alive,' Jane said carefully, remembering that High Court battles had been fought over less. But her heart was starting to race.

She anxiously refreshed her emails, and the phone buzzed in

her hand. 'Argh! Oh no. Oh my god, oh my god!' She met Simon's eyes, hers filled with horror and surprise. 'I got a second interview at the gambling place. They want me to come in in two days.'

Above them, the ceiling creaked from one side all the way to the other, as if somebody was walking across the roof.

PART THREE

20

Present Day

Spring was the best season to leave – new life growing everywhere while you journeyed into a new life.

The woman looked around her bedroom, wondering if she'd sleep better or worse in the next one. That was just a packing thought; packing involved a chain of dull tasks that left her prone to overthinking. She unzipped the empty holdall and put her hand inside, checking for any items that might have been left there from last time, but really just to roam around in the shell of her new existence. The holdall was battered from many journeys into new lives, but the zip still worked, and that was the most important thing for bags.

Nothing could stay the same, that was the lesson of spring. Or so she'd been taught every year. Change was hopeful and could lead you somewhere better than where you'd begun. They never explained why, if spring was so hopeful, each new one inevitably turned back into winter. How did you pack necklaces without them getting tangled?

Outside, an ageing car engine gave a gravelly, sputtering cough. It kept running while the door slammed shut, and the footsteps made their way towards her ground-floor window. *TAP-TAP-TAP!* The knock on the glass made her jump.

'Excuse me!' said the driver. 'I've not got all day. Or have I got the wrong place? Car for Miss Daisy Brown?'

She tipped the necklaces loose into the holdall. Whatever they were destined for, she would just have to work out how to unpick them at the other end.

21

Tuesday 16 April – Present Day

'... The break in the case was when we had our big idea: joining the Thames Beachcombing Society. The river has two low tides per day, and we had to catch both daily. Sally from Hove, a beachcomber of thirty-seven years, found the laptop sitting on a bit of driftwood near Greenwich Pier on day two. After that, we enlisted Pierre from our local U Crack We Fix on Mitcham High Road, who was able to retrieve the contents of the hard drive despite waterlogging. And that was how we found the child pornography.'

There was a patter of applause from the class. Gavin stood up from the small desk on the front row where he'd been perching.

'Well done, Hans,' he said, clapping the bald bouncer on his leather shoulder. He turned to the class. 'This was exactly how I found the stockbroker's laptop back in 'oh-six. Did it start the chain of events that led to the financial crash? Some say no. But these things are tricky to gauge, and I still think...' He shrugged. '... it's possible. Now, obviously, I made a placeholder folder labelled CHILD PORNOGRAPHY, but when you opened it, you found...?'

'Your holiday pictures, Gdansk, February last year.'

'Correct! Proof that he found the same laptop I deposited in the river last week, by the Slug and Lettuce in Canary Wharf. Now, I'll still need to see the write-up, but I have to hand it to you, Hans, you're on track for a very good coursework score, a very good score indeed.'

In the Naughty Seats, Simon whispered to Jane, 'Why does Hans keep saying "we"? Is he using the royal *we*? Does he have a grandiosity complex?'

Jane had a face as sour as lemon vinegar. 'It's him and his wife. He roped her in to help with the investigation. They're adorable. I've been following them on Instagram.'

Under the desk, she showed Simon a selfie of Hans the bouncer and his pretty middle-aged wife, all smiles, gleefully holding up a wet laptop on a crisp blue day.

'They've captioned it: "Bosh! Might become full-time detectives!"' she said. 'Isn't that a bit insensitive? Given what's on that laptop?'

'Maybe,' considered Simon. 'Though it is just pictures of Gavin eating pierogi.'

'Not to mention they've stolen your idea of having a catchphrase. I mean, "bosh"?! It's not exactly original, is it?'

'You two!' said Gavin sharply. The Naughty Twins looked up. 'If you've finished your conversation, it's your turn.'

'Oh,' said Simon involuntarily, his throat going dry. The class turned to them, waiting.

The last twenty-four hours had been a scrabble. They'd left the inn at Tonbridge and had boarded a homeward train, where Jane had begun making the presentation she had to give to the gambling app people, and Simon had opened his laptop to begin the detective coursework, which was due today.

He'd suggested they swap these tasks, as Simon had once got sucked into matched betting on Canadian women's hockey, and Jane was the obvious propelling force behind their coursework. Jane had suggested she might do both, which had hurt Simon's feelings. She'd then dithered with the idea of withdrawing from the gambling app job entirely, before realising that this, ironically, would be a gamble, since she didn't have a plan for next month's rent and this application was the furthest she'd got in her job hunt so far.

When Simon had suggested asking for an extension on their coursework update, Jane had nearly thrown him off the train. After that, it was a simple matter of connecting to the in-train wi-fi, which had taken them the rest of the way into London.

So the presentation had been Simon's responsibility alone, and now his wobbling legs carried him to the front of the classroom, where he put his laptop on Gavin's desk and plugged it into the projector. He was trembling not so much with nerves, but with excitement about the roof of this case, which was about to be blown off. Jane tentatively followed him and stood by the projector screen. She put her hands behind her back and tried not to lean against the wall.

'Good evening, lady and gentlemen,' said Simon to the class, as a loading wheel spun in the centre of his screen. 'Ahem.'

The class members frowned in anticipation.

Onto the screen popped a scowling demon, skinless and sinewy, eating a person. Simon had used AI to generate this image, and it had come out almost as disturbing as he'd hoped.

'I present to you . . . the Demons of Kent,' he said with great gravity, and then, to break the ice: 'Jane used to play drums for them.'

Simon had worked on this at their kitchen table into the early hours of the afternoon. At his elbow had been a can of energy drink and a cup of Earl Grey. The breakthrough had been so exciting that he hadn't even told Jane. He stood in a confident pose, legs apart.

'Get ready to come with me, travellers, on a journey into Kent's demonic secret. Because it may be the Garden of England . . . but at night, when the shadows fall over the gnomes' faces, and the foxes come out to scream, gardens can be very spooky indeed.'

He clicked onto the next slide: the Wikipedia picture of Tonbridge, a photo of Dev taken from far away while he'd been unaware, and a stock photo of a woman pulling a scary face.

'But first, I'll explain the basics of the case.'

22

Wednesday 14 May 1997

Gavin walked with purpose. His legs had a destination. His sunglasses protected him from the spring's strong sun. The British Isles were in business. A new government, employment at a high, the concrete pavements hoarding sticky-smelling heat, and every party pub and lorry radio pumping the boppy beats of acid house, Primal Scream, and 'I'm a Barbie girl'. Gavin had just decided to officially change his name from Gavin MacCrimmon, which stuck out like a sore thumb and bore the ironic syllable *crim*, to the one he'd been using for a while: Gavin Smith. Smith was a name guaranteed to fly under the radar like a Man in Black's lasered-off fingerprints. For Gavin, it was an exciting step towards the mid-career.

His stride took him under the lime-green canopy of the one tree growing on Thornton Heath High Street. He turned left at a bleak Brutalist box of apartments which seemed cheerful today, its ground-floor walls covered in colourful graffiti. A group of women in strappy tops exited it, holding tote bags and tinnies, heading for the station and then a day lounging in the park. Things were good; the nation was happy. Except in Tonbridge, where there'd been a murder.

Gavin fare-dodged again, not so much out of penury this

time, more out of *joie de vivre*. His plan was to get down to the crime scene and establish quickly whether the victim was Nellie Thorne. The odds seemed high – a missing woman, a body turning up – the case was a story writing itself.

Leaving Tonbridge station, he bounced with energy. He felt a sense of purpose, or whatever it was in this world that kept you feeling on track instead of a bit depressed. Gavin had now been to Tonbridge a few times; it was home to Terence's closest police station, and Gavin had expanded his car search and general enquiries there. He'd begun to like Tonbridge, every building shorter and smaller than in London, with green hills comfortingly in sight in the distance. It was the sort of place you could stop and take a breath, begin to feel at home. Or maybe get a bit bored.

While it would, of course, be sad if Nellie had died, it would be a leap forward in the case. Gavin had cross-checked Terence's list of number plates with every car that had parked in a four-mile radius of the flat for a fortnight. Despite all that effort, he hadn't found the car that had taken Little Miss Perfect away. He'd come to know the other cars in Terence's notebook, like side-characters popping up here and there. They made him think of the TV show for kids with the yellow car that drove itself around, getting into trouble. According to Terence's notebook, the car Nellie had got into on the day she'd disappeared had only been seen on the street once – it did not appear in the book again and had never appeared before.

Gavin's first thought had been that she'd got into a taxi, so he'd checked with the three nearest taxi companies. None of them had had that number plate on their books. After that, he'd wondered if it had been a stolen vehicle, that could be traced back to a known criminal. But of course, he couldn't get the police's list of stolen cars in the area. If only people put posters on streetlights like they did for cats: 'Ford Mondeo, missing since Tuesday, generous reward, answers to Wotsit.'

The body had been found in a field, on some farmland outside town, and it was refreshing for Gavin to tread a new path from Tonbridge station. He tried not to think about how much the murder had improved his day and his mood.

The crime scene was in full swing under a cloudless sky. It seemed at odds: the weather for a festival, but the mood of a funeral. Even worse, the cows hadn't been cleared from the site but had just drifted to the other side of their field, away from the inner cordon around the forensics tent and parked-up vehicles; they chewed and stared like voyeurs. A ring of officers guarding the cordon stared back, possibly wary of a stampede.

Gavin approached slowly from the public footpath. He'd begun wearing suits, to embody seriousness, and he'd found today's in a sale at British Home Stores. It was dark grey and a bit shiny, the whole lot for a tenner. In the heat, it was making his crotch sweat, and the cloth was folding weirdly, more like plastic than fabric. He scanned the crowd of police for his contact, but all the faces were small and indistinguishable. He suddenly worried that in the suit he might look like a man going to a *Reservoir Dogs*-themed party, rather than a smart professional who might work shoulder-to-shoulder with the Criminal Investigation Department.

He reached the border of the scene, a wire fence that ran along the edge of the cow field. A female officer in uniform was putting tape up. Gavin looked down at its instruction – DO NOT CROSS.

'Hello. I'm here to see Bernard.'

For a moment, she just looked at him with the correct amount of disdain for this stupid statement, but he kept going.

'Bernard Parker, I mean. I'm an informant, and he's asked

me to come down and give a statement as urgently as possible. I'm . . .' He paused, hitting the energy barrier of his don't-give-your-identity rule. '*Tch*. I'm Gavin Smith. I'm a private detective and I have important information.'

She looked him up and down, possibly wondering if this important information could be 'I'm your guy', and if she might be able to just arrest him. But she said, 'Wait here. I'll have a look.'

'Thank you!' said Gavin to her back, which had already walked away. Was it better to be nice and polite to them, or act stony and show them he was a hardman? Perhaps he should take it on an officer-by-officer basis?

He realised he should be using these precious moments to take in every detail he could see at the scene. His first observation still held: this was a lot of officers, even for the most serious crime. Near the body there were about half a dozen people, crouching, walking, conversing seriously. But many more were pacing around the perimeter inspecting the grass, trying to look occupied. Gavin bobbed and craned to see past the forensics tent to the location where the body must be, a centre of gravity that was creating an invisible pull on every person present. But on this side of the fence and the tape he couldn't see anything. Radios were fuzzing in some of the cars, and officers leaned awkwardly through the windows to answer. Indeterminable speech came out of the handsets at a pitch just below what Gavin could hear. Up in the clear sky, an osprey wheeled in circles. Very insensitive, he thought.

'MacCrim?' Gavin's contact approached him, a big lumbering man in uniform. He wore the bucket helmet even on this sweltering day.

'Not my name any more, Bernie.'

'I prefer the ring of the old one. Makes you sound like a fast-food detective. Caught that Hamburglar yet?'

Gavin had met Bernard Parker at some point on his Thorne journey. He couldn't pin down exactly when, but it had been on one of his visits to the police station in Tonbridge. There was never any information for Gavin, nothing he could be told or given. But Bernard had been the officer most often assigned to the reception desk, and they'd struck up a little bonhomie, especially after Gavin had referred to Nellie as 'the Thorne in my side', which had made Bernard laugh. Finally, at some point, they'd gone for a pint. He was Gavin's first proper contact. Bernard insisted they weren't 'contacts', just two blokes who happened to share a liking for Kentish urban legends, going to the pub and interesting facts. Gavin felt his career would come to rely on people like this: almost-friends, unofficial contacts, and especially people who were as bad at lying as Bernard.

'Look MacCrim, you can't come and ask for me here,' Bernard said, leaning over the fence and talking quietly. 'It looks like we're in cahoots.'

'Come on, Bernie. You never know, I might be some help.'

Bernard shifted and looked around him to see if anyone was watching.

'You know I can't tell you anything. Hop it.'

'What's the maximum you can tell me?' In pleading, Gavin noticed he had crouched a little, making himself even shorter than usual.

'Police are investigating a body found on Pagett Farm at oh-five-hundred hours. The individual in question has not yet been publicly identified.'

'That was the line on the morning news, Bernard.'

Bernard's expression was even and calm.

'But she's been privately identified. Hasn't she?'

'Gav, you know I can't, mate.'

'Is it her? Is it Nellie?'

Bernard tapped his nose. But his tiny, grim grin told Gavin the answer was no.

'Oh, thank god.' Where had that come from? Was Gavin relieved?

'What do you mean, "thank god"? I haven't told you anything! Look, Gav, I don't even know anything about this myself, I'm basically just a crime-scene bouncer, so I haven't said anything, alright? Now, you'd better piss off before you get us both in trouble.'

'I needed to know if it was her. This is my case. A missing person, and now a murder, in the same small area? Bit of a coincidence, isn't it?'

Bernard rolled his eyes.

'And I know murders do happen, unrelated to the Nellie thing. I mean, there was that woman last year . . .'

He meant the Tonbridge resident who'd been found murdered in her home the previous summer. Tragic scandal in leafy suburbia: it had caused a fluster of tabloid headlines, before being bumped off the front page by a football tournament the following week.

'But if you do find that whatever this is' – Gavin pointed to the tent – 'is linked to Nellie, and you want to chew it over with someone, I'm your man.'

'There's no way I could confirm or deny anything about this case, or about the totally separate investigation into the disappearance of Ms Thorne,' said Bernard.

'So that means the murder victim *definitely* isn't her!'

Bernard sighed, kicking himself. Gavin decided to keep going.

'Bernard, I can help you. I know this area like the back of my hand now. I might have something useful. Just please keep talking to m—'

'You alright there, Parker?' a plainclothes copper shouted from a nearby car, which he'd reached into for a pack of cigarettes.

'Yes, Sarge, just advising this member of the public to clear the area,' Bernard shouted back. 'You can't work with us on a case this big, Gav. PIs stick to burglaries and chasing up child support. You're not on the payroll.' He looked around again. His boss was still watching suspiciously, puffing on a Rothmans. 'I can't be talking to you.'

Bernard shooed Gavin away with his hands like a cat. Gavin nodded. No hard feelings. Never any hard feelings with your important contacts. Gavin backed away, left at the bottom of the food chain again. Although the body in the field did not belong to Thorne, he could sense she was connected to this chaos somehow. He felt that anything odd happening anywhere in Kent was likely to be connected to her. Moreover, he was beginning to realise that being a detective was like being a psychoanalyst, or an artist – you had to learn to listen to your intuition. And his intuition told him it was time to dig deeper. At least down here, at the bottom of the food chain, you could grub around a bit.

23

Tuesday 16 April – Present Day

Simon was in full presenting flow, embodying his idea of a Steve Jobs keynote, despite never having watched one. Jane stood beside him like the silent half of a magician's act.

'I know what you're thinking. Is Nellie Thorne real? If she's real, is she alive? If she's dead, was she murdered by the only suspect we've been able to identify, Dev Hooper? What was his motive, especially if Nellie was pregnant? Is there any truth in the police's theory that this is all a hoax? Or is it a terrible miscarriage of justice? What links these women through the years who share the same name? Is it a coincidence, or part of an elaborate scam? Yes, it's a scam.'

At 'yes', Jane stood up straight.

'A scam for romance. Powerful, paranormal romance that robs the victims of their very lifeforce. But let's begin with some important written evidence by Bernard Parker, formerly of Kent Police. This is an almost-direct quote from a novel he wrote about the case.'

A quote appeared on the next slide: [You'd] better ... call ... Ghostbusters.

'Slightly abridged, sure, but reading between the lines, he's saying that this is paranormal,' Simon continued. 'Let's go further and hear from Tonbridge's premier ghost expert, Mark Sweeney, with whom I recently spent a night in the woods.'

On the next slide a quote, made in WordArt, read: She is not a human being but a powerful force roaming the countryside seeking the life energy of men on which to feast.

'And finally, from the man himself, our teacher, Gavin Smith.'

The next slide read: Kids used to think she was a ghost and would wind each other up.

Simon took a deep breath which puffed up his chest, and spoke in a powerful voice he'd developed in his school drama club days. 'Three wise men. All of whom believe Nellie is something beyond the natural. But what is she up to? The answer came from my own mother.'

Captain Alex and a couple of the others near the front exchanged glances.

On the next slide: a photo of Penny Mash, at a roadside bar drinking a fishbowl-sized Aperol spritz, wearing large sunglasses and a pashmina.

'Penny's from Kent, so I phoned her to see if she could add any local insight. Instead, she reminded me of an incident that happened when I was thirteen. One night, she caught me up past my bedtime watching a documentary about succubi.'

'Suck your what?' asked Captain Alex with a smirk. Simon continued as if he were a professor outlining his research at a conference.

'I'm glad you asked. *Succubi*,' he repeated, 'are female demons who feed off the energy of men. It tripped my memory, because this is exactly what Mark the paranormal expert thinks Nellie is.'

He clicked onto the next slide: a cartoon woman with horns and wings, perched on a rock, baring snarly fangs and wearing a tattered micro bikini.

Jane covered her eyes, the sort of motion a person might make if they were about to see two boats crash. While she'd been busy preparing for her job interview, Simon had given her every reassurance that he'd 'got this' and had sworn on David Bowie's memory that it would be a simple, no-frills recap.

'These demons can possess the bodies of normal human women. Then they seduce a man to steal his energy, leaving him tired and lethargic. The next time you're feeling a bit under the weather, it's worth bearing that in mind.

'We've spoken to several witnesses in the Tonbridge area, including ourselves, who have seen mysterious women dressed all in white doing some kind of ritual in Wylebrook Woods.'

Next slide: a picture of the 1990s girl group All Saints wearing all-white outfits: cargo pants with boob tubes, halter tops with miniskirts.

'Apologies, I googled "group of women wearing white" and this was the closest picture to what I had in mind.' His voice rose in pitch with passion: 'Who casts spells, does rituals, and wears robes?'

'S Club 7?' jeered somebody from the middle rows.

'Demons!' Simon announced, proudly. 'Or demon-*worshippers*. Which brings me back to the documentary. Succubi will often get pregnant by their human boyfriend while they're busy stealing their lifeforce. Because succubi don't care about birth control, and well, you know . . .'

Simon formed a ring with his thumb and forefinger. He stuck out the index finger of his other hand. Jane realised what he was about to do. She met his eye, held his stare, and slowly shook her head. There was a pause of standoff. He grinned, and in slow motion, pushed his index finger into the hole of his other hand.

As he moved the finger in and out, Jane began to quietly

hyperventilate. She watched every face in the class turn to each other with a mocking smirk. She wondered if she could go and sit back down, divesting herself of this mess, but that wasn't in the spirit of a long-term relationship. Her wagon was hitched to Simon's, and for the first time, the convoy had hit a pothole.

'Could these succubi be roaming the mortal plane, possessing ordinary women?' Simon carried on. 'Here I present to you: My Theory, trademark Simon Mash. Imagine you're an ordinary woman.'

Simon flicked back to the photo of his mother. Jane squinted, wondering why *she* wasn't a more immediate example of an ordinary woman.

'One day, you're going about your business. Then you fall into a weird sort of sleepy trance: the possession. The next thing you know, you're waking up in a bed you don't recognise. Bleary and confused, you sit up, reach for your phone to get the time, and find . . . one year has passed.'

A couple of the Hells Angels nodded at each other sympathetically.

'Even worse, something feels different in your body. You look down, and you're pregnant!'

The Angels raised their eyebrows.

'What are you going to do? The only logical thing. Leave, take anything you recognise as yours, say nothing to anyone, and try to find your way home. Once you get there, you'll seek medical help.' Simon paused for a breath. 'But what happened wasn't a mental breakdown or a memory lapse. You were possessed by the spirit of an angry demon, hungry to regain her ancient powers. The moment she invaded your body, you began believing your name was Nellie Thorne, the succubus's earthly alias. You left your life as you knew it, said your goodbyes, quit your job and moved to a new town. Where your goal was to meet a man, regain your power, and then fly away into the night. Ready to possess the next innocent girl.'

Simon stood, waiting for applause. The room stayed silent.

Gavin sighed. 'You two. See me after class.'

24

Wednesday 14 May 1997

Grubbing around was a key technique in the detective's toolbox, and Gavin always felt determined to enjoy it. Because if you didn't enjoy grubbing around, you might as well be sitting in an office in Croydon filing pensions paperwork. Or whatever it was people with nine-to-fives did.

He considered his strategy as he wheezed up a hill next to the cow field, his suit making him look like he'd been dropped through a portal from an Italian mafia wedding into the British countryside. Despite what Bernard had said, Gavin couldn't shake the feeling that this was connected to Nellie. He probably only had, say, half an hour before the police search expanded like a mushroom cloud all over the surrounding area, with maps spread over bonnets and junior coppers assigned grid squares, looking for the smoking gun or the tell-tale ciggy butt. Gavin wanted to see if he could find it first. Locating a clue related to the murder and quietly handing it over to the up-and-comer Parker could only solidify their relationship. Couldn't it? And if he found something that linked all this to Nellie somehow, even better. He reminded himself not to drop any cigarette ends today.

From his hilltop vantage point, he observed the lay of the land. In front of him was the crime scene, but on the other side of the hill was a little road, one that came out of Tonbridge towards Tudeley. Was this the closest road to the scene? It seemed likely that the murderer had arrived by car. The smart move might be to get down to the road and look for tyre marks that could indicate a vehicle swerving off. But that would mean climbing all the way back down the hill. Bugger.

It was a quicker journey down than it had been up, with a few little slips and the odd low moment when Gavin considered rolling the rest of the way. At the bottom, he shook the mud off his suit, lit a cigarette, and tried to think of this walk in the country as therapeutic. All the exercise and fresh air must be good for him. His hip had clicked on the way down, and he was walking with a slight limp.

Gavin crouched, his eyes scanning the tarmac. It didn't take long to spot the faint arcs of rubber tyre marks veering off the road. His theory might be dead-on: the murderer had fled Tonbridge by car, cutting through the cow field to dispose of the body. Gavin rose to his feet, veins humming with adrenaline. There was nothing like solving a puzzle before all the pieces were laid out. He pulled a compact camera from his jacket pocket and began snapping photos of the trail. The tyre marks cut through the soil and grass, and wildflowers lay squashed in parallel lines leading back up the hill, toward the edge of a patch of woodland.

He reached the end of his cigarette and just managed to stop himself from dropping it on the ground. He looked around for something to stub it out on. Feeling antsy about leaving his ash at the crime scene, he took his house keys from his left pocket and tried to stub the butt out on the circular end. It made an odd burning smell that lingered in the air, even after Gavin wiped the key on his trousers and put the set back in his pocket. What *was* that? It was the stink of a distant bonfire, with stringent top notes of rubber and plastic.

He finally noticed what he'd been hearing but tuning out, in among the bird coos and rustling leaves: a low crackle. Gavin knew this was a clue; the instinct was tugging on him like a fish on the hook. He picked his way through the trees and the crackling got louder and louder, until he saw it: a black burnt-out car wedged between two saplings, still smoking and smouldering. The number plate had survived, though was slightly bent and very dirty. Could it be . . . ?

Gavin's mind raced, replaying Terence's words about the day Nellie disappeared: *She left in a car I hadn't seen before.*

He reached into the top pocket of his shirt, pulling out a dog-eared page torn from the notebook of number plates that Terence had been tracking on his street. Could it be the car Nellie had got into the day she'd vanished? His eyes darted to the one Terence had circled. It was not a match.

Heavy disappointment sank through his body. But instinct made him check the paper a second time. Oh.

There was that drug-hit of excitement again. Because the number plate did match one of the other ones on Terence's list. One that had a star drawn next to it. Nellie's boyfriend's car.

25

Tuesday 16 April – Present Day

'Well, you two went totally off-chops there.'

After class, the group had trickled out slowly, hoping to overhear the roasting Gavin was about to give the two weirdly dressed blunder-muppets who sat at the back. Once they'd given up and gone, Gavin had told the pair to wait there, and had left the room.

They'd spent a while wondering if this was a mind game, but when he'd returned, he'd been holding two takeaway cups of grey coffee with some of the powdered milk still undissolved, courtesy of the training-centre coffee machine. He'd pushed them across his desk to Pye and Mash, who were sitting in their plastic chairs like naughty kids.

'Would you like to tell me what that was all about?' he said.

'Gavin,' Jane leapt in, using his name for ingratiation purposes. 'We're really sorry, and I just want to reassure you that we take this course seriously, and we respect you, Gavin, highly, as a professional.'

'And I just want you to know, Gav,' added Simon, 'that all theories presented here were generated in good faith, and I think before we jump down anyone's throats' – he looked at Jane – 'perhaps we should remember that detecting is not about apportioning blame, or singling someone out to say, "Hey, you messed up."'

'Simon, it's literally about that.'

'OK, but *learning* detecting isn't about that.'

Gavin raised his hands to take the volume down. 'OK, both of you. I don't want any "It's her fault" or "It's not my fault." You're not kids.'

He let a moment of blessed silence linger in the air. 'And you're not in trouble. Why do you think you're in trouble? This isn't the army. You've paid to be here. I just want to bump you back in the right direction.'

Jane knew what was coming next, but it still pierced her soul like a wasp's stinger in a bare foot.

'There's no such thing as ghosts. Or demons, or witches, or possession. OK?'

'Well, we can agree that science hasn't adequately explored some of these areas,' Simon replied.

'Whatever you like, son. But I can tell you, my ninth personal rule of detecting is: If you have a theory that relies in any way on the paranormal . . .'

They were all ears.

'. . . for god's sake, don't say it out loud.'

Jane started to speak, 'Yes, yes, absolutely, and I just want to say that I didn't have as much of a hand in this as I'd have liked, since I have a job interview tomorrow—'

Gavin raised a finger to stop her. 'Stop blaming each other. Come on, lads. Answer me this: how many Nellies went missing in total?'

'Loads!' blurted Simon.

Gavin breathed a deep sigh. 'How many Nellies have actually been reported as missing?'

'Four!' said Jane quickly.

'Well done, Janet.'

'Five if you include Dev's girlfriend,' Simon added helpfully.

'OK, five,' said Gavin. 'Now this is, relatively speaking, a lot of women in the small area we call Kent. If they'd woken up in a strange bloke's house up the duff, they'd have called the police, because it's serious kidnapping and serious spiking. That's a case with evidence that the police would follow up and solve. That is the story we'd be hearing. Not "I had a girlfriend, but then she vanished into thin air."'

'Right. Of course,' said Jane. Simon nodded.

'So, what are your key takeaways?' Gavin prompted.

'Chinese, Indian and pizza?' offered Simon. Jane worried that Gavin might hit him.

'Your theory is rubbish. Now, because I'm an extremely nice bloke, I'm going to give you another chance to present your findings. You can re-present at the extra coursework session on Friday. So you've got until the end of the week.'

'That's big of you, Gavin,' said Simon.

'I also wondered . . .' said Jane. 'Is it possible to set up as a detective agency without the qualification we get from passing the class?'

'It is technically possible, but you won't be able to join the National Register of Private Investigators, and you will, as a result, find it difficult to attract clients without the proper qualifications and experience. Plus, you won't have a scooby what you're doing.'

Jane looked at the floor and couldn't seem to look anywhere else. A keen observer of the human condition, Gavin picked up on her distress. 'Look, I'd be happy to give you a small discount on taking the course again, if you can't present your findings properly on Friday.'

'When are you next going to run it?'

'It'll be next year, probably. Unless I take any more cases in Tenerife. If that happens, it could be longer.'

'Oh,' said the would-be detectives.

'And look,' said Gavin comfortingly, deciding to play his feel-good ace, 'some people just don't finish the course. And that's OK. It's not for everyone. You had a rough hand, getting the only unsolved case, you took the easy way out with the ghost theory, and I don't blame you for it, but let's just call it a fail. Bob's your uncle, Fanny's your aunt. You're welcome to sit in for the last session and watch the others present their cases. I won't even make you take the exam.'

'There's an exam?!' said Simon.

'We'll be there for it. Three days is a long time in detecting,' said Jane, and she put on a big smile, stood up, and swung her backpack onto her back. Simon followed her out of the room, giving Gavin a friendly little wave before the door closed on him.

It hadn't worked. Gavin hadn't banked on any tenacity from those two. He thought he'd seen their type before, people who turned up for the first couple of weeks but then fizzled out when the classes began clashing with after-work drinks or after he'd done the slideshow on retrieving evidence from hospitals' medical waste bins. He rooted around in his overcoat for his vape, which this week was Candied Grapefruit.

He took a long, serious puff, but it didn't dislodge the guilt. Maybe it would still be OK. Maybe three days wasn't long enough for the intense girl and her weird boyfriend to get as deep and dirty into the case as he once had. As he packed up his things and turned off the classroom strip-lights, he looked forward to failing the two of them. It was for their own good, after all.

26

Present Day

Daisy had never used a taxi booking app before, but was pleasantly surprised by the sense of freedom and autonomy it gave her. Life 'on-grid' was easier than expected. The ride that had brought her to the nightclub had cost under a tenner, not too big a dent in the wad of cash she'd been given to live off while she got set up.

Tonight was her night to celebrate. She paid the entry fee, and the woman stamped her wrist without a word. As Daisy queued for the cloakroom, she studied the inky mark before making her way to the bar.

Everyone here seemed to be with someone else, but there wasn't much she could do about that. She leaned on the cold stainless-steel surface and waited for a drink. The music throbbed like a heartbeat. At the end of the bar a man was looking at her. Staring at her, actually. Shaggy-hair, buttoned-up shirt, in his thirties, he looked like so many others, except for his unwavering gaze. Unsure what to do, Daisy stared back.

The man smiled and leaned forward to speak to the bartender. His mouth moved, but his eyes stayed fixed on her. Flustered, Daisy looked away. Her high heels pinched painfully. A moment later, the bartender came across and put a shot of something down in front of her.

'From the man over there,' he said.

'Thanks,' she replied, the word getting drowned in the music.

Daisy picked up the clear shot, examined it briefly, then knocked it back in one go. It burned her throat, but she hid the wince. She glanced at the man. He was pointing his phone in her direction. Her face flushed. Was he taking a picture? She checked again, but he was staring at his screen. Unsettled, she ordered a vodka-and-Coke before pressing her way into the crowd, looking for a spot to blend in.

There was a commotion in a group of women next to her, everyone done up in tiaras and sashes and wedding veils. They jostled themselves into a line, opposite a man with a professional camera. 'Come on, love – get in,' said a total stranger, grabbing Daisy's shoulder.

'But I don't know you,' said Daisy. Nobody heard.

'Smile!' the group cooed. Daisy tried to grin, but she blinked and recoiled as the camera flashed.

The thumping music was starting to disorient her and a nearby circle of shirted lads stank dizzyingly of aftershave. There was that man again. Standing at the far end of the dancefloor, staring at her. What was his problem? Was this how people flirted – stare at you, then follow you around? She weaved between dancers, trying to disappear once more.

The staring man had a theory, and he was almost dead sure. A woman by herself in a nightclub in Kent. Tall and skinny with long brown hair. She'd flinched like she'd never had a shot before. He'd got enough photos of her to do a proper check later, plus the club photographer would post that group shot online. He'd finally found one in the wild. He couldn't wait to post about this on the message board. The others would be thrilled, and jealous.

Especially Mark. Out of everyone on the message board, only Mark had spoken to a real one. But tonight, it was his turn. How could he get closer?

The night was unseasonably cold. The fire escape served as a smoking area, crowded with shivering women and men offering warm arms while puffing on multicoloured vapes. Daisy stumbled out and tried not to panic. Everywhere she went, there he was. She needed to escape, take a breath. But then he appeared in the doorway, smiling an unsettling smile. He stepped towards her, and she instinctively stepped back. Too far. The world dropped away and she fell, her spine slamming into the metal stairs with a shocking *CRACK*.

'Ooof!' said the smoking crowd as one. Every single person turned to see what had happened. She was lying, winded on the fire escape stairs, her hair splaying downwards.

'Are you alright, love?' someone finally said, a drunk dark-haired woman wearing a bright pink dress. 'Don't move, love. I'm a nurse – just stay there and we'll get you some help . . .' She began teetering towards the steps on her tiny fluorescent stilettos, hands out for balance.

But Daisy was feeling more animal than human, and she rolled onto her front and bounced up. 'I'm fine.'

She ran down the rest of the stairs. The crowd's mouths hung open as they watched her hobble across the car park and duck under the barrier to get out onto the street.

Everything ached and everything stung. Daisy's tears had melted mascara into her eyes, and her back throbbed. As the wind whipped her bare arms, she realised she'd left her coat in the cloakroom. Maybe she could just leave it there. She wouldn't need a coat if she was, as she planned, never going to go out again.

'Hey!' A voice shouted towards her.

Oh no.

'Look, I'm sorry about tonight. Are you alright?'

It was the man from the club. He was walking towards her, but Daisy didn't answer, looking around wildly for an escape route. Here, out in the open street, she was trapped.

'I'm sorry I was staring, I didn't mean to be creepy – I really didn't. You just look so nice, and I had a breakup a few months ago and I thought it would be nice to talk to someone who— Wow, OK, I'm babbling. You didn't need to know about that.'

She watched him as he got closer. His features were softer without the intense stare.

He stopped a couple of paces away from her. 'Anyway, look, I'm sorry about your fall – they should really put a chain across those stairs! I've nearly done that myself. Fall down them, I mean. Anyway, I brought you a glass of water.' He held out a plastic pint cup.

'Thank you.' She smiled thinly at him, but didn't take the water.

'I just—' His voice broke with nerves. 'I needed to ask your name.'

She hadn't been prepared for a single thing that had happened tonight. But there was one point that had been drilled into her, again and again and again. *This is your name. This is your new name.*

'I'm Daisy Brown,' she said.

And the staring man beamed like he was meeting a celebrity.

27

Wednesday 17 April – Present Day

'Simon, why do we even have one of these?' Jane asked, stuffing a large multicoloured parachute into a bag for life.

Simon had hoped a good sleep would help Jane recover from Gavin's damning feedback. He had been wrong, and she had spent the morning sitting on the living-room floor surrounded by piles of their belongings. She'd dragged every bag and box out of their storage spaces – cupboards and drawers and underneath anything that had an underneath.

'Well,' said Simon, watching her from the breakfast bar, spooning granola into his mouth and talking through it, 'it was for a workshop I ran on "reclaiming your inner child". It was a huge success, but difficult to pull off. You remember, I told you about it? The catering team refused to serve Party Rings?'

Jane looked at the parachute's bold primary colours; it was one of those ones used at kids' parties, where the adults billow it up so the children can run underneath. Jane only had bad memories of early birthday parties, as the adults had always sat her next to a small, thin girl, who they'd decided was Jane's best friend, and who'd thrown up every time she'd seen Silly String.

'Well, maybe you can take it back to work?' asked Jane. 'The flat's getting cluttered, and how you do one thing is how you do everything.'

'What?' said Simon.

'Exactly! My thoughts are all over the place. I can't even make sense.' The parachute was too big for the bag and Jane punched the brightly coloured fabric to make it fit.

'Aw, I'm sorry, Jane. But the good news is I don't have to take the parachute back to work. I bought it on my credit card. Thought it might be fun for us to have.'

Jane had been sitting cross-legged, but decided it was time to lie on the floor for a bit. There was nothing like a good lie on the floor. Lately, she liked them so much she had trouble getting back up.

'By the way, love,' said Simon gently, 'do we really need to have a clear-out today? I mean, are you confident you've finished preparing for this interview?'

'Sure, sure: I've made the presentation, I've finished the online test, I've Glassdoored the company – I'll be fine. I know my strengths and weaknesses.'

'Is stress-cleaning a strength or a weakness?'

'It's neither! But I am stressed about our money situation. If I don't get a job, we won't be able to keep paying our rent here, and then inevitably we'll have to move in with Penny for a bit. And if that happens, I don't want to arrive with bags of old tat, because that's embarrassing. And also, she'll definitely rummage through them at the first opportunity she gets.'

'We won't end up at Mum's house. Not if I've got breath left in my body,' said Simon. 'But actually, if we do have to move, we will have to paint the walls back to magnolia.' He looked around at their trendy tomato-soup-coloured walls. 'Could take a few coats. Maybe we should move all the furniture into the middle of the room, so we're ready to paint.'

'Oh dear,' said Jane, knowing that having to weave around their displaced furniture to get across the flat would make her mental state much, much worse.

'Come on, Potato,' said Simon, setting his breakfast on the counter and getting up to help her to her feet.

'You're right,' she said, hugging him and breathing in the nice smell of his jumper: rarely washed, but layered up with many sprays of maturing eau de cologne. 'We're not quitters! And Nellie's still missing. We've got to keep going with the investigation.'

She reached down to untie a plastic bag and find out what was inside it: more plastic bags.

'So, what do we know? Number one: the Nellie cases aren't paranormal. It's time to move past that.' She said it with a little cringe, but Simon seemed relaxed and pensive, a man who viewed his failures as something external, something that existed but didn't reflect on him personally, like groceries, or time.

'I'd still love to know what was up with that little goblin ghost we saw in the woods,' he mused.

'Ah. I think I've solved that one,' said Jane, and she got out her phone to show him an article she'd found: WYLEBROOK WOODS TOPS POLICE LIST OF 50 DOGGING SITES IDENTIFIED IN KENT.

'Oh,' said Simon. 'Just a person then. Christ . . .' Simon squinted at the article. 'Fifty?!'

'So that light we saw must have been a car headlight.' Jane crammed her phone back into her pocket.

'It's uncanny what you think you're seeing when you're in a state of fear, isn't it? Now I'm wondering if that wave might have been more of a "come hither"? Anyway, all the questions the paranormal theory attempted to answer are still open.'

'Right!' Jane opened up another bag that she'd hauled out

from under their bed earlier. This one was hers, and it was full of her old discoloured and holey trainer socks. When Jane was little, her parents had made socks talk to her, and now she found them particularly hard to throw away. Or at least, this was what she told Simon whenever he hinted about getting her an OCD assessment for Christmas. 'We need to answer some questions. We think Dev's Nellie is alive. So where is she?'

'Where is she?' echoed Simon.

'Why did she leave?'

'Why did she leave?'

'Did I hear a woman talking in Dev's house, and if so, why would he be cagey about it? If it was his sister coming round to help, or a friend, why wouldn't he just say so? She might've been someone I could interview. So that is suspicious.'

'Suspicious,' mused Simon, examining a box of books Jane had marked CHARITY SHOP and picking several self-help volumes back out of it.

'Simon, I love you, but you're repeating everything I say.'

'Everything you say?' Simon replied, pleased with himself.

A while ago, the two of them had agreed that for jokes like these, Jane would try to manage a polite smile.

She continued, 'Why wouldn't she leave a note if it was a breakup, and why didn't she tell Dev she was pregnant?'

'Actually,' said Simon, thumbing through a book about to-do lists, 'we don't technically know she didn't tell him.'

'God, you're right. We've got to stop making assumptions.' Jane was pacing now. 'Oh! In fact, we don't even know if that pregnancy test was hers.'

Simon sat back, thoughtful. 'Oh, wow. It could have belonged to the mystery woman in Dev's house!'

'What if he was having an affair with Mystery Woman, she

did a pregnancy test at his house – which is why the test was so well hidden, flushed right down the toilet—'

'It was *right* down the toilet,' Simon confirmed.

'—and so Nellie had to go! So he killed her.'

'Wow,' said Simon. 'But why would he kill her? Surely he'd just break up with her?'

'You're right. It's a TV-show motive, not a real motive.' Jane rubbed the dry skin on her lips: her thinking tell. 'And on top of that, we've got no other evidence against Dev. And it wouldn't explain why Nellie's Depop is still active.'

'Well, she didn't reply to my message about a men's whiskey-scented bubble bath set,' said Simon, sniffily. 'I'm wondering if her appearing online was just a technical glitch. Again, to keep our assumption hygiene spotless, we can't assume that she was the only person with access to that account.'

'Hmm,' said Jane, wondering if she should question the phrase 'assumption hygiene'. 'Speaking of replies, have you heard from Dev lately?'

Simon shook his head. He and Dev had discussed keeping in touch about a shared interest of theirs, ancient Roman Stoicism podcasts, but neither man had gone first in sending a text to the other.

'I dropped him a line after the ghost stakeout asking if he was going to put some missing posters back up. But that was two days ago, and he's left me on read,' said Jane, checking her phone screen as if that would materialise a reply.

'He's a busy man. Maybe he's got evidence to hide.'

'And who took down the missing posters?' Jane continued. 'Nellie herself, maybe? If she didn't want to be found?'

'Maybe. But surely a better bet for her, if she didn't want to be found, would be to leave town. Not hang around in the places the police are looking for her.'

'People aren't always logical. But you're right, we have to think about what's most likely, so we don't go down something like the ghost route again.'

'And don't forget the second part of the mystery,' said Simon. 'What's with the bloody name?'

'The bloody name! And the fact the police have never found a shred of evidence connected to the disappearances. Just like us now.' She frowned. 'This is too much. We need to get this down somewhere, visually. Simon, do you have a pinboard?'

He looked blank, as if this was an odd question for a man who owned his own play parachute.

'You know,' Jane said, 'like a corkboard, pins? A ball of yarn? We should organise the case! I'm organising the flat, but maybe that's a distraction from the task I really need to do, which is organise the case!' Jane had her job interview today, so she was half right.

'Sorry, hun, I've never bought a pinboard,' said Simon, but he half-heartedly looked around their piles of stuff for one just in case, overturning a box full of scuba gear and another one containing all his uni notes.

Jane scanned the flat for surfaces. 'The fridge! We've got sticky notes and paper...' She cast around for them. 'Is it OK if I use the backs of your old bank statements?' she said, grabbing a pile of Simon's financial records that had been destined for the shredder.

'Thank goodness I never made the effort to go paperless.'

Jane made her way over to their fridge door, which was covered in magnetic Scrabble tiles and tasteless magnets from holiday destinations, a literal collection of the worst magnets in the world. She scribbled down notes on strips of paper and unscrambled the Scrabble word SMASH to stick a few pieces of paper to the fridge:

'pregnancy test', 'scam?', 'the bloody name'. Soon, everything was on there.

'Food for thought,' said Simon. 'Because it's on the fridge? So it's full of actual food, but on the front is . . . you know.'

Jane smiled politely. 'Very good. So, you know what we need now?'

'A bigger fridge?'

'Well, yes, but I was thinking about some other suspects. And more leads. We need to find the Nellie that Mark the Wizard met. *Claims* to have met.'

'I don't think he actually considers himself a wizard, just to be totally accurate,' said Simon.

'Sure, but it's a shorthand. Quite a few people are mixed up in this now.' She stopped for a quick muse. 'Gavin knew absolutely loads about the case.'

'Well, he gave us the case.'

'No, there's something going on there. When he assigned it to us, he talked about it as if it'd just dropped into his emails the day before. But yesterday in class, he knew the details off by heart, like how many disappearances there were.'

'Here's another thing,' said Simon. 'Why isn't this the most famous true crime case in the country? You'd never heard of it. It's the weirdest disappearance I've ever heard of. Why is it such a tiny story on the news websites?'

Simon was right; the story wasn't making waves, hidden beneath political headlines and celebrity gossip. A couple of true crime TikTokers had turned up in Tonbridge for a day last week, but that hadn't helped things.

'I've been thinking about that,' said Jane. 'Up until this disappearance, there wasn't even a picture of her. There were no sad parents making appeals. No new clues to push the story back to the top of the news cycle. I hate to say it, but people are only interested in good stories. Ones with characters, and a tragic, pretty heroine. But in the old cases, because there were no photos of Nellie, she was hard for people to picture, so she never caught the breeze. I mean, there are over five thousand long-term missing people in this country. And yes, the pretty young white women are the most likely to make headlines. But in this case, there have never been enough hooks to keep people . . . hooked. Maybe I need a yoghurt.'

'Anyway, I did *try* getting the contact details for the Nellie Mark met,' said Simon. 'Remember the message board I found him on? I sent him a load of messages on there. He told me he'd managed to track down a Nellie's address. Isn't that great detective work? And a bit creepy. But now he's saying he can't tell me the address, or anything else about the Nellie he met due to data protection laws and also for our own safety. I've told him I'm not worried about my essential lifeforce, but I think he's just gatekeeping. I mean, telling these spooky stories is his thing. Why would he just give away his sources?'

'We need to find her.' Jane sighed. 'She could be one of the women who disappeared between the seventies and the nineties. So that's the first thing we need. The second is new suspects. People who might have kidnapped or even killed Dev's Nellie.'

'New suspects.' Simon stroked his smooth chin, and carefully moved the bag of old socks into the 'bin' pile while Jane was distracted. 'Right: what about Dev's neighbour you interviewed?'

'Possible.' Jane tore off a small piece of bank statement and wrote 'Ian Neighbour' on the blank side. 'But he was very keen to speak to me, which doesn't suggest guilt. He even offered me a ride on his tugboat.'

Simon's eyes lit up. 'I'd love to go for a ride on a tugboat.'

'I'm worried the tugboat might be figurative, Simon,' replied Jane grimly.

'Oh,' he paused. 'Who else do we know that's involved?'

'The creepy librarian I met. Oh my god, the police too!' Jane tore off more paper and wrote 'POLICE' in large letters. 'I mean, if they were involved in . . . I don't know, covering something up – that would explain why this case is so weird.'

'So weird.' Simon nodded solemnly.

'But how . . . ' Her gaze settled on their kooky wall clock, which had forks for hands. 'Oh, balls! I need to go in fifteen minutes. Shit, I need to get changed.'

'I'll walk you to the station,' said Simon. 'I've got to go to my mum's this afternoon. Think I'll have to do a client call in her utility-room-slash-wine cellar.' He rubbed his eyes heavily.

'Five-minute shower each?'

And as Simon went off to take his, Jane couldn't help but look back at the fridge. She was still holding the piece of paper saying 'POLICE', and for no reason she turned it over. On the back, on the side that was once Simon's bank statement, were printed a few words and numbers that left her cold.

PAYMENT IN – JUNIPER MARSH-BRIDGES – £2,000.00

28

Lavender Hill was the main road between Simon and Jane's flat and Clapham Junction station. It sloped downwards from the direction of their place, which meant they always had to walk home uphill after long working days or drunken nights (or sometimes both). People bustled in and out of glass-fronted restaurants, salons, colourful general stores, a party shop, and Golden Pie, a traditional pie-and-mash restaurant where Jane had enjoyed the pie but had refused to try the eels.

The pavements were wide and dirty, and red double-decker buses docked carefully in and out of stops. Mopeds sputtered past. There was no lavender in sight. As Jane and Simon walked towards the station, Jane's mind was spinning like a fruit machine. Who was Juniper Marsh-Bridges? Was Simon having an affair with an incredibly posh woman? Where was Mark's living Nellie? And – because she might be asked this one later – what was her greatest professional achievement?

'You're in one of your thinking moods,' said Simon as they marched down the hill. 'But honestly, just keep thinking of my mantra: Smash! And hey, even if you don't do great, what's there to lose? Why would you want to be in any club that doesn't want you as a member? Isn't that the saying?'

'I think the saying is, "I don't want to be part of any club that *would* have me as a member."'

'Well, sounds like we can't join any clubs at all, then. My point is, don't worry about the job interview. You can get back to applications after we've finished the coursework.'

'Thanks, Simon.'

'You're bound to find something,' he continued. 'Any company would be mad not to hire you.'

'Thanks, Simon.' She wanted to add: *And by the way, who's Juniper Marsh-Bridges?* But for some reason, that part was impossible to say. Whenever she tried to ask, she felt like her mouth froze up. Simon was so dorky, so open and easy to read. The idea of him cheating on her was as ludicrous as discovering he secretly built pipe-bombs.

'Jane!' He stopped suddenly, causing a pile-up as a couple of teenagers behind them walked into him. 'What on earth is wrong? Why won't you talk to me?'

Jane hesitated. He could always sniff out feelings she was trying to hide. 'I'm fine, honestly, I'm fine. Come on, why are we stopping? We've got places to be.' 'Places to be' had come out more acidic than she'd planned. They were at the big junction now, a huge four-way meeting of roads, waiting for the green man.

'Is this about me going to my mum's house a lot? I'm sorry, and I promise I am focused on the coursework, and on you.'

She started walking again, and he followed her.

'I . . . I can't get my head around the fact that I'm not good at something,' said Jane. 'Something that I really want to be good at.' The green man beeped and she half jogged across the road.

Simon easily kept up with her in long strides. 'Really? That's it?'

She nodded.

'So then, why are you angry at *me*? There's nothing else you want to tell me? I can tell when you're being cagey—'

BANG. The world disappeared.

'Oh, Christ on a bike, Jane!' On reaching the other side of the road, Jane had walked straight into an outside pub table, slopping the pints of a couple of young guys.

Simon steered her away from the people staring and into the doorway of a defunct burrito shop. 'Are you alright?!' He hugged her.

'I'm just a . . . kind of . . . so stupid . . .' She'd started crying, and was snivelling too much to talk.

'Come on, have you got a tissue?' He patted his pockets. 'I've only got Post-it notes. Do you want to use my shirt?' He started untucking it from his trousers. The shirt's fabric was decorated with tiny cheerful flowers.

'No.' She laughed a little, opened her bag, and started rummaging in it. Jane carried lots of useful things that accumulated in every bag she owned: at least two half-packets of tissues, paperbacks on detecting, three different kinds of hand sanitiser, half a dozen pens, and antibacterial wet wipes.

'Oh my god,' she said as her hand grazed one of the books that had found its way in. She handed it to Simon.

'*The Tonbridge Strangler?*' he said, leafing through the shiny pages.

'Linda gave it to me. You know, the woman who works at Tonbridge Library? But this is – well, we were talking about serial killer books, and this is about a Kent serial killer, so really, whoever this murderer is, they're another suspect, right? Or at least, they're another avenue of investigation to cross off, aren't they?' She was barely stopping to breathe. 'I haven't read it. Well, I thumbed through a bit of it on the loo. Either way, it's a huge lead!' Jane's mood was lifting.

'Yeah, it's exciting!' said Simon, not totally following.

'What I mean is, this is a Kent-based serial killer who was operating at the same time as some of the Nellies. And possibly still is! I mean, again, I'll have to finish reading it . . .' She cursed herself. She could have easily read it on the train home from Tonbridge on the day Linda had given it to her. She'd probably scrolled Reddit instead. If only she was more driven.

'To be fair, it won't take you long,' said Simon, flicking through all thirty-two pages.

'Let's say they didn't ever catch this guy. Or if they did, perhaps they got the wrong person. What if he's specifically going after the Nellies for some reason, and now he's struck again?'

It wouldn't explain the odd naming convention of the victims, but Simon was too nice to point this out. 'Great lead, Detective. Smash! Come on, say it with me. It helps.'

'Smash,' said Jane, a little weakly.

'That's right, soldier. Look, here are some tissues.' He took a packet from her open bag and offered them to her. 'Now let's get your face cleaned up, get you to your interview, and then later on tonight we can read the little book and see if it sparks anything off.'

They walked the last few yards into the station. Simon had to jog for his train to Hartwell. Jane scanned the boards for the quickest departure to Farringdon, twenty minutes' walk from the gambling company's offices, but the thin book weighed heavy in her bag. Questions were still racing in her mind, but this time, they were questions she wanted to ask Linda.

She couldn't help but notice LONDON WATERLOO, in its big bright letters, in five minutes' time. From there, she could go across to Waterloo East, and then on to Tonbridge. But obviously, that would be stupid. She stood still in the busy concourse, people weaving and pushing around her, sticking out, at odds with the world. If she wanted to make the interview, she'd have to go now, and even then, she'd be late. She had to be sensible.

What would a driven detective do? Knowing that someone was missing, maybe in danger? What would Gavin do? And what about Simon – was he really going to his mum's house, or to see Juniper Mystery-Mistress? Which platform was it going to be? She took a deep breath, beeped her debit card, and went through the barriers.

29

Sunday 3 August 1997

Throughout the summer of 1997, Gavin Smith took on more cases – a potential insurance fraud here, a missing employee there, and memorably, a cuckolded man who wanted to make sure that his wife was, as per their arrangement, going out and cheating on him.

But through everything, he couldn't stop thinking about a woman. Or four women. Whichever it was. After he'd found the burnt-out car in Tonbridge, he'd had a grateful slap on the back from Bernard, and a politely phrased instruction to piss off.

He could now assume that Nellie had been in a relationship with a murderer, and that she hadn't been seen for months, but nobody seemed to care or want to help him with it. Bernard's line was: 'We're going to find the bloke, Gav. I'd bring you in if I could, but I've got no power.' Gavin had given in and bought one of those mobile phone devices so it was easier to check in with Bernard – even though the phones were stupid, and expensive, and throughout most of the 1980s had made grown men look like they were talking into Tonka trucks. But there was no news, no arrest of Nellie's probable boyfriend, and increasingly, there was no answer to his calls. Like the one he was making just now, which had been re-routed to Bernard's slightly too perfunctory answer message.

'Ahem. Parker, Bernard. *BEEP.*'

Gavin meant to slam the end-call button, but accidentally hit the loudspeaker button, and recorded several seconds of expletives onto Bernard's answering machine.

It was nearly midnight. He was standing on the shore of the River Thames at Erith, one of London's eastmost fringes, where the suburbs were bland and the river was wide and glorious. From the pier or the stretching sand flats, you could look back at the behemoth city on the water. Tonight, its twinkling twilight lights bejewelled the skyline.

He was meant to be investigating two stripclub owners who kept setting each other on fire. Well, bits of each other's stripclubs, anyway. Two nights ago, Jackie Pinto, the owner of the illustrious Club 2000, had been informed by staff that the bins were ablaze in the alley behind the club. The furious Pinto knew this was the work of one person: the owner of the nearby South East Pole. How could he be so sure? Because last month he'd torched a brown paper bag of human faeces in the car park of the South East Pole.

It was just meant to be a warning, to stop the club from poaching his staff, his girls, and some of the regulars. After all, it had been a bold move for the South East Pole to set up shop earlier in the year. Club 2000 had been there first, since the days when the millennium had seemed distant and exotic, and Gavin had to agree that two stripclubs seemed too many for a suburb of Erith's size.

On this particular night, Gavin was on his way to scope out the chicken shop across the road from the South East Pole. He'd spent a few obligatory nights in both clubs, trying to get a handle on the key players: handymen who might be up for carrying out some freelance crime, that sort of thing. But he'd soon discovered that one of the most uncomfortable things you could do in a stripclub was strike up a chat with the other punters. Plus, the food was terrible.

The owner of the chicken shop wasn't too forthcoming about his knowledge of the competing clubs either, but he seemed happy for the detective to sit with a bag of chips and try to chit-chat with the other customers. Gavin spent most of his night tracing his finger around on the Formica table, and then remembering he was meant to be watching for guys coming from the club to the shop.

Like this guy. Gavin sat up to check the man out as he opened the Perspex door, causing the bell to ring. He was on his own, wearing a zipped-up burgundy jacket, and looked to be only about twenty, with bad acne and blonde hair like a bronze brush.

Gavin made his approach. 'Alright, mate? Just wondering if you could help me with something? I'll buy your dinner.'

Some people took this with suspicion, but the young man's eyes brightened. When his chicken and chips had been fried, he stayed and ate his food with Gavin.

'So, mate,' Gavin started, 'I just wanted to ask a bit about Club 2000. You know, the other stripclub. You're not in trouble, I'm just investigating the fire that happened the other night. You can be anonymous; you don't have to tell me your name or anything.'

'It's Paulie.'

'Oh, right.' Over Paulie's shoulder, through the glass front of the shop, Gavin thought he saw quite a few people leaving the South East Pole at once. He rose and squinted – why the exodus? A fight perhaps? An unpopular performer? 'Sorry, got a bit distracted there. So did you hear that there was a fire incident in the car park of the Pole recently?'

'I did, yeah,' said Paulie, stuffing hot chips into his mouth. 'Heard it from my mate who works behind the bar sometimes.'

'So do you know anything about the fire? Did anyone see who might've started it?' Gavin pressed further.

Paulie considered the question. 'Hmm. All I really know is that there's a fire in there right now. In a booth.'

A siren sounded, getting closer. Gavin leapt to his feet, looking between his new informant and the club, where there was now a stream of panicked punters leaving.

'Paulie, who did it? Did you see anything? Anyone suspicious?'

The boy shrugged. 'Can I come with you?'

Gavin was halfway out the door. 'Sure.'

Gavin assessed the situation on the street. The fire engine pulled up on the kerb at the same time as he did. Firefighters poured out, getting into formation, two of them rolling out the hose. A few people straggled out of the club, coughing. A light haze of smoke emerged from the doorway. Just as with any fire in any neighbourhood, rather than running away, people had pooled around to look on both sides of the street, many of them punters who'd just come from the club. Gavin saw a lick of flame escape the roof.

Paulie jogged across the road and stood a metre from Gavin, waiting for further instructions like a pet.

BZZZZZ, – Gavin's pocket vibrated. He pulled out his mobile phone and saw it was a text message from the owner of the rival club, Jackie Pinto. Gavin looked from the phone to Paulie. At some point in the chicken shop, a sachet of mayonnaise had backfired on the young man's jacket.

Gavin took a deep breath. 'Paulie, could you start chatting to some of this lot? The ones on this side, who came from the club? Just ask if anyone saw anything dodgy.'

Paulie ran off, eager to help. Gavin opened the text message:

Dear Gav. I hv torched the Pole. If ur inside, u'd best get out. Ha ha ha. Jackie Pinto (Club 2000) xxx

'Jesus.' Gavin would probably have to destroy this phone with a hammer, as he didn't know how to delete a text, and this was evidence that might hold up in court. He began pressing buttons, hoping to phone the man and beg him to stop confessing to his crimes, when Paulie jogged back, a little out of breath. Gavin pocketed the phone. He'd have to aid and abet later.

'I found somebody you should talk to,' said the young man. 'What was your name, by the way?'

'Eric,' said Gavin. 'Who and where are they?'

'Over here. Girl who'd come to meet her flatmate after her shift.'

Paulie steered Gavin's elbow to a woman on the edge of the crowd, and the moment he saw her, he felt like he'd been punched. He'd anticipated being punched on this particular job, but he hadn't expected to finally find her. *Don't be stupid,* he thought. *Lots of women have long hair. Why would she be here, in South-East London?* Or was he close enough to her . . . territory?

'Evening, madam,' he managed to say. 'Were you inside the club when the fire started?'

'Yeah.' The woman looked down at her hands, playing with her fingers nervously.

'Did you see anything unusual?' His pocket buzzed again, but this time he took the mobile phone out and held down the power button. The girl watched him do it.

'What's that?' she said. Her eyes were blue and huge. She wore a loose brown dress and a scuffed black denim jacket several sizes too big. Her straight brown hair hung over her shoulders.

'It's a phone,' he said, waving it in her direction. 'You said your friend works here?'

She nodded. 'Amber.'

'Is there anything else you can tell me? On the way in, did you see anyone acting suspiciously?'

'He's a private detective,' said Paulie helpfully.

'What?' He hadn't mentioned that to his young friend. Was it that obvious? The last thing a PI wanted was to be obvious.

'A detective? Will I have to talk to the police?' She was backing away from him.

'Absolutely not,' he lied.

'Well, anyway, I didn't see anything. Sorry.' She started fiddling with her long hair. 'I'd better go.'

'Wait! What's your name?'

'You don't have to tell him,' said Paulie, who was hovering.

Gavin glared at him. 'I would really, really appreciate it though.'

She thought for a second. 'It's Nellie. OK, goodnight.'

There was the breath, gone from his body again. And there was Nellie Thorne, about to be gone, because before he could think, she backed into the crowd and slipped away.

'Wait!' He was hot and panicking. He turned to Paulie, got out his wallet and peeled out a fiver, trembling and fumbling the note.

'Thanks, mate, off you go now.' He scanned the street. There she was, the denim jacket and long dress, halfway to the T-junction. How had she got there so fast?

He followed her, stopping to hide behind scenery, first a shrub protruding from a garden, then, when he was more exposed, he ducked behind somebody's front wall. He waited, ready to observe which way she would turn at the end of the road. Paulie watched Gavin, suddenly wondering if he'd got involved with the village pervert, before drifting back to the chicken shop to get some more chips to eat while he stood and watched the fire.

Gavin trailed Nellie through several streets that became more residential, with progressively fewer good spots to hide in. He was rattled that he seemed to have the words PRIVATE DETECTIVE tattooed across his forehead. He also fouled up when, having found another low garden wall to crouch behind, he trod on an empty Carling can, making a loud crumpling noise that caused Nellie to turn around. In the end, and feeling short of breath and also like a total creep, he reached a street of low Georgian houses. She let herself into a house with a purple door, and Gavin breathed out as it smacked shut behind her.

He counted down the road: number 71. This was it. The holy grail. How did it feel? He wasn't sure what the feeling was called, but his heart was pounding.

30

Wednesday 17 April – Present Day

The first interviewer yawned, and this set off the second one. Jane tried to ignore them.

'... As you can see, my earliest experience was integrating APIs, in this case weather APIs, with campaign microsites that ran between six and twelve months.' Jane sounded boring even to herself. But this was the right thing to do. After yesterday evening's disastrous class, she'd foregone working on the detective coursework to prepare a portfolio of her previous projects, then had stayed up the rest of the night tackling the online assessment. There was no way she could have skipped the interview.

The woman who'd greeted her at the reception desk wore a full suit and hadn't cracked a smile yet. The man, who was apparently the founder and CEO of the gambling app, sat back in his chair casually, red shirt unbuttoned slightly too low, his legs wide apart, his hair a long blonde streak swept back over buzzed sides.

'Let's move on to the assessment we sent you,' said the serious woman seriously. 'How long did it take?'

'Oh, gosh, well, I have to admit I did it quite late at night, but...'

The interviewers looked at each other. The instructions on the test had said 'should take one hour to complete', which had been a mild relief to Jane, as she'd only started it at 3 a.m. But she'd still been struggling with it when her morning alarm had gone off, one pot of coffee and a teacup full of icing later.

'See, we put on the instructions that the test should take an hour,' the CEO said, smirking. 'But it was meant to take about two. We wanted to see who'd last until the end.'

'Right. Clever,' said Jane through a pretend smile. The test results were in: she was both a slow programmer and a mug.

She waited while the interviewers stared at their laptops, appraising her work with damningly blank faces.

'How many cars are there in the car park at Heathrow Airport?' said the CEO, smiling like a proud cat.

'Pardon?' Jane blinked.

'Have a think about it. But don't think too much.'

This was definitely a psy-ops move: seeing how she'd react under pressure, being asked a nonsensical and pointless question. He watched her, waiting for an answer.

'Well, um, I would say, Heathrow Airport probably has a rudimentary piece of software that counts the number of times the barriers are raised on the entrances and exits to the car park. Or cameras that track number plates. Probably a combination of both.'

He laughed, clapping his hands together once, which made Jane's skin crawl. 'Very good. But think outside the box, Jane.'

'Well, I think you're meant to stay inside the box in the car park at Heathrow Airport, or you'll get a ticket.'

No laughter this time. The CEO spoke slowly: 'It's a critical thinking exercise. You're meant to work it out from scratch.'

'Right, I see. Well, I've only been to Heathrow a handful of times, but I remember the car park being . . . quite big? No, it was very big.' She was trying to sound confident.

'How many planes take off per day?' he said sternly.

Jane had missed the part of her computing degree that covered air traffic control.

'Heathrow has how many runways?' he said, as if to a baby or fool.

'Two,' said the besuited woman, programmed to answer.

'Look, the thing is, I didn't take a flight until I was sixteen,' Jane began. 'My dad doesn't fly, so if you were asking me: "How many places can you get a pub lunch on the Isle of Arran?" I could list them by name. But I've always felt less confident navigating airports, because not everyone has had the chance to, well, use them that much.'

The man made a noise that sounded a bit like *ew*. The woman scribbled down an extremely long note and showed it to him.

'Let me get a Word document open, because I can think better when I write things down.' Jane minimised her presentation, revealing her bare desktop, which had a large folder in the centre labelled GAMBLING TWITS – STUPID PRESENTATION.

The serious woman now looked like she was witnessing an execution. A younger version of Jane, maybe even the version that was a few weeks younger, would have turned red and grovelled, and tried to make something up about always bringing a light-hearted attitude to her work. But that Jane was gone.

'You know what? You are twits. Both of you. And I feel sorry for whoever it is that gets this job. Perhaps I'll warn the next candidate on the way out.'

And she shut her laptop, unplugged it from their screen, and left.

As she walked to Waterloo, Jane felt shaken up, so she bought a coffee that would shake her up more. Giddy and picturing a scenario in which she'd punched both her interviewers, she went through the barriers and down to the platforms at Waterloo East. In her ears, headphones for some full-volume music; on her nose, big sunglasses for the first real sunshine of the year.

31

Monday 4 August 1997

It was only eleven in the morning, but Gavin was sweating. This was his sweatiest summer, which must have been to do with the heat and the polyester of his suit, and not at all related to his caseload or the marathon runaround he'd been taken on looking for Thorne. A chase which might finally, in this moment, be coming to an end. He had with him a bunch of cheerful yellow flowers wrapped in dotty pink cellophane. He didn't know what they were called, but they'd begun wilting as soon as they were out of the petrol-station bucket, and they'd dribbled plant-smelling bucket water up his sleeve. He was gripping the bunch so hard it had buckled in the middle.

His stride was fast and he soon reached the purple door. He had a sudden cold feeling, as if despite his urgency, he didn't want to do this after all. But he swallowed hard to eat the feeling, and knocked on the door.

'Yep, what?' said the woman who answered. She was wearing a vest and shorts that looked like pyjamas and seemed to have just woken up. So this was the flatmate. Gavin remembered the name Nellie had told him the night before.

'Amber?'

She looked at him suspiciously. 'Who are you?'

'My name's Gavin, I'm a friend of Nellie's — I'm just wondering if she's in?' His quaking voice and limp flowers must have made him look like a suitor. He hoped Nellie didn't have an actual boyfriend, inside, pumping iron.

'Well, she's not here. She's gone. Sorry.' Amber began to shut the door, but Gavin stopped it with his hand.

'What — permanently?'

Amber shrugged. 'I just heard the door slam a few minutes before you got here.'

'Do you know where she's gone? When she'll be back?'

Another shrug. 'She doesn't really talk to me about stuff.'

'Well, do you know if she left in a car, or . . . ?' Gavin kept one hand on the door.

'Yeah, I think I heard a car . . .' Amber thought about it. 'There was an engine.'

There was a good chance Nellie was at the shops, or on a date, or had gone to get a corn professionally dug out of her foot, or any number of trivialities. But she was gone; Gavin just knew. He didn't even say goodbye to Amber, just turned and sprinted back the way he'd come, a total act of guesswork. If he was a car, where would he go? There was one idea he could try, but it was a long shot.

Back at the petrol station he banged through the door with an energy that startled the man at the till.

'Are the flowers OK, sir?'

'Did you see . . . ?' Gavin huffed, wheezing and holding his chest as if he thought it might try to escape. Maybe he should set himself a fitness test every year, like the police? He pictured buying his own personal multicoloured cones and running between them, by himself, in Norbury Park. 'Did a car come through here five to ten minutes ago for petrol?'

'Yes, a few did,' said the man, in a voice that a waiter might use on someone asking if their restaurant served food. Gavin hoped he didn't have a panic button under the counter.

'I'm sorry,' he said, holding up his hands the way a sane person would. 'I'm looking for a specific car. Number plate AAD 566F.'

The burnt-out car he'd found in the woods a few months ago, Nellie's boyfriend's car, had long been crushed into a cube by the police. But he was still looking for the second car: the one that had appeared on Terence's street only once. The one that had taken Nellie away.

Gavin craned his neck to look outside. 'Do you have cameras?'

This was about a fifty/fifty chance, as a few businesses had just started investing in expensive CCTV and the clunky tape machines that needed to be wired up to the office. But the man nodded. 'We have one.'

'Oh god! Can I see it please? The footage?'

The man looked uncertain. 'I'd need to stop it recording now if you wanted to take a look. Normally we stop the tape six times per day, then rewind and re-record, the next scheduled stop being at two p.m.'

Gavin wanted to tear out his hair, or maybe the garage owner's hair, which wouldn't be that difficult, as it looked like a toupée. He thought about how far a car could've got in the few minutes he'd been discussing the finer points of VHS technology. Nellie was probably halfway over the Dartford Crossing by now.

'Please. I'm begging you. I'll buy anything. I don't have a car but . . . how much petrol could you put in a bucket? I just need to see the last five minutes of the tape. Ten minutes tops.' Gavin started loading chocolate bars and mini packets of gummy sweets onto the counter, hoping he had enough cash with him as he opened his cracked leather wallet. 'I'll take all of these. By the way, I *am* a detective.' He should have led with that. He got out his detective ID card, which was homemade, but looked legitimate, and flashed it at the owner. 'I work with the police – I'm working with Kent Police on this case actually, and I'd rather not have to come back with a warrant.'

The owner looked down at the scattered brightly coloured chocolate wrappers in front of him, sighed, and beckoned Gavin behind the till.

The setup in the back room was impressive, and made Gavin feel for a moment like he'd stepped into a government secret-service control room, albeit a very small one. It was dark and cool, with a freestanding air-conditioning unit that blew cold air over the gigantic PC, video machines and screens.

The garage owner pressed the video machine's STOP button heavily, with a bit of annoyance. But he started rewinding the tape, scrubbing backwards past cars which now appeared to reverse into the spaces by the pumps. Gavin contemplated getting a better VHS machine. He liked to tape golf tournaments to fall asleep to, but often found himself woken by the smell of burning plastic as the machine ate the video.

'Don't touch anything. Please come back out when you've finished,' said the owner, leaving Gavin alone with the precious tape.

Gavin immediately ignored his briefing and touched the machine, fast-forwarding to the point he suspected Nellie's car would have come through. It was probably at the moment he'd knocked on her door, which (he'd checked) had been at 11:00 a.m. precisely. As Gavin watched the footage reach 11:00 a.m., in a bit of luck that he didn't dare to believe, an unusual car pulled onto the forecourt.

It was a surf-blue Austin 1100, which Gavin recognised immediately. They were the flagship granny cars of the 1970s. His own grandmother had owned one, and had totalled it by driving it into the back of a parked ice-cream van.

He could make out two faces in the front seats. If his theory was correct, one of them must be Nellie. Since this car was the one that had picked her up from Terence's building on Elm Crescent, the other face – the driver – was likely to be the same person who'd picked her up there. Now they had taken her away from a second address. But who was it? The footage was so grainy, it was impossible to make out anything more than a blur of pink. How did the police get any decent leads from this technology? It would never catch on.

As Gavin kept watching, the driver got out and began to pump petrol. He could tell almost nothing about the person except that they were white, wore dark baggy clothes, and would be about medium height for a man, but tall for a woman. He paused the tape, squinting at the screen, hoping to get the car's number plate.

He knew the plate he was looking for by heart now. Every day he took the crumpled piece of paper out of his pocket to check he still had it right: AAD 566F. Whether he was working on a job, taking a disinterested girl to the cinema, or going to collect a chow mein in the middle of the night, he checked every number plate of every car he saw, each time hoping vainly that it would be AAD 566F.

It wasn't a dead cert. But the very specific shape formed by the repeating AS and then the D was obvious on the plate of the Austin.

'Yes! Come on!' Gavin slammed his hands down on the desk in victory, making the screen shake and the tape skip. A moment later the garage owner, who had obviously been listening nearby, poked his head back in.

'Thank you!' said Gavin, standing up. 'Thank you so much.' He had to hold back from hugging the man. 'Let me just see which way they went.'

He bent down to scrub the footage forward, but the camera didn't catch the direction in which cars turned out of the forecourt. Still, this was a huge step, a lottery win. If not a full jackpot, the detective equivalent of being able to buy everyone a round. He'd found the car that had taken Nellie away from Terence's building. He now knew what it looked like, the make and colour. Gavin had also seen the driver, though that didn't help him much. He knew Nellie had looked quiet and still in the passenger seat, so in all likelihood this wasn't a kidnapping, and whoever was driving her away, Nellie knew them.

It seemed more probable than ever that this Nellie – the woman who Gavin had met last night, and who'd passed through this garage forecourt just fifteen minutes earlier – was the same woman as Terence's neighbour: the real Nellie Thorne. But of course, he'd known that already, deep in his gut, the moment he'd seen her. Gavin followed the garage owner back out into the shop, bouncing with delight.

'If possible, could you tell me everything you remember about the person who came in to pay for petrol for the blue Austin at eleven a.m.?'

'First you can pay for this,' said the garage owner, reaching under the counter and heaving up a pungent bucket full of semi-unleaded onto the counter. 'Five pounds fifty.'

32

Wednesday 17 April – Present Day

Jane considered her plan as she watched streets and offices morph into fields and trees through the train window. She'd managed to snag a whole table to herself and felt like the queen of the carriage. With nobody opposite her she stretched her legs right out (but no feet on the seat; never feet on the seat).

The forty-minute journey to Tonbridge would give her time to read *The Tonbridge Strangler*. Then she'd head to the library, where resident Nellie expert and archivist Linda could hopefully explain any links between the historic Tonbridge murders and the Nellies. Or if there was no link, then at least that avenue would be ruled out. Plus, Jane had a feeling there was something else Linda would be able to shed light on, if Jane could be clever enough to extract the information from her.

It did seem a little unlikely that this book, which had been given to her on a plate, would be the key to cracking the mystery open like a refrigerated Easter egg. But on the other hand, this was the first time Jane had been able to indulge her guilty pleasure for a good cause: reading about horrible real crimes. And she remembered something that Gavin had taught them, which he called his tenth rule of detecting: Be creative. Solving a case might seem like following a thread through a series of logical steps, he'd said. But sometimes it was more like hundreds of little pieces of thread you kept reaching the end of, and you might have to go all the way across town to find the next one.

Gavin even carried with him a set of homemade cards designed to beat creative block, that said things like WHAT IF THE BUTLER REALLY DID DO IT? and DO A HANDSTAND TO GET MORE BLOOD TO YOUR BRAIN. Jane thought about the intensity in his eyes when he'd had her rattle off the stats about the case. The certainty when he'd said, 'The Nellie cases aren't paranormal.' She remembered something he'd said right at the start. That this was 'the only case in the room that I haven't already solved'.

She took out *The Tonbridge Strangler: Local Legend, Local Man* and opened up the cheap, shiny cover, which confusingly had a picture of a large butcher's knife on it. The length of the tome, the occasional unexpected changes in font, and the fact the title had been made in WordArt were all hints that this masterpiece was self-published. Jane now realised it must be by Tonbridge's premier crime writer, under one of his many pseudonyms.

THE TONBRIDGE STRANGLER: LOCAL LEGEND,
LOCAL MAN

BY PERNARD BARKER

Prologue

Occasionally, we all entertain thoughts of murdering one or two of our fellow townmates. But most of us won't actually go through with it. Not so for the local man who murdered two Tonbridgers back in the late 1990s (and possibly more). Some details have been changed here for fictionalisation purposes. For example, the modus operandi (strangling is only the sixth most efficient murder method according to experts). But the central thematic question is the same: what was the Strangler so angry about?

(NOTE TO B: Maybe he hadn't had sex in a while? Really enjoying it so far! Jennifer x)

Jane felt she was going to get a look behind the crime writer's curtain here. She flicked to the meat of the story.

Chapter One: The Woman on the Kitchen Floor

On an unspecified day in 1996 (although it was a Tuesday, and quite overcast), Kent Police were called to a crime scene. PC Mike was still loving his work on the ground, but was starting to think ahead, and had a decent shot at sergeant in the next year or two. He arrived at the crime scene and closed the car door with confidence (but not too much, because, given the unusual strength in his shoulders, sometimes when he did a big slam it could damage the vehicle).

Only the officers who were there could really understand how shocking the scene before them was. For some of the team, it was the first body they'd seen. They had to enter the house by force through the front door with a battering ram. The history of the battering ram in British policing is fascinating, and many of the public won't know this, but the police refer to it as The Enforcer, or sometimes, colloquially, the big red key . . .

Jane flicked through the pages, skipping quite a lot of rambling and then several paragraphs about the stylistic evolution of Kent kitchens, handleless cabinets and white-tiled countertops.

Eventually, she learned that the first victim of the Strangler was a fifty-something librarian, who was murdered in her own kitchen. A quick online search using the key terms informed Jane that the serial killer's modus operandi had been stabbing, which explained the knife on the front cover. Oh god, a librarian . . . Jane realised what might have attracted Linda to her current post.

The next chapter concerned the murder of a teenage girl who seemed to have been chosen at random the following May.

> That was when PC Mike knew they had a multi-person killer on their hands. (The term 'serial killer' only applies to a murderer of three or more victims, according to the FBI, who developed the designation.) Which brings us on to . . .
>
> ### Chapter Three: The Steakout
>
> *(Bernie, is 'steak' a typo? Think you might have dinner on your brain! J x)*

Jane had never seen a book chapter prefaced by 'Which brings us on to . . .', but she admired the sense of flow.

> After the second murder, in May 1997, where the victim's body was found in a cow field on the outskirts of Tonbridge, despite the lack of a fingerprint match PC Mike knew who their guy was. Fingerprinting was first used by the force as far back as 1901, when the fingers of crims would be dipped in the fat of geese.
>
> Tonbridge isn't a large town, and the local force knew exactly who it was who'd spent their teenage years dissecting hedgehogs, cats, even baby foxes, and leaving the organ-less

corpses on the doorsteps of their teachers and employers. The young man in question was Alexander Reeves (not his real name in the real case). He currently lives at HMP Full Sutton, in Yorkshire, rubbing shoulders with other, similar murderers.

Jane smiled proudly – HMP Full Sutton was only a few miles from where she'd grown up in York.

Reeves was the prime suspect. But there was only one real piece of evidence. His car, which he'd attempted to burn at the site where the body had been found. The car's plates were run, and it was established the vehicle had been stolen from a local falconer the previous year (which accounted for all the feathers in the boot.) There were no leads in that case either (but the force had a terrific day out, flying kestrels. PC Mike would thoroughly recommend it). There was nothing to concretely prove Reeves was the owner of the car, besides a sighting by an old man, which wasn't enough to stand up in court.

More evidence was needed. So, Reeves's house on Parkway Avenue was staked out. When officers work on a stakeout, they sit in unmarked cars for ten-hour shifts (or longer, if the bloke who's meant to be relieving you at midnight doesn't turn up!). Their job is to watch and log the suspect's every movement and follow them wherever they go. Plus, occasionally go out to get chips and coffee. When it came to Reeves, the days were long and the suspect did not visit many places, as at the time he was unemployed and did not seem to be in a relationship.

PC Mike followed him on two occasions to the outskirts of Tonbridge, to the house of an old man on Elm Crescent, where he was seen having a verbal altercation. The old man – let's call him Clarence – was also known to the police, as he was in regular contact with them about a number of gripes. Clarence reported to the police that the suspect had been looking for his former girlfriend, who had failed to say goodbye to Reeves before leaving town entirely with no forwarding address. Clarence had, apparently, told Reeves that he had already spoken to the police and to his own personal private detective, and wouldn't comment any further on the matter. PC Mike reflected on the interesting story of the disappearing girlfriend, a separate story entirely which could, perhaps even will, become an interesting book of its own one day.

Jane looked at the book's author again: Pernard Barker. There was no doubt this was the mighty wordmanship of Bernard Parker.

Chapter Four: The Day We Caught Him.

Before I get too far into this chapter, I'd like to salute a man who was not on the Kent police force at the time, and still isn't, but who was helpful and pointed the police in the direction of Reeves's car. He was working on the case of the Strangler's disappearing girlfriend, whose name was – well, let's call her Shirley Bourne. In looking for a link between the girlfriend and the two murders, he led us to some important evidence. This man, who's asked the author to use his real name for advertising purposes, is a private investigator called Gavin Smith. Thanks, Gav!

Oh god. Jane felt like her brain was full of jigsaw pieces that had been shaken up, thrown in the air, and had landed, somehow, in their right places. So Gavin had worked on the Nellie case, back in 1997! But why would he lie to them about it?

'The next station is Tonbridge. We are now approaching Tonbridge.'

There was only one way to find out: but it would involve reading while walking.

33

Sunday 10 August 1997

Gavin knew he was gaining PC Bernard Parker's trust because when they went drinking together, Bernard had finally stopped pretending to like beer.

'Thing is, Gav, it gives me gas. And I'm on this job at the moment that . . . well, obviously I can't say what it is, but I'm in the car all day every day with Louis. If one of us has a bad takeaway, it's game over.'

Gavin nodded sympathetically, 'I hear you, mate. How about a sherry?' Was that a rib too far?

'Red wine, please,' said Bernard in a faux-snooty voice.

This was going well, much better than when Gavin had tried to establish rapport by switching their usual handshake to a high five. He glanced at the bar, where a large bald barman was polishing dirty glasses, a massive England flag hanging up behind him. Gavin guessed it wasn't to celebrate the FIFA Youth Cup.

Gavin stood up and started to move towards the door. 'Tell you what, I know somewhere that does better wine than here. Follow me.'

Bernard had asked to meet in South London, away from anyone he might run into from Kent Police, so Gavin felt he could slip into the role of host, a slightly higher-status role that helped even out the playing field between them. Gavin picked up his jacket from the little pub stool and kicked it back under the table with a scrape. He swirled his jacket open and shrugged it onto his arms with a magician's flourish, a move he may or may not have been practising in front of his daytime TV.

'Just over the street. Come on.'

The evening was still light as they crossed the road. Bernard stayed a step behind, looking around himself much more than necessary, as if he expected a speeding car to appear at any moment from a vortex and run him over.

'I know I'm a bit of a stuck record,' said Gavin, as a scooter zipped round the corner and wove past them. Bernard held his hand to his chest.

'Sorry,' he said. 'Been drinking a lot of coffee. Feeling pretty edgy at the mo.'

'Right,' said Gavin sympathetically. The edginess was catching, and he was starting to feel his neck sweat, like there were some red-hot eyes watching him. 'So, I've been back to Nellie's house in Erith every day this week. Her housemate, the stripper, hates me now, reckons if I'm going to drop by that often I should pay Nellie's rent arrears. But either way, she hasn't come back. Nellie's given us the slip again.'

Gavin led them onto the pavement, where they dodged sprawling arrangements of al-fresco diners. He stopped suddenly at their destination, a bijou French restaurant called La Perruche, a small brightly painted jewel nestled between a hardware store whose wares spilled out onto the pavement, and on the other side, a black-fronted tattoo and piercing parlour called Satan's Nipples.

'Well, this looks nice,' said Bernard cheerfully. Inside, candlelit diners were visible chatting comfortably over neat red-and-white-checked tablecloths.

Footing the bill at a nice French restaurant was quite the choice for Gavin when there was a brand-new water bill lying on the mat at home. But for the last three nights, Gavin had had takeaway pizza for dinner. Yesterday, he'd considered taking it back out into the night to his local chippie and having it deep fried just for a change. Sometimes he longed for a person in his life who would nudge him towards a less lethal diet. Maybe a neighbour who left homecooked shepherd's pies on his doormat. But he told himself that tonight was an important investment in a professional relationship, and on top of that, he really needed Bernard to come through on a favour.

Inside, the light was pleasantly low and most of the tables were crammed with diners. Framed French cartoons covered the walls, and violin music played from somewhere – probably a tape player, but amidst the cosy ambience, it seemed possible there was a small violinist hiding behind the thick velvet curtain near the till. A waiter in a waistcoat showed Gavin and Bernard to a table for two, with chairs that were just a bit too narrow. When they'd sat down, the men's knees stuck out from under the tablecloth at wide, awkward angles.

'A bottle of house red, please,' said Gavin confidently to the waiter, who poured water into tiny glasses and left them to it.

'Well,' said Bernard, looking around. 'Don't get many opportunities to go to French restaurants with the boys.'

'What have they got you on at the moment? You said you're out in the car every day? Have they got you training for the Grand Prix, or . . . ?'

'No, no. I probably shouldn't say, really.' His gaze drifted off around the restaurant, but he was thinking. 'So, let's recap. You found Nellie.'

'Right. But nowhere near her last place, which we know was Elm Crescent in Hildenborough.'

Bernard nodded. 'Our turf.' He downed his little glass of water in one, then started on the bread basket, ripping into a dainty piece of white baguette like a giant.

Gavin continued: 'Her neighbour there was Terence Hancock, who lives in the flat upstairs. Old bloke. Bit of a one-man Neighbourhood Watch.'

'Oh, we know him well. And you don't think he's got anything to do with it?'

'No, no. I think he's harmless. Unless you run a customer complaints department and have a fear of letters.'

Bernard nodded as if he did, on both counts.

'He actually seems very keen to find her,' said Gavin. 'But as you know, I'd drawn a blank. Apart from linking her to the Tonbridge Ripper.'

'We don't like calling him that in the force.'

'Why not?'

'Well, according to the latest official vocab guidelines, we should be calling him the Tonbridge Knife User.'

Gavin laughed. 'So, fast-forward to a couple of weeks ago, and I was out in Erith for a job. You know – South-East London, virtually Kent. And I met her. I still can't believe I met her, Bernie!'

The waiter arrived like a gliding ghost, filled their wine glasses, and left the bottle.

'What did she look like?' Bernard asked this not like a policeman, but like a boy with an autograph book waiting in the dank alleyway behind a theatre. Despite the fact he was taller, he seemed to be looking up at Gavin.

'Oh, well, she was . . . you know. Very normal.' Gavin took a long sip of wine. He realised he'd gained some cultural capital here, as if he'd met Meat Loaf, or Gandhi. Could he use it to his advantage? 'She wore quite baggy clothes.'

'That's fashionable.'

'I wouldn't say she was fashionable.'

'Did she seem like a demon?'

She'd seemed more like a spaced-out teenager. 'No.' Gavin chuckled.

Bernard took a long drink of wine, as if he were hydrating for a race. At a nearby table, a grey-haired man in a brown tweed suit spilled beef-cheek butter on his tie. He raised his hands as if to say to his horrified wife, *Don't worry, I've got a plan*, and then pressed the tie into his mouth to suck out the buttery goodness.

'Here's the thing,' said Gavin, his mind working on the case while his eyes stayed locked on Tiegate, 'I'd been worrying that Nellie was killed by the Tonbridge Ripper. Because they were dating. I know, I know, you can't possibly comment. But hear me out: say you're her. You've just figured out your boyfriend's a creep. And I mean, he sounds like one. Long hair, grumpy, unwashed, always wore a leather jacket.'

The agog copper nodded, confirming that the description given by Terence was correct. Bernard was opening up like a can-can skirt. The detective poured more wine.

'Right! Well, say you've just linked your boyfriend with the murders. The first one, anyway, as the second hasn't happened yet. You've heard him talk in his sleep about disembowelling. Maybe you've found blood on his collar. He goes out and won't tell you where he's been. He's starting to scare you.'

'We've had about a hundred women call in who think their boyfriend might be the killer,' Bernard added as a fun fact. Gavin felt sorry for Kent's women.

'Right. Well in Nellie's case, she's correct, because it's her boyfriend's car that eventually ends up at the second murder scene. So in this scenario, what do you do?'

'Talk to a helpful policeman?'

'You run. You don't tell anyone where you're going. Easy for Nellie – she's a rolling stone. The only person who noticed she'd gone was her doddering neighbour. You relocate, somewhere far, far away. The last place anyone would think to look for you.'

'Timbuktu!'

'Erith. A place so dull that when the council held a competition for its residents to name its new leisure centre, the winner was "Erith Leisure Centre". And you stay there, until you think your boyfriend might have tracked you down. Or he's sent a weirdo friend-slash-private-detective to come and find you on the false pretence of investigating a nightclub fire. So perhaps I sent her on the run again.'

'Oh! So you think you startled her? She thought you were . . . something to do with him?'

Gavin shrugged. 'Maybe. I spooked her, and so it's not a coincidence that the next morning, when I came back, I'd missed her by five minutes.'

'Shame she thought you were a creep. All you did was start talking to her on the street and then follow her home.'

Gavin rolled his eyes. 'But it all adds up,' he said. 'Amber, the housemate in Erith: she said Nellie had only been there a few months. That's how long it's been since Nellie disappeared from Hildenborough. She was cagey with Amber about where she'd lived before. She was cagey about everything, apparently.'

'Sounds like her,' said Bernard.

The pitch of bubbling restaurant chatter was rising as the restaurant filled up. The two men drinking their fancy French wine didn't even notice the bell above the door ring as a man in a black bomber jacket entered and was shown to a table alone.

'Which brings me to the little matter of that thing I need your help with,' said Gavin. He smiled, trying to pitch the smile at 'conspiratorial' without pushing the dial to 'simpering'. He pulled a business card from his jacket pocket, slid it across the table, and flipped it to reveal a handwritten memo: 'Surf-blue Austin 1100, AAD 566F.'

'Come on, Gav. Why do you need to get me in trouble?'

'Are we ready to order?' the waiter interrupted.

'Oh!' said Bernard, blushing.

'Are we ready to . . . ?' said Gav.

'Are we?' The men deferred back and forth, like polite ladies passing in a doorway. Gavin asserted dominance and filled the power vacuum.

'*Je voudrais le sole Dover, s'il vous plait,*' he said, in a mangled accent that had more Dover about it than France.

'Huh? Do you mean the Dover sole?' said the waiter.

'Yes.' Gavin died inside.

'Any vegetables?'

'No,' Gavin mumbled.

'None? Because otherwise it will be, like, just a piece of fish.'

'Fine, I'll have the mixed greens,' said Gavin, who had turned a mixed red.

'And you, sir?'

Bernard lifted up his menu and in a very loud and confident voice said, 'Steak tartare, please.'

'Very good.' The waiter wrote this down.

'Well done, please.'

The waiter laughed at that, and then left.

'And another bottle!' said Gavin to his back.

'Funny bloke, isn't he?' said Bernard.

'Look, Bernie . . .' Gavin downed his wine and refilled both glasses, finishing the bottle. 'You know me. You can trust me. We're both rooting for Nellie, aren't we? I've come to sort of . . . care about her. I'm not going to tell anyone you did this for me. It's like a journalist and their government sources. It benefits us both if I don't dob you in.'

Bernard rolled his eyes. 'I know, I know, and in return for favours, when you get deep into gangland, I'll get to put one of those little wire microphones up your arse.'

'Don't they traditionally go under the shirt?' asked Gavin.

'Either way.' Bernard sighed and looked out of the window. 'I'm sorry, Gavin. This would be a step too far. I can't just run a number plate for someone outside the force. I'd get done for corruption.' He slid the card back across the table towards Gavin.

'Bernie! This is our only lead. Out of all the cars, houses, people, animals, minerals or vegetables in the world, this car' – he jabbed the card – 'is the only thing we can consistently link her to!'

Bernard shrugged. He looked sorry, at least.

'Well, you're about as much use as factor-ten sun cream.' Gavin rubbed his forehead. 'If you can't ever tell me anything, why bother meeting up with me?'

'Because . . .' Bernard still couldn't look him in the eye. 'Because you're my friend.'

Gavin stopped massaging his forehead and looked at Bernard. He felt a pang of guilt for the ulterior motive behind every phone call and meet-up.

Bernard continued, 'And while it's a bit unorthodox for us to be friends, you do come up with some good information.' He gestured at the card. 'I do want this case solved. And I do appreciate your help. It's just . . .'

'Well, I can't solve anything unless you run this plate! If we can find out who owns the blue Austin that took Nellie, we might finally have a decent lead for where she's gone. It could even be the Ripper!'

'We found his car burning in the woods, Gav.'

Gavin fought the urge to remind Bernard that actually *he* had found the Ripper's car burning in the woods. 'People can have access to more than one vehicle. Maybe the Austin is his kidnapping car?'

'He's not involved. I would know – I've been sitting outside his bleeding house for two weeks watching him eat Pot Noodles in front of the naughty channels. Shit, I shouldn't have said that. I should not have said that.'

Gavin's eyes glinted. 'Then I need to know who does own the car. They're at the centre of the whole bloody mystery! They know where Nellie is, and whether she's dead or alive, for Pete's sake. I'm on my own here, and you've got the weight of Kent Police behind you!' He wasn't sure if that had sounded dramatic enough. It didn't have the same ring as, for instance, 'you've got the weight of the Met behind you'.

People on the surrounding tables were starting to look at them, which wasn't great form for a moonlighting police officer and a private detective.

Gavin finally spotted the man who'd been staring at him longest. The man in the black bomber jacket, sitting alone. He was drinking red wine too. For a moment they held eye contact, longer than the polite split second you might lock eyes with a stranger by accident. Gavin's thick brown brows formed one long frown line across his head. He noted that Bomber Jacket hadn't ordered any food, and hadn't even touched the bread.

Two plates were put down in front of them, a skeletal blanched fish for Gavin, and a block of raw mince for Bernard, its square shape hinting that it had been emptied onto the plate directly from the packet.

'What the tits is this?!' said Bernard. 'And where's the tartare sauce?'

'Bernard,' said the detective darkly, as if he was about to propose something serious, like marriage. 'Don't look behind you, but a man is watching us.'

'Hmm?' Bernard turned round.

'No!' Gavin knew that one was on him. 'We're going to need to get out of here, immediately.'

'What?' Bernard looked at his plate of refrigerated mince. 'Yeah, you're right, let's go to the chippie.'

'No, I mean...' Gavin rubbed his forehead with his short fingers. 'I might have done something a little bit bad. Dangerous.'

Bernard eyed him. 'What is it?'

'Can't explain now.' Under the table, Gavin pulled out his wallet and started flicking through notes. 'Do you have a tenner?'

'I hoped this one was on you, Gav!'

'Can you please stop being jovial, Bernard – this is serious.' Gavin's red-wine buzz had turned into a dark anxious headache. He waved over the waiter.

'Hello, yes? Look, I know we're prats, but I need you to do us a favour.'

'What can I help you with, sir?' The waiter couldn't have been more than twenty, and he smiled sideways, pleased for some drama on a boring night, and maybe a big tip.

'In a minute, I want you to try and swap us with that table there.' Gavin nodded towards the man in the brown suit with the butter-stained tie and his wife, who hadn't spoken to him in ten minutes. 'Blame it on me, say I insisted.' He slipped a twenty-pound note into the waiter's waistcoat pocket. 'Then, when they refuse to swap, I'm going to ask to see the manager. You're going to take me over to the kitchen, and then I'm going to go out the back. There's a door out the back of the kitchen, isn't there?'

The waiter nodded, not quite computing what he'd heard, until Gavin patted his arm and nudged him back to work.

Gavin leaned close to Bernard. 'Our tail won't get up and follow me if he thinks I'm busy complaining, and then I'll be out the back and gone by the time he eventually checks. At which point, Bernard, you can slip out the front.'

'No way: I'm sticking with you,' said Bernard, eyes gleaming. Gavin felt it was noble of his friend, but also hoped he wouldn't get in the way.

The waiter slowly walked over to the older couple's table and said something they couldn't hear.

'Stop looking!' Gavin told Bernard, who kept looking.

The couple looked confused, but they began politely standing up, gathering their plates and cutlery.

'Shit,' muttered Gavin. 'Was hoping they would put up a fight. OK, Plan B.'

He looked around, scanning the room, then got up and walked conspicuously fast between the tables towards the back of the restaurant, through the velvet curtain that roped off the corridor to the kitchen, with Bernard close behind.

Bomber Jacket decided it was time to blow cover. He strode through the sea of diners, past the curtains and banged through the kitchen door to find an assortment of white-clad chefs who all turned to face him at once. The back door of the kitchen hung open, and as he took a step towards it, against the grumbling of the distracted French chefs, the fire alarm went off.

In the dining area, everyone observed normal fire-alarm protocol: waiting fifteen seconds, looking at each other confused, and covering their ears, wondering if it was real. The waiters flapped their hands to signal everyone should evacuate, and the rush to the door became a crush as everyone tried to squeeze through at once. In the kitchen, the chefs flopped down their tea towels and tools in resignation and filed out of the back entrance.

Gavin's plan had worked. He'd created the illusion of having left out the back, but in reality, he'd sardined himself and Bernard behind the velvet curtain and waited until Bomber Jacket had stormed past them into the kitchen. Gavin had then pulled the fire alarm to create some extra chaos, and the pair had bolted to be the first out the front door.

Out on the street in front of the restaurant, with about thirty seconds' head start, Bernard and Gavin leapt onto the first bus they saw, panting, and thinking about all the cardio they'd have to do, for Bernard to pass this year's fitness test, and for Gavin to escape the man who'd been sent to kill him.

Memo: to all officers in the search for Nellie Thorne – 11 August 1997

An anonymous informant has tipped us off to a recent sighting of Miss Thorne on 4 August in Erith, London, when she was seen in the front passenger seat of a surf-blue Austin 1100, AAD 566F.

Police National Database shows this vehicle was reported stolen in 1976 from a farm in Kent. Consequently, the car's current ownership is unknown. However, based on this recent sighting, the individual currently in possession of the vehicle is now a person of interest in the disappearance of Miss Thorne.

J. D. BRINKWORTH

ANPR has located the Austin leaving the M25 via Junction 5 in the direction of Kent on 4 August at 11:35 a.m. After that, the vehicle has not been picked up by cameras. Door-to-door enquiries are taking place in an effort to locate the car. Unfortunately, the area of the county served by the motorway exit the vehicle took is large.

Very, very large.

34

Wednesday 17 April – Present Day

Jane power-walked out of Tonbridge station, the wind whipping her face. She had three objectives.

The first was to ask Linda what she knew about the Tonbridge Ripper. Jane had read most of Bernard Parker's book, and with a little help from Wikipedia she had managed to separate fact from flourish. She could now summarise it easily – creepy man stabs two women, confesses to more, goes to jail – but she wouldn't have recommended it to a book club. The grisly murders seemed at odds with the low-rise leafy landscape, the concrete 1960s block that housed Lidl, the bridge over the river – all the little things that were starting to make her fond of Tonbridge. Bernard's book suggested that the murderer had been dating a Nellie, but hadn't made any mention of her being murdered or meaningfully involved. Was it possible Bernard wasn't putting two and two together? Had they caught the right guy? Could the Ripper somehow be the missing link between the Nellies?

The second objective was to find out if Linda knew Mark, the paranormal expert. He was refusing to tell Jane and Simon how or where he'd met a Nellie, beyond the fact he'd somehow found her home address. Needing another way to get this information, Jane was hoping that his path had crossed with Linda's.

They seemed like a pair who might get along well, or poison each other, it was hard to be sure. Even if they had met, Jane wasn't yet sure what use that would be, but she was kickstarting a healthy new habit called 'asking for help'. Asking for help didn't come naturally to Jane – she'd even missed a flight out of Charles de Gaulle airport once, unwilling to admit just how much GCSE French she'd forgotten.

The third objective was to get a chocolate croissant, which she'd need after having to ask Linda for help.

The five-minute walk into town was becoming so familiar to Jane that she barely saw her surroundings now, absorbed in thoughts of knives, police stakeouts, and possibly a cappuccino with the pastry. So when she strode through the grand brick entranceway of the old Victorian building, she fully bumped into the man blocking her path.

'God, sorry, I . . . Oh.' She disentangled herself and looked at the man properly. 'Dev! What are you doing here?'

'Hi, Jane! Oh, I was, er, just returning something.' He waved a spotty reusable shopping bag lamely.

'A book, maybe?'

'Yeah!' He laughed. 'A book, and they actually have some pretty sweet VHS tapes you can borrow here if you have the right card, so . . .'

Dev was doing the conversational version of sweating: fumbling his words nervously, waving his arms in big gestures.

'Anyway, I've got an appointment at the police station, so I really ought to . . .'

'Is there any news?'

'No, nothing yet.' He pulled a theatrically sad face, as if the missing party were a cat he'd been pet-sitting. 'But, you know, I'm hopeful. We've just got to keep doing all we can. Good to see you, Jane, but my appointment is at one o'clock, so I should . . .'

'Of course,' she said, and as he was leaving, 'Text me back! Hope you've got your crime number!'

So Dev had become a weird variable in the mystery again. Jane looked at the cork pinboards that lined the library entrance: his missing missing posters hadn't been replaced. Why wouldn't Dev put new ones up if he was here anyway? And what was the bereaved boyfriend doing borrowing a stack of Jodi Picoults? It seemed a far cry from the man who'd sniffed around in the dirt with a borrowed dog the week before.

Neither of these questions fitted into Jane's objectives, so for now, she proceeded towards the library desk. Linda had her hair styled in braids that were wrapped into a large bun, matching the black Victorian-style matron's dress she wore buttoned up to the neck, with fishnet sleeves. She had a new, quite sore-looking lip piercing. Behind the desk, she was putting romance novels through a shredder.

'Not a fan of the happily ever after?' Jane asked.

'I can't accept stained donations,' said Linda, taking a pristine-looking cowboy novella from a stack of books, ripping out a chunk of pages, and feeding them through the teeth of her machine. On the other side of the room, the noise was causing mums at a storytime session to turn round and glare. The shredder began gnashing at the book's cover, mangling the handsome cowboy's Stetson. Two or three babies started grizzling.

Jane took a deep breath, 'Anyway, hi, Linda. Not sure if you'll remember me, but I'm Jane Pye from the Pie and Mash Detective Agency.'

'Oh, I remember, darling. I've been thinking about you a lot,' said the librarian, pausing her destruction to look up at Jane with big brown eyes. 'Couldn't find your website though.'

Was she flirting? Jane wished there was an alarm for it, or a sort of badge you could wear if you were on the flirt.

'Well, I'm back because I need your expertise . . . hun.'

'On what, sweetheart? Need a Martin Hansen recommendation?'

'No, I've read them all, and I've got the new one on pre-order. I'm actually here about the *Nellie Thorne case*.' She whispered the last part. 'Through our investigations, a few questions have come up, and I wanted to come back and speak to you due to your interest and expertise on the case.'

Linda seemed pleased to hear this.

Jane continued: 'I've been reading the book you gave me on the Tonbridge murders, and I'd like your take on that too. But my burning question is about Mark Sweeney. Do you know him? Big Liverpudlian guy who runs the Haunted Tonbridge tours?'

'Oh yes,' said Linda, leaning back. 'We dated.'

'Oh!' It shouldn't really have been surprising that the paranormal community was insular. How many people in Tonbridge shared an interest in night-time walks and ectoplasm?

'He wears the wizard robes to bed,' Linda continued.

'Very interesting,' said Jane, wondering how to swerve this conversational car back onto the road.

'I'm only joking.'

'Well, he claims he found a living Nellie in Kent. One who never disappeared, and more than that, he claims to have her contact details. Do you happen to know anything about that? Even better, if you have the address . . . ?'

Linda stretched out both arms behind her head and looked at Jane with a catlike smile. Over at mum and baby storytime, several babies had become unsettled in a sort of mass panic, and Linda clicked her fingers in their direction.

'Hey! Hey! Shhhhhhh.'

Linda pointed at her library computer, an unremarkable mid-range PC with a slim black screen. 'Tonbridge Library is run by the Britfit Leisure Group, which operates libraries in thirty-one counties. It means that our data is shared across library groups.'

'Cool fact,' said Jane.

'What I mean is, I probably have the address of every woman in Kent in this little beauty.' She tapped the PC like a middle-aged man might slap the rump of his brand-new Porsche. 'The ones who can read, anyway. But there's no way I could give them to you. Sorry.'

Jane wondered what to do with this data brag. She wished Simon were here. He was unavoidably detained, assembling a wine rack at his mum's house, so she'd come prepared with some Mash magic up her sleeve. Or more accurately, in her tote bag.

'I brought you a Twix,' she said, offering it to Linda. 'It matches your personality, which is complex and has, um, at least two fingers.'

'Aw, that's so sweet of you, babe. But I'm lactose intolerant.'

'Oh. Sorry. Your hair looks nice.'

'Thank you.'

'Wait, did *you* give Mark the living Nellie's address? From the library database?'

'No!' said Linda so loudly it set one of the babies off again. Jane glanced over and saw one of the mums was crying too.

'Well, how else could he have got hold of it?' said Jane. 'He doesn't even have a private detective qualification.'

'I would never willingly compromise library users' data,' said Linda firmly, although she seemed to be enjoying the accusation.

'Well, if you didn't give it to him . . .' Without realising she was doing it, Jane began unpeeling the Twix. She broke a chunk off and chewed it while she thought. '. . . he must have stolen the data.'

'No!' said Linda falsely.

'He did!' After flattery, there was only one route left for Pye: extortion. 'And I bet if I went on your computer, I could go into the directory, access the database's query logs and see your searches, even if you think you've deleted them. It might take me a while if I haven't used the specific software before, but it's probably quite a simple build ... The point is, this is a serious breach of GDPR laws, and I'm sure it would be upsetting for Britfit Leisure to hear about, seeing as it could cost them four per cent of their turnover in fines!'

As yet, the European High Courts had not fined a company millions of euros for the leak of one woman's address, but anything could happen.

Jane continued: 'I'd hate to see you get in trouble, Linda. But as a PI, I've got to do right by the law. That being said, I don't think this needs to be an official part of my write-up. If you co-operate.'

Linda crossed her arms. 'Fine, fine. But I didn't give it to him on purpose. I'd set him up downstairs with the archives, like I did for you, and I went off to Febreze the Ann Cleeves section. The pages get musty in the popular Veras. Anyway, I went back down there to find him, because, you know, sometimes we'd get a bit hot and sweaty down there.'

Jane shuddered, hating everyone.

'But he was gone,' Linda continued, 'and when I came back up, he was here, *at my computer*! I chased him out, told him I'd kill him, et cetera. When I got back on to see what he'd been up to, he'd looked up the Nellie addresses.'

Bingo. 'The Nellie *addresses*? Plural?'

Linda seemed resigned. 'There are two registered in the Kent system. Obviously I'd looked her up before. Could be the same woman registered at two different addresses. I wouldn't know.'

Jane knew this could be the only existing official data on the Thornes.

'Oh, Linda. Data breaches are such a *turn-off*. Well, like I say, I really wouldn't want to go to your employer about this. But I suppose there's another way to make it right.'

Linda bit her lip excitedly.

Within a minute, a slightly disappointed Linda was watching Jane write down the two living Nellies' addresses on the title page ripped from *A European Prince: One Hot Summer in Valkonia*, as Linda had insisted there could be no digital trail of this second serious data breach.

'You might not want to find her, you know,' said Linda. 'Don't you remember what I said about her being a highly dangerous shapeshifting ghost?'

Jane folded the piece of paper with the addresses and tucked it carefully into her bag.

'I'll take my chances.'

'It's your funeral,' said Linda, and Jane suddenly pictured Linda at her funeral, having a wonderful time. 'Would you like to take the rest of *A European Prince*?'

'... OK.'

35

The automatic doors opened for Jane on her way out, and just as she was starting to think about getting some lunch and maybe calling Simon, her phone buzzed with a call from him.

'Babe! Just calling 'cos I've got a bit of good news,' he said.

Jane stepped out onto Tonbridge High Street and made her way up towards the shopping centre, admiring the rickety window display of a charity shop and considering a comfort mooch into Boots.

'The flat downstairs is completely infested with bed bugs!' said Simon victoriously.

'Congratulations?'

'Thank you! So the landlord is getting our whole building fumigated, and we're getting half off the rent this month.'

'Oh, that actually *is* great news.'

'But it comes with a little side order of catastrophic news. We have to go and stay with Penny for a bit.'

Jane stopped walking. She had reached the fishmonger, and stared dead-eyed through the window at the slabs of silver fish.

'I've thought it through, and it has to be Penny's, I'm afraid. Your folks are a bit too far for me to commute, so . . .' Simon trailed off.

'We couldn't just breathe in the toxic chemicals?'

'I did ask the landlord about that, but apparently it's not legal for him. Unless you think you might have got the gambling job?

Because if we're feeling more flush for cash we could check into a Premier Inn?'

'No, I . . . I think I threw that actually. But I've got some good news! I've got a job on an oil rig instead. It's not remote, obviously, so I'll have to move to Senegal.'

'Wow! Oh my god, Jane!'

'That was a joke, sorry, because compared to living with Penny it's actually . . . Never mind. I actually have some real good news too. I've got the address of the living Nellie that Mark found!'

'Oh, wow!' This wow was stronger than the previous one.

'And it's even juicier than that. I've got two addresses. Mark must have found a second Nellie. Two for one. It's either that or it's the same woman who moved house and signed up to a new library. So I think that's the next thing on our priority list. Hit both these addresses and see if we can really find her.'

'That's amazing, Jane. Do you think one of them could be Dev's Nellie?'

'I don't think so,' said Jane, remembering the weird encounter with Dev at the library. 'Something definitely seems off about him now, doesn't it? Did you let him know we saw that Nellie was active on Depop?'

'I texted him about it, but he just replied "Great!"'

'Also, it sounds like Mark got access to the addresses a while ago, not in the last week.'

'OK, well, cracking. Well done, Jane. How did you get them?'

'From the library. Linda had accidentally let Mark steal library data, so I threatened to report a GDPR breach.'

'Jane! You did a power play! I'm so proud!'

'I don't know if it was really a power play, I just had power.'

'Don't do yourself down. Now, there's one more bit of news, which I wouldn't want to label as either "good" or "bad" . . .'

'We have to go to Penny's tonight, don't we?'

'Tomorrow. The fumigators arrive at three.'

'Fine.' Jane sighed. She felt bad for Simon. He'd been with Penny all day, doing odd DIY jobs, and now he'd get less than twenty-four hours' break from her before they had to go back for an extended stay. 'I'll see you back at ours, then. Love you.'

'Love you!'

As she hung up, her thumbs went to Instagram, her fried brain opening it automatically. Right there, at the top of the feed, was a picture of Penny, in a massive straw hat, on a white sand beach, the blue sky spotless behind her. Captioned: So sad to leave Corfu today, mwah for now! Posted this morning.

If Penny was currently on a flight back from Greece, where was Simon? Jane groaned out loud. She had forgotten about the mystery woman Juniper Marsh-Bridges, whose name she'd found on Simon's bank statement this morning. Maybe, stuck with Simon in his mother's converted barn for several nights of psychological torture, she might be able to get to the bottom of that one too.

36

Saturday 30 August 1997

Gavin nearly called the bomb squad when he discovered a brown paper package on the doorstep of his South London flat. But when he poked it with a stick from his shared front garden, flinching against death, he noticed that something was rolling around inside the parcel un-bomb-ishly.

He decided to open the box, and inside he found a bottle of red wine and a copy of the *Tonbridge Gazette*. It was dated a few days ago, and the front-page headline had been circled. Bad handwriting next to it spelled out: 'Thanks Gav!!' and a smiley face.

SUSPECT APPREHENDED IN TONBRIDGE MURDER CASES

Two nights ago, an arrest was made in the search for the 'Tonbridge Ripper', the murderer of Margaret Taylor, 52, and Colleen Loughlin, 16. Alan Reed, 27, of Kelvin Street, is now in police custody having been apprehended for drink-driving on the Shale Way. Arresting officer PC Bernard Perker, 29, told the Gazette, 'On the night of 25 August, Kent Police found several items in the suspect's car, including three kitchen knives, a length of rope, and an angle-grinder. In the suspect's home we very sadly found human remains, some of which were in the freezer, and some of which had been fashioned into a rudimentary lamp base . . .'

So that was the end of a chapter for Bernard, who now owed Gavin indefinitely. The stakeout had been taking too long and costing too much. For a fortnight, all the prime suspect had done was sit in front of the TV drinking bottles of cash-and-carry whiskey. Fears had been growing that he might be a strictly annual killer, who wouldn't even think about striking again until the weather had properly cooled off.

Gavin had crossed the Ripper off the suspect list in the Nellie case. Nothing had linked Reed to the surf-blue Austin, the car that had been spotted twice during Nellie's disappearances. At the French restaurant, Bernard had even let slip that Reed had been under his watchful eye while Nellie had made her trip through the petrol station in Erith. Still, while Gavin had had no professional interest in busting Reed, he preferred it when strangers avoided untimely deaths. Perhaps he'd also felt guilty about the exploitative nature of his pseudo-friendship with Bernard. Whatever the reason, Gavin had stepped in to help with a bright idea: it had been his suggestion for Bernard to slip the suspect a note saying: 'Alan, we need to talk. Meet me tonight at the skatepark, Nellie x'

This trick had lured Reed away from his home. He'd sourced a new car since setting fire to the old one at the crime scene in May, a black Toyota, and as soon as it rolled off the driveway, the police were able to pull him over and breathalyse him, knocking over the first domino that led to his arrest for murder. Great for Bernard, who was now almost certainly in line for a promotion.

If only things had been going so well for Gavin. He had a hunch about who'd followed him to the restaurant that night he'd met Bernard. Perhaps the request he'd made of Jackie Pinto, his stripclub-owning client, had been a stupid one. All he'd wanted was an introduction to a particularly unsavoury type of criminal, so that he could ask them a question. But there was still no word on the meeting, and Gavin felt he was already in over his head.

In the days since the restaurant incident, he'd been trying to keep his head down. He'd kept the curtains closed all day and had stayed inside as much as possible. When he'd finally had to go out to the corner shop for urgent supplies of toilet paper and cereal, he'd worn a hoodie and sunglasses over a balaclava, looking around him so much that he'd attracted more attention than he'd avoided. Rather than being followed, people had moved out of his way, keen to dodge the man wearing a balaclava in summer and twitching on the edge of a breakdown. Plus, he'd had to take the balaclava off before getting to the end of the road so that the shop's owner didn't mistake him for an armed robber.

One morning, after a particularly good episode of *Art Attack* had moved him to tears, he decided that enough was enough. He sent Jackie a text message.

> Dear Jackie. The human trafficking man you promised to introduce me to is having me followed. Got chased out of a restaurant by one of his thugs. Feel I am in danger. Also, it ruined dinner. Can you call him off?

Gavin waited nearly an hour for the reply, making cups of tea, deciding he was too nauseated to drink them, then pouring them down the sink.

BZZZ-BZZZ

> Gav. Ya stupid clot. Dn't mention the trafficking clots on the phone. The fuzz cld be reading the txts. Hvnt u seen Goodfellas? Anyway, he wsn't going 2 kill u. U were jst being followed. Mr Death's just sussin u out. U'll be fine. As long as ur not a snitch or undercover copper. LOL.

Gavin swallowed a lump of rising panic: he'd been followed to a romantic evening out with a police officer. He began typing out: I've changed my mind when the phone buzzed and bleeped in his hand.

> Meet Robbie 2nite, Canada Water Docks. 11pm. Opposite new Café Rouge.

> The docks? Is he fitting me in between heroin shipments?

> The less I kno, Gavvie, the mre bits of my face I'll get to keep xx

Gavin had his meeting. He hoped it wouldn't be his last.

At night, Canada Water docks looked a bit like a black tar pit. The perfect place to sink a body. The jetty opposite Café Rouge was deserted, and all around the edges of the water, red cranes were parked up for the night, guarding over the skeletons of half-built high-rises.

Robbie was an enforcer for an East London criminal organisation that specialised in human trafficking, and Gavin cursed the bastard's vanity for choosing such a dramatic meeting place. This introduction was part payment for the stripclub job: in return for a discount, Jackie Pinto had put Gavin in touch with this serious ganglander. Because, having exhausted numerous other theories, Gavin now wanted to enquire about the possibility that 'Nellie Thorne' could be an alias, a fake name for women falling victim to this type of crime.

When Robbie eventually stepped out of the darkness, from between a cluster of building-site portacabins, it wasn't clear how long he'd been hiding, observing. He was about five foot five, a little shorter than Gavin, and his triangular face was ratty. He smirked, brought a cigarette from the pocket of his black tracksuit, and lit it from a small packet of matches. Although his name was anglicised, when he spoke, his accent was European.

'You are Gavin?'

Gavin nodded, as if speaking would lose him points.

'What's the game then, Gavin? We don't usually hire like this, you know. We have enough enforcers. And you are not the usual type of client.' He half laughed.

Gavin was shaking. He put his hands in his pockets. 'I want to know if you use the alias "Nellie Thorne" for the girls you work with.'

'What?' Whatever Robbie had been expecting to hear, it wasn't this.

'I'll try phrasing it more simply,' Gavin continued. 'Have you ever heard the name Nellie Thorne?'

Robbie didn't give away any sign that he recognised the name. In fact, he looked like he was getting bored. He flicked his cigarette away. 'A girl's name? Let me get this right. You are a detective, and you have made contact with my organisation to ask me if I have heard a girl's name?'

Out came the snarl-toothed grin again. 'Yes, it is my mother's name, back in home country, how I miss her.' Robbie made a 'boo-hoo' gesture and laughed, and this time another laugh joined him in stereo, coming from behind Gavin.

Gavin spun round; on the jetty was the man in the black bomber jacket who'd trailed him to the restaurant. How long had he been there? He was walking towards Gavin, who turned back to find Robbie was an arm's length away.

Gavin was close enough to see his gnarly yellow-brown teeth as he said, 'Now you have your answer, we have a message from the boss. He doesn't like two things: friends of police, and stupid questions. Keep your nose out from our business, or we'll break it again.'

Again? The last thing he saw was Robbie's arm swinging. CRUNCH.

He didn't feel pain at first. Just the raw force and the rush of air as he toppled backwards. Bomber Jacket caught him. Gavin staggered, scrambling to run, but Robbie's foot hooked his leg. He went down hard, slamming into the jetty with a grunt as the impact drove the air from his lungs. Then the pain hit. Warm blood trickled from his split lip, and began to drip onto the weathered wood of the jetty.

Bomber Jacket aimed a hard kick at his hip.

'Argh!' Gavin growled.

'You're a lucky bitch – we feeling lazy tonight,' said Robbie.

But more kicks came. Gavin's only thought was worry about his kidneys. A kick in the spine caused another crunch, and the last one – the last one he remembered – was the one to the back of his head.

PART FOUR

37

Thursday 18 April – Present Day

'What if we get there and she's gone?' said Jane. 'I've got a weird feeling that could happen.'

'We should stay optimistic,' said Simon, who was at the wheel with his driving glasses on, the ones that didn't have real lenses in the frames, because his eyesight was perfect. 'You don't want to will something like that into existence.'

Simon's driving posture was hunched, giving the impression of an old hawk perching on a falconer's glove. This was partly due to his being too tall for the car, and partly due to intense concentration, on account of his being an appalling driver.

HOONK! Another car balked as he swerved into the lane he needed in Gravesend's one-way system. The first address Jane had swiped from the library was far away from Tonbridge, up on the scenic north Kent coast.

'You really ought to put the windscreen wipers on when it's raining,' said Jane tartly. She still hadn't asked where Simon had spent yesterday, when he'd lied about being with Penny.

'One thing at a time!'

That morning, in their flat, Jane had bundled their bags of tat back into their storage spaces, and put away their few important items ready for the fumigation. Their map of the case was still stuck to the fridge; Jane had taken a photo of it before they'd left, but now she was trying to look at it the words were too blurry to make out.

'How about this,' said Simon, taking his eyes off the road: 'one life point to whoever sees the sea first?'

'Did we ever speak to someone called Nedborough?' Jane squinted at the picture of their case notes.

'What?' asked Simon, running a red light, causing someone behind him to brake and toot curses.

'Oh, it says *neighbour*! Dev's neighbour. We should add that to the list: go back and check in with Dev's neighbour. Maybe he's seen something since last week.'

'Jane, I think we're letting the to-do list get out of hand. It's not strategic thinking to just add things willy-nilly. You've got to prioritise. What will create eighty per cent of the impact with twenty per cent of the effort?'

Jane found a tin of mints in the glove box and stress-ate one, crunching it like a giant might gnash a cow.

'When we get there,' she said, 'I think we should take a good cop/bad cop approach. I was wondering if you could be bad cop, because I don't like being bad.'

'We don't need to plan our dynamic in advance, Jane. Our strategy should be human-centred, bespoke for each individual. We'll feel it out in the moment.'

'You do talk a lot of nonsense, Simon,' said Penny Mash in the back seat. 'Did you bring a bottle of wine? Why didn't you bring a bottle of wine? I always taught you, never show up to a friend's house empty-handed.'

Penny had let them borrow her car on the condition that they swing by her exercise class on the way home, and also that she be driven around in the back seat, where she sat with her big sunglasses on like a celebrity. Jane suspected Penny's tagging along was less to do with the timing of her class and more about nosing into their strange errand. She'd been adding plenty of unhelpful commentary and was also preventing Jane from asking Simon about Juniper Marsh-Bridges, the mysterious woman who'd been dropping a small fortune into his bank account. Or what he'd been up to yesterday, when he'd claimed to be with Penny, who Jane now knew had been on holiday in Corfu. Jane was sad at the thought of Simon having a sugar-baby type affair, but was content to kick the confrontation can down the road.

'She's not exactly a friend, Penny. She's a woman we've been trying to track down as part of our detective class. We've been using specialist detective skills to investigate several leads over the last few weeks,' Jane explained. She couldn't help it: on some level, she was still trying to impress her potential future-mother-in-law. This was only the third time they'd met, but she had the measure of the woman. The last meeting had been at a village fete, where Penny had won the marmalade competition and had referred to Jane in her acceptance speech as 'my son's unemployed girlfriend'.

'Oh, I see. Do you get paid to do this "detecting", dear?' Penny eyed her in the car's rearview mirror.

'Well, maybe one day!' Jane smiled flatly.

'It's even worse to turn up empty-handed if you don't know her very well.' Penny adjusted her pashmina over her expensive athleisure wear. 'Are you sure you'll be able to get me to Pelvic Pilates by four?'

'God, Mum might be right,' said Simon. 'Can you google if there's a corner shop on the way?'

'I think we just need to get there.'

Simon sensed a low mood in the vehicle. 'Aren't you a little bit excited that we're finally going to meet a real Nellie Thorne?'

'I just don't feel like she's really going to be there.'

'Why don't I put on my latest playlist? "Bangers and Mash". It's taken me months to perfect.' He fumbled with the controls before giving up. There was a silence as they waited for a traffic light. Raindrops sputtered onto the windscreen.

'Maybe we should have a talk when we get home,' said Simon. 'About positivity. And proactive communication.'

'So, Penny, how was Corfu?' said Jane, watching Simon's face carefully.

'Oh, lovely, darling. Full of sexy Greeks. I only got back last night—'

'Can we stop chit-chatting please?' Simon's smile had disappeared. 'I need to focus on the road.'

And so the only sound was the rain, and the crunch of another mint.

They pulled up at an address in the heart of suburbia, a cut-and-paste residential road that could have been anywhere. The grass verge and pavement lined a string of semi-detached post-war houses, some pebble-dashed, some red-brick and cream, some with added porches, all double-glazed. Cars and vans sat on the brick driveways that used to be front gardens, and neat pairs of wheelie bins stood by the doors. The sky was grey and the mood in the car was sour. They parked on the road and Penny waited in the back seat, doing her brain-training exercises.

At the front door, Jane pressed the bell and found her stomach flipping. She looked at Simon to see if he was nervous, but he just looked miserable.

The front door opened with a click, and there was a woman.

'Hello – yes?'

'H-hi . . .' Jane stuttered, forgetting all about good cop/bad cop. 'Are you Nellie Thorne?'

'That's right,' said the woman. She was blonde and cheery, about fifty, and her round face was layered with makeup. Her perfume was strong and sweet, and she wore the season's latest Per Una blouse accessorised with gold jewellery.

'Can we come in, please?' Jane asked.

'Well . . . who are you?' The woman examined the pair.

Simon seemed to suddenly remember who he was and what he was capable of.

'We're private detectives. Nothing to worry about, but we'd love to ask you a few questions. We'd be happy to ask them on the doorstep if you'd rather we didn't come in.'

And then he smiled, and Jane smiled, and their little chipmunk faces looked youthful. Simon was wearing his orange tartan trench, but Jane was in her usual sensible all-weather clothes, and together they looked like Doctor Who and a companion he'd just found in a camping shop.

'Come on in then, loves. It's about to rain again anyway.' She waved them into the living room, which was airy and cream-coloured, clean but cluttered, decorated with plants, ornaments of little angels, a big bookcase and a basket of blankets. Two squashy off-white sofas dominated the room, and Jane and Simon sat down on the left-hand one by the door. There were too many throw cushions to properly sit down, and while Nellie made coffee, Jane rearranged them around her. Not wanting to put any of the artfully mismatched little pillows on the floor, she ended up making a sort of fort with them, while Simon perched on the seat's edge, taking everything in.

'To be honest, I think we all know Amanda's husband is

cheating,' said Nellie sadly, re-entering with three coffees in flowered mugs on a tray, with a separate jug for the milk. 'She didn't need to spend her money on detectives. Well, hopefully she's spending his money. That's what you're here about, isn't it?' she said, placing down the tray on the coffee table and taking a seat on the other sofa.

The detectives looked at her: she didn't fit the Nellie profile at all. She was so normal, so nice, so glamorous.

'I just can't think what else it would be. It's nothing to do with Malcolm, is it?' Nellie asked.

'No, it's not about Malcolm,' Jane said reassuringly, wondering who Malcolm was.

'Oh, thank god!' said Nellie. 'I keep telling him, you've got to pay HMRC twice a year now, and he's the one who should stay on top of that, but I have to remind him. I'm so worried he'll get in trouble. Just by forgetting something, I mean! He'd never fiddle his taxes on purpose, honestly.'

'The thing is, Ms Thorne, we wondered if you happened to know anything about the Nellie Thorne legend?' asked Simon, taking a coffee and burning his mouth on it.

'Hmm?' she said, smiling.

'Quite a lot of other women have had the same name as you,' said Jane. 'And we wondered if you knew anything about that.'

'Well, that's normal, isn't it?' She'd tensed up a bit.

'We're working for a man whose girlfriend recently disappeared. Her name was Nellie Thorne, like yours, and we want to find out if there's any connection between you and her.'

'How did you find out where I live? God, are you anything to do with that man?'

'That man?' said Jane.

'The man – the big, tall man with the Liverpool accent!'

'Mark the Wizard,' said Jane and Simon as one, meeting eyes.

'He came here last year asking me all these questions: am I a witch, have I ever been up to the woods and taken my clothes off, all kinds of rubbish! He accused me of some terrible things. The kids were back from uni at the time, and they had to come down and help me get him to leave!'

Jane looked at Simon worriedly: kids, a husband? None of this seemed to fit.

'We certainly don't want to accuse you of anything, Ms Thorne,' said Simon, hoping the calm note in his voice would soothe her nervous system, a bit like with horses.

'This might sound strange,' said Jane, 'but have you ever been abroad?'

'Yes . . . ?' said Nellie slowly.

'And you don't have any issue with registering for things, being on-grid?'

'Sorry, I don't understand what you mean.'

'I'm just wondering if you have a passport, or a driving licence?'

'I do, but I'm not quite sure why I should show you. Perhaps I should have asked you for some ID before inviting you into my home . . .'

'Oh, my driving licence expired years ago,' said Simon.

'Simon, you've been driving us around!'

'Look,' said Nellie, 'if you must know, I have heard something about this. The police have been round before, years ago, checking on me, but I've got nothing to do with missing women. I've got to go out in a minute. Is there anything else? Because I really need to get on.'

She wanted them out as quickly as possible. Jane wished they'd pre-prepared their questions in the car. Clearly she'd learned nothing from bungling the interview with Dev, and right now, it felt like they'd learned nothing from seven weeks of detective classes.

'Nellie,' said Simon, 'I don't want to pry, but what did the police say to you? It's just, a few women with your name *have* gone missing, and we'd obviously hate to think that you were in danger too—'

'Right, please can you go now.'

They stood up and started moving towards the door. 'We promise, this isn't a scam, or a prank, or anything like that,' said Jane. 'We just want to warn you.'

'It's not even my real name! I just read it in the paper years ago and liked the sound of it, so . . .' She spread her hands out. 'I was an actress, and my real name wasn't any good, so I changed it. Jane Binns. I did the paperwork and everything.'

'My name's Jane!' said Jane cheerfully.

'Well, no offence. I just thought, *Jane Binns is more likely to be a bin lady than a Bond girl.*' She looked around her living room at her ordinary life. 'I wanted a name that would give me a fighting chance, at least.'

'Well, I'm very sorry to have scared you, Ms Thorne,' said Simon. 'If it's not your real name, you're probably OK?' He shrugged and looked at Jane for confirmation.

'We're not really sure how this works, but you'll probably be fine.' Jane nodded.

'Thank you,' she said sarcastically. 'What a weight off my mind. All this bloody nonsense. I didn't realise when I chose that name that she was in the paper because she was bloody missing. It's been a load of hassle. I'm tempted to change it back.'

Outside, a car horn honked aggressively.

'We must have forgotten to crack the window,' said Simon.

*

'Well, that was a bust,' said Jane. 'I just knew we weren't really going to meet a Nellie.'

'Hmm,' said Simon, fiddling his phone into a holster on the windscreen. 'Where's the next address, Robin?'

'What?'

'Like we're Batman and Robin. I'm trying to get the mood up.'

'God, Simon, just get on the road,' said Penny. 'I'm starting to need a wee. I really can't sit in the car for hours like I used to, you know, thanks to a little thing called *birth*! Do you think she'd let me pop in and use hers?'

'No!' said the detectives at once.

'Well, you'll have to get me to the community centre early.'

'Mum, we can't, I told you. We've got two stops. We've got to go to— Jane, where are we going next?'

She looked at the picture she'd taken of the precious addresses. 'Dungeness.'

So the second Nellie had chosen the coast, but the coast on the other side of Kent.

'Right.' Simon strapped himself in. 'Only another hour and fifteen minutes.'

On the second Nellie's doorstep, Jane didn't even feel nervous. She expected the door to be opened by a prankster or another PhD student in Paranormal Studies. But the woman who stood there was pale, with long light brown hair that was let down loose almost to her waist. Jane felt winded, as if she was recognising somebody she'd never met.

'Oh god,' she said out loud.

'Good afternoon,' Simon swooped in. 'We're looking for Nellie Thorne?' Somehow Simon was keeping it cool, even though he must have had the same pang of recognition.

The woman looked up and down the street. She fit the profile exactly, except for the fact she wasn't in her twenties. It was hard to tell, but she was probably around forty.

'Who's asking?' she said carefully.

'We're friends of a friend of yours . . . who's being cheated on.'

Jane looked at Simon, perplexed at his angle.

'I don't really have time to talk now,' the woman said, looking back into her hallway. She was keeping the door cracked open as little as possible. 'I've got the kids.'

'No worries, we'll be quick,' said Simon, deflecting the hint. 'You *are* Nellie, right?'

She thought a moment before answering. 'Yes.'

Jane thought she might faint. She should have drunk some water in the car.

'That's a lovely smell in there, Nellie – what is that smell?' said Simon, craning for a look inside.

'I'm just burning some candles.' She relaxed her arm, and the door opened a fraction more. On a table in the hallway was a bunch of flowers, and a red candle on a gold saucer.

'I'm going to level with you, Ms Thorne,' Simon continued. 'We're actually here because several women with your name have been reported missing over the past few decades and we just wanted to check that you're OK.'

'Well, I don't know anything about that,' she replied.

Jane frowned. Was that a strange answer?

'We're just concerned you could be in danger,' said Simon. 'There's no way of knowing who could be next.'

Her face didn't change. 'Well, thank you, I'll bear that in mind.'

She began closing the door.

'Wait!' said Jane out of instinct. How could she be more thorough? What had she forgotten to do? Was there any way to keep the door open? 'Can we get a picture?'

Now Nellie looked startled. 'Of me? Um, no, I don't think so.'

But before the door slammed shut, Jane had raised her phone and snapped a photo.

'Go away!' came Nellie's voice from behind the door. 'I've got my kids in here. I'll call the police!'

'Come on,' said Jane, and they ran back to the car. 'Wow. I've never done anything somebody told me not to before.'

'Though, to be fair,' said Simon, leaping into the driver's seat, 'if she did call the police, they probably wouldn't be able to find her.'

'How did that go?' said Penny, who was applying powder from a makeup compact.

The two detectives looked at each other. 'I'm not sure,' said Jane. Her face was red, and her heart hammered. It felt a bit like a hangover.

'Well, anyway, I'm going to have to use that woman's toilet.'

'Oh, she definitely won't let you in,' said Simon, pulling his seatbelt on.

But Penny was halfway out of the car and tiptoeing up the driveway, about to be rejected spectacularly by the real Nellie Thorne.

'Shall we leave her here?' joked Jane.

'Yes,' said Simon, starting the engine. 'With any luck, she'll disappear too.'

38

'Welcome to my humble abode!' they heard Penny say at the front door, and then there were squeals and air-kisses.

Simon, Jane and Penny had only returned from their driving tour of Kent an hour ago. But at Penny's house, there seemed to be a non-stop twenty-four-hour party going on, punctuated by Pilates. Yet another person was on the doorstep, coming to join the three glamorous sixty-somethings who were already lounging in the back garden drinking rosé. Two of them had already been there when Simon, Jane and Penny arrived home.

The house, Green Haven Cottage, was a luxurious converted barn in a winding leafy one-way road that was also, apparently, home to a retired cricketer. The house was full of countryside accoutrements: decorative watering cans full of garden flowers, sculpted wooden hedgehogs, and arrangements of fridge magnets detailing how much wine had been drunk by the chef. Simon and Jane sat at Penny's farmhouse kitchen table and Simon poured coffee into twee rustic mugs.

'Would you like the mug with the gingerbread men or the . . . What are these? Aliens?' said Simon.

'I think they're ducks,' said Jane.

A woman in a bright fuchsia sundress banged on the patio doors from outside. Penny swept into the kitchen from the entrance hall, followed by a skinny short-haired lady in a denim dress and FitFlops who was holding a bottle of champagne.

'Coming, Deborah! Must have locked her out,' she added to Simon and Jane. 'I wasn't expecting her at all, it's a miracle she came. She's been a real flake since her husband died.'

Deborah smiled and waved through the glass doors.

'Yes, I'm bringing another bottle!' Penny turned to Simon and gestured at the short-haired lady beside her, 'Simon, darling, you remember Annie, don't you?'

'Hello, Simon!' chirped Annie the champagne-bringer, lifting her sunglasses onto her head. 'Delightful to see you again. Gosh, you're so handsome.'

'And this is his girlfriend, Jane, she's a real studious little thing, aren't you Jane?'

'Yes, I guess so,' said Jane's mouth, which was smiling without her consent.

'Jane? Gosh! Who would've thought?' said Annie.

'That's right,' Penny confirmed in a theatrical whisper. 'Simon *isn't gay* any more.'

'What?' said Jane. 'Penny, Simon was never gay, he's bi.'

'One minute he's gay, the next minute he's not.' Penny rolled her eyes. 'I think he's just trying to keep us on our toes.'

'Penny!' said Jane sharply.

'Don't worry about it!' Simon smiled. 'Let's just have a drink and not worry about what I am.'

He got up from the kitchen table and went to a cupboard to get Annie a glass. She was swept into the garden and the champagne into the fridge. As soon as all the women were outside, Simon whispered, 'Annie's the one who kissed me at a school disco when I was fifteen.'

Jane grimaced. 'Oh dear. I'm sorry about that. And your rude mum!'

'Oh, well...' Simon brushed it off. 'I stopped trying to make her understand after the fourth or fifth attempt. Imagine how she reacted when I tried to explain the word "neurodivergent". For years she's been boasting to her friends about how my "special needs" got me a free laptop at school.'

Jane shook her head.

'So where are we at now?' He reached for a chocolate Bourbon that Penny had put on a plate earlier while telling them how unhealthy biscuits were.

'Well,' said Jane, 'we've found two women. One wasn't a real Nellie, and the other one was, but she's probably getting a restraining order on us as we speak. Still, I can't believe we found her.'

'Yeah, that's huge,' said Simon through a mouthful of mushy crumbs. 'We found the Nellie who Mark met. And without his help! Why did you take a photo of her, by the way?'

'Well, I just sort of panicked. I was thinking about what we'd put in our coursework presentation. It might be a bit better than another stock image.'

'What else are we going to put in it? The presentation is tomorrow night.'

Jane stared out of the patio doors, watching fuchsia-dressed Deborah open a bottle of frizzante with a small sword. 'Our task was to find Dev's girlfriend Nellie. We didn't find her, but we've found *one* of the Nellies. And she looked a bit like the pictures of Dev's girlfriend, didn't she?'

'Mm.' Simon thought about it. 'They had the same hair.'

'And blue eyes.'

'But a different nose.'

'Maybe they're related.' Jane sat back in her chair. 'I could believe they were mother and daughter, for example. But that's not enough for the class project. We still don't know what's going on. Can you ask Mark if he found out anything useful when he met her? He may as well spill the beans now we've got the addresses.'

'Sorry, he's blocked me on the message board,' said Simon. 'He said all my questions were "draining his vibration". Could the woman we met today have been the 1997 Nellie? If she was about twenty in 1997, she'd be forty-seven now.'

Jane considered it. 'I thought she looked younger than that.'

'Did you get her date of birth from the library?' asked Simon.

'I just got the address. I'm an idiot.' Jane massaged her forehead.

'Don't worry, Potato. So the Nellies are possibly related, and often disappear. Could they be some sort of co-ordinated crime family?' Simon reached for another biscuit and handed it to Jane, who ate it in two bites and kept speculating with her mouth full.

'Sure, but if they're up to no good and trying to disappear, then why have the same alias, and keep using it over and over again? It's the name thing that drew us into the case. People who are trying to stay under the radar normally come up with all kinds of different names.'

'What would your fake alias be? Mine would be Barnaby Pumpernickel.'

'Is that a pseudonym for when you start making porn or artisanal bread?' asked Jane.

'I like that it's multi-purpose. What about the little book you showed me yesterday outside the train station? The one about the murderer from Tonbridge? Do you think he's involved?'

Jane sighed. 'I was so excited to have got the addresses at the library, I forgot to ask Linda about it. But the book really doesn't suggest that Nellie was killed by the guy. She was his girlfriend, but according to the book, he was confused and angry when she disappeared. He went to her flat to look for her, and he wouldn't have done that if he'd killed her.' Jane reached into her bag, which she'd dumped on the chair next to her, dug out the book and passed it to Simon, 'It's by Bernard, by the way. You should read it, see if you find something I missed.'

'I really won't. No offence to him, but what an awful waste of time for us both to read the same book. No, Jane, if you say you're not keen on the murder victim theory, we'll throw it out the window.' Simon placed the book on the table and slid it away from him.

'But if we throw it out the window, there's nothing left in the house.' Jane picked up a small box of toothpicks that were waiting to be turned into pre-dinner cheese-and-pineapple sticks. 'Have you looked at Nellie's Depop lately?'

'It's been deactivated. I did buy a good Mickey Mouse hoodie from someone else though. I'd better ask the fumigators to keep an eye out for it.'

Simon began texting the landlord, and Jane's attention wandered once more to the carefree retirees on the patio. The sun was starting to get low over their revels, turning the sky a shade of rosé. Simon and Jane's last chance to present their coursework was tomorrow at six. They'd found so many answers, all of them wrong. If detecting was about following threads, as Gavin said, they'd just tugged on their last loose end. Yet the solution felt so close, like the truth was pushing up against a dam. Something was stirring among Penny and her friends, and they began getting up out of their seats, some swaying a little.

'Simon?' said Jane. 'Is one of those women called Juniper?'

'Yeah!' he said, looking up from his phone with a smile. 'How did you know that?'

Jane's stomach froze. Why didn't he look guilty?

'Daaaaaarlings!' bellowed Penny, swooshing the slide doors open. 'We're going to Vita Italiana!'

'Great, have fun,' said Simon, continuing his text.

'But we need you to drive us, pudding,' she said, coming up and pressing Simon's nose with her finger like a lift button. 'We've all had one or two tiny drinks.'

'It's the cougar bar,' Simon informed Jane. 'They go there to drink wine and meet men.'

'Simon!' said Jane, checking his mother's face for offence, but Penny had gone to rifle through a tray of letters, looking for her purse.

'No, they call it the cougar bar. They love it.'

Which one of the women was Simon's mystery donor? They queued for the downstairs toilet, while Annie put a half-drunk bottle in the fridge, taking a good swig first.

'Found it, sweetheart!' Penny waved the purse around. 'Drinks on me!'

Everybody cheered. Since nobody seemed to be listening, Jane said, 'We'll be able to think more clearly when you're back from dropping them off. A bit of peace and quiet. And we can have a proper talk.' Jane's stomach did a rollercoaster drop at the thought of asking Simon which woman was Juniper, and what he'd been up to with her yesterday when he'd claimed to be with his mother.

'Why don't you come with us, darling?' said Penny to Simon. 'Both of you! You've been working so hard, you need to let your hair down, have a little fun. We'll get a cab for the way home.'

Simon seemed interested. 'It would be funny,' he said to Jane.

'That's right, sweetie, it's so much fun!' said Penny, finding her handbag on the kitchen island. She took out a lipstick and applied it without a mirror like an old pro. 'Come on, get in the car. Chop-chop.'

'I think shaking things up could clear our heads, Jane. Vita does have quite a nice ambience,' said Simon.

'And I won't be making any dinner tonight, darlings, so if you want to eat, you'd better come with us and have an aperitivo platter or something.'

Jane wasn't sure what an aperitivo platter was, but the way to her Achilles' heel was through her stomach. And so it was that they got into the car, with Jane somehow ending up on Annie's lap, out to experience more nightlife on their first night in rural Kent than they would in an average week in London.

Simon had been right. Not about everything, of course. The cougar bar didn't have a particularly nice ambience, and it seemed unlikely that 'shaking things up' here would solve the case, but it did seem to be the social hub of Hartwell for men and women over fifty.

Inside, the decor was dark and up-lit by blue and purple lights that were hidden everywhere: under the bar, in the corners, and behind the fake plants. It was a look that had been very fresh and fun in the early-to-mid-2000s. Bar stools lined a long bar at the heart of the room, and there were cosy booths upholstered in black velvet around the walls. The only thing that seemed to remotely connect Vita Italiana and the real Italy were the little round al-fresco tables and faux-wicker chairs laid out on the pavement of Hartwell High Street. At these you could sit smoking Silk Cut and watch the simple beauty of the world passing by: bored teenagers sipping long-expired Kahlua stolen from parents' cabinets, or the family-run stationery shop across the road letting down its shutters for the night.

Jane ended up sitting next to Annie, Simon's teenage harasser. Penny and her friends had crammed into a booth with a table that was slightly too small for their party of seven, but rather than split up, they had chosen to squeeze, with Simon enveloped in the heart of the group, and Jane on the end, on a tall bar stool they'd had to pull up specially. As Annie spoke, Jane's face loomed down from above, and she began to get a crick in her neck from trying to maintain eye contact.

'Hartwell is a village, but it's technically big enough to be a town,' said Annie. 'Mind you, we might not want that upgrade. It's not all fun and games being a town. We'd lose our status as the village with the highest proportion of elderly people in west Kent.'

'That's very interesting,' said Jane over the din at the table.

'Still, it's not as idyllic as it seems round here.'

'Oh, really?' Jane was drinking her cocktail a bit too quickly. She'd chosen the house special, a Gin Garden of England: Italy by way of the M25.

'Somebody's been skimming cards at one of the cash machines,' Annie fake-whispered.

'Oh dear,' said Jane, sucking as much gin as she could from her crushed ice through a disintegrating straw. 'Yes, Simon's mentioned to me before about Penny's M&S card.'

'Would you like another, Jane?' said Annie.

'I'm fine, thanks.' Jane knew she didn't have enough money in her account for a drink, or to return a round later.

'You don't need to be polite. Why don't we get a bottle of something? Do you drink Australian Chardonnays?'

'I'm not sure, I've never checked. I'm happy to give them a go.'

She was definitely feeling the buzz now. Every song sounded amazing: why had she never heard any of them before? Maybe it was time to make a new playlist. If they could just get out of this place, and back to London, everything could be made right again.

At the bar, Annie continued to talk about the big local drama. 'Deborah over there had her card skimmed. After everything she's been through this year! Terrible. So did Sarah and Teresa. And dear old Tony, who's over there with Penny. Soon it'll be a nationwide crisis!'

Annie waved over to the dancefloor at the back: Penny had given her friends the slip and was now by the loudspeakers grinding on a man in a bright orange shirt. They were the only two people on the dancefloor.

'We don't use the cashpoints in town any more,' continued Annie. 'We think it's the one outside the big bank up the street that's doing it. It's very scruffy. Covered in chewing gum.'

Jane nodded, her face contorting in a repressed yawn.

'I got a brand-new card, of course,' said Annie, pulling a fold of cash out of her wallet and handing it over to the bartender. 'But they're so clever these days, they managed to skim the new one before I'd even used the cashpoint with it! Thanks, sweetie.'

When they brought the bottle back to the table, they found Simon watching his mother and her friend, who looked like they were now competing to see who could suck each other's chins the hardest.

'I don't mind,' said Simon as Jane wiggled into the booth next to him. 'If she's happy, I'm happy. The thing that bothers me is that it looks like a bad kiss. Is my mum a bad kisser?'

'That's what I found out last night. Eyo!' said Jane.

Disco lights on the dancefloor lit up his mother's smooching in technicolour.

'I'm sorry she's been a bit sassy today,' said Simon.

'Was she being sassier than normal?' Jane sipped her wine.

'No, actually she was on quite good behaviour.'

'She takes a lot of risks for a woman who's eventually going to rely on us to wipe her bum.'

They watched Penny unclip her hair and shake it dramatically loose to the music while Tony spanked her rhythmically on the bottom.

'It is a bit of a difficult watch,' admitted Simon. But neither of them found they could stop. They both took a long drink of wine.

'Darling, darling!' Penny came over to them, teetering a little on heels that Jane would never have attempted. 'Tony's going to drive us home. Because you've been drinking – naughty, naughty!'

'You said we were going to get a cab! You bought me the drink!' said Simon.

'Well, now Tony's going to drive because he's lovely, and he's only had three Italian lagers.'

'Wh—' Simon began to argue.

'They're very light, love, the Italian ones, he'll be fine,' Penny said, waving Simon off.

'I wonder if we should get a taxi,' said Jane. 'Might be safer.'

'Oh, that's very easy for you to say, madam. You're happy to spend money when it's not yours, aren't you?' said Penny briskly.

'Pardon?' Jane wondered if she'd misheard.

Penny picked up Simon's drink and took a long sip. 'I wonder why you could be so interested in Simon, with his good job, and being generous to a fault!'

Jane froze with rage. She looked at Simon, hoping he'd help.

'Come on, Mum,' he said quietly.

'Some people have taken advantage of him, you know,' continued Penny.

'Oh yeah? What are you trying to say, Penny?' said Jane, completely unable to stop herself, propelled by wine. 'Yeah, some people do take advantage of Simon, because he's so nice, and so simple.'

'Hey!'

'So you admit it, do you?' said Penny. 'I always said to him, "Don't stay with an unemployed girl. She'll be leechy."'

'You know who takes advantage of him the most?' Jane stood up in the booth, hoping to reach Penny's height, but she was still several inches shorter. 'You! He does anything you want, and he tolerates all your horrible comments. You're so demanding of him, and not very nice to me, all the time! Why do you think we'll put up with it?'

'Because that's what families do,' said Penny.

'No, it's because we're nice! Nicer than you! We actually think it's important to be nice!'

Everyone in the booth had stopped to watch this now. In the silence, Jane's thoughts had both sped up and stopped entirely. She was full of molten lava, and she realised all these women were probably a bit scared of Penny. What was she going to do? Scream? Start a fight? Cut Jane's head off with the bottle-opening sword?

'Sounds boring to me.' She sniffed. 'Come on, Tony, we're leaving.'

Penny turned and left, walking as haughtily as possible. Then there was a strange silence. A part of Jane had hoped for a round of applause.

'I think Tony was meant to be giving us a lift too,' said Deborah.

Earlier in the evening, Simon had parked Penny's Peugeot in the car park belonging to the church, about halfway up the high street. The two detectives trudged back to the spot in a sombre, quiet mood.

'You'll see,' Simon said, trying to sound bright. 'They'll have taken Tony's car and left us the Peugeot. I've only had half a glass of wine, and the fight really sobered me up, so I'm probably OK to drive. Then we'll find her at home, waiting for us to apologise, and we'll all make up and forget about it.'

'Are you sure? Isn't it really, really bad?'

'Honestly, Jane, she does this with everyone at some point.' The evening had got chilly, and Simon walked with his shoulders hunched and his hands in his pockets.

'Did this ever happen with any of your exes?'

'No, I wouldn't... Not that I can think of, no.'

They reached the car park, but found that the space where the Peugeot had been parked was empty. Beside it was a small, fresh pile of sick.

'Oh dear. Well, she's left her calling card,' said Simon.

'Oh god, Simon! I've really upset her!'

'No, no, she'll have been sick because of the wine – it happens all the time, honestly.'

Simon shivered in the chilly air. Jane's eyes were red and hot. She really didn't want to cry in a car park. She opened her phone to look for a taxi.

'Ah, you won't find any of those around here, I'm afraid,' said Simon. 'We'd have to ring up the company, or flag one down. The old-fashioned way. But I don't have any money – do you?'

'Simon, of course I don't have any money! I've spent weeks complaining about not having any money. Haven't you heard any of that?!' Jane heard her voice rising.

'Alright! I just meant that I didn't bring my wallet. There's no need to unleash the dragon on me too.'

'The dragon?! I thought you thought that I was totally justified!'

'Well...' Simon squirmed.

'Well, what?' She had her hands on her hips now.

'Obviously, the situation's unfortunate.'

'Why *don't* you stand up to her? Why have you been putting up with this for so long? And why didn't you help me out back there?'

'What do you mean?' Simon looked innocent. A pair of crows squawked in the yew trees around the church and swooped over the car park, as if coming to see the argument unfold. The detectives stood square to each other, facing off.

'Well, I wouldn't have had to do all that if you'd stood up for me instead. She could be my mother-in-law and she's going to hate me forever now!' Jane waved her arms widely, to indicate *forever*.

'Jane, please, don't yell at me. Someone might hear us.'

'Oh, great! You care about what strangers think, but not about what I'm saying?'

'Alright, well, maybe it's fine that you're yelling, because it's better than what you usually do, which is lie to me.'

Jane jabbed herself in the chest with a finger. '*I* lie to *you*?'

Simon's eyes were starting to look wet now too. 'You never tell me how you really feel or what you're worried about. You don't tell me the truth. I have to prise it out of you like a grumpy little clam.'

'That's not the same as lying,' Jane spat.

'Well, how is it different?' Simon spread his palms open. 'If I ask what's going on and you say, "I'm fine, leave me alone, Simon," then that's not exactly the truth, is it? I don't mean you have to tell me everything. But you don't tell me anything! You've been so anxious lately, even more than usual, and it's killing me that I can't do anything to help.'

'Well, it's your fault! Do you have any idea what I've been through these last two weeks?' Jane yelled thickly, through tears.

'No! Because you don't *tell* me! And if you can't tell me the things you're worrying about, then what chance do we have? As a couple?' Simon huffed.

'Well, I'll tell you this! I found out about the affair with your sugar mama, her sending you all that money which you're spending on god knows what.'

'What are you talking about?' Simon whined.

'Juniper Marsh-Bridges! If you're going to do something like that, you shouldn't leave your bank statements lying around.'

There was a pause, and Jane noticed she was shaking. She'd avoided conflict for years and now she'd had two fights in one night. The adrenaline was making her hot. But Simon smiled.

'Oh my god, what? That's so funny,' he said.

'What?' Jane watched him cover his mouth and laugh into his hand.

'You think I'm having an affair? And you think it's with my mum? Juniper Marsh-Bridges is my mum's name, you heritage tomato! Penny is short for Juniper.'

'Oh! Bloody posh people.' Jane put her face in her hands.

'And Marsh-Bridges is her original surname. From before she got married to my dad. She's using it again now because she thinks it sounds better.'

'So I shouldn't have been calling her Penny Mash this entire time?'

'She sort of goes by either. That's what most people know her as.'

'Well, why's she giving you all that money then?'

'It's such a stupid reason.' He sighed and rubbed his forehead. 'It's 'cos she won't get cash out any more. There's been a card-skimming scam around here. They think it's happening at the cash machine up at the bank on the high street. It's happened to Annie, and Deborah – after the year she's had!'

'I know, babe, I know all about it.'

'Now she transfers the money to me in big chunks and I take it out in cash, and come down here from London to give it to her.'

'Three grand in cash? What does she even spend that on?'

Simon pulled a face and nodded back up the street, in the direction of Vita Italiana. 'I mean, it lasts a while. She prefers to use cash for most things now, after what happened with the card.'

'What about yesterday? You said you were coming here to fix Penny's wine rack, but she was on holiday. So where were you?'

He looked down at the ground. 'Yesterday I did it for Annie too.'

'I probably should have just asked you about it.' Jane felt her chest un-tighten.

'I'm sorry,' said Simon, and he hugged her. 'I should have stood up for you at the bar. And I hated hiding the money from you. Mum didn't want anyone to know her card was cloned, I think she's a bit squeamish about it. But none of this would have happened if I'd put you first all along and just told you.'

'I'm sorry too, for being so . . . generally annoying. I don't think I realised how much pressure I was putting on myself, about the job, and the detecting. I think – well, my parents aren't perfect either. They only really said nice things to me when I passed exams.' She hugged him back, hard. 'I think they were trying to do positive reinforcement or something. That might be why I got so invested in the detective classes. When things got tough, I found another exam to do.'

'Maybe that's why you *started* the detective classes.' Simon released her from the hug and looked her in the eyes. 'But you love this. You really do. You're stressed because of the deadline, and because this is a hard case. Especially for a first case. But you're really, really good at it.'

'Thank you. But we're totally out of real leads, and out of time. I love you. Despite everything, I'm lucky to have you.'

She hugged him again, so hard he stepped backwards, and he leaned down to bury his face in her neck.

'Oh no,' he said after a while.

'What's wrong?'

'I've trodden in the sick.'

39

'Car!' yelled Simon.

'Car!' repeated Jane, as if she had to pass the message down the line.

'Don't get run over!'

And once again they pressed up against a dark, sharp hedge as a gleaming black BMW slowed down to pass them.

Between Jane and Simon there'd been no money for a taxi and Penny's phone was resolutely off, so a midnight ramble down country lanes had been the only route home. Jane had thought the village was small, as it had only taken Simon ten minutes to drive a car full of rowdy women here from Penny's house. But walking back seemed to be taking hours. There were no pavements, no lights, and barely enough room for two cars to pass on the road. On this stretch of the lane the trees met and touched above the road, transforming into a tunnel of vegetation that enclosed them. Simon's phone torch, pointed down at the ground in front of them, was doing nothing, diffused easily by the darkness.

'The thing is, Jane,' said Simon cheerfully, 'even if your balance hadn't been at zero, and even if I'd had my card with me, we couldn't have got any cash out anyway. Because of the problem with the cash machine.'

'Oh, Simon. You know it's nothing to do with the cash machine, don't you?'

'It's not?' Simon swung the torch light into Jane's face, making her flinch.

'What's the one connecting thread between all the people you know who've had their card details stolen?'

Simon thought about it, stepping around a glob of fox poo. 'Calcified arteries?'

'It's obviously somebody or something at the bar. That's why it happened to Annie twice, even after she stopped using the cashpoint.'

'Oh! The bar! That's amazing news. I think our client will be very happy.'

'What client?!' Jane could hardly see him in the darkness, but it was obvious he was grinning.

'Well, I was going to save it as a surprise, but I was telling Annie about the detective agency, and she said she's sick of complaining to the bank, so she's hired us to catch the scammer!'

'Simon, that's incredible! Our first paid case?'

He smiled and raised his hand for a high five, which Jane missed.

'I mean, we'll still have to gather the evidence,' she said excitedly, 'figure out whether it's a member of staff, or possibly somebody who hangs out there with a gadget scanning people's handbags— CAR!'

'Car!' They backed up against the hedge again. Jane put her arms out wide like someone in the movies navigating the ledge of a tall building. A red hatchback crawled past them, honked loudly, and then sped off into the night.

'What was that for?' said Jane, finding she still had some anger left over from earlier.

'Oh, nothing. That was my Uncle Nick. He was honking hello,' said Simon, who was waving at the back of the car. 'Must be coming back from the pub.'

'Couldn't he have stopped to give us a lift?!'

'Hmm. Didn't think about that.'

And they watched the red lights disappear round a corner.

Luckily, Green Haven Cottage was only another two lanes over, and their feet crunched a slow trudge up the gravel driveway.

'Simon?' said Jane through a yawn. 'Why does your mum call the house Green Haven Cottage when it's not a cottage, it's a massive barn?'

Simon shrugged, indifferent with tiredness, and found the key in his back pocket. 'If we're going down that road, Jane, it's not really a haven either.'

In the hallway, several candles had been lit and arranged on the side table, giving the space a golden glow. To the left of the hallway was Penny's ornate, maximalist living room, and standing in its doorway was a fully naked man holding a candle and a long barbecue lighter.

'Oh, sorry, Tony.' Simon grimaced.

'Not to worry, champ,' said Tony, and he closed the living-room door to the sound of Penny giggling within.

'See?' said Simon. 'She's fine.'

And then they both laughed so hard that they had to sit down.

'Wait!' said Jane. 'The candle! Did you see the candle?'

'I wasn't looking at the candle,' said Simon, wiping away tears.

'It was red!' Jane continued, 'It could be nothing, and I don't want to get us all excited over nothing, but I think it could be a lead. Do you remember right at the beginning, when I found that red candle buried in the woods opposite Dev's house?'

'Oh yeah! That was weird.'

'And then when we were at Nellie's yesterday – the real one –

she was burning one in the hallway! It smelled sweet, remember? You were the one who pointed it out!'

'So,' Simon was beginning to understand, 'we can link the same brand of red candle to two of the Nellies?'

'Possibly. Like I say, it's so small, but . . .'

'Jane, you're a genius. And my mum's got one! God, do you think she'll disappear too?' He looked hopeful.

Jane got up and went through to the kitchen with her coat still on. 'Does she have any more of them?' she asked, shuffling through a stack of letters, and then looking in the store cupboard, and then the fridge.

'Here!' Simon replied, finding one on the shelf above the sink.

They crowded around the red candle and turned it over, looking for anything. It was just like the one Jane had found in the woods and had brought in her suitcase, wrapped in tissue paper and some clean underpants. On the underside was a small sticker that said: SCARLET POMEGRANATE – PLUTO. HANDMADE AT FAWKE WOOD SANCTUARY.

'Fawke Wood Sanctuary,' said Jane. 'Have you heard of it?'

Simon shook his head. 'Sounds like a craftsy local farm shop. Wait, isn't that the wellness retreat we saw the flier for in Sainsbury's?'

'Maybe,' said Jane, giving the wax a sniff. 'I think we'd better pay them a visit.'

40

Wednesday 17 April – Present Day

Over the last few weeks, there'd been a buzz in Tonbridge Library, as if it were the secret headquarters for the French Resistance. It had become a conspiratorial nest. And today, in had walked the latest mysterious stranger. The exact type of person the library had come to attract. The shelf-stackers had watched as he'd crossed the threshold and shaken the rain off his grubby ankle-length mac onto the foyer floor. They'd watched him limp towards the desk, his eyes fixed on Linda, who was pretending to read a thick biography of Rose West.

'Linda, I take it?' Gavin stood up as straight and as tall as he could.

'Gavin Smith, PI. Welcome to my war rooms.' She put the book down on its front and folded her arms.

'I found your blogpost on Nellie very illuminating. Wish I'd found a Linda back in the nineties. Might have saved me a lot of headaches.'

'So what's put the case back on your radar? The new disappearance?'

'Something like that. Colleagues of mine have got involved and it got me thinking again. I suppose, in a way, I've been chewing on it for a quarter of a century, somewhere in the back of my brain. And then when you least expect it, inspiration hits.'

'So, you think you've got the answer now?' said Linda, leaning towards him.

'A hypothesis,' said Gavin. 'But I'd like to see if your research supports it.'

'I guess we ought to take this down to the basement then?'

Gavin looked behind him. 'I reckon we should.'

Gavin had brought his own torch – his nineteenth rule of detecting was: Never enter somebody else's basement without a torch. He used it to help him read through Linda's file, since she'd left several dead bulbs in the light fittings to create a 'sense of atmosphere'.

As Gavin read, he didn't react, but once Linda had finished guiding him through the key articles, he looked at her and said, 'This all fits perfectly.'

Linda grinned. The enthusiasm didn't match her dark eyeliner, or the fake-blood tear she'd painted on her cheek.

'I'm used to non-believers when it comes to my many Nellies theory. My MNT,' she said.

Gavin nodded. 'In 'ninety-seven, I met a bloke in a pub who'd met a Nellie at a greyhound-racing track. She'd disappeared, of course, but he never reported her missing. It got the idea in my head that there were more. More than we officially knew about. Then I had a revelation – my new idea. Quick search online, found your post, and it all fell into place.'

'I almost didn't post,' said Linda. 'I'm careful with the internet. So, what's your idea?'

Gavin looked at her. He'd never seen a goth look so hopeful. He thought of all the work that had gone into compiling that folder, but he knew that if he told her what he was thinking, there was a chance she might post about it online. And he couldn't risk tipping *them* off.

'I'm sorry. I can't tell you just yet.'

Linda's smile dropped.

'And – the other thing you mentioned in your email?' said Gavin.

'Right,' said Linda heavily. She might've been hoping for a quid-pro-quo information swap. 'Yes, there's a network of us who keep an eye out for sightings. We're all part of a message board about Nellie, where we post our information and theories. And there's been a new one this week.'

Excitement buzzed in Gavin's stomach. 'A Nellie sighting?'

'Well, no. As my folder shows, only some of them are called Nellie. But yes, somebody matching the description was seen falling down the stairs in a nightclub in Canterbury. There's plenty of false positives, but I looked on social media for photos taken in the club that night. She's in a couple of them, and she looks bang on.'

'I hoped there'd be a new one,' said Gavin. He'd just needed to know which town she was in. 'Thank you, Linda. Really, thank you. And I'm sorry I can't tell you what's going on yet. But I promise, as soon as I nail the bastards, I'll let you know.'

Thursday 18 April – Present Day

Gavin sat in his car in a multi-storey car park in the centre of Canterbury, swiping on a dating app. He'd set up his profile with a false age (twenty-five), plus a nice picture of him from when he was young and, as private detectives went, handsome. It was after he'd started out as a PI, but before he'd been duffed up by the human-trafficking gang, because after that, his nose had never been straight again. The photo was ancient, but he hoped young people would just assume it was a filter.

You couldn't choose what you became obsessed with: whether it was a video game, a pet, the language of a country you'd never visited, or a person you adored. Dev's email had brought the case back into Gavin's life, and just like before, he couldn't let it go. And as he'd got increasingly worried about his students, he'd found himself chewing on it more and more.

A few nights ago, he'd had a brainwave while watching a documentary about cicadas. Each generation of the noisy insects pupated in the ground for up to seventeen years before burrowing their way up to the surface. And after that, like so many sheltered seventeen-year-olds, they followed the drive to mate. This had got him thinking: Nellies were known for disappearing. But where did they appear from in the first place? Not underground, of course, but it had to be somewhere. Once Linda had keyed Gavin in on how many women were wrapped up in this mystery, he'd realised there could be another one out in the world already, fresh from the Nellie factory, wherever that might be. When he'd emailed Dev asking how he and Nellie had met, the answer had come back: a dating app. Gavin had tutted: of course, his methods of looking for a girl were outdated.

The population of Canterbury was 157,400. Using a couple of statistics websites, Gavin had estimated that about 12.6 per cent of the UK population was between the ages of 20–29. Of those, 51 per cent would be female, roughly another half might be single, and – at a very rough estimate – three-quarters of those might use a dating app. According to the calculator on Gavin's phone, this left approximately 2.4 per cent of Canterbury's population to swipe through, or 3,778 women. With the right distance settings applied, and a swipe rate of one profile every thirty seconds, the project should take him just shy of thirty-two hours. Yesterday he'd managed ten hours of swiping. Today he'd come back with a supply of energy drinks and a determination to double his swipe rate. If he found her, he was going to hit a button called SUPER-LIKE, for an extra fee of £1.29. Nobody had ever accused Gavin of being a romantic.

Young women were certainly pretty these days, but Gavin found himself totally disinterested in the idea of matching with them for fun. He felt more like he was smiling well-manneredly at graduation pictures of his friends' daughters. Occasionally, he refreshed his memory by opening the photo Linda had sent him from the nightclub: a hen party who'd posed for a group shot with the target. He might have been imagining it, but he thought she looked like the woman he'd met in Erith all those decades ago.

A young Romanian family on holiday were unpacking their double buggy from the boot of their hire car when the suspicious man parked next to them started hooting and punching the roof.

'I've found her!' cried the man in a voice so loud it was audible through his window. There were tears in his eyes, and on his phone screen, the dating profile of a twenty-year-old called Daisy.

'Come on, kids,' said the toddlers' mother, shooing her children in the direction of the cathedral, and making a mental note to warn her friends that the UK wasn't the hot holiday destination of the year.

Gavin drove for an hour or so to the next person he needed to see. Pulling up outside the house and cranking on the handbrake, he regretted all the years he hadn't bothered with birthday pub trips or phone calls. He should have made the effort to remember all the news about the kids, or at the very least, what their names were. But at least he'd stopped at a supermarket on the way over.

'Alright, mate. I've brought you a little something,' said Gavin when the door opened, and he held up an expensive-looking bottle of Bordeaux, which had actually been on offer.

'I suppose you want something then?' said Bernard, but he was smiling. He wore a ratty old polo shirt and dad jeans. The smell of something delicious wafted from inside the house.

'I'm afraid so. But I think you do still owe me a favour. The capture of the Tonbridge Ripper, 1997?'

'Ah, of course. I never did repay you for your little spark of inspiration.'

'I need some help writing a message on a dating app.'

'Gavin! You reprobate.' He laughed. 'You can't have come all the way here for that.'

'I might also possibly need some top-secret police intelligence.'

'Some things never change.'

'It may or may not interest you that I've found the newest Nellie.'

Bernard's eyes opened wide. 'Ah. Well, you'd better come in. I'm trying my hand at a chicken congee.' As Gavin crossed the threshold, Bernard slapped his old friend on the back. 'But it won't go with a Bordeaux, I'll tell you that,' he said, closing the door behind them.

41

Friday 19 April – Present Day

It was a new morning, and Pye and Mash were on the road for their first ever proper undercover mission. They were packed and prepared. They were full of a fire and fury that only possessed detectives when they were a feather's breadth from the truth. They were driving a massive advert for a rental service called SwiftCar. It couldn't be helped. Penny was out at a friend's divorce-iversary and needed the car.

Fawke Wood Sanctuary was truly in the middle of nowhere. They bumped the rental car over a potholed country lane for miles, under a clear and unseasonably hot sky, past fields of disinterested sheep and cows. The sat-nav kept telling them to turn around, as if it knew there was nothing good here.

Off to the right, a dirt track opened onto a patch of bare ground with a couple of parked cars in front of a one-storey red-brick hut. The hut looked like it had grown from a bed of wild and unruly herbs and shrubs, and scattered around the front were rusting pieces of vintage farm equipment, buckets of fresh flowers, and baskets of rhubarb. A cheerful chalkboard read: FARM SHOP, FRESH PRODUCE, CRAFTS, YOGA ☺

'Right, well, this looks nice!' said Jane. 'So, what's the plan – go in there and look for the candles? Is there anything else we should ask? Even if we just end up with the candles link, that might still be enough to present for coursework tonight. It's better than nothing. And this was a really difficult case. Don't you think?'

Simon was absorbed in his phone.

'Are you alright?' she asked. 'You're not nervous, are you?'

'No, no, it's just . . .' His face reflected a man in turmoil. 'I've got to do some work today. Day-job work, I mean.'

'Oh dear. That's bad timing. But hopefully we'll be in and out.'

Simon took a call, put an 'excuse me' finger in the air, and politely ducked out of the car. He took some long strides towards a field of sheep.

'Yeah, Neil, I saw it. I've touched base, and they've downselected the option they feel the most comfortable with, from a psychological safety point of view . . .'

Jane needed to get back into the workforce quickly, before she could no longer speak corporate dialect, like those children who never learn to talk because they were raised by bears.

She entered the farm shop, which was cooler inside than the hot car park. The whitewashed brick walls were lined with neat pine shelving. Daylight shone in through the roof's panels of corrugated see-through plastic. About half the shop, nearest the door, was given over to seasonal vegetables: nubby new potatoes and bags of curling rocket were marked with handwritten labels, and along the floor were cardboard boxes packed with varieties of lumpy squash. The shop also stocked stacks of second-hand books, and a whole picnic table of wood carvings. The carvings were of animals, little otters and owls, and they'd all been given mismatched buttons for eyes, creating goofy expressions probably not intended by the person who'd spent hours carving them.

In the far-right corner, near the till, Jane spotted a collection of candles laid out on a table with a black velvet tablecloth. She went over and started picking them up and turning them in her hands. There were plenty of shapes and sizes, but the main stock was thick red pillar candles. The sticker on the bottom matched the one in Penny's kitchen: SCARLET POMEGRANATE. Jane had the stub of the candle she'd found in the dirt in Tonbridge, and she took it from her pocket to compare: it was missing the sticker the others had, but in size and colour it was identical.

There was nobody else in the shop apart from the girl behind the till, who Jane finally looked at properly.

'Hello,' the girl said.

'Hi.' Jane smiled weakly. The girl looked like she was a teenager, and wore a plain oversized T-shirt, scuffed jeans and an apron. Jane noticed her tall skinny frame and mouse-brown hair, which was up in a bun. All of that, plus the slight arch in her nose... Jane opened her phone to pull up a photo of Dev's Nellie. They didn't look totally alike. Maybe a little.

Fawke Wood Sanctuary had a website, which Simon and Jane had checked the previous night when they'd found Penny's candle. The website was so old and badly built it had made Jane's heart hurt. Maybe she should offer to make them a new one? The site hadn't made clear what the place was about: while the homepage had displayed a picture of the shop, it hadn't listed any products or opening hours. It had claimed that you could get a massage, realign your chakras, and stay overnight in one of the guest rooms, but you couldn't book online. It gave the overall impression of a trendy rustic boutique hotel that might be mentioned in a Sunday supplement, but with the added feature that you were likely to be murdered.

Someone else entered the shop; not Simon, but an older man in a straw sunhat.

'Mornin', Hayley,' he said.

'Hello, Patrick,' the girl replied, and Jane felt suddenly self-conscious, noticeably a stranger in these parts.

She waited by the table of red candles while the older man got a pint of milk from a fridge near the till. He wore a Barbour jacket over an old checked shirt, and gave the impression of a retired rambler who enjoyed supporting his local farm shop over the big supermarkets.

After Patrick had counted out the coins for his milk, he didn't hurry to leave, but began assessing the vegetables. Jane brought a red candle up to the till. She noticed a handwritten sign on the desk saying CASH ONLY. How did this place survive?

'Hi!' she said again, with confident cheer. 'I was just wondering if you could tell me about this candle, please?'

'Certainly,' said Hayley. 'These are our best-selling candles. The scent is Scarlet Pomegranate, and they're soy wax candles poured here by hand.'

'Great! And what does this mean – "Pluto"?'

'Well, this candle is also infused with corn oil and some herbs associated with the planet Pluto. Pluto rules over the changes in our lives. It's our own interpretation, really, but Pluto also rules the underworld, so, pomegranates.'

'OK,' said Jane, feeling she'd learned net nothing. 'And is there a reason somebody would ever burn this candle, and then bury the last bit of the wax in the ground?'

'Oh, yes,' said Hayley. 'You might do that if you'd used the candle to cast a spell. With this candle in particular, you might burn it to protect you through a period of transition or new beginnings. Burial is a way to dispose of the candle that doesn't affect the benefit of the spell.'

'Right,' said Jane. 'So, if I was going to leave a relationship, or have a baby or something, I might use this?'

'Maybe, yes.' Hayley smiled. 'Or if you liked the smell of pomegranate.'

'Right, thank you. Have you ever heard of somebody called Nellie Thorne?'

Hayley's face froze with fear. 'Um, no, no, I haven't. I don't know anybody with that name.' Her smile was now that of a bank teller pressing the emergency alarm under the desk. 'Is there anything else I can help you with?'

'Yes,' said Jane, not wanting to drop this thread. 'Is it possible to book in here and stay a night or two?'

'No,' the girl said quickly. 'Sorry, we're fully booked.'

'Well, thanks anyway,' said Jane, and she put the candle back. Which was a shame. If she'd had the money, she might have bought one, so she could wish for a change in fortune.

'Simon!' Jane called, striding across the car park. He was still on the phone, pacing, but began trying to end the call when he saw her. He angled the phone further and further from his face as he said his corporate goodbyes.

'OK. Yep. Thanks, Neil. Yeah, let's square the circle and circle back later. OK. Bye.' He squinted in the bright spring sun. 'Yikes. Sorry, babe. I think I'm going to have to take a couple of calls later, which isn't ideal, but—'

'Simon, get in the car!' Jane interrupted.

'Is something wrong?'

'Just – quickly, quickly!' She waved him into the passenger's seat, looking back at the shop hut and its small curtained window. She couldn't see Hayley looking, yet.

'Duck down, Simon, I don't want her to see you!'

'Jane, what have you done?' he said, squashing himself into the car and leaning his head into the footwell as best he could.

'Stay under the window. We're going to drive out of here, and then a bit later you're going to come back and book us in for a spa weekend.'

'That is what I do best,' Simon muttered.

Now Hayley came to the doorway and watched Jane get into the driver's side. Jane gave a little wave and mouthed to Simon like a ventriloquist. 'Keep hiding. Don't move. Don't speak. We're going to get out of here.'

And the ventriloquist drove away, back down the dirt track, with her boyfriend folded up in the front seat like a dummy in a box.

Back on a country lane about a mile away, they found a gap in a hedgerow to pull the car over.

Jane turned to Simon. 'As soon as I said the words "Nellie Thorne", she looked like I was calling in a bomb threat. I totally rattled her.'

'So we're definitely in the right place. Or at least, getting warmer,' said Simon.

'We're getting scorching hot, Simon. The problem is my cover's blown now. When I asked about staying there tonight, she said they were booked up, but I could tell she was lying to get rid of me. She didn't want me nosing around.'

'Jane, that's great! You can never normally tell when people are lying! So you need me, a person she hasn't seen, to go back up there and book a room for us.'

'Exactly! That's why I had to hide you in the car. Sorry about that. I think we should invite Dev along too – one of us can sleep on the floor if needed. I really feel like we've iced him out of the investigation lately.'

'I think he's been icing himself out.'

'Can you call him anyway?'

'No problemo. But Jane, this is very out of character for you.'
'What?'
'To be missing detective class tonight.'

Jane's stomach sank. She'd forgotten the final deadline to present their coursework was tonight's class. There was no way they could go back to Croydon this evening and lose this red-hot lead.

'I'm going to email Gavin and ask him if we can please, please, please have a coursework extension. Next week is the final exam, but he might let us present our case afterwards. We might just squeak it in under the buzzer.'

'OK,' said Simon. 'That's a plan, Stan.'

'I do think we should leave it a good couple of hours until you go back. Otherwise she might connect the dots between me and you.'

'Do you think?' Simon looked at Jane's cat jumper and his own psychedelic floral shirt.

'The only thing is, what can we usefully do until then?' she said, looking at the rural idyll around them.

'Pub?' said Simon, and, knowing now that his instinct was rarely wrong, she answered,

'Pub.'

'Coffee, good sir?'

'Yes, thank you, uh . . . my lord.'

It hadn't taken Gavin and Bernard long to fall back into their old ways, and after staying up late trying to draft the perfect dating-app opener, Gavin had agreed to stay over in the spare room of the Parker family home, a little holiday from his South London bachelor flat. The spare room was small and loaded up with stacks of bags and books intended for the charity shop, but it was pristinely clean. The bed had been made up with bedding left over from the kids' childhoods, and Gavin had secretly enjoyed a night under a dinosaur duvet.

Now, back at the dining-room table with the morning light filtering in, Bernard carried a tray supplied with mugs, milk and a tall pot of coffee. He sat down, put his glasses on his head, and looked at Gavin to deliver the news.

'We've got it,' he said.

'You've got the name of the place?' Gavin felt like it was Christmas.

'Somewhere in this list, yes. So, naturally, I can't access what the National Crime Agency has on cults. But I've got a mate who's a criminologist at Portsmouth University, who happens to have written a few papers on the subject. She's just emailed me back and attached some of her articles. Between her investigations, and the work she's done with colleagues and journalists, she thinks she's found thirty-six cults operating across Kent.'

'Oh,' said Gavin, slightly disappointed.

'Well, it's a big county. Try policing it,' said Bernard, pouring two coffees. 'What made you think of cults after all these years?'

Gavin shrugged. 'A documentary on cicadas.'

'Oh, right, naturally,' said Bernard, stirring sugar into his coffee.

'They live in the ground for years, and no one has a clue. Then *BAM*, they're there in droves. There are so many more Nellies than we knew about. And we were so busy asking where they went that we never asked where they were all coming from. What kind of place might generate a steady supply of innocent young women who exist off-grid with no documentation? A cult.'

'Great! Now you just have to look into thirty-six cults,' said Bernard.

'It'll be a lot of work, but . . .' Gavin started on a bit of freelancer maths: how many valuable workdays he'd have to sink into investigating thirty-six organisations, just to prove or disprove his hunch. 'Anyway, thank you, Bernie. I do appreciate it.'

'Well, some days you accept the favours, other days, they get called in. Anyway, drink up. I'll go and print out her email. Then maybe we could pop out to the cafe for a full English.'

While his friend was gone, Gavin mooched over to a bookcase. It was packed with flimsy novels, some of which seemed to have been home-printed. 'What's this, mate? *Double Yellow: An Epic Parking Offences Saga?*'

Bernard didn't hear him. Gavin put the book back and idly checked his emails. One dropped in: VERY VERY VERY SORRY, from Jane Pye.

'Bernie!' he shouted through to the room that was Bernard's study. 'Can you print a map as well?'

'A map of what?'

'Of Kent!'

'Oh, right, well, that's all part of room service.'

As the noisy printer whirred, Gavin mouthed Jane's email aloud.

'"Hi Gavin, I must apologise . . ." blah blah blah, "very sorry . . . missing class tonight . . ." blah blah blah. "This morning we tracked down a place that we believe connects all the Nellies and are going to infiltrate it tonight. Sorry again. Wish us luck."'

He read it again. 'Oh god.' He could barely reply quick enough.

> Tell me where? Be careful. Could be dangerous. Please send address and your mobile number. Sent from my iPhone.

Bernard came back in with a slim handful of still-warm pages. He stopped when he saw Gavin's face. 'What's wrong? You look like you've driven over a cat.'

'Bernie, how dangerous are these cults? Are they just hippy-dippy linen trousers, or . . . ?'

'Well, some of them will be, yes. The problem is we don't know. If the police know an organisation is linked with crimes, they can go in and bust them. But as you'll know, you can't turn up at a church meeting on a university campus with the K-9s on suspicion of coercive control. Not if there's been no incidents reported.'

Gavin rested his forehead in his hands and began massaging his eyes. 'I think some of my students have found the place I'm looking for. Cults don't kill people, do they? Not in the UK?'

'Well, yes. It has been known to happen.'

Gavin wilted even more. 'This is my fault; I've sent them there. I shouldn't have given them the bloody case. It's been nothing but a curse.'

Bernard raised his eyebrows. 'Sounds like we should probably find them then, doesn't it?' He pulled the printed map from between the other pages and put it down on the table, smoothing it over with his hand.

'I've just emailed them to ask them where they are. But what if they don't see it before it's too late?' said Gavin.

'Well, luckily, you more or less have a direct line to somebody who should know which of these thirty-six places we're looking for.' Bernard nodded at Gavin's phone.

'You mean Daisy from the dating app?'

'Do you have any other options? Better send her that killer message we've been working on.'

42

Simon and Jane parked up behind the nearest village's pub, the Buck's Head, a rickety Tudor inn painted white with black beams, and accessorised with hanging baskets of pink and purple petunias. Although it was only two minutes past twelve, there was already a small queue outside the front door. Several men of retirement age stood outside patiently, wiping sweat from their foreheads, except the man at the front, who was knocking on the door's glass panes and pointing to the bit of his bare wrist where a watch could have been.

'Simon, I know one of these guys!' whispered Jane. 'He bought some milk in the farm shop earlier!'

'Well, there you go, see. A trip to the pub is always worthwhile.'

They queued up quietly behind Patrick, the man with the straw hat from the Fawke Wood farm shop, until the door was unbolted.

Once inside, the men filed towards a corner of the main bar, where a cluster of stools bore the arse-prints of their regular patronage. Gradually, gingerly, they all got established on their seats. Luckily, Patrick's seat was at a separate table, where he went and put his hat down before getting a newspaper from a rack in the corner.

Jane saw the ringleader of the bar-stool men, the one who'd knocked on the door, order two ales and a Guinness from the barman. The other two blokes watched Jane and Simon enjoyably, like lazing lions might watch some stupidly dressed antelopes.

Jane and Simon took it all in: the men, the furniture, the grubby patterned carpet, the dark wood tables and stools, the low ceiling beams, and the horse gear and scythes hanging decoratively from them.

'Jane, did you know that there are nearly a thousand Wetherspoons in the UK now, and that each and every one of them has a uniquely designed carpet that's inspired by the pub's history?'

'I don't think that can be true.'

'It is true, look it up.'

'You want me to look it up right now?'

'No, no. Come on. Let's buy your friend a drink,' Simon whispered in Jane's ear.

'On it,' she said. 'But I'm going to do a power play. I think I'm good at them now.'

She went to the bar, looked the hung-over middle-aged proprietor in the eye and said, 'Three house ales, please.'

'No such thing, love,' he replied.

She thought for a moment. 'Dealer's choice, then.'

'God, there's absolutely no phone signal here,' said Simon, coming over to the bar. 'Do you have wi-fi?'

'No wi-fi,' said the barman, pumping the pints. 'Talk to each other instead.'

'Bit of a shame though,' said Simon. 'How do you run your Instagram?'

The man didn't reply to that, and went off towards the till.

'Sixteen-fifty, please.'

Simon handed over his credit card: the answer to all their problems now, the cause of all their problems tomorrow.

'One day we'll be rich,' mused Jane, 'and I can go back to the farm shop and buy one of those red candles.'

'Don't you have a credit card, Jane?'

'No, my mum always warned me against them.'

'You really should – they're good for your credit score.'

'Not if you use them like we do!' They carefully brought the drinks over to Patrick and put them down on the table.

'Hello,' said Jane, mistaking volume for confidence. Patrick lowered the local paper.

'I saw you this morning,' he replied. 'In the shop.'

'That's right,' said Jane, encouraged. 'And it would be my honour to give you this beverage, if we can ask you a few questions about Fawke Wood Sanctuary.'

Patrick laughed. 'Well, I wouldn't touch that stuff, but for a double rum and Coke you can grill me 'til dinnertime.'

Jane went bright red. 'Simon, can I have the credit card, please?'

'Of course, babe.' He handed it to her, then sat down and happily lined up his pair of pints.

'I'm Simon,' he said, offering his hand, which Patrick shook.

'Patrick,' he said.

'So, Patrick, I hear you're a fan of local dairy. Are you a farmer, or . . . ?'

'I'm a retired software architect.'

'Oh, brilliant.'

Jane returned with a rum and Coke that had a little blue cocktail umbrella in it. When Patrick saw this, he gave the barman a thumbs-up.

'Thanks, Tommy.' The barman saluted.

'I'm not surprised you want to ask me about Fawke Wood. It's bloody weird.'

The young detectives nodded. Patrick admired a shaft of sunlight that was coming through the window and illuminating some dancing dust.

'It's been here longer than I have. We moved here in 1985. I'm allergic to cities,' he continued. 'Fawke Wood's just a farm-shop type place. Or so you think at first! Did you see any of the buildings round the back?'

The detectives shook their heads. 'I didn't see anything, but I guessed there must be more buildings, because they have rooms you can stay in,' said Jane.

'That's right. Well, I've seen round there because I had a kundalini yoga phase. It's like a little village of its own. It must have started as a farm at some point, what with all the land they have. They've got the old farmhouse, which is where the guests stay, but listen to this: I think people are living in the barn. And on top of that, they've got all these portacabins. You know, like where the offices are on building sites.'

'And do they produce the milk there?' asked Simon.

'No!' Patrick scoffed. 'It comes in on a lorry like any shop. Some of the veg too, I think. They pay for it in cash, you know. In a little brown envelope. I've seen it happen. No, all that farmland, they've let it go wild. It's a mess back there. They've got some goats and pigs, I think, because you could hear them from the yoga studio.'

'And where was the yoga studio?' said Jane.

'Bottom floor of the farmhouse. They like to keep any visitors just to the farmhouse. No deeper into the site, everything else is boxed off with hedges, but . . .' Patrick looked around cheekily. '. . . I used to peek through the hedges. It's obviously huge.'

'Why did you stop going to yoga?' said Simon. 'Did you get a strange vibe about the place?'

'Because I strained a trapezius. Also, I prefer that woman from YouTube. Adrian? But to be honest,' continued Patrick, 'I'm fascinated by the place. That's why I still go up there for bits and pieces sometimes. There's something there that pulls me back.'

'Have you ever heard the name Nellie Thorne?' asked Jane.

Patrick thought about it, but then shook his head. 'No. Why?'

Jane sighed. 'The truth is,' she said, 'we're looking for the girlfriend of a friend of ours. She's gone missing.'

'Oh dear, terrible,' said Patrick, sipping his drink. He removed the umbrella and put it in his shirt buttonhole.

'But the only thing we know is that she owned a candle from that shop,' said Jane. 'Even that's a bit of a guess.'

'Show him the picture, Jane.'

'Might as well.' She got her phone out and found the picture they'd used for Nellie's missing poster. 'Have you ever seen this girl?'

Patrick squinted and took the phone. 'That's Claire!' he said.

'What?!' The detectives looked at each other.

'Yep, definitely Claire. She used to work in the farm shop. Haven't seen her around for a while though, mind.' He handed the phone back to a speechless Jane.

'Are you sure?' asked Simon. Patrick nodded. 'Hold on, how about her?' said Simon, taking Jane's phone again and finding the picture she'd taken of the Nellie from Dungeness.

Patrick had another good squint. 'Oh! Oh . . .' He thought about it. 'Yes, she's familiar. Slightly familiar. Couldn't come up with a name, though.'

'But it's possible you've seen her at Fawke Wood Sanctuary?' Simon pressed.

Patrick shrugged. 'It's possible.'

'Is there anything else you can tell us about these two women?' asked Jane.

'Sorry. I really don't know anything else. Claire worked in the farm shop for a few years, and I always used to ask how she was. What was she reading, what was she knitting behind the till, that kind of thing. But I didn't really know her at all.'

'No,' said Jane. 'As far as we can tell, nobody did.'

They thanked Patrick, and Simon downed the spare pint.

Out in the car park, they leaned on the hot bonnet of their car. 'Incredible thought. Would you rather have hands for feet, or feet for hands?' asked Simon.

'Obviously hands for feet,' said Jane. 'Think of the tree-climbing.'

'Strong answer. So her name's Claire?'

'I suppose so! Unless she's got a secret twin . . .'

'We should have expected this. We always knew Nellie was an alias!'

'Did Dev reply to you?' said Jane.

'Not yet. I just sort of assumed he was at school.'

'He will be,' said Jane, looking at her watch. 'But it's lunchtime now.' She rang his number, but there wasn't enough signal for the call to connect.

And so the two detectives swung the saloon door open for the second time, causing a sudden silence to settle over the punters, who'd obviously been discussing them, and negotiated using the pub's landline.

'Hello, Dev?' said Simon into the receiver. 'I think we've found her.'

At Bernard's, the two middle-aged sleuths had put on their reading glasses to consider their next move. They pondered every detail, nuance and subtext of the reply they'd received from Daisy: Good, you?

'How about: "That's a lovely summer dress"?' offered Bernard.

'Which one? She's got dresses on in at least three of her pictures,' said Gavin, always the man for attention to detail.

'Good thinking, best change that to be more accurate.' Bernard typed carefully, poking the keyboard with one finger. '"That's a lovely summer dress in your second picture." Sent.'

'Careful, Bernie. One wrong move and we could scare her off.'

'From what I hear from my sons, we're very lucky she's even replied to us once.'

'Christ, look at the pair of us,' said Gavin, flinging the glasses off his face and onto the table. 'It's like Cyrano de Bergerac squared.' He rubbed his eyes.

'Oh, look! Those little dots mean she's typing,' said Bernard.

'She is?' There was a *bloop* sound as her message dropped in. 'What does it say?!' pleaded Gavin.

'It says: "Thanks."'

'Well, what do we do now?'

'Another message, I suppose.'

'You're right, we've got to keep her talking,' said Gavin. 'Get on to her emotional level. Start mirroring what she's thinking and feeling.'

'Sounds a bit deep to me,' said Bernard. 'How about: "What have you had for your breakfast?" I always used to ask the missus that when we were first going out.'

'Maybe. Let's keep thinking.' Gavin rubbed his forehead. 'What do we know about her? That she's probably just left home, that . . . What's that in the background of her pictures? Is she in a field? Maybe she likes fields?'

'Well, she's on a dating app,' said Bernard. 'We know that.'

'Of course!' Gavin grabbed the phone. '"How . . . have . . . you found . . . online dating." Question mark. What do you think?'

'Hit send,' said Bernard. And sure enough, she started typing back. 'Read it out, Gav.'

'She says: "Dating's hard. I've been trying to meet people, but it always goes wrong. The other day I fell down the stairs at a nightclub." Ouch.'

'Say you wish you'd been there to catch her!'

Gavin typed it down. Bernard's wife put her head into the room to see what was going on, decided against the vibe, and backed out again before anyone had seen her.

'She's typing again!' Gavin had the bit between his teeth now. 'Oh, she's just reacted with a little crying face.'

Bernard leaned over to have a look. 'That's laughing, mate. Does no one laugh at your texts?'

'No, I'm a miserable bastard. So is she laughing at us?'

'Can't blame her, can you?'

'Oh, I'm sick of this,' said Gavin, and started typing again. 'I'm going to go with: "This could sound strange, but you look like you grew up somewhere with good energy." Cults love energy, don't they?'

'No question?'

'No, I don't want to ask. If we start asking "So, what cult did you grow up in?" she'll clam up. I want to goad her. Make her feel like she's giving the information up without even being asked. You know, Freud would leave a long silence after patients answered his questions, so that people would just start blurting things out from their subconscious to fill the gap.'

The message tone sounded again. 'What has she said?' said Bernie.

'"Thanks."' Gavin growled.

'How's your missus, Gav?'

'We got divorced.' Gavin looked off into a corner of the room, then decided to look at his hands instead.

'Oh, I'm sorry, mate.'

'It's alright.'

'What happened? Did you psychoanalyse her for Valentine's Day?'

Gavin turned back to the printed map of Kent. They'd marked the thirty-six known locations in which Kent's cults operated, and had crossed off some of the less likely ones, like the Church of Scientology, whose UK headquarters were just across the border in Sussex, and a Doomsday sect who targeted the student union in Canterbury.

'If we can just get her to name the nearest town . . .' Gavin picked up the phone again. I'm from Faversham, how about you? he lied.

She replied: I don't really like talking about where I'm from.

'I've got one!' said Bernard. 'Why don't you ask her where she went shopping as a kid? These places are all quite remote, so she'd have to go to the next town over.'

'Good thinking,' said Gavin, and he got it down.

The reply came back: I didn't really go shopping. The two men sighed. But I used to love going to the fair at Hucking Green when it was in town.

The lightbulb pinged on. Gavin's finger raced across the map. 'That's it, that's it! And the closest cult is . . .'

And at the same time, they yelled: 'Fawke Wood Sanctuary.'

43

Pye and Mash were almost ready to check in for their night at Fawke Wood Sanctuary. To avoid compromising Simon while he booked their room, Jane had parked round the corner. Simon had made up an unnecessary story about how he and his wife were in town for a tennis tournament and, in the excitement of qualifying, had forgotten to book accommodation.

However, before their stay, they had one more important stop to make. They got the car back on the road, knowing that in the next hour or two – if they played it right – they could unlock the penultimate piece of the puzzle. It was so exciting they couldn't bring themselves to talk about it.

'I feel better now we've made the reservation,' said Jane, who was taking a turn at the wheel while Simon balanced his work laptop on his knees.

'You'll feel double better once you've cleared out your throat chakra,' he said, dragging a stock image into a deck.

'What are you actually doing there?'

'I've got to run an event next week for some CEOs from Belgium. I'm thinking that for the icebreaker, I'll make them all roar like lions? I know it sounds mad, but men in business absolutely love that kind of stuff. It makes them feel powerful.'

'And it never backfires?'

'Oh, yeah. Sometimes it really backfires.' Simon laughed thinking about the times it had backfired. 'But you've got to go for it.'

'You really do,' agreed Jane, and she nudged the accelerator over the speed limit.

Their very important stop was Dungeness, where they pulled up for a second time in the driveway of the real, possibly-47-year-old Nellie Thorne.

'Not you two again,' said Nellie when she opened the door. 'Look, I'm sorry, I meant what I said about the police.' She began shutting them out.

'No, you don't,' said Jane quickly, 'because we know you don't have any paperwork or records. We know you grew up at Fawke Wood Sanctuary.'

Nellie opened the door again. 'No, I didn't,' she said.

Jane looked at Simon. 'I can tell she's lying.'

'Nice assessment.' Simon attempted to fist-bump her, but she turned back towards Nellie, leaving him to awkwardly punch her shoulder.

'We know your name's not Nellie, too.'

'It bloody is,' said the woman.

'Look,' said Simon, falling into the role of good cop, 'we don't want to cause trouble. It's just . . . a very good friend of ours has gone missing. Her name was Nellie Thorne too, and although we only knew her for less than a year, we're worried. It wasn't easy to find you, if that makes you feel better. And any secrets you're keeping, we'll keep them too. If you can help reassure us our friend's OK.'

She twisted her lips, thinking about it.

'My kids are doing homework, so you can't stay long. I'll have to explain quickly. And if you repeat any of what I'm about to say, I will find you, and I will end you.'

And with that, Simon and Jane were allowed in.

The detectives were lucky enough to check in to Fawke Wood Sanctuary in time for Sacral Chakra Flow, which was due to start at six-thirty. Thankfully, a different girl had rotated onto the farm-shop till, so nobody recognised Jane. Her disguise – a big pair of sunglasses, a face mask and a deerstalker hat belonging to Simon – had been unnecessary.

'If anything,' Simon whispered to her as they were shown through the farm shop's back exit, 'you're drawing more attention to yourself. They probably think you're Taylor Swift.'

'Don't be silly, Simon,' she said. 'I'm half her height. Also, I doubt cult members listen to pop music.'

'Everyone listens to Taylor,' Simon whispered back.

They arrived in the belly of the Sanctuary's lush grounds. The farmhouse was right ahead as they exited the shop. It was a three-storey red-brick box of a house, Georgian and pretty. The yard between the shop and the house was planted up in neat squares of flowerbeds and vegetable patches. As Patrick had promised, the shop, farmhouse and the yard between them were lined on all sides by a thick laurel hedge. You could visit and never know there was any more to the grounds than this, unless you were as nosy as Patrick.

A young woman led them up a path through the vegetable patches, explaining the facilities and staying a few steps ahead. Her long hair was loose, and she wore a green linen dress down to her ankles.

'We have massages in the potting sheds over to the left, there,' she said, pointing to a pair of wooden sheds on the left side of the garden's hedge. 'You can book those with me in the shop once you've got settled.'

'Wow,' said Jane. 'Maybe we should stay longer.'

'They're probably always looking for new recruits,' said Simon quietly.

Jane started to wonder how they were going to find their target, but her instinct was growing stronger. Dev's Nellie, aka Claire, would be here.

'Oh, look, Jane!' said Simon, reading the labels in one of the herb patches. 'Nightshade! As in, deadly nightshade?'

Jane wondered if they should have brought some cereal bars to live on.

Inside the farmhouse, the girl showed them to a room called Tarragon. It was simple and decorated like Jane's childhood bedroom, with purple curtains and two pine-framed single beds. On one, a woollen granny-square blanket was tucked across the duvet. It was made of clashing multi-colours and looked like it had been hand-crocheted.

'Funny!' said Simon, as he put down a bag for life on the blanketed bed. 'How did you know tarragon was my favourite herb?'

The girl pointed out a complimentary bottle of wine on the windowsill and left them to get comfortable. 'What do we do now?' said Jane.

'Well, I've got to take a work call,' said Simon, getting his laptop out of the carrier bag. 'But I think you should go and get a massage.'

'Hmm.' Jane thought about the idea of Simon working while she lay down, listening to twinkly music, getting the permanent ache rubbed out of her left shoulder. 'I suppose it couldn't hurt to check the place out a little more.'

She decided to do a lap of the farmhouse on her way out. The sun was starting to sink lower and grow golden. She went down the side of the building and tried to look through the laurel hedge, like Patrick had done, but the vegetation was thick. Perhaps he'd done his snooping in winter when the branches were sparser.

At the farm shop, Jane booked the next available massage slot, which was in ten minutes. For a moment she forgot she was undercover on a dangerous mission, and as she wandered back into the grounds she imagined the online review she'd write about the excellent service. In truth she hadn't had a massage before. They were a part of Simon's world. She could imagine her parents saying, 'Ooh! He's taken you for a *massage*, has he?' as if it were a bad thing.

The potting sheds were a pair of standard garden sheds. Ivy had crawled up the sides and sunk its tendrils into the wooden slats. The sheds were roughly the same size as the one Jane's dad fiddled with car engines in, except these ones were rotting in the corners and rusting at the hinges. Jane heard somebody moving around in the left-hand shed. On the door was a little wooden sign saying: DO NOT DISTURB, CHILLOUT IN PROGRESS! A gingham curtain was drawn over the dirty window.

That's good, thought Jane. She wouldn't want a passing cult member to see her bottom. Were you meant to get naked for this? Or would that upset the masseuse? Suddenly she felt a bit nervous. She was determined not to back out, though. She didn't want to explain to Simon why she'd changed her mind. Sometimes in life you had to steel yourself and go through something stressful, like a massage.

But when the door creaked open, Jane's confidence vanished.

'Hi. If you'd like to come in now,' said the masseuse. As she spoke, she recognised Jane, and panic washed across her eyes.

Jane was sure it was her: the woman she'd mentioned Nellie Thorne to earlier in the farm shop, Hayley. She had tried to get rid of Jane as fast as possible and had lied and told her the place was fully booked. But now she plastered a new smile on her face.

'Thanks,' croaked Jane.

Inside there was a massage table, an incense burner, and an antiquated cassette recorder playing tinny meditation music. Jane spotted a row of old gardening tools hanging from the walls: trowels, sharp forks, even a rusting pair of scissors. Jane wondered if it was time to run. Then her cover would be truly blown. Should she fake a medical emergency? She didn't want to risk incurring any herbal healthcare procedures. All she had to do was stay alert and be ready to reach for the scissors before Hayley could. Or a fork.

But the girl seemed relaxed again, as if the encounter in the shop hadn't happened at all.

'I'll just step out for a moment.' She smiled. 'If you'd like to take your clothes off.'

'All of them?' said Jane, struggling to get words out.

'It's up to you.' Well, at least that was an easy decision. If she was going to die, Jane at least wanted to keep her underwear on.

Simon was trying to wrap up his call, but none of the other participants seemed cognisant that it was long past six o'clock. The Tarragon room was starting to lose its charm. Neither of the twin single beds were big enough for Simon's long, anxiously shifting legs, on which he was having to balance his laptop. The smell of old pine and mothballs was making him irritated. The saving grace was the large window looking out onto the grounds, which he kept getting distracted by.

'That's more Simon's area,' said Simon's boss, once again deflecting a difficult question onto him. 'Could you explain the timeline of engaging the catering crew when booking a team social? Simon? Are you with us?'

'Mm! Yes, sorry,' he said. 'It might be easiest if I summarise that one in an email for you.'

The two clients looked miffed. 'Sorry, everyone,' said Simon. 'It's the end of the working day now, and — well, as you know, our team is here to help other teams work more creatively. And I feel I wouldn't be aligning with our core values if I didn't remind everyone that the brain is like a well-cooked piece of meat.' They looked confused. 'It needs to rest. In the name of creativity, I'd suggest we come back to this fresh on Monday and give it our very best energy.'

This play was a long shot, and as it hung in the air, he glanced out towards the potting shed. He wondered how Jane was getting on, and whether she'd managed to choose a relaxing type of massage instead of a painful one.

'Of course, Simon,' said one of his clients, beaming. 'Thanks for keeping us on the right track.'

He couldn't believe it had worked. He was free!

'But if nobody minds,' the client continued, 'I will pop a little catch-up in the diary for Sunday afternoon, so we can get a head-start on the week.'

'Sure, of course,' said the devastated Mash cheerfully. But he finally got to say his goodbyes and slam his laptop shut.

Desperate to escape the room, he wandered out into the hallway, which smelled musty, like Simon's primary school. Perhaps the people here ate school-dinner food, boiled vegetables and lumpy custard. He was unsure where to go next; what would Jane want him to do? He noticed there were two more bedrooms on this floor, plus the shared bathroom with the old-fashioned chain-flush toilet. He crept up and put his ear to the doors of the neighbouring bedrooms but couldn't hear anything from within.

He made his way down the farmhouse's stairs. There was activity happening on the ground floor: people were filing through the big farmhouse front door and into one of the downstairs rooms. Magnetically, Simon clicked into the group and followed them into the front room, to whatever it was they were about to do.

The front room was painted entirely white. The ceilings were high and the windows large, just like in the bedrooms. He looked around at the rest of the group, hoping for evidence that this wasn't going to be a ritual group sacrifice. There were about fifteen other people, mostly women over fifty, plus a couple of white-haired elderly gents, and an extremely lean bald man in his forties. He was tanned, muscular and hardy, how Simon imagined a fisherman might look beneath his overalls.

Everyone wore leggings or harem pants, and the lean fisherman removed his shirt. A couple of small groups of the women were chatting to each other comfortably as they mooched towards the back of the room and started getting exercise mats out from a wooden cupboard. Fisherman got into a cross-legged position and began loudly humming a drone note. While Simon was relieved to realise he'd gate-crashed a yoga class, he slightly regretted that he'd come downstairs in his buttoned floral shirt and tweedy tailored trousers. He'd have to negotiate carefully around the trousers' crotch seams to avoid another ripping incident. He took a yoga mat and a couple of hard foam blocks out of the cupboard, and the rubbery smell of the old mats once again took him back to school, this time to the endless gym classes.

Simon hadn't been naturally sporty, but his long limbs had made him a serviceable runner. When it came to yoga, he'd tried plenty of classes in studios all over London but had never quite had the spiritual awakening he'd been hoping for.

The class yogis were well trained: they'd unrolled their mats and limbered up before the instructor had even arrived. When she did enter, Simon recognised her as the woman he'd booked the room with earlier in the day. The public-facing side of this operation was obviously small. The woman was tall and wore a full-length brown linen dress. Simon wondered how this outfit would work once the yoga got into full swing.

'Hello, everyone,' she said, purposefully peaceful. 'My name is Calla. Welcome once more to Sacral Chakra Flow: Advanced.'

Simon swallowed. But then, pretending to keep up with advanced people was his strong suit. The group went straight in with a stretch that looked a bit to Simon like the splits, before rolling around through a quick series of poses designed to get heat into the body. Simon began sweating, and wondered if he could follow Fisherman's lead and take his shirt off. But the tanned man had so little fat on his body that his sinews were visible, and Simon settled for undoing a couple of buttons. When they moved into the downward dogs, someone let loose a long, parping fart. Nobody laughed. Simon felt far from home.

The door opened, interrupting the focus of the room like a shark's fin interrupts a day at the beach. Everybody turned to look, and a woman who'd been balancing arrogantly on one wrist fell over. A hunched dark-haired man in a shabby coat shuffled in.

'Gavin!' said Simon out loud. Gavin shot him a 'shut up' look. 'Sorry,' Simon mouthed. Of course he shouldn't have blown his teacher's identity. He squirmed, and wondered if this was what it felt like to be Jane.

'Apologies,' said Gavin to Calla, raising his palms. 'I'm a bit late this week.'

She scrutinised him, knowing she didn't recognise this stranger. Every person in the room watched as the mysterious man made his way to the back of the room, sat on the floorboards and, forgoing a mat, began to stretch his legs out bareback. He realised something must still be wrong, as people's heads had not turned back in the direction of their own business, so he unlaced his Doc Martens and placed them on the floor next to him.

'Welcome, namaste, and soul greetings to you all,' said Calla. 'While punctuality is important, so is welcoming new friends to this sacred space where we clear blocked energy from our bodies.' Simon felt more gas had been released than blocked energy. 'Let's continue,' she said, 'and as we do, say a silent prayer to your soul asking for the healing you came here for.'

And so Simon got his head down, dangerously attempting the same headstand as the rest of the class, saying a silent prayer for the crotch seams of his and Gavin's trousers.

'What are you doing here?!' said Simon as they filed out of the class. It had lasted an hour, and both he and Gavin were red-faced and gleaming with sweat.

'Alright, mate, first things first: have you got a room? Somewhere private?'

'Sure, up here.' They went upstairs, noticing how many Kentish yogis were still watching them.

'Let's get up before she sees us,' he said, meaning Calla, who was sitting patiently in a meditative state until the last of the class left.

Simon got out his key and let them into the Tarragon room.

'Nice place you've got here,' said Gavin, looking around carefully.

'Thanks!' said Simon, missing the sarcasm.

The detective teacher pressed his ear against the wall and

tapped it with his hand. He opened the wardrobe and patted down Simon's spare Tommy Bahama shirt. He opened every drawer, unscrewed every lightbulb, and if there'd been a phone in the room, he would have unplugged it. Gavin reached into his biggest pocket and pulled out a grey handheld device with a digital screen. He pressed a couple of its buttons and the screen lit up, flashing as he scanned it over every piece of furniture and most of the walls. Simon stared, wondering if there was a way he could use this attention-grabbing magic in the office.

'Right,' said Gavin after a while. 'No mics, no cameras. I think we're clear. Now, are you alright?'

'Yes!' said Simon, his eyes alight at the spycraft.

'Nobody here's tried to hurt you?'

'Well, that low lunge was a killer, but I've always had tight hamstrings, so it's to be expected.'

Gavin sighed and sat down on one of the twin beds. The mattress sank low. 'I suppose you want to know what I'm doing here?'

'I didn't think it would be that big of a deal for us to miss class tonight,' said Simon, sitting on the other bed.

'God! I forgot about that.' Gavin rubbed his forehead. 'No class tonight. I need to call the training centre again. They're short-staffed and nobody's answering the phone.'

'I have so many questions.'

'Go on then, son. Shoot.'

'Why did you come to yoga?'

'Starting with the easy ones. Well, as you'll have found out, to get further than the farm shop you need to book a room. But apparently two nosey yuppies booked out the last one earlier today.'

'So the only option was to come in for a yoga class.' Simon felt sorry for him. 'Would you like a glass of wine?' Simon offered.

'I'm on duty. So yes, please. Just a sharpener.'

Simon got the bottle from the windowsill. There were no glasses, except for the toothbrush holder by the sink, which he filled and handed to his teacher.

Gavin swallowed a mouthful and winced. 'I haven't been completely honest with you, Steven.'

'Simon.'

'Sorry, Simon. When I handed you two your coursework assignment, I pretended I didn't know about the Nellie Thorne case. Even worse, I pretended it wasn't real. The truth is, I investigated the case myself back in the nineties, and it turned out to be a dangerous road.'

Simon was rapt.

Gavin continued: 'I'd hoped it would keep you busy, but that you'd run out of road and let Dev Hooper down.'

They passed the toothbrush glass back and forth as Gavin explained the rest of his story; how he'd thought the Nellies might have been ghosts or murder victims, maybe even murder accomplices. How he'd finally met a Nellie himself but had given up after being left bleeding on the road in East London. He'd been taken to hospital after a dawn jogger had found him. His hip had shattered, causing the slight limp he had now. Just a few days ago, he'd realised what was going on, making the connection that the Nellies could have been off-grid if they'd come from a cult.

'It was the only thing I didn't think of back in the day. I know cults sound exotic, but there are over two thousand of them in the UK right now. They don't always look like you'd imagine. Sometimes it's a really hardcore church. Some only have a handful of members. At least half are thought to use emotional abuse to isolate their victims, but I think that statistic is on the low side. Why else would people stick around in a cult?'

'Perhaps the rent's cheap.'

'The thing is, Simon, *this* is a cult. This place.' He gestured around.

'Wow! We did know that though.'

'You did?'

'Yes, we followed a pensioner to the pub, and he told us he had his suspicions. He recognised Dev's girlfriend! Her real name's Claire. She used to work here, in the shop. Then we went to Dungeness to interrogate a Nellie we tracked down, and what she said basically confirmed it.'

Gavin shook his head grimly, buzzing with joy. 'I knew it,' he said.

'So.' Simon was still taking it in. 'Why did you lie to us?'

Gavin shifted on the bed and held his hand out for the cup of wine, which Simon passed over.

'Well, I suppose I'm proud. I never solved the case, did I? It annoyed me. I just palmed it off on you. I thought if I couldn't solve it, you wouldn't either.' He looked at Simon, at his wide-open shirt and glazed look.

'But we have solved it now,' said Simon.

'Nearly,' said Gavin, finishing the wine. 'We haven't found her though, have we? And we still haven't figured out *why*.'

'Ah,' said Simon. 'I think I can help with that.'

He explained to Gavin what Dungeness Nellie had told them when they'd visited earlier that day.

Gavin shook his head. 'Really?' he said.

Simon nodded. 'Is that why you came all the way here?' said Simon. 'To find that out? The final piece of the puzzle?'

'No, you dolt – I came to save you! Jane emailed me earlier today saying you two had found Nellie HQ somewhere, and you were planning to infiltrate it. I had a duty of care to find you.

Nobody knows how dangerous these cults can be.'

'Well, thank you,' said Simon. 'But we're doing great.'

'Are you? Then where's Jane?'

Simon looked around the room, as if she could have somehow evaded the bug sweep. She should have returned from her massage a long time ago. 'I don't know,' he said finally.

44

Hayley had no mercy on Jane's back.

'Ow,' said Jane, as a finger pressed deep into her neck.

'Is the pressure OK?'

'Yep, absolutely fine, thanks.' She couldn't tell if this was punishment for rumbling whatever scam this cult was running, or just how a massage was meant to feel. Hayley finally took her hands away. The massage didn't seem to have lasted an hour, but rather a torturous twenty minutes. Jane had survived until the end, although she would have been surprised if Hayley had ever massaged anyone more tense.

Hayley clicked the tape player's off button abruptly. 'Can you stay here for a moment, please?'

'Oh, of course,' said Jane, getting up and pulling on her T-shirt as quickly as possible. She planned to sneak out of the shed and back to the room once Hayley had left, but as Hayley closed the door behind her, Jane heard a series of metallic clicks. She felt sour panic in her stomach. She tried to open the door, even though she knew it had been padlocked from the outside.

Should she shout for help? That would only work if Simon happened to be walking past the shed, and even then, she doubted his lock-picking skills. If she ran at the door, would it come off the old hinges? That was the best chance she had.

She took a run-up and smacked into the door shoulder-first. 'Ow!!' A few more of these did nothing. The walls wobbled, but the door stayed sturdy. How was the shed so strong?

Jane waited for what felt like forever, until she finally heard somebody outside. She earwigged as hard as she could, catching most of the words.

'. . . Claire was told *expressly* not to use the name . . .'

'. . . Might not have been Claire.'

'Please. It's hardly going to have been a coincidence . . .'

There were two voices. One was Hayley's. The other belonged to an older woman, who sounded angry.

'Go and find her now . . . Take her to the cabins. I want to talk to her after we're clear . . .'

Jane was unable to hear any more over the clunks of the padlock being unlocked. She grabbed the rusty scissors from their hook on the wall and held them behind her back. The door was opened by a woman in a long brown dress. Hayley hung around behind her, pale and nervous.

'Hello, Jane,' said the older woman, smiling. 'Bad news, I'm afraid. We're going to have to evacuate everyone. Please come to the farm shop as soon as possible and we'll be happy to refund you for your stay.'

'Oh,' said Jane.

'We're very sorry about that, but it can't be helped.'

'Can I ask why?'

'Asbestos,' said the woman.

'Asbestos? Isn't that normally found during building work?'

'Please come through to the farm shop as soon as you can. You might want to get dressed.'

'Oh, right, yes,' said Jane, who'd forgotten to put her trousers back on. She was left to gather up her things. A moment ago, she'd been desperate to escape. Now she had to scheme a way to stay.

Up in Tarragon, Simon tried to call Jane, and a pillow started ringing. 'Oh god!' he moaned. 'I told her to leave her bloody phone here, so she could enjoy the massage!'

RAP-RAP! A knock at the door.

'Hide!' he hissed to Gavin, who squeezed himself between the sink and the wardrobe. 'Isn't inside the wardrobe better?'

'Seventeenth rule of detecting,' Gavin whispered. 'Inside the wardrobe leaves no manoeuvrability.'

The knock at the door came again and Simon unlocked it to find Calla the yoga teacher. 'Oh, hello,' he said.

'Good evening, Simon.' She must have got his name from the check-in details. It startled Simon to have his own neuro-linguistic-programming techniques used back on him.

'I'm afraid to say we're having to close the guesthouse for the night.'

'Ah. So, I'll just stay put here, shall I?'

'No, Simon. I'm afraid I'll need you to pack up and meet me in the farm shop for your refund, with our apologies.'

'Not a problem,' said Simon, deciding to leave her feathers unruffled while he figured out what was going on. Calla gave him a small bow and he closed the door.

'What was that about?' he said to Gavin, hoping the teacher had all the answers.

'I think they're on to us,' he said. 'Who else is staying up here?'

Simon shrugged.

'Those other two rooms must be occupied,' continued Gavin, 'because they told me they're fully booked. Those are the only other rooms I've seen, unless they have people sleeping in the garden sheds.'

'No, that's where Jane's being murdered,' said Simon whimperingly. 'Well, massaged. But maybe murdered.'

'Right, I'm going to go and leverage some persuasion on the other guests. You go and find out what's happened to Jane.' Gavin strode towards the door.

'What about packing?' said Simon.

'Don't worry about that,' said Gavin. 'You won't need to after I've had a word with our neighbours.'

'You're not going to hurt them, are you?' said Simon, picturing the shabby little man bending back pensioners' fingers.

'No!' said Gavin, and he got his wallet from an inside pocket, peeling it open to review his wodge of cash. 'But I am going to hurt my bank balance. Off you go, mate.'

Simon headed towards the massage sheds, boldly trying both the doors. The sheds were empty inside, and he was relieved to see an absence of blood splatters. The garden was deserted, the yogis having long since left. Now they were starting to lose the sun, and his view of the garden was getting murky. His only remaining option was to go to the farm shop, as he'd been instructed.

In the shop, ugly strip-lights had been switched on, the kind that were able to bore into heads and cause migraines.

'Simon!' said Jane, now fully trousered, putting down a cross-eyed wooden duck and running to hug him. Calla sat at the till, pretending to write in the shop's ledger, but it was clear she was keeping an eye on the Sanctuary's infestation of detectives.

'Are you OK?' asked Simon, handing Jane her phone.

'I'm fine.' Jane glanced at Calla, unable to tell him what had happened. 'I'm honestly fine. Good massage!' She said the last two words loudly, so they would be overheard. 'Look at this.' She showed Simon an incoming message on her phone screen.

Dev Hooper: Thanks Jane. On my way now. ETA about 9pm.

Simon widened his eyes. He took out his own phone and started typing, one eye on the screen, the other on Calla. Jane's phone buzzed.

World's Sexiest Man: Gavin is here. He's going to help us not get kicked out tonight.

Calla eyed them – two youngsters on their phones – and went back to the diary.

Jane (Girlfriend): How? Where is he?

World's Sexiest Man: Not sure. How much was that wooden duck? Might look good in our toilet. Like it's swimming on the cistern.

Just then, a couple entered the room. They were both grey-haired, slim to the point of fragile, and wearing sensible walking clothing. The woman wore a sunhat with a cord that tied under her chin, and their sandals were reinforced for off-road use. They seemed the type of couple that had been married forty years and had spent most of those years making hearty lentil stews. They were short, but the woman stood at her full height as she walked up to the till.

World's Sexiest Man: Look sharp, Jane. These must be some other guests. I think Gavin's bribed them.

'Excuse me, madam,' said the woman to Calla, her sensible sunhat shaking. 'I'm not happy that we have to leave our rooms. It absolutely will not do.'

'I apologise,' said Calla. 'You didn't seem quite so upset when I broke the news to you earlier?'

'Well, I've had some time to think about it!' said the woman. 'Where do you expect us to go tonight? It's already getting dark, and my husband and I have nowhere else to stay. We've come here all the way from Nottingham, and I'm telling you – not asking you – that we'll be staying in our room tonight.'

> World's Sexiest Man: I feel like we're being saved by my mother.

'I'm sorry about the inconvenience, of course,' said Calla, who seemed untouched by the woman's anger. 'But this is a safety issue, due to a gas leak on the premises, and I will have to insist. My apologies again.' She opened the till and started counting out cash. 'Please accept a full refund.'

> Jane (Girlfriend): I told her the asbestos excuse sounded like nonsense, and now she's changed it!!

'You can stop there,' said the woman. 'If there's a gas leak, we'll just sleep with the windows open. Though I suspect that's nonsense, because earlier you said it was something to do with hornets.'

'We don't want the money back; we want to stay for our holiday,' her husband cut in, before handing back over to his wife for the *coup de grâce*.

'I have a terminal illness. We don't know how long I've got left, but let's just say I'm not buying any Christmas presents. This could be our last holiday together, and you have destroyed it. You may as well have stuck the knife in my back yourself and twisted it.'

Jane (Girlfriend): Wow. That is savage.

World's Sexiest Man: Did you see any aloe vera in the garden? She's gonna need some for that BURN!

'My apologies again,' said Calla, stone-cold.

'Well, you've left me with only one option,' said the woman. 'If your premises are really so dangerous and poorly maintained that you have hornets *and* a gas leak—'

'And asbestos,' added Jane.

'—and asbestos, we'll have to get in touch with the police.'

'The police?' said Calla.

The woman nodded towards her silent husband. 'Bruce here was an assistant chief constable up in Nottinghamshire. He'd certainly pull a few strings to check all your safety certificates are in order. And I'm sure the police would be very happy to alert HMRC to the fact you only deal in cash.'

'Alright,' said Calla with an exhale. 'Well, you can stay the night. Will that work?'

'And our friends, too,' said the woman quickly, pointing at Simon and Jane. 'Or I'll call the police.' She was losing conviction.

Calla stood up heavily to address the room. 'Everybody will stay the night tonight. But there will be no massages or classes, and I must ask everybody to stay in their rooms. No wandering around. We'll be requiring you all to leave by an hour after sunrise.'

'Claire?' Hayley called out.

'What is it?' Claire groaned quietly. She was sitting in a camp chair by the fire, hoping that watching the sunset in silence would help her headache. Some of the other women mingled and chatted, others fired up the barbecues for dinner. Soon the whole family would gather here to eat.

'Calla wants to talk to you. You're in trouble.' Hayley stuck her tongue out.

'Urgh. Shut up,' said Claire. She tried to lift herself out of the chair, but sank back in. Hayley frowned. Claire knew it was too early to be acting like this, that it was only normal to struggle with moving in the final months before the baby came. And her headaches had been getting worse.

'Come on,' said Hayley, and she took her sister's arm, hauling her up. Together, they walked baby step by baby step towards the cabins.

'Is your friend sure there's not really a gas leak?' said the woman to Jane as they left the shop.

'A hundred per cent,' said Jane. 'They told me it was asbestos.'

'Oh!' she said, looking at her husband. 'Isn't that even more dangerous, if they're combined?'

'You're not really ill, are you?' asked Jane.

'No, no, dear. We're doing very well for our age. Just the bunions and high blood pressure. And Bruce's heart condition. And my colonoscopy last year. And the dizzy spells.'

'Were you really that high up in the police?' said Simon to the man.

'Oh, no. I'm a second-hand car salesman. Did a few years in the big house, actually. A long time ago, of course. Tax issue. It was my idea to bring up HMRC.' The couple grinned with pride. 'Your friend liked that one.'

A pair of forty-something men wearing brightly coloured shirts crunched up the gravel pathway from the house, wheeling their suitcases.

'It's alright, we can stay now!' said the sunhat woman cheerily. The men shrugged and turned around, and the six guests made their way back up to the house.

'Now we've got to deal with the next issue,' said Jane. 'How to get our old friend Dev Hooper into Midsomer Fort Knox.'

'You still think he should come along?' said Simon, rubbing his chilly arms. Night had fallen while they'd been arguing in the shop.

'Absolutely,' said Jane. 'The more the merrier. Tonight we're breaking into the heart of the operation.'

45

'Yes, there's a burglar alarm, but luckily, burglar alarms aren't foolproof,' said Gavin, suddenly remembering he was talking to fools. The young acolytes leaned in to listen. They were sitting on the beds in Tarragon, scheming.

The customer-facing part of Fawke Wood Sanctuary had been built for security. The site was a square: the shop at the front, the farmhouse at the back, the vegetable garden in the middle, and the two sheds along one side. The back three sides were lined by the laurel hedge, but across the front – built on to either side of the shop – was an eight-foot-high brick wall. Since the three detectives had failed to find a ladder in the farmhouse, they were looking for a plan more fitting of professionals.

'One of us will disarm the shop's burglar alarm,' Gavin continued, 'while another one picks the locks. We'll have to hope they don't bolt it because I only brought my portable bolt-cutters.'

'Really?' said Simon.

'No, not really. There's no such thing as portable bolt-cutters, nitwit,' said Gavin. He took another sip of wine from the toothbrush glass. Jane and Simon had let their guest have exclusive use of it now, while they swigged from the bottle.

'Never say "there's no such thing" until you've checked on Amazon,' said Jane.

'We should put that on a motivational poster!' said Simon.

'The locks on the shop doors are old-fashioned, the easiest kind to pick,' continued Gavin. 'They've probably been there since the place was built. I didn't spot an alarm panel in there, so I'm hoping it's in the fuse box. Which, luckily for us, has been built on to the back of the shop on the outside. Stupid, but not unusual for buildings that have had electricity put in as an afterthought. And I suppose they didn't think about people trying to break *out*.'

Jane was in awe of her teacher's observational skills, and resolved to pay more attention to her surroundings. She looked around the room: sink, wardrobe, window.

'After all this effort to break Dev in, we'd better hope we find his girlfriend. What are you charging him, by the way?' said Gavin.

'Charging him?' said Simon.

'Amateurs,' said Gavin, shaking his head. 'Though to be fair, I don't normally teach people how to destroy burglar alarms until the Level Five course, so in some ways you're speeding ahead.'

'So we're going to be better equipped as detectives than the other people in the class?' said Jane hopefully.

'On second thoughts, I think most of that lot probably already know their way around a burglar alarm. Well, no time like the present,' said Gavin, standing up.

Jane felt cold inside. Was it excitement, or a fear of prison?

At the back of the shop, Simon popped the front off the fuse box, and Jane used Gavin's Christmas-cracker mini screwdrivers to prise open the fused spur of what she really, truly hoped was the fuse for the burglar alarm. After that, she looked for the red and black battery wires, like Gavin had told her, and snipped them with the scissors she'd taken from the massage shed. The three of them were wearing their darkest clothing, which for two of them wasn't particularly dark.

Simon gave a thumbs-up, and Gavin clicked around in the lock of the shop until the door swung open.

'Still got it,' he muttered.

They waited a moment for the burglar alarm to go off, and after five long seconds, breathed a sigh of relief.

'The poor old thing was probably busted anyway,' said Gavin.

They crept into the shop, not daring to switch the lights on. 'Ow!' Simon tripped on a basket of marmalade.

It took a quick click of the lock on the front door for it to swing open. Dev stood like a shadow in the doorway. Jane's heart leapt, even though she'd been expecting to see him there. 'Dev!'

He came in and hugged her, and then Simon. Gavin went to shake his hand. 'Dev Hooper?' he asked.

'That's right.'

'Gavin Smith. Good to put a face to the name.'

'Dev, have you been drinking?' said Jane, sniffing around Dev's chest area. Dev lifted his sweater over his nose and took a deep inhale.

'Oh, that!' he said. 'No, that's my men's bubble bath. Whiskey-scented.'

'Goddammit,' said Simon, stepping forward to get a whiff of Dev's coat collar. 'That is lovely.'

Gavin watched them for a minute before clearing his throat. 'Ahem. Now, unless anyone fancies some last-minute blackberry jam, I suggest we crack on.'

'How are you?' Jane asked Dev in a whisper as they crept round the edge of the hedge. The moon was nearly full, and the hedge was casting a useful shadow. It couldn't hurt to not be visible from the house.

'I'm good, Jane. I'm really good,' said Dev, smiling. Jane wondered what he was so happy about. 'How are you? Well done for getting me in here. What is this place?'

'It's a cult,' said Jane. 'We haven't seen Nellie yet, but she used to work here a few years ago.'

'By the way, her name's really Claire,' said Simon. The smile dropped off Dev's face.

'Claire?' he said, trying it out.

'Yeah,' Simon said. 'Nellie Thorne isn't anyone's real name. Well, apart from that actress in Gravesend who changed it by deed poll. I'm sorry, man. Didn't mean to upset you.'

'Well, I should have realised it wasn't a real name by now,' said Dev. 'Oh well.'

'Oh!' said Jane, a bit too loud.

'Shhh!' said the others.

'You've moved on!' said Jane.

'W-what?' said Dev, looking flustered.

'Something's been up with you, Dev, and I've been trying to put my finger on it. You've found someone new, haven't you?'

Gavin and Simon turned to look at Dev; even in their present situation, this was red-hot gossip. 'Well, ah, I wouldn't quite say, um . . .' Dev stumbled.

'Long way to say "yes",' muttered Gavin.

'Come on, who is it?' said Jane.

'Well, I haven't actually said that there is anyone, and I mean, wouldn't want to label something that . . .'

'Oh my god, it's Linda from the library! That's why I saw you there!' Jane was alight with vindication.

'That's why you've been swerving my texts,' said Simon. 'You've gone off Nellie!'

'Well, look,' said the embattled man, 'it was you two who kept saying she'd probably left me! Obviously I didn't want to just give up, but when you told me she was back on Depop, I guess that was the final straw. I accepted she'd had enough of me. I didn't want to say anything, because . . .'

'Bit of a quick turnaround,' Simon filled in the gap in the sentence.

'It is Linda though, isn't it?' said Jane.

Dev gave in. 'I went in there to ask if I could put the posters up. Turned out Linda knew all about the Nellie story, and then she showed me the archive, and . . . well, she's a very flirtatious and appealing person. We hit it off straight away. I can tell this one's special.'

Jane recognised the tone of voice he'd used to talk about Nellie during their first meeting. 'God, I'm so stupid,' she said. 'Linda said something like, "You're not even the first person who's come in asking about Nellie this week." I thought it was weird, but I didn't question it. It was you! And she must have been the woman who I heard in your house!'

'She brought some Nellie files round with a bottle of wine. Things just sort of went from there.' He was appropriately sheepish for a man who'd moved on from his missing girlfriend within days.

'Dev, you dog! You're a bigger dog than Hotdog!' Simon slapped him on the back.

'But she'd been flirting with *me*!' blurted Jane, incensed.

'What?!' said Dev and Simon.

'As interesting as I'm sure Mr Hooper's personal life is,' said Gavin, 'he's only engaged us to snoop into one specific part of it. Calla could be out any moment with a shotgun, and we don't have time to waste. But there's one thing I need to say first. If we keep going, there could be trouble. This is your last chance to back out of this and just call the fuzz instead. Speak now or forever hold your peace.'

Everyone looked at Dev, who shrugged. 'They haven't been much use so far. If you say she's here, then let's do it.'

Gavin nodded. 'Personally, I agree – if we call them, that would be the end of our involvement. We'd never find out the truth about this place.'

'Much better story for our new website if we finish the job,' said Simon, and he looked at Jane to read her face.

'We have to finish the coursework,' she said resolutely.

'Coursework?' said Dev.

'Shoot,' said Jane. 'Sorry, Dev. That's another thing. We're just detective students. We don't really know anything.'

'Oh, for god's sake!' But he didn't get angry. 'Well, for students, you've done a good job, I suppose.' It was the best thing Jane had heard in weeks.

'Well, then,' said Gavin. 'On we press.'

Near the farmhouse, the plan was much simpler. There was to be no breaking into fuse boxes or picking locks. Just a simple insight from country boy Simon Mash, who stood explaining the plan like the conductor of his criminal string trio.

'Laurel hedges,' he explained quietly, 'are very easy to climb through. It just doesn't occur to adults to do so. As a child growing up in the countryside, however, climbing into laurel hedges was a core pastime for my brother and me.' Dev and Gavin exchanged glances.

'The leaves' – he pointed to them with a wide arm wave, like a magician introducing a punter about to be sawn in half – 'are only thick here, on the outsides. The interior of the hedge is basically just sticks. There are plenty of gaps to move through. So one of us is going to go first – I suggest myself – and get a visual of what's happening on the other side. If our twelve o'clock position is compromised, I'll move up and down along the hedge until we've got a safe point to exit. Then we'll all come through one by one.'

Dev raised his hand. 'And what happens if we get taken out by a crack squad of badgers?'

'Good one, Dev,' said Simon generously, and then raised a lanky leg up to waist height and entered the hedge like a man folding himself into a barrel.

The procedure was loud. Sticks cracked, leaves shifted, the man in the hedge grunted and swore. 'Shit!'

'What is it?!'

'Spider's web!'

The other commandos shuddered on their leader's behalf.

Jane followed, and found the inside of the hedge exactly as Simon had described: full of dead twigs, which whipped her in the face, and on the spacious side, but not as spacious as it would have been for a couple of ten-year-old boys. Simon's memory might have betrayed him slightly, as she looked up to find he was stuck. She moved towards him carefully, swimming through branches, and bent down a bough so he could dislodge his leg.

'Thanks, babe.' Simon rubbed at a scratch on his arm.

Gavin was faring well as the second shortest, except his coat kept getting caught on the undergrowth. Dev was surprisingly agile but had an air of disbelief that any of this was not, in fact, a dream. From the outside the hedge must have looked alive and wriggly.

'Can you see them?' Dev asked.

Everyone held their breath. Jane peeked through twigs.

Beyond the hedge was some scruffy wild land overgrown with bushes and littered with oil drums, a wooden log store covered by tarpaulin, and an abandoned car. Off in the distance was a cluster of portacabins ringed by a low wire fence, the kind used to pen in cattle.

'I can smell fire,' said Simon.

'Are they burning their stuff? Destroying the evidence of something?' said Gavin.

'Maybe,' said Simon. 'Or maybe it's a ritual. I can't see, it's too far off in the distance.'

'It's like Patrick said. There are cabins. I think I can maybe see the roof of a barn,' said Jane.

'Can you see Nellie?' asked Gavin, remembering the primary directive.

'Claire,' corrected Jane.

'Yeah, can you see her?' echoed Dev.

'No, we're way too far away,' said Simon. 'We'll have to get closer.'

'I think we should go and hide behind the abandoned car,' whispered Jane. 'Then we can regroup and work out the next steps.'

Gavin joined her, scanning the area. He nodded. 'Yep. Let's do that.'

Jane bloomed with pride. 'I'll go first,' she said, and immediately regretted it. Her chest filled with hot adrenaline. Trying to breathe at a normal pace, she stepped out of the hedge. The world didn't end, and nobody tried to shoot her, but a branch scratched the back of her thigh. She bent down low and started crab-crawling towards the car. Once she'd made it the others followed, Gavin, then Simon, then Dev.

Jane crouched behind the right-hand-side door, a spot where

she could pop up and watch the cultists through the car's broken window. The car had been defunct a long time; the tyres were gone, the chassis was held up on bricks, and tall weeds had grown up through the driver's-side seat. Gavin crawled on his hands and knees, keeping a keen eye out for CCTV cameras or people on a night-time stroll. But when he got near the car he stopped, stunned. He could only have been more surprised if he'd looked up to discover Jane was hiding behind his ex-wife.

'Oh my god,' he said, crawling the last of the distance and running a hand along the car's rusted blue paintwork. 'It's the Austin.'

'Yeah, it's . . . a nice model,' said Jane.

'No, I mean . . .' Gavin looked like a cowboy stroking a horse who was also his best friend. 'I was looking for this car back in the nineties. I knew it belonged to somebody who was driving the Nellies around, but I had no idea who. It must have been one of the women here. Driving her home. I gave the plates to Bernie, but—' His eyes lit up. 'Christ, maybe he tracked it to the area. On the ANPR cameras, back in 'ninety-seven. They might've come door-to-door asking if anyone had seen it. That's why it's rusting out here, scrapped! He rattled them.'

Gavin looked awed. He couldn't take his hands off the car now he'd finally caught it. Dev and Simon shuffled up as quietly as they could.

'What's going on?' said Dev.

'Gavin's a car pervert,' said Jane.

'I knew there'd be something like that,' said Simon.

Gavin got back into action mode, peeping up from behind the bonnet. Jane took up her observation point at the window. She scanned the wire fence and the ring of buildings. Now they were closer to the portacabins, she saw a slight glow behind them, like a bonfire. There were still no people in sight, but if she strained, she could hear a light hum of chatter.

'Earlier, when I was in the massage sheds, I heard Calla say, "Take Claire to the cabins."' Jane put on a stern, deep voice for Calla. 'She must be in one of these. We need to get closer.'

'Just one issue,' said Dev, pointing at a sign on the wire fence. Everyone squinted their eyes to see the lightning bolt symbol. 'How do we get past the electric fence?'

Claire had never known Calla to be angry until today.

'All of these years of trying to impress upon you the importance of secrecy,' Calla fumed, 'for you to do something so naive.'

Claire didn't answer. She didn't know what to say. She looked around the cabin. It was one of the living cabins, with two old sofas, throw blankets and fairy lights. It looked cosy, but nothing stopped the cold from bleeding through the thin walls. 'May I put on the storage heater?'

Calla tutted but didn't reply. Claire got up carefully and clicked the machine on. Its panels lit up orange. Even though Claire was only halfway through the pregnancy it had been much harder than she'd expected. Her ankles were swollen and painful, and her head ached. She was dizzy often. The other women said that the first part was the hardest, with the sickness. But Claire hadn't had any of that. In fact, things were getting harder with time. It was part of the reason she'd come back. And since she'd returned home, she'd been treated as special, a delicate ornament. Until now.

'Your entire upbringing,' continued Calla, stressing the words sternly, 'has been about preserving the secrecy of our life from the powers outside that would destroy it. The men, and their poison, and their violence.'

Claire knew this to be untrue. Her upbringing had also been about living with nature and embodying the essence of peace. About doing chores, fixing the springs on the old farm-shop till, experimenting with candle spells, building forts out of scrap wood, and getting told off for fighting with her sisters, because she was meant to be embodying peace.

'If our way of life is discovered, men will come, and they will tear down our buildings, our homes, because we did not complete their paperwork. They will force their poisonous medicine down our necks. They will drag us into their ambulances and take us to their hospitals to die with tubes down our throats. They will ransack our rooms and say this home is not fit for our children.' She gestured around the cabin. 'And they will take all our children away. They will take *your* child away. Our family will be torn apart.'

Claire stared at Calla. These were familiar threats. But they'd never seemed likely to come true. For at least three generations, life at the farm had maintained a balance. The story of the outside world destroying their lives seemed as likely to be true as the stories of the monsters who lived under the bed.

'I'm sorry,' said Claire.

'So tell me honestly, because I need to know,' said Calla, making an effort to restrain her fury. 'Did you use your mother's alias?'

'I . . .' She'd known it was against the rules. But her mother had always told her: this name runs in our family. It's one of the lucky ones. You'll come to no harm if you use this name. Claire's head spun.

'We chose a new name for you, Claire. A safe name,' Calla lectured. 'One that hadn't been used before and couldn't be recognised.'

Claire closed her eyes and massaged them, trying to stop the spinning, but even with her eyelids shut her vision was full of bursting stars. She started to panic, but Calla didn't notice.

'Did you inform your partner you were leaving, as we repeatedly told you to do during your preparation period?'

'Please, Calla. I don't feel well.'

'It was your mother who brought the police to our doorstep during her time away. I had to pick her up and rescue her from danger, twice. And now you let her talk you into tempting fate again? Why?'

But Claire couldn't reply. Her head fell back. The world went black.

46

Jane wondered if she could negotiate extra coursework points if she threw herself at the electric fence first. The group of intruders had left the safety of the car and moved to a patch of mushy ground, closer to the circle of portacabins but still on the wrong side of the electrified wire. Through the gaps, they could see a small crowd sitting around a large campfire, women chatting and carrying plates, children toddling and tripping.

'I brought a pair of fleece-lined gloves,' said Dev. 'Maybe they'll insulate us from the current?' But nobody volunteered to try.

'I've got a stick we could throw at it,' said Simon, returning from a nearby patch of ground he'd been investigating.

'Right, and why would we do that, champ?' asked Gavin.

'Well, you know, like in the movies. I'll throw the stick at the fence and then it'll go *brzzzz*!! *Brrrrzzz!!*' Simon did an impression of a twig being electrocuted.

'I don't think that's quite how it works, Si,' said Jane.

'We could try to turn off the power at the mains?' suggested Dev.

'Plunging the whole place into darkness isn't subtle,' said Gavin.

'Guys,' Simon whimpered. 'I don't want to worry anyone, but I think I've just disturbed a burial site.' Simon's stick, which he was now holding very far from his body, was more like the slat of a wooden fence. As the team looked around, they saw more of them, maybe thirty, sticking out of the ground. They marked mounds grown over with grass or planted with flowers. Some were ornamented with trinkets and tea lights.

'Shit,' he muttered. He read a small inscription on the stick. '"Cheryl, return to the land you loved: 1971 to 2019."'

Everyone watched as Simon tried to put the stick back where it had come from, wobbling between different spots, then, at a loss, planting it in a randomly chosen final resting place.

Gavin shuffled between the graves, assessing. 'Oof,' he said. 'This ain't legal.'

Dev walked between the grave markers, crouching to read them. 'Are they killing people?' he said nervously. 'Is Nellie one of these?!'

'Claire,' Jane corrected him.

'No, mate,' said Gavin. 'With murder, you don't mark the spot.'

'But they're young,' said Dev. 'Mostly.'

'Come on, lads: task at hand.' Gavin continued. 'If Nellie's in one of the cabins, which one would it be?'

'Ooh!' said Jane, shooting her hand up. 'The one with the lights on.'

'Bingo,' said Gavin, and Jane lit up with pride.

'It's that one.' She pointed. 'Let's go and stake it out. See if we can see Claire.' Jane started to move in the direction of the cabin, with the gang following close behind. They crept the 200 metres or so along the back of the cabins, but still behind the electric fence, making sure to stay lost in the shadows. In the gaps between the huts, they glimpsed the campfire.

'Is that a barbecue?' said Simon. 'It looks quite cosy.'

'Like a festival,' said Jane.

'Is there such a thing as a nice cult?' Simon was really craning to look. They reached the lit-up cabin and hung back behind the next building along, peeking in the gap to see if anyone was coming in or out.

'Look!' said Dev. Someone approached the lit-up cabin, holding a flask. Jane squinted, recognising her before ducking back into the dark.

They held their breath and listened as the girl knocked on the door, and as the hinges squeaked to let her in.

'Dev,' whispered Gavin, 'do you remember Nellie—'

'Claire.'

'Thanks, Jane. Do you remember *Claire* being anti-medicine at all?'

Dev frowned, wondering. 'Um . . . well, there was one thing,' he said. 'I got a subscription to a company that takes a blood sample, analyses your whole genetic ancestry, then gives you a gummy vitamin supplement to improve your mental health.'

'That sounds amazing,' said Simon. 'What was it called?'

Gavin held a hand up in the direction of Simon's mouth. 'What happened?'

'Well, Nellie threw all the gummies in the bin.'

'Claire.'

'I remember because it was basically the first fight we had. The subscription was really expensive. *Claire* said that what you couldn't grow, raise or cook yourself was poison. It was a bit trippy, actually. I was worried she might be, like, a . . .'

Jane raised an eyebrow. 'An advocate for alternative health choices?' she said.

'Yeah, something like that,' Dev said. 'It was ironic really, 'cos I was sixty quid out, and Ne— and Claire and I weren't talking, and the whole point had been to improve my mental health.'

'I can't wait to try them,' said Simon brightly.

'Thought so.' Gavin nodded. 'See, I heard about a 'ninety-seven Nellie who swapped out her boyfriend's kidney medicine. Maybe it's their thing.'

'Hold on,' said Dev. 'Is that why my hair loss medication started tasting like Smints?'

'I think the guy died, actually . . .' Gavin was looking off into the distance.

'They're having a conversation in there,' interrupted Jane, nodding towards the cabin. 'Can you hear Claire's voice, Dev?'

They all listened hard. There was definitely a conversation being had, and an angry one at that, but the words weren't audible. Gavin looked back in the direction of the graveyard.

'Not such a nice cult after all.'

Hayley handed Claire the flask. 'Raspberry-leaf tea,' she said. 'Iris says if you drink this you'll be right as rain.'

Hayley squeezed onto the small sofa next to Claire. Claire opened the mouth hole of the flask and drank, burning her lip and the tip of her tongue.

'Have you been feeling bad for a while?' asked Hayley.

'I'm fine.' Claire winced.

'Yes, she is fine,' said Calla sternly. 'Tomorrow we'll begin an energy cleanse. I'm sure it's nothing to be alarmed about.' Hayley didn't look reassured. She pulled Claire's swollen foot onto her lap and stroked it.

'Now, Claire, you'll stay here and rest; Hayley, you stay with her. I'll bring a plate,' said Calla, standing up.

'No,' said Claire. 'I want to have dinner outside, with everyone. I'm fine. Help me get up.'

*

'I can hear the door again!' whispered Dev.

The intruders stayed quiet and watched as the yoga teacher, Calla, climbed down the step from the cabin. Simon and Gavin met eyes, bonded in their chakratic trauma. Next, two young women took the step carefully. Jane recognised Hayley from her massage. And the woman in the blue dress, the one she was propping up . . .

'Nellie.' Even in the dark, Jane could make out her pretty side-profile. It felt like seeing a celebrity. 'She used to wear that blue dress around the house,' said Dev, his eyes getting a bit wet.

They watched as Hayley and Claire walked hand-in-hand towards the fire. 'What do we do?' Jane asked Gavin.

'Well . . .' Gavin thought for a moment. 'The thing is, we've finished. There she is, mate,' he said to Dev kindly. 'Found her!'

'So that's it?' said Simon.

'Sounds like it,' said Jane. Her face had a spaced-out look. There was a moment of pause, like a respectful silence for the end of their mission. Jane felt it was a bit of an anti-climax.

'So, I guess the best way is just to walk back as far as the car, check we're not being followed, then go through the hedge again?' said Simon.

'Guess so,' said Gavin.

Dev looked back at his ex, perhaps thinking about arguing. But Gavin gave him a consolatory slap on the back, and he began trudging through the mud with the others.

Simon broke the dull silence with some whispered chit-chat: 'I hope she's not anti-painkillers too. That'll be a hassle when she gives birth.'

'What?' said Dev.

'Oh,' said Simon.

'Shit,' groaned Jane. 'We were temporarily keeping that one under our hat.'

'She's pregnant? I've got to talk to her!' Dev was panicking.

'Easy, mate.' Gavin put a hand on his shoulder.

'Wait, are you sure?' Dev said to Jane.

'We found a pregnancy test in your bathroom. We didn't want to say anything until we'd figured out what was going on. I mean, I did hear a mystery woman in your house, so . . . didn't want to give you any false information. But I assume it isn't Linda's, or some kind of innocent mix-up?' Jane said.

'No, it bloody isn't!' Dev began taking deep breaths, on the verge of a panic attack.

'Come on, champ: breathe,' said Gavin. But Dev started pacing back towards the fence perimeter.

'Don't get seen!' hissed Jane, but he was too far away to hear. There was nothing for the other three to do but follow him.

'Claire's breaking off on her own,' said Dev when they'd joined him back behind the cabin. 'Look.' He pointed – Hayley was letting go of Claire's shoulders. Jane looked in the direction Claire was heading: towards a small shed, away from the portacabins, and in front of a large septic tank.

'Toilets,' she said.

'Makes sense,' said Simon. 'Pregnant women wee all the time, don't they?'

Dev grimaced. Now they were closer, and Jane was thinking about it, she could see a slight curve around Claire's stomach through the fabric of her blue dress. She'd only been gone a few weeks. How had Dev not noticed?

'How are we going to get over the fence?' asked Simon. Gavin didn't say anything, but he had a very Gavin look in his eye as he began jogging up towards the electrified wire.

'Woah.' Simon's mouth hung open. Jane wondered if their teacher had finally given up on life. But Gavin slammed his left hand down on a metal fence pole, swung both legs over at the same time, and remained un-barbecued as he landed heavily on the other side.

'Come on, tosspots,' said Gavin quietly, and for the first time ever, they saw him grin.

'How did you know it wasn't on?' said Jane, inelegantly vaulting the fence herself.

'Price of energy bills these days,' he said, helping to haul Dev and then Simon over by their bums. 'A bunch of yoga teachers who run a farm shop aren't leaving the fence switched on.'

The four of them hid behind the last portacabin, the one nearest the toilet shed. Nellie cut a lone shadowy figure, hugging herself in the cold.

'Nellie! I mean – Claire!' Dev shout-whispered, and Claire looked round.

'Dev! What are you doing here?' She looked terrified. She glanced around, on the edge of sounding the alarm.

'Please, don't panic, Nell,' he said.

She took a few steps towards them. 'Who are all these people?'

'We don't mean any harm – please. We just want to talk, and then we'll leave, I promise,' said Dev. 'Nobody needs to know about this place, or anything . . .' His sentence ran out of road.

She didn't speak. She just stared with her cool blue eyes.

When Dev spoke, his voice wobbled. 'So, have we . . . have we broken up?'

'Yes,' she said peacefully.

'B-But—' His stutters were explosive. 'Why wouldn't you tell me? You could have left me a note, or an email, or anything!'

'Careful of the volume, mate,' said Gavin in his horse-whisperer voice.

'I'm sorry about that,' said Claire. 'I intended to leave a note, but in the stress of the move, I forgot.'

Dev put his face in his hands. 'Of course,' he said. 'Of course, you have no idea how to behave. You grew up in a cult!' He waved his arms to indicate the premises.

'It's not a cult! We are a collective of women attuned to nature,' she said forcefully. 'We're a family.'

'So were the Mansons,' muttered Jane.

'It does explain the resemblance though. Between all the Nellies,' said Simon.

Something occurred to Jane. 'Did the women here go into Tonbridge and take all the missing posters down?'

'My sister did that. I'm sorry, Dev,' she said, but she didn't sound rueful. 'Perhaps I should have told you about the decision I'd come to.'

'Perhaps you should have told me you were pregnant!'

She touched her belly. 'I'd known for a little while. I wasn't sure what to do. I did care for you, Dev. But it was always the case that I'd have to choose between you and my family.'

'Your family,' Dev echoed. He looked around, starting to take in what she meant. 'No wonder you never wanted to talk about your bloody parents!'

'You literally never asked,' she said. Dev began to cry. Unmoved, Claire continued her explanation, gesturing to her stomach. 'You can see that it's becoming obvious. I'd already been wearing baggy clothes to buy myself more time to think. But I reached a point where I couldn't hide it any longer and I had to make my choice.'

'You burned a Pluto candle to support you in your change,' said Jane. 'And then buried it in the woods, away from the house.'

'How do you know that?' said Claire, staring Jane cold in the eye.

'Intuition,' said Jane, just as cool.

'Yes,' she said. 'I'm going to raise my child the way I was raised. She's going to be a daughter of Fawke Wood.'

'It's a girl?' Dev asked.

'I believe so,' said Claire.

'Sounds like a guess,' muttered Simon.

'What about me?' pleaded Dev. 'She's going to be my daughter too.'

'That's never been the way it works here,' said Claire. 'We don't have fathers at Fawke Wood.'

'Well, you're going to now,' said Dev through angry tears. 'I'm going to be the first one. I'm going to know my child.' Claire shook her head. 'I'm going to fight you for this, Nellie.'

She paused for a moment, putting her hand to her forehead.

'Are you OK?' said Dev, reaching for her arm. 'Are you ill? Have you had a check-up? Hospital appointments, scans?'

Nellie didn't reply. The atmosphere dropped. The domino had fallen. She opened her mouth to yell. 'HELP! HELP! OUTSIDERS!!'

'Oh, tits,' said Gavin.

47

Women poured around the sides of the portacabins from the campfire, surrounding the group. They were stuck. Within seconds, Calla arrived, striding to the front of the women. She looked from Claire to Dev to the detectives. 'You two,' she said. 'I should have got rid of you when I had the chance.'

'There's no need for this to get out of hand,' said Gavin, carefully taking a step forward with his hands in the air. 'How about you just step back and let us walk away before any serious crimes are committed? We've got tracking devices on our phones. People will miss us.'

'Regardless,' said Calla, fury on her face, 'for the protection of our community, we cannot let you leave.'

They were at a standoff. Nobody moved.

Jane suddenly felt like an over-inflated birthday balloon on the verge of popping. She spoke in a voice she didn't recognise. 'We can't leave? Well, what are you going to do?'

Calla turned to the woman next to her. 'Get the guns.'

'Shit,' said Jane. 'RUN!' She tried to slip between the two women behind her, but one grabbed her by the elbow. Without hesitation, Jane clenched her right hand into a little fist and swung her body round hard, punching the woman square in the face. She couldn't believe how soft and yet crunchy a face felt. Jane's punching-bag let go and staggered backwards; several others rushed to attend to her, giving the intruders a narrow gap to run through.

'Turn on the fence!' Calla shouted behind them, and someone fled to the barn to flip the switch.

'Quickly, quickly, let's get over!' yelled Gavin. Dev threw himself clumsily at the fence, but only managed to get one leg over before Gavin shoved the rest of him. Simon went next, suffering a similar lumpy landing in the mud. Everyone was finding the fence a lot harder to climb over knowing it was a race between them, the woman who'd gone to find the on switch and the woman grabbing the guns.

'Get up – run!' Jane screamed at Dev and Simon, as she and Gavin made it over a bit more gracefully. They ran an adrenaline-fuelled sprint back over the dark ground, through the makeshift graveyard, praying not to trip. The cult members hadn't followed them over the fence, instead going the long way round. This had bought the escapees some time, and they had a hundred metres or so on the first women who emerged behind them.

CRACK! They were nearly at the Austin, their chests burning, when they heard the first shot.

'Shit!' said Simon.

'Are you hit?' Jane shouted behind her.

'No, it just scared me!'

'I'm hit!' shouted Dev, who had slowed pace and was limping.

'Where did they get you?' yelled Jane.

'My Chelsea boot!'

CRACK! DING! This time the shot scattered as it hit the chassis of the car. Jane squeaked. Dev forgot about his limp and picked up the pace again.

Gavin risked a look backwards. 'Shotgun range is... up to... couple of hundred metres!' he panted. 'Keep running!'

The cult members didn't seem to be gaining on them. Maybe it was survival instinct; maybe the epidemic of jogging among the yuppie classes had made them fitter. Maybe, for Gavin, it was those little cones he really had gone out and bought, and all the running he'd done between them every week – hip injury permitting – since the late nineties. But as shots thundered behind them, they managed to stay ahead and reach the hedge.

'IN, IN, IN!' screamed Jane like a sergeant major. She pushed the other three's backs as they scrambled into the foliage.

The Fawke Wood women didn't follow them into the hedge, but Jane heard one of them say, 'Go through the gate!' There must have been a gate somewhere in the brick wall. Jane plunged into the scratching branches, and soon she joined the others falling through the other side of the hedge.

'I left the shop doors open,' panted Gavin. But Simon was running in the wrong direction, back towards the farmhouse's front door.

'The car keys! I've left them in the room! *Get to ze chopper!*' Simon roared, disappearing into the guesthouse of the beast.

'Oh god,' said Jane. She ran into the farmhouse after him. Simon's adequate runner's legs carried him like a bullet train up the stairs. Jane waited at the bottom, wondering what kind of a head start they'd gained by getting through the hedge.

But in seconds, Simon was back, leaping down the stairs two at a time, with their carrier bag of belongings, and their two precious trench coats over his arm. He thrust Jane's coat at her and threw his arm into the sleeve of his own, swooping it round his back dramatically before popping the collar. Jane followed suit.

'Smash?' she asked.

'SMASH!!!' And they started running.

They pounded the path through the vegetable gardens, past

the deadly nightshade and past the deadly massage sheds. Jane wondered how much energy a person's adrenaline could give them before death. Gavin was at the shop door, holding it open like a soldier. 'Go, go, go!' he yelled.

They got through the shop and out the other side into the car park. Dev was in the driver's seat of his car, revving.

Simon and Jane bundled into the Pie-and-Mash-mobile and Simon fumbled the keys into the ignition. The Fawke Wood women started pouring out of the shop, long dresses billowing, hair twisting around their faces. Three of them aimed shotguns at the escapees. Jane made sure to lock the doors as Simon crunched around, two-point-turning in the dirt. There was a *THUNK* as a round of shot hit Simon and Jane's car. The back window cracked into a spiderweb pattern.

Dev led the convoy's charge, accelerating up the dirt track, and swerving into the road without looking, or even signalling. In the car park, Simon skidded a wide circle around the women, spraying a cloud of dust from the wheels. The turn was so sharp, two of their tyres might have left the ground.

'Duck!' screamed Jane, as more shots clipped the roof of their car from the back. Simon accelerated out onto the road.

'My SwiftCar rating!' muttered Simon under his breath. The women chased them out into the lane, but it was too late. They were free.

'Where are we going?' said Simon, following Gavin, who was following Dev. Here in the dead of night, the roads were empty and the convoy hit seventy miles an hour.

'I don't care,' said Jane through panting breaths. 'Literally anywhere but here.'

The Fawke Wood women were left straggling in the rearview mirror, until they disappeared in the darkness.

48

Tuesday 23 April – Present Day

'Dev Hooper came home from work to find his front door hanging open. His girlfriend had disappeared without a trace.'

Jane and Simon stood at the front of the classroom presenting their case. They brought up the headshot of Dev they'd found on his school's website, to which they'd added an arrow marking him VICTIM.

Unlike Friday, the students of Gavin Smith's detective class had turned up today to find that their teacher was actually there. This was a relief, given it was the final session of the course.

'My apologies,' Gavin had said gruffly at the top of the hour. 'I was unavoidably detained last week, and due to staffing shortages at the centre, was unable to let you know in advance that class was cancelled.'

'You could have sent us an email,' Captain Alex had said.

'I couldn't,' Gavin had shot back, 'because I was on a dangerous undercover mission at an active underground cult.'

'If they were a bit more active, they might have caught us,' Simon had whispered to Jane in the Naughty Seats, and she'd laughed.

Now they were wrapping up their case and tying the final bow.

'Fawke Wood Sanctuary is a collective of women living

off-grid in central Kent,' Jane explained. 'They're a spiritual community who don't believe in medicine. In fact, we believe they meet all the criteria to be classified as a cult. Kent Police has had them on a watch list for some time. While this may sound a little far-fetched, there are in fact over two thousand cults in the UK.' From his chair in the front row, Gavin nodded approvingly.

'There were always two major strands to this mystery,' said Simon. 'The first was simple: where is Dev Hooper's girlfriend, Nellie Thorne?'

He clicked onto a picture of Claire, the one from her missing poster, labelled PERP. Every member of the class was rapt.

'We managed to track her down to Fawke Wood Sanctuary, where she'd been raised. She left Dev when she realised she was pregnant, as she wanted to raise her child in her peaceful community. It makes sense. If you'd been raised by a village, would you want to embark on motherhood almost on your own?'

'Also, their relationship seemed just so-so,' added Jane. 'He's literally already dating someone else!' Craniax gasped.

'But there was a second part to the mystery,' said Simon, moving the presentation onto a question mark with eyes. 'Dev's former girlfriend wasn't the only person with the name Nellie Thorne. Why had four women with that name been reported missing before?'

'We worked through a few theories,' explained Jane. 'Some of them you've heard. We wondered for a while if the Nellies were the victims of a Kent-based serial killer, the so-called Tonbridge Ripper. The cases were, briefly, intertwined. But that turned out to be an odd quirk of fate. In 1997, one of the Nellies was romantically involved with the murderer, but in April of that year she left him and moved to Erith, where she only stayed until August, before returning to the cult for good. Prior to that, we think she'd tried a stint living in Wimbledon too. Gavin met a man in a South London pub who'd recently been dating a Nellie Thorne. She'd tried to stop him taking his medication, and before long, she left without a trace. In fact, we have Gavin to thank for most of this intel.'

Gavin bowed his head humbly. 'Get on with it, you two.'

'So, the murder victim theory was out,' said Simon. 'But what was the real solution?'

'We used library data to find a woman living in Dungeness under the name Nellie Thorne,' said Jane.

'We presume she's been living under a married name all these years, but she must have registered for the library before getting married and never bothered to change it.'

'And we persuaded her to spill the beans: at some point between the ages of eighteen and twenty-five, every woman at Fawke Wood is given a choice. To go out and live in the world for a year and see if they prefer it to living in the Fawke Wood community. They're encouraged to find a partner and see if settling down into a traditional life is right for them. Of course, most don't stay out of the cult for long, due to the awkwardness of navigating the modern world, having not been properly socialised growing up.' Jane paused.

'While they're out in the world, to preserve the secrecy of their community, they take on an alias. Over time, those tried-and-tested names were re-used. They often run in families, and get recycled by sisters, or passed from mothers to daughters. Along the way we found more than one "Lily Jones" and "Daisy Brown". But the most popular name? Nellie Thorne. Our woman in Dungeness just happened to really like her new life. She fell in love with her husband and couldn't face telling him it wasn't her real name.'

Simon moved on to the next slide: a picture of a group of Amish people. 'The Amish have a sort of gap year similar to this. It's called Rumspringa. Though I should say, they're a religious community, not a cult.'

'And if, during this year, the Fawke Wood women happen to get pregnant,' said Jane, 'then great. They're encouraged to. The cult only continues if new members are born. In fact, any Fawke Wood woman wanting more children can venture into the world again. For a sort of . . . boyfriend sabbatical.'

Simon re-took the lead. 'We found the cult by tracing their popular handmade candles back to Fawke Wood Sanctuary. Gavin came to a similar conclusion by thinking through the type of people who live off-grid.'

'It all clicked into place when I watched a documentary about cicadas,' said Gavin. 'You know, those bugs that appear out of the ground. I kept asking where the women were going, when I should have been asking where they were coming from. I'd also considered that it could be something to do with the travelling community, or trafficking victims. That last one led me down a particularly sore path.'

A class member put up his hand. 'Why would some of them use the same fake name?' he said.

'Good question,' said Simon. 'We believe that superstition has a big part to play here. A researcher at Tonbridge Library has found several examples of what she thinks are repeat Fawke Wood names. They often come from the ancestors of the cult members. The original Nellie Thorne, apparently, was the grandmother of one of the Fawke Wood founders. She's buried in a cemetery in Westerham, and when people found her gravestone in the 1990s, it made the Nellie Thorne legend much spookier.'

'Then, like we mentioned, it got passed down the family,'

explained Jane. 'For example, Dev's ex-girlfriend is the daughter of the woman who went missing in 1997. She says that in her family the name's considered lucky. She wanted some good luck on her journey into the outside world.'

'Bit careless though, isn't it?' their classmate continued.

'It definitely brought more attention in their direction,' said Jane. 'The cult banned its members from using that name after the 1987 Nellie disappearance became relatively huge news. But not everyone took the ban seriously. Claire's mum was breaking the rules by using it in 1997, and that nearly led the police to them. The fact Claire chose to use it again now is the reason we caught them.'

'So, are there any questions?' said Simon cheerily, clapping his hands together. Almost every hand in the class went up.

'Why do most Nellies choose not to stay with their romantic partners?' said a bouncer at the back.

'I think that's one to mull over,' answered Jane. 'But remember, these women are being asked to choose between the person they have their first relationship with, and the only home and community they've ever known.' She shrugged.

'And are these cult birds going to prison?' said the bouncer's deskmate.

'Maybe,' said Simon. 'The police are still figuring out the details of their operation. They've been denying their members access to proper medical care. Plus, they kept a stash of illegal weapons, and interfered with a police investigation by taking down missing posters.' He flipped the presentation to a picture of Dev and Claire in hospital. Dev was giving a thumbs-up to the camera. Claire was smiling weakly, but looked only half conscious. For the first time, Jane noticed a frowning Linda lurking in the background of the shot, and jumped.

'And it's a good thing we managed to get there when we did,' Jane added, 'because Claire was suffering from undiagnosed pre-eclampsia. It's a common and treatable complication of pregnancy, but without treatment, it can be fatal.'

There was a tear in Captain Alex's eye.

'We knew something fishy was up when we found a DIY graveyard on site. Plenty of ailments are a killer when you ignore modern medicine,' Gavin chimed in.

'If the cult's made up of women, what happens when they give birth to little baby boys?' asked Craniax, hot on the ball. It was something that had occurred to Simon and Jane.

'We don't know,' said Simon, grimacing. 'But Kent police know lots of cases of baby boys being left on the doorsteps of churches and nurseries. They're going to explore the link.'

'This stuff is a bit above the junior detective's pay grade,' Gavin jumped in, turning to Craniax. 'But don't worry, everyone. Luckily, the good men and women of Kent Police are going to take it from here.'

'Now,' said Simon, 'I've prepared a very interesting slide on what SwiftCar says if you return a car that's been attacked with a shotgun . . .'

For the rest of the session, Simon and Jane fielded more questions about the library archives, Gavin's brief adventure in gangland, candle spells, and how the midnight red-candle-wax rituals in Wylebrook Woods had got the cult mistaken for bloodthirsty ghosts.

The questions overran the session by half an hour. Eventually, the cleaner could be seen lingering outside the classroom door with a mop and bucket, glaring through the glass.

'Well,' said Gavin stiffly, getting up from his plastic chair and going back to the front of the room to reassert dominance. 'That is our final coursework presentation of the class. And for the observant among you, which isn't many, you'll have noticed this is the end of the course.' There was a collective disappointed murmur.

'You'll be pleased to know a couple of things,' continued Gavin. 'The first is that, due to us moving the last few coursework presentations to today, we no longer have time to do the end-of-course exam. So you all automatically pass.' A rousing cheer went up among the men.

'The second bit of good news is that the training centre's staffing shortage is at an end. Please welcome their brand-new reception coordinator, Jane Pye,' said Gavin, pointing towards her. There was a reluctant spatter of applause.

'Oh,' added Gavin, 'and also, I escaped the cult alive. Clearly.'

The class left for the last time, and the cleaner came in to mop the floor. Simon and Jane hung back.

'So, you two,' said Gavin. 'What's next?'

'Well, we passed as well, right?' asked Jane.

'Yes, you passed.' He chuckled. 'And I trust I'll see you back some time for Private Investigation Level Two: Further Detecting?'

'Definitely!' said Jane. 'And I think a discount on the classes here is a perk of the new job.'

'I've already enrolled in Introduction to DJing,' added Simon.

'Good,' Gavin replied, giving them a rare smile. 'I'm off to Tenerife to rest the old war wound for a bit, but you'll hear from me when I'm back.'

'Don't worry, we won't miss enrolment. This little pie is now in charge of scheduling all your courses!' said Simon, slapping Jane proudly on the back.

'It's just a nice job to have while we get the agency off the ground,' she said, grinning.

'Ah! So you're going to launch the detective agency after all? I usually advise people to wait until after Level Five, but you two have proved you know your way around a case. It's not always the right way, but still.'

'Absolutely,' said Simon. 'In fact, we're putting together the finishing touches on a credit fraud case in Kent.'

'And Dev offered to pay us for finding Claire!'

'I hope you said yes?'

'We did.'

'Smart,' said Gavin. 'What's he going to do about his cult baby?'

'We don't know,' said Jane, 'but the police are helping him learn about his rights.'

'Well, it sounds like you two are well on your way,' said Gavin, and he swung his backpack onto his back and made for the door. 'I just hope you remember my twenty-first rule of detecting.'

'What's that?' said Simon.

'Celebrate your wins. Well done, kids,' he said, and when he was halfway out the door, he paused and mumbled something that sounded like 'I'm proud of you.'

And then he was gone.

Simon turned to Jane. 'I reckon we can call this the hard launch of the Pie and Mash Detective Agency. Wouldn't you say?'

'Yes,' said Jane. Her eyes welled up a little. 'So, what now?'

'Pub?' said Mash.

'Pub,' said Pye.

And they went off into the evening hand-in-hand, a little bit more qualified as detectives, and more certain than ever that they were on the right road.

THE PIE & MASH DETECTIVE AGENCY

www.pieandmash.com

THE PIE & MASH DETECTIVE AGENCY
Homepage   About Us   Detective Outfit of the Day
Crime(s) We Have Solved

Welcome to the homepage of the Pie & Mash Detective Agency!!!!

(Jane, can you make that bit all colourful and wiggly like WordArt? Retro!! S xxx)

We are Simon Mash and Jane Pye, detectives extraordinaire.

(Simon, I keep telling you, my name needs to go first! Nobody cooks a Sunday dinner of Mash and Pie. FFS.)

We have studied under a brilliant London-based detective teacher who has asked us not to mention his name here because he doesn't want to muddy his brand.

Why should you work with us? I'll tell you for why. We've solved a case that bamboozled Kent Police for over 50 years, creating fantastic outcomes for all our stakeholders, except for one man, whose Tonbridge ghost tour we slightly ruined.

Having barely escaped the Nellie Thorne case with our lives, we're now busy with our second case, which involves financial fraud and a number of sexy ladies.

(Jane, pleeeeeeeease let me invent a couple of other cases xxx.)

(NO. Also, don't refer to your mum as sexy. She is, but it's gross.)

We NEED more cases!! ☺ Contact us now on hotdetectives@pieandmash.com, or call 07700 900612.

(Simon don't put your actual mobile number!)

Jane Pye and Simon Mash live in South London with no beautiful kids.

THE PIE & MASH DETECTIVE AGENCY

https://www.reddit.com/r/actingjobs/

liz_honeymead

Butler Needed Immediately!!!

Are you an actor looking for a JOB? Do you mind being MURDERED??!

My murder mystery production 'A Killing Most Chilling' runs every weekend and we are looking for a Butler on very short notice. After an 'incident' last weekend, we are very motivated to hire and keep our show running.

Perks: You get to come and live at our remote countryside mansion every weekend alongside an incredible cast, meet interesting people, and get stuck into a murder case over and over again!

Cons: None!

Contact liz@honeymeadproductions.co.uk

(Top Comment) interested_whale32

Guys, do not take this job. My friend worked there. The role is cursed.

> **yellow_ephemera11**
>
> I heard this too!! People get sick, people get hurt, people disappear. Do not audition lol :((
>
> **yang_basics46**
>
> 😳 Trying to put other actors off applying. Curses aren't real, ppl.

mixed_lollipop45

'an incident' – this was my friend. Was only in the job a few weeks and it gave him a nervous breakdown. He's still in hospital.

liz_honeymead

to everyone saying the role is cursed, I will kindly remind you that this is libel, and if such allegations persist, I will be happy to take legal action.

ggh67667

from what I hear about you and your company, Liz, you're going to need to hire a defence lawyer. Won't be long until somebody looks into your unethical practices.

graham_glisson

Everyone in theatre knows something's very wrong at Honeymead Productions. Does anyone know a detective who'd be happy to take on a curse?

Acknowledgements

Thank you so much for reading our book. We sincerely hope you enjoyed it, but if not, no refunds! Well, maybe some refunds, depending on where you bought it and their return policy.

People are often surprised that we write as a pair. The truth is, the absolute best way to write a book is with a team. You'd be amazed how many people you can squeeze around one keyboard. We'd like to thank them all.

The legendary Selina Walker, and the whole team at Century and PRH (listed on page 359). The marvellous Michelle Vega at Berkley, for being Simon and Jane's US ambassador and editor. Louisa Burden Garabedian, for championing new voices in publishing. Mike Taylor, for generously sharing his invaluable police expertise and insight (any mistakes are entirely our own).

Charlotte Osment, our original editor, who rooted for Simon and Jane from the first thousand words. Her dedication, expertise and hard work are woven into every page.

Daisy Chandley, our fierce and fabulous agent, who is the constant wind in our sails.

The shady online university that certified us as private investigators.

Our friends, in particular our writing support network: Mr DJ, Alex Walker-Smith, Michael Lindsay, Swéta Rana, James Bugg, Jo Wiggins and Joe Barnes.

Our family for their support and, in some cases, DNA:

David Dinkin, Gill Hagon, Charlie Dinkin, Ben Sutton, Sheila Hagon and Louie the Pug. Helen Brinkworth, Rob Brinkworth, Andrew Brinkworth, Stewy Brinkworth and Fred the Tortoise. Bernard Carter, Jean Carter, Eileen Carter, Pat Gargan, Matt Carter, Elaine Tindal and Steve Carter. Michael, Lea and all the Brodies; Ruwan, Michelle and all the Weerasekeras; and Anne and Holly Wayman.

SMASH!

Bringing a book from manuscript to what you are reading is a team effort, and Penguin Random House would like to thank everyone at Century who helped to publish *The Pie & Mash Detective Agency*.

PUBLISHER
Selina Walker

EDITORIAL
Charlotte Osment
Laurie Ip Fung Chun
Alice Brett
Mary Karayel
Eugenie Woodhouse

DESIGN
Dan Simpkins

PRODUCTION
Helen Wynn-Smith

INVENTORY
Lizzy Moyes

UK SALES
Alice Gomer
Kirsten Greenwood
Rhian Steer
Phoenix Curland
Emily Harvey

INTERNATIONAL SALES
Anna Curvis
Barbora Sabolova

PUBLICITY
Hana Sparkes
Georgie Townley

MARKETING
Sophie Shaw

AUDIO
Brónagh Grace

FILM & TV
Jenna Brown

RIGHTS
Amelia Evans